THINKWELL BOOKS

THE DISAPPEARED

David Stephens was born in 1950, in Woking, Surrey. He graduated in 1972 from the University of Reading with a degree in Modern History & Politics and went on to gain a PGCE at the University of Southampton, picking up his M.Ed. in 1976 and PhD in 1982 – both from the University of Exeter. He has worked in Afghanistan, Laos, Kenya and Sierra Leone as a professor and researcher, spending the past six years in Lima, Peru. He is the eldest of five siblings, son of two teachers, and author of *Purely Academic: A Satire*, *The Disappeared* and *Under Andean Skies: Living and Writing in Peru*. He is a snazzy and natty former Ten Pound Pom who has filled his life with an awful lot of adventure.

I0747695

'The [Quechua] revolution's ferocity has given the Corner of the Dead a new and chilling resonance. Journalists, at first mystified by the theatricality and macabre ritual of Sendero's violence, groped for clichés, something to help box the complexities of peasant insurgency and Maoist revolution into the requirements of the six hundred-word news story. They came up with 'the Khmer Rouge of Latin America'. The tag stuck, but like all such tags does more to hinder than enhance understanding of the nature, causes and trajectory of Sendero's revolution.'

Ronan Bennett, author of *The Catastrophist* and *Havoc, in its Third Year*

'On 26 December 1980, residents of Lima woke to a gruesome, incongruous sight: dead dogs had been strung up from lampposts in the city centre, some bearing pieces of cloth scrawled with the words: 'Deng Xiaoping, Son of a Bitch.' It was the work of Partido Comunista del Peru-Sendero Luminoso. Sendero (or Shining Path, as it's referred to in English) was an ultra-orthodox Maoist group which had a few months earlier launched an armed insurrection against the Peruvian state. The combination of ideological rigidity and violence was to become Sendero's hallmark.'

Tony Wood, Assistant Professor of History at the University of Colorado Boulder & author of *Chechnya: The Case for Independence*

'Shining Path's first 'armed action' took place in 1980, timed for maximum visibility, on the day of a national election. The movement fell apart 12 years later, after Guzmán was captured in Lima...hiding in a flat above a ballet studio. But over the years...there were savage battles between Shining Path, the Peruvian army and the *rondas campesinas* – paramilitary patrols...intended to repel the guerrillas.'

Peter Canby, author of
The Heart of the Sky: Travels Among the Maya

'He refused to condemn it, did not call it barbarism or give any pejorative spin at all to his descriptions of its cruelty. Tadek, in Rey's view, was the antique precursor to the absolutely modern system of justice now being employed by [Peru]. Wartime justice, arbitrary justice, he contended, was valid both ethically (one could never know what crimes were lurking in the hearts and minds of men) and practically (swift, violent punishment, if random in nature, could bolster the cause of peace, frightening potential subversives).'

Daniel Alarcón, author,
extract from *Lost City Radio*

'Drawing on five years' research into Peru's violent guerrilla conflicts of the 1980s/early 1990s, David Stephens compels us to explore the emotional depths of a father's fearful uncertainty following the disappearance of his son, an investigative journalist. Fuelled by first-hand testimonies from victims' relatives and members of Peru's judiciary, this novel is as fast-paced as the infamous rapids of the Urubamba.'

Patricia Khan, author of *A Thousand Witnesses*

David Stephens

THE

DISAPPEARED

THINKWELL BOOKS

Edited by J. David Simons.

Cover design by Alejandro Baigorri.

Interior formatting by Rachel Bostwick.

Published by Thinkwell Books, U.K.

First printing edition 2023.

.

For Benjamin

"A desaparecido is someone who is 'absent forever' whose destiny is to 'vanish'."
- Roberto Viola, Army commander, Argentina, from a speech on Army Day, May 29th, 1979.

CONTENTS

FOREWORD

During the final two decades of the twentieth century, Peru experienced one of the greatest outbreaks of political violence seen in the history of the American continent. According to figures from the Report of the Truth and Reconciliation Commission, it is estimated that during those years around 69,000 people died or disappeared, and that, unlike other internal armed conflicts in Latin America where state agents were in the main responsible for the loss of human lives, in Peru the highest number of fatalities among the civilian population (54%) was caused by a Maoist subversive group: the Communist Party of Peru – the Shining Path or *Sendero Luminoso*.

The state counter-offensive, for its part, was not up to the complexity of such defiance, and it was unable to contain the expansion of subversion in those years. Civilian rulers agreed to militarize the conflict and leave their struggle in the hands of the Armed Forces, an act that left a huge gap in terms of the protection of fundamental rights and opened a space for the systematic violation of human rights by the forces of order, who, together with the paramilitary groups among other actors, were responsible for 37% of the dead and disappeared of that period.

All of the above acquires an even more gloomy nuance if we consider that the said violence took place in some of the poorest provinces and areas of Peru, with Ayacucho recording the highest number of dead and disappeared. Those Peruvians who were the target of the violence produced by the subversion and its counter-offensive, mainly Quechua-speaking citizens and mostly dedicated to agricultural activities in rural areas, lost their lives before the unjustifiable indifference of that other urban, modern and Lima-centered Peru, a fact that deepens and aggravates the dishonor experienced.

The political violence suffered in Peru came from various actors. On the subversive side, in addition to the Shining Path, cruel in its beginnings to all forms of political or public authority and soon ruthless with innocent civilians, we also witnessed the Túpac Amaru Revolutionary Movement operating in those same years, a sequel to post-Castro guerrilla factions that appeared in the 1960s, and which, although it did not share the former's ideology (and in most cases distinguished itself in procedures and geography from the aforementioned Maoist group), it was also ruthless and joined the excesses of the Shining Path. On the counter-subversive side, were the various official institutions of the Peruvian State and those made up of clandestine officers. A third group with a much lower incidence of oppression was formed by self-defense committees managed by local residents.

The meeting of all these forces, located in the scenario described above, gave rise to the hardest chapter in the republican history of Peru, which, due to its myriad forms, episodes, legacies and perhaps generational proximity, beyond the taxonomic hierarchies granted by the coldness of statistical equivalences, has been compared by renowned scholars to the Rwandan genocide at the end of the last century, or the Cambodian genocide of the Khmer Rouge in the mid-1970s, superlative milestones of human impiety in contemporary times.

In more than two decades that have followed this infamy, culture and art, as well as academia and social studies, have been able to collect the painful history and indentation of this time, and record - with greater or lesser degree - the extensive and changing wake that this left us. Collecting testimonies, episodes, sequels, remembrances or findings, the effort of non-fiction writing has bestowed an important - and still growing - bibliographical production that allows us to educate new generations and helps to move us away from the painful disgrace of recidivism.

But it is, however, in the unlimited reality of fiction, where memory complements fantasy and vice versa, that both merge into a parallel reality that is often the one to tell the private history of nations and the one that prevails and is embedded into the popular imagination.

The Peruvian cultural industries and literature in particular, have been able - for more than two decades - to delve into this horror and collect material that has nurtured innumerable fictions narrated from very different angles. It is tempting to think that such a prerogative should be in the hands of those who have closely known and perhaps suffered from the shrapnel of that time, and it is not strange that many fiction writers are disqualified for daring to enter the space that some gatekeepers, out of prejudice, might believe reserved for a select group of local storytellers. Nothing could be more wrong than the latter, not only because those who write do not always write about what they know but also about what they do not know precisely in order to know it, but above all because the gaze of every writer is always arbitrary and external and sometimes even unfair to a reality that ends up turning until it is, over time, the unpredictable amalgamation of all this arbitrariness. And that is where reality lies, as a paradox, the line between the chronicle and art.

In this sense, the story that David Stephens gives us in *The Disappeared* is part of a tradition of writing on political violence that does not remain in the superficial account of the description of the damage or the social and political phenomenon that Shining Path meant, nor of the recurrent stereotypes of amassing drugs, corruption and underdevelopment to achieve one more episode of an exotic failed republic, but instead dives into the complexity of the multiple actors and drivers that are the backdrop to one of the most heartfelt and universals of the human condition: filial love and its scope to exercise it and live it where the scenarios are painted in adverse and insurmountable colors.

There will be little that has not been said, since the time of the pre-Socratic writers and even from outside or before Western civilization, about the loss of a loved one, and worse still, about the uncertainty that follows a disappearance and the eternal ghost of uncertainty and waiting, but each new story, each *good* new story, is a valuable excuse to look at ourselves from the outside again and surprise ourselves or reform ourselves as a civilization, or die attempting to.

The Disappeared is a novel that crosses the Peruvian landscape and some of its most critical spaces in recent decades in the same way that it traverses possible episodes of a history caused and populated by different authors that here - be it through feasible testimonies or the voice of a narrator eager to understand and revive the hidden genealogy of a wounded country that sheltered him for several years - seem to come back to life.

The British presence and influence in our republican history and culture is huge, and now it will continue growing with a story that imagines and narrates Peru from within Peru itself. David Stephens has taken a universal theme, knowing how to give it that individual and particular tint that is the essence of every writer and which provides his passport to enter a tradition - the tradition of an art and a country he has recently joined thanks to this vigorous novel.

Pedro Llosa Vélez, Lima, author of *La medida de todas las cosas*

Introduction

What does it mean to disappear? This is a question explored in some detail in Stephens' latest novel -- a story of loss and hope that encompasses generations of Peruvian history. There are many disappearances in the novel, both physical and metaphorical, and each layers inside the next in a tightly structured and cleverly formed narrative. There is, of course, Hugh's son Adam, whose literal disappearance sets in motion the exciting and page-turning mystery that is the thrust of this story. In the ensuing search, we are treated to the highs and lows of Peruvian society: drug-runners and guerrilla fighters, corrupt politicians and cocaine fields deep in the Andes. All these ingredients have the makings of a gritty international thriller, with heart-stopping excitement and unexpected twists.

But underneath this tale, there are other disappearances. The spectre of Hugh's dead wife Sarah looms over the story and injects a powerful tenderness to the prose. Even as the urgency of the narrative pushes us forward, the touching insights into grief and loss make us pause, inviting us to share in the emotional depths that come with such tragedy. Just as there are disappearances, Stephens explores the blank spaces that they leave behind, whether the distance between father and son or the loneliness of losing what you love, and how we fill these, if we ever can.

The Disappeared is also a novel with a clear sense of its literary and historical context. Keenly researched, Stephens' recognition of the South American traditions from which his story is born and the written and oral histories that have informed it, lead to a world that feels utterly real. The novel transports the reader almost entirely to a different land, one in which the rules are different and the stakes higher.

Finally, it is a story about those things which do not disappear, despite the world's attempts to make them so -- the love for family, the tenacity of hope, and, even amidst a hotbed of drug-running and corruption, a sense of justice being able to prevail. There are many layers to this novel and Stephens ties all of them deftly together to craft a story that will sit with you for a long time.

Nicholas Binge, Scotland, author of *Ascension* and *Professor Everywhere*

Prologue

Hugh looked beyond the old sewer pipe towards the distant shoreline. It was early evening, but dark storm clouds were coming in from the east giving the Norfolk saltmarshes a translucent sheen, bunches of pink sea thrift and sea lavender providing the only splashes of colour. A skein of Brent geese was flying east to their nesting grounds in the Russian arctic.

Coming towards him were two figures, dark, indistinct shapes, moving slowly across the creeks in a purposeful, almost solemn manner. They appeared to be walking side by side, but he couldn't be sure. They seemed unaware of his presence. He was distracted for a moment by the shriek of a corncrake. When he looked again, he saw a solitary figure now, a shapeless silhouette advancing and receding, appearing, and disappearing.

One

H e took the marsh road out from the village and found himself in an open, liminal landscape of sea lavender and samphire. Ahead, he could make out the shore, and beyond, a row of wind turbines, slowly turning. The man walked out across the marshes, taking advantage of the low tide, his path guided by a series of wooden bridges that crossed the deeper gullies and lagoons. Sarah had enjoyed this walk, striding ahead, stopping every now and then to admire a particular bird or to spur him on before the tide turned. At the first bridge he stopped, momentarily startled by the call of a red shank soaring out towards the sea. She was right though, if he didn't get a move on, he'd be in danger of being caught by the rapidly advancing tide. He also didn't like the look of the scurrying bank of rain clouds heading westward. He looked towards the rusting sewer pipe that stretched out towards the distant shore. Time to turn back.

During their second holiday he'd tried walking along the whole length of the pipe, something that had entered into the folklife of family life. They'd come every summer and, without fail, he and Adam would attempt the pipe, his son racing ahead with an agility that never ceased to amaze him.

He rested for a moment. The lagoons and creeks were filling fast, the skies darkening. He pushed on towards a line of oak trees that shielded the church from the north wind. Beyond the bridge, he crouched down and quickly picked a bunch of light-blue sea lavender. He could make out the southern wall of the church between the line of trees. He pushed open the gate into the church yard just as the heavens opened. 'God's tears,' Sarah used to say, her faith more apparent in landscapes such as this.

He knew his way and walked quickly towards the north-east corner of the field. There were two new plots, their shiny granite headstones incongruous and out of place. He moved towards one of the headstones, unadorned, except for a brief inscription, *Sarah, ever present.* At the foot of the grave was a small vase. He knelt and wiped the rain from his face. Into the vase he placed the small bunch of light-blue flowers.

***

For him, a pleasure of being out on the marshes was being alone, away from all forms of human interaction, except for the occasional walker who might grunt a brief greeting or nod as they passed. Walking up the gentle hill away from the churchyard, his thoughts were interrupted by a short ping from his phone. He was in no hurry to respond. They had both enjoyed the isolation of the marsh. 'Being alone together,' she had once quipped. He skirted around the closed-up campsite and headed in the direction of the pub. He'd check his phone when he was out of the rain.

She'd order a glass of dry white and he a pint of best. It was another ritual that had entered family life. Like most things in life, they'd found this tucked-away corner of the country – and each other – by chance. He liked to think that their first meeting had been likewise: destined, eyes meeting across the room, that kind of thing. But in fact, it had been chance, pure chance. If such a thing existed.

Lady Luck had played her hand in a small bar, *El Flamenco*, in one of those Latin American towns, that would never make it into the guidebooks. She was working behind the bar and hoping for an early night. A few stragglers were drinking up. He looked like every other backpacker: tall and gangly with a thin, wispy beard. Clearly, he was in a tizz about something. He was muttering, *passport, passport, passport*, as if just saying the words would make it miraculously appear. She walked over and crouched down beneath the table.

'Is this what you're looking for?' she said with a laugh. He had the good grace to look embarrassed. *Chance, luck, circumstance,* he told her later, offering to buy her a drink at a rival bar in the general direction of his hostel. Chance or luck, she agreed.

He remembered her order. 'A large glass of dry white wine, please,' spoken in an accent that suggested a privately educated Home Counties girl. In fact – as with most things he discovered about her – she was very different from how she first appeared, the only daughter of Derbyshire sheep farmers who just about managed to keep a roof over their heads. She'd done badly at the local comp, had scraped into one of the new polys where she'd studied geology – a subject which she considered a natural extension to a life spent mostly outdoors.

Geology – or as she liked to remind him, geomorphology – had left her with a fascination for all things tectonic, a particular interest being the San Andreas fault than runs down the Andean spine of Latin America. Working in a bar in a small town along a route favoured by backpackers, was not a matter of chance, but one of necessity. Her father had presented her with the air ticket, how she funded the rest was up to her.

She'd been in the country for six weeks and had managed a couple of solo hikes up into the mountains.

Over the years his love of a good story had changed the narrative of their first meeting. *I'd left the wretched thing in the bar – I was absent-minded then – and Sarah had run after me and...well...the rest is history.* Not strictly true he'd admit, but a different kind of truth to that found amongst rocks and tectonic plates. What *was* true was the serendipitous nature of their first meeting.

The path soon narrowed as it left the fields and entered an ancient holloway providing him with some shelter from the rain. He stamped his feet on the mat at the back door of the pub and entered. His phone pinged again. For a moment he wondered where he'd put the thing. Must be Adam calling to say he'd arrived safely in Lima, and was no doubt resting up after the long flight. It was a text, brief, and to the point.

'I've found your son's phone. He's disappeared. Please call me. Cristina.'

***

Two

He read the text again. Adam had disappeared. Whoever this Cristina was had clearly got hold of Adam's phone – stolen it more likely – and was about to scam him. But he would call back if only to try and reason with her. He hastened his step as the pub came into view.

She picked up immediately. She had found the phone on a dirt track that ran around the back of the hostel where he was staying. Diego the hostel owner could unlock any phone. She'd called the last number he'd called. Had enquired with Diego and had worked out who the likely owner of the phone was.

'Of course, maybe he threw away the phone and bought a new one?' Her voice was heavily accented, and he wondered what she looked like. 'But it is not damaged, so I think he threw it for some reason.' He interrupted her and described Adam in case she had seen him. No, she didn't know him, though there were quite a few guys who fitted the description: tall, bearded, *kinda* nice. She used the word *kinda* and *nice* a lot. Told him not to worry. Where was she calling from?

'I'm in Huacachina, the desert oasis. It's in the centre of Peru. Famous for its lagoon and sand buggying.' She paused. 'Many like your son come here.'

'You live there, in Huacachina?'

'Yes, it's my hometown, though for a town it is very small. My grandfather lives just outside in a place called Ica. He has a vineyard and I come to visit him.'

There was a short silence. He thought he could hear the revving of motorcycles in the background. No, she didn't know him, but there were quite a few guys who looked like him: tall, bearded. *Kinda* nice. And he wasn't to worry. He had probably dropped the phone on the way back from the lagoon. She told him again that she was calling from the oasis village of Huacachina, in the centre of the country, about four hours from Lima. Famous for its lagoon and dunes. He waited for her to say something else. She knew he was called Adam from his phone. She wanted to help which was why she called. He heard her laugh nervously. He was probably looking for it right now. She would leave the phone at the front desk of the hostel, not far from where she'd found it. She had to go but if he called her back on her number in an hour or so, she'd check if he'd picked it up. And he was not to worry.

'Thank you, Cristina but why did you call me? Maybe he has just lost or has thrown away his phone?'

'Yes, thank you, *senor* Hugh. Before I sent you the text, I spoke with Diego who runs the hostel near where I found the phone, and he told me your son, Adam was staying at the hostel but had not returned last night. The hostel owner, Diego looked into his room this morning and found no sign of him, just a few of his things. No passport or money. And so, when I found the phone this morning, I decided to call you.'

'Thank you, Cristina. You are very kind.'

'I hope I am not intruding senor, but when I texted you, I thought it was for the best. Of course, maybe he has moved to another hostel and is looking for his phone right now.'

She sounded nice, relieved perhaps to be talking to him, a slight American accent. For a moment he tried to picture her, perhaps in her mid-twenties, dark hair, bright smile, clearly kind. She told him she was going to leave the phone at the front desk of the hostel, but that if he called her in an hour or two – she gave him her number – she'd check if the phone had been picked up. Before she said goodbye, he detected a faint hesitation in her voice, as if she wasn't telling him everything she knew.

'But please not to worry, senor Hugh, I am sure he is well, and all is fine.'

But he did worry. Something wasn't right. Adam had thrown a tantrum once when Sarah had banned all electronic devices from the table. He must have been about thirteen or fourteen. He loved his phone. And Hugh knew enough of journalists to know that losing a phone was like cutting off a limb. Perhaps Cristina was right, and he had deliberately discarded this one for a newer model, but it still didn't explain his sudden disappearance from the hostel. He walked over to the bar and ordered a pint. *Where on earth was he?* He carried his drink back to a small table overlooking the back of the pub. The rain was clearing.

He'd taken a room above, at the back and away from the road. It was late Autumn and there were few guests, just a couple of regulars downstairs, occupying the saloon every evening until closing time. Food was good, though he hadn't eaten much since the funeral. The place was quiet which suited him. An occasional bus trundled past the front and that was it. A semblance of peace and quiet. Until the call from Cristina. He finished his beer and ordered a burger and chips which he'd carry up to his room. He'd put the hour until he heard from Cristina to good use.

A click of a mouse takes you into the world of the disappeared and the missing. It was both fascinating and appalling. Something like a quarter of a million people go missing every year, or, to put it another way, someone disappears off the streets every ninety seconds. Dear God, that was equivalent to a city the size of Plymouth disappearing every year. Most return home but it meant that something like 16,000 individuals remained missing for more than a year. And of those who disappear abroad, most are never found.

He sat back in his chair and picked at his food. For once he was glad, he'd brought his computer with him. His plan had been to catch up on emails, reply to those who had expressed their condolences. Perhaps do a little work.

Never found. But never searched for either? He clicked on a link. There were further links to the Foreign, Commonwealth & Development Office. Here there was something about *contacting the appropriate British Embassy when checking to see if a missing person had come to notice,* whatever that meant. There was also a link to various organisations set up to help in the search. The Lucie Blackman Trust was one of them. Lots of advice, and a somewhat chilling interpretation of what constituted a missing person. He took down their details and then those of the Embassy in Lima. Doing something – anything – helped assuage the rumblings of anxiety. He took a mouthful of the burger. It tasted of nothing. He should have asked for some gherkins or a couple of sachets of mustard.

He jotted down the Trust's opening lines, *A missing person was a person in limbo, neither alive nor dead, in a shadowy no-man's land, until a Presumption of Death certificate can be obtained from the High Court seven years after the date they were last seen.*

He looked up from the screen. *Seven years? Did those looking eventually give up exhausted or maybe became resigned to the inevitable?* Amongst the statistics and weblinks were the occasional life stories of a missing person, as if to remind you that these were real people lost and not found.

He then peered at a blurred photograph of a middle-aged man smiling awkwardly towards the camera. His name was Andrew Johnston, happily married with four daughters, who had 'popped out to buy some cigarettes from the corner shop' and had never been seen since. *Never been seen since.* He thought of the birthdays he had missed, the anniversaries of the day of his disappearance coming round like clockwork, the messages posted on social media, his daughters' anguish – four daughters! –

and wondered whether they were still looking. He looked happy enough in the photograph, but then you'd have said the same about Adam until Sarah had died. Then he had become gloomy and withdrawn. Understandable though.

No, Adam wouldn't do such a thing, whatever crises he might be going through, whatever anguish he was experiencing. He had been close to Sarah – perhaps less so to him – but he knew enough of his son to know that he'd would never inflict such cruelty or unkindness on his father. Or on anyone.

He ate some more of the food. Being hungry wouldn't help. There seemed to be two possibilities. The first was that it really was some kind of mistake. Losing a phone is quite common – though he had never lost his own – but then he was extra-careful when it came to possessions. The young woman, Cristina was clearly trying to be helpful – and she said there was nothing to worry about. In a day or so Adam would call on his old – or a newly bought phone – to apologise for any anxiety he had caused. End of story.

The second was that something unfortunate *had* happened to him. He'd been mugged, kidnapped or worse. He didn't like to think what *worse* might entail, at least not until he had more evidence to go on. But weighing it all up, he decided that the first possibility was the more likely. It was clearly some kind of mistake.

But he was worried. Something wasn't right, something still niggled. *All would be well*, Sarah liked used to say, when she saw he was worried or at a loss at what to do. He walked over to the window and looked out towards the church. *All will be well*, he said quietly in the direction of the graveyard.

Grief, when it came, seemed to ebb and flow like the tide. It also stopped him thinking straight, which for an academic, he found somewhat unsettling, almost unprofessional. He knew the cause of his malaise of course, it was perfectly rational to feel uprooted, adrift – what was that word she liked to use? – *discombobulated*. He'd read somewhere that grief reconfigures time, its length, its texture, even its function, a little like falling in love – pushing you into a new geography, a new cartography, a realignment of familiar tectonic plates, a new landscape in which the bearings are unfamiliar, the road ahead unknown.

He stayed by the window and looked out. It was dark but possible to catch a glimpse of the churchyard and the beginnings of the path that led out across the marsh to the distant shore. Looking more closely, he saw a slightly stooped figure walking slowly through the gate that led from the marsh into the field where Sarah lay. The woman was dressed in a mid-length skirt. He couldn't make out the colour, but in her right hand she seemed to be carrying a small bunch of light-blue sea lavender.

***

Three

H e had more or less retired – more rather than less – his university suggesting he move from fractional to emeritus status following Sarah's death, which meant he kept a desk in a shared office and more importantly, maintained some semblance of an institutional identity. *More or less retired, more or less disappeared.* He bought into that and knew that Sarah would have agreed. 'Leave while you still enjoy it,' she'd said the last time they had discussed what she called *transitioning* from working for others to working for yourself. Not that he ever saw academic life that way. For him it was a bit of both. He genuinely felt he was serving both his students and himself when he embarked on the preparation for a lecture or spent long hours over a research application. Ok, so committee-time was different, all jobs had their downsides, but if you played your cards right it was possible to keep the balance tilted towards the positive.

Telling people what he did had always been problematic. In the early days when he was a humble graduate student, he played up the poverty and precariousness of his chosen career, reminded whoever would listen, that a lectureship in cultural history – though an important part of the fabric of civilised life – was never going to earn you big bucks, but at least it gave you the chance to see a bit of the world. It had taken him to Latin America – he'd written his dissertation on 'the Cusco School of Art and its influence on Peruvian national identity', an interest which had landed him a temporary lectureship at one of the old polys and then a more established position at a middle-rank university on the south coast. Occasionally, he'd glance at his name on his office door, and smile. *Haven't done too badly*.

In the early days, he had toyed with the idea of applying for something in a more prestigious university but once

Sarah became more established as head of art at a local secondary school he – they – had decided to put down roots in the form of a Victorian three-storey terrace in a street that ran close to one of the city's parks – and which they were assured by the agent – was close to the best schools, 'when the time is right'. They had smiled at this remark, remembering its veracity, when Adam came along.

As he settled in at the university, he began to learn the art of saying 'no' without offending those in positions above his. He soon gained a reputation for being a safe pair of hands, perhaps not the shiniest academic in the pack, but reliable, a man you could trust. Now, part-time, he was mostly left alone, welcomed when he was seen around campus, usually on the occasion of a leaving-do. Then questions were asked about how he was occupying his time, condolences offered for his loss, an offer made of a pint if he felt like *getting out*. He would smile benignly, developing an air of gentle diffidence which he found agreeable since Sarah had gone. *Gone?* What a strange word. He had no idea *where,* exactly, she had *gone,* preferring to think she had *left* – or worse – had *passed on* to somewhere out of reach. When he did think of her – which was most of the time – he would sigh and shake his head. Theatrical, yes, but it gave him something to do. The simple fact was, she had been there and now she wasn't. She had disappeared.

For a moment, thoughts of Adam intruded. *Where had he gone? And more important, was he coming back?* He continued to look out towards the marsh. The rain had stopped but it was completely dark. No moon. Soon he would call Cristina, and if the news was good – Adam had retrieved his phone – he would climb the narrow stairs down to the bar and reward himself with a large scotch.

***

She answered immediately as if she'd been expecting his call. Adam hadn't returned to the hostel. When he pushed her to say more, she told him – again –not to worry. It was only five or six hours since she'd found the phone, and it was unlikely Adam would immediately think it had been found and left at the front desk of the hostel. Give it another two or three hours. He agreed and said he'd call her around midnight his time, early evening where she was. He thanked her, wondering again what she looked like. She sounded friendly, sensible; or was certainly acting so.

The bar was almost empty, a fire lit in the grate. He carried a pint of Adnams – it was too early for whisky – and sat a table nearest the window. She was right, there was nothing to be particularly worried about. This assumed, of course, that she'd found the phone shortly after Adam had dropped it. But what if Adam had dropped it shortly *after* he'd arrived – some forty-eight hours *before* she'd spotted it? And if that was the case, it would make his disappearance all the more serious, and a plan to find him all the more important.

The hostel owner. What if this Diego person had been mistaken about the last time he'd seen Adam, which raised the possibility he'd been missing for at least twenty-four hours? On the other hand, the few things Adam had left behind in his room suggested he was intending to return. But it was late. He'd promised her he'd call her at midnight, so he decided to make good use of the time he had by drawing up a plan of action. There was no need to rush, but at some point, he might need to catch a flight to Lima. He had no commitments at the university, and, in fact he'd be acting on the well-intentioned advice that he should get away, take a break, recharge his batteries. If he needed any further excuses, he'd tell those who asked that he was re-visiting old haunts, returning to where he and Sarah had met, a run-down bar in a run-down place in the foothills of the Andes. He wondered if it still existed. Only one way to find out. Chance, luck, and circumstance marshalled into something more useful.

Thinking it through cheered him up. When Adam reappeared – which he was now certain he would do – any disquiet on his son's part about what he was doing following him would be assuaged when he told him it was all about Sarah. She might have gone, but where they met, he was sure, remained. He'd put off calling the Embassy until it really did look like an emergency. Equally he would call the hostel once he'd got a flight booked and he had some idea of when he might arrive. They would be able to recommend somewhere nearby to stay, somewhere quiet. After a twelve-hour flight, he would need to catch up on his sleep. The same with the hostel where he hoped to stay. That too could wait.

Sharing his plans with someone was more problematic. He was an only child and with just Adam the family circle was very small. Plus, he had an instinctive desire not to burden any of them with more bad news. Best if he kept his plans to himself. And the paper. He'd need to call them at some point to see if they'd heard anything, but he also needed to be careful. On university open days he had seen enough of helicopter parents to know that the closer they hovered, the quicker their beloved offspring wanted to escape.

But something still niggled. If Adam *had* dropped the phone accidentally, he would have traced his steps back to the hostel, if only to put up a notice asking local residents to look out for it. And if he had deliberately thrown it away – to be off-grid for some reason – he'd leave himself with no way of communicating with his editor, unless he had in fact discarded his old phone and decided to buy a new one? Or borrow someone else's? For a journalist that seemed out of character, unprofessional even.

He resisted the temptation of a second pint – he needed to be cold sober when he talked to Cristina – and instead, drew up a shortlist of things he had to do when he arrived home. Ticket, dollars, passport, pack. For a moment he considered calling Avril, one of his few colleagues who had seemed genuinely upset when she had learnt of Sarah's death.

'It's so ghastly, Hugh. There's nothing I can say, except give me a buzz if you want company or just drop round. We can sit in total silence for an hour if it helps.' She paused and gave him a lop-sided smile. 'But if that's the case bring a large bottle of malt with you.'

He'd said he would think about it, and there was the occasional evening when he did consider walking round. But his natural reticence prevented him taking up her offer. On reflection – and he noticed he seemed to be doing a lot of reflecting these days – he decided he'd only call her if he really needed to. Since the funeral, explaining and justifying and avoiding the wave of compassion that flowed towards him, was exhausting. He'd put on a small spread for those who came – mostly her family – a buffet and some wine which he'd laid out on a trestle table in the garden. One or two speeches were made, and then as the afternoon faded, they had drifted away, offering support but sensing he was best left alone. As he'd cleared the table, he'd looked at the apple tree that had started to drop its fruit onto the ground. He'd walked over the lawn, which he had mowed the previous day, and had run his hands over the bark. He had leaned in close, his hands pressed firmly into the bark. Solid, permanent. He looked back towards the kitchen window –half-expecting to see her beckoning him in. He wasn't alone, he just wasn't with her. And there was Adam looking out. He had moved back into his old room at the top of the house, just for a few days he had said, just the two of them now.

It had been later in the evening when he'd come down and told him about the article he was going to write, 'A long piece, Dad, something about Peru – off the beaten track - that kind of thing'. The paper would cover costs, a chance to make his name, maybe a book in it – and he'd added with a smile, 'chance to check out your old stomping grounds, Dad, find that bar, *El Flamenco* wasn't it, where you say it all started'. He had smiled at his father, 'passport, passport, passport! Who knows, maybe I'll manage to lose mine like you did, and like you, find the love of my life?' Father and son sharing something. It hadn't happened like that in a long time. Perhaps never.

'When will you leave?'

'Tomorrow night. I've spoken to Max, and he's keen I should go. I'm on compassionate leave anyway, but this'll clear my head and get me thinking about work.'

He hopped from one foot to the other, a gesture he'd carried with him into adulthood.

'What will you write about?'

'Cocaine, the *Shining Path,* corruption – you know – run-of-the-mill kind of stuff.' He had looked excited and energised. 'I've done a bit of the preliminary groundwork and have a few names and contacts I can interview when I get there.'

He would travel light, no laptop, just a clutch of Moleskin notebooks – 'good enough for Chatwin, good enough for me' – his mobile, and enough clothes for three, possibly four weeks. He had patted him on the shoulder. It was the closest he'd got to displaying affection.

Where it had all started. A chance encounter in a faded bar in a dusty Andean town. It was good he was going. Nothing like work to distract. And he was young, the future ahead of him. Opportunities too, for some chance encounters of his own.

***

He drank up and carried his empty glass back to the bar. Rather than return to his room and wait until twelve, he decided to walk the mile or so back to the marsh. Clear his head, collect his thoughts, think about what news Cristina might bring.

Checking the mobile was in the inner pocket of his windcheater, he set off from the front of the pub taking the tarred road for a short distance until he met the uphill track that led towards the campsite and then the marsh. They must have taken this route hundreds of times but still he was glad he'd had the foresight to bring along the torch. It was pitch black, the only light coming from the pub windows to his right and a faint glow from the ground floor window of a newly converted barn. There was no moon, but he could see enough to not need the torch. The track would take him past the western edge of the campsite with its gate into the churchyard, and then down towards the row of oaks that separated the edge of the marsh from the fields. At the trees he'd stop and retrace his steps back to the pub. It was comforting walking a path he knew so well, connecting him in some way to the time when his family was a perfect triangle of equal sides. Somehow, the loss of one side created just a jagged intersection between two points, sharp and indefinite.

He thought about the call he'd make in a couple of hours. He felt certain it would be good news. If she had nothing new to say – the phone hadn't been collected and Adam hadn't made contact, it would be clear what he had do. *A man of action and not a man of thought.* How often had Sarah said something similar? Melodramatic but true. *philosophers have sought to interpret the world...* and all that. He kicked at a stone which spun off into the ditch at the side of the road.

When he reached the line of oaks, he stopped to catch his breath. He could hear the distant rumble of breakers crashing onto the shore way out beyond the marsh. To his right he could make out the narrow track that led down to the church. On an impulse – he had at least an hour before the call – he turned right towards the church. He could walk around the building and take the path back via the graveyard.

It was then that he saw her, standing amongst the graves, bending low, her back to him, as if she was looking for something on the ground or tying a lace. She was dressed in the same long brown skirt but was now wearing a red shawl on her head that looked a little like a bonnet of past times. He picked up speed and shone his torch on the path ahead. He walked quickly between two large trees which for a moment obscured his view of the field. When it came back into sight she had gone. He pointed his light in her direction and back the way he'd come in case she'd run around the far side of the church. There was no sign of her. She had disappeared. He walked over the grave of his wife, and knelt. 'Sorry, Sarah, I've been such a fool, such a stupid old fool.'

He arrived back just before eleven thirty and left his walking boots on the wooden veranda outside his room. On the dot of twelve he called. No response. He waited fifteen minutes and called again. Nothing. Five hours behind UK time, seven p.m. her time.

Why hadn't she picked up? It didn't make sense.

He waited another hour and called again. Nothing. If the bar had been open, he'd have gone down for a scotch, if only to help him sleep. When sleep eventually came it was fretful, peopled with indistinct human forms, beckoning him from the furthest reaches of the marsh, one wearing a bright red shawl over her shoulders, another of a young man grinning at him, one eye permanently closed, the other unblinking in the intensity of its gaze.

***

Four

The house – it was no longer a home – felt cold and unwelcoming. He gathered up the mail, mostly junk, but opened two cards expressing regret at missing the funeral and hoping he was OK. For a moment he half-expected to see one in Sarah's handwriting, 'Sorry I had to leave in such a rush, Hugh.' He threw the junk mail into the bin and wandered over to his chair next to the window that overlooked the garden. 'What do you think, Sarah, should I rush over there and make a fool of myself when we meet up or be patient and give it a few days?'

He glanced at his watch. Not quite the sun over the yardarm, but no harm in a scotch and an early night. 'That's right, darling, sleep on it. I'm sure he's just fine.'

The next few days were surprisingly busy. A decision he had taken quickly whilst walking across the marshes had been to put the house on the market. He'd even gone as far as glancing at properties for sale in some of the places he could imaging living: Blakeney, Wells-next-the-Sea, Cley. And it was something to do, activity to fill the emptiness inside.

***

'Your reason for visiting?'

To find my son who's gone missing, who has disappeared into thin air.

Instead, he said, 'tourism' and was waved through. *Thin Air?* He waited for his bags by the carousel. There had been no calls from Adam or Cristina. Nothing. Just before he'd left, he'd called Avril – to be honest she'd called him twice asking if he was alright – and had met up for a drink.

'There's no point me trying to persuade you, Hugh, because you can be a stubborn bugger at the best of time, but promise me this, you'll call me every now and then, and if you do meet up with Adam – which I'm sure you will – you won't quiz him on why he didn't call or why he threw away his phone'. He had nodded, taken aback by the concern she was showing for him. He'd discussed another reason for flying out, to revisit the country where he and Sarah had first met. Avril had touched him gently on the sleeve. 'Good for you, Hugh, good for you.'

Now he had arrived, he did feel in a funny kind of way nearer to Sarah.

He'd returned to her bar the following day, just before they closed. She was putting glasses away and didn't see him enter.

'Hi, stranger?'

'Hi, Sarah,' he said, and added 'You're working tomorrow?'

'Actually, I'm not. A couple of days off in lieu of working all last weekend. Why do you ask?'

'If you're free, maybe …'

She interrupted him. '…Whatever you're proposing I'd love to, but I've promised myself a two-day hike up into the mountains above Titicaca. I'm told it's a challenge, altitude and all that.' She placed the last glass on its shelf above the bar. Her hair was tied back in a ponytail. 'Fancy coming along? You look fit enough.'

The carousel continued to spit out the occasional bag. His was the last to arrive. The airport had been completely transformed. Then it had looked a little like a set from *One of Our Aircraft is Missing,* now it was all gleaming steel and duty-free shops.

Halfway up the mountain they stopped to admire the view.

'God, this takes my breath away, 'she said, laughing. They were sitting on a low wall that overlooked the lake.

'*You* take my breath away,' he said boldly, surprising himself. She smacked his hand.

'Repressed Englishman is getting flirty? Must be the lack of oxygen or the potent effect of the coca leaves!'

And that's how he remembered their early days, walking – the occasional attempt at a hike – her evenings working at the bar, he joining her at closing time, the late meals, more nights at her place than his. Her employer, Ricardo, gradually relied increasingly on her opening and closing, calling by at the end of the week to cash up and pay her wages. He was friendly enough but seemed to have other more pressing concerns away from the bar. Only once had he joined them for a Friday evening drink and talked about the rebels, the *Shining Path*, who didn't take kindly to *gringoes* flaunting their wealth. But he reassured them. They'd be fine. Clearly, they had no wealth to flaunt.

***

The modernity of the airport soon gave way to the chaotic and frightening mix of heavy traffic, aggressive drivers, and perilous roadworks that seemed designed to thwart any driver hurtling towards their destination. His own taxi driver seemed unconcerned, turning around to shout ask him about how he intended to spend his days and whether he needed a driver to show him around. He said no and rolled down the window. Avenida Faucett, if he remembered correctly should take him down to the seafront, then left along the Malecon to his hotel in the more upmarket district of Miraflores. He took in a lungful of air and coughed. But it was good to be back in a foreign land that was familiar, and which was special for him and Sarah.

He'd decided on one of the best hotels with acclaimed views of the ocean. He dumped his bags in his room and made his way up to the bar.

'What would you like?' the barman asked in perfect English.

'A large scotch,' he replied, using a phrase taken directly from the guidebook.

'Please sit, senor, I will bring it to you.'

He sat at one of the small tables next to the window that ran from floor to ceiling giving him an amazing view over the Pacific. It was on the thirteenth floor, his room one floor below. One night here would give him a chance to catch up on sleep and adjust to the time difference. And, if he was honest, some luxury way beyond his budget all those years ago. At one end of the room was the bar with its swivel black stools and granite surfaces, at the other an ultra-modern restaurant. He placed his phone on the table and looked out. The ocean was a dark blue, almost black, illuminated by a huge cross erected on a headland to the left of the hotel.

'To commemorate the visit of a Holy Father,' the barman said, placing his whisky and a small plate of pretzels on the table. 'The owner of one of our largest casinos pays for the replacement bulbs.' Hugh looked at his phone. Nothing. The day after he had left the pub, he had called her twice, but nothing. It was as if the events of the night before had been swallowed up in the swirling sea mist rolling in across the marsh.

Why had she contacted him and then severed all communication? Had something happened to her, or worse, to Adam?

There was a text from Avril. He'd relented called her from Heathrow telling her he'd checked in and that he would call her every few days. Their outing to the pub had ended well. She'd hugged him as he'd turned to leave.

'But, Hugh, just so you know, I'm not getting on a plane to rescue you from some guerrilla movement deep in the Andes.'

He had assured her he'd be fine and had practised the story about visiting *El Flamenco*. He also rang the paper, and after holding for ten minutes, was put through to Max. He seemed surprised at the call.

'Sorry to trouble you, Max, but small family matter. I've tried calling him but he's not picking up. Just wondered if you've heard anything. Not to worry.'

Max said he'd heard nothing, but added pointedly that the paper's policy was to let their journalists – especially the experienced ones – have their head.

'But fear not, if he breaks cover, I'll send you a text. Keep well.' And with that he signed off.

Despite his room being directly below the bar, it was, like the rest of the hotel fully soundproofed, the only noise the gentle hum of the air conditioner. He fell asleep immediately and woke just before breakfast, an achievement considering it was something like mid-afternoon his time. Nothing on his phone, no miscalls. *Where are you Adam, what's happened?* They were now in the same time zone, the same country. Such an odd state of affairs, so unlike him. *And Cristina? What's your role in all this? First a friendly good Samaritan, then changing your tune. Strange and perplexing. Worrying too.* He lifted himself out of bed and wandered into the en suite.

One thing of the few lessons he'd learnt about parenthood was the disconnect between what you thought they were up to and what they were actually doing. Knowledge of this came through Sarah, who had the ear of her only child. When Adam was upset or fearful, he went to her. When he sought praise or the answer to some homework question, he came to him. And so, like many families they settled into well-defined roles that seemed to work, that complemented each other. But perhaps he should have been more like Sarah, closer to him?

He went down for breakfast. Once the article was written, he'd be the first to offer his congratulations, and encourage the longer piece, the book with his name on the cover, more than he had ever achieved at his age. He entered the restaurant and saw one or two guests helping themselves to the buffet. There would be coffee. It was a good coffee country. He entered, showed his room key, and made his way over to a window that looked down upon a park of tropical trees and bougainvillea. So much of his life had been spent looking out of windows. A paraglider floated gently over the Costa Verde, warm currents carrying him towards the endless expanse of sea. For a moment he envied the person, drifting alone and looking down on the people below.

From the North Norfolk coastline to the edge of the Pacific. Was all this some wild goose chase in search of a lost phone? Still, Sarah would approve. At least he was *doing* something.

And if it turns out that chucking away the phone was in an idle fit of pique. What then, Sarah?

He knew her answer. 'He's a grown man, Hugh, a professional journalist employed by a leading newspaper, and quite capable of looking after himself, phone or no phone.'

The waiter brought him his coffee and a small wicker basket containing an assortment of rolls and French bread. He decided he would call the Embassy when he was certain his son really was missing. All he had to go on for now was the word of a young woman who had found his phone and hadn't called him back. Hardly a crime. For all he knew, Adam could be anywhere, off-grid for a while, and ready to resurface at a time of his choosing. He refilled his cup. A plausible explanation, but one that didn't account for the unease he still felt. Something *had* happened to Adam; of that he was certain. To find the answer he would need to travel to where she said she had found the phone. On the plane he'd looked at the map. The desert oasis where Adam was, was mid-way between the capital and the dusty town where he had met Sarah.

*****

Though she was older than him by a couple of months, she was much fitter. He looked the part though: beard, rangy limbs, bushwhacker hat, but years of smoking was now beginning to tell.

'Hang on a minute, Sarah, let's stop and catch our breath,' he said. They'd only been walking for an hour, but at just over ten thousand feet, the climb was taking more out of him than he'd expected. It was chilly too and he was glad of the windcheater. She stopped ahead and sat down on a large flat boulder by the side of the road. Though the climb up to the summit was gentle, they'd started from a high base. It was his mother who'd said, 'if you want to know what someone is really like, take them camping.' Hiking a trail in the Andes seemed a good alternative. 'Looks like you've done this before,' he said, as he sat down beside her.

'Yes, Dad loved the Cairngorms. We went every summer. Highest about four thousand feet, so nothing like this, but fun. Here chew some of these.' She handed him a few *coca* leaves she'd picked up from reception just before they left. 'Supposed to help you cope with the altitude,' she said.

'Did your mum share his love of climbing?'

'To be honest, I think she enjoyed making the packed lunches and sorting out all the gear before we set out, but it wasn't really her thing. Not that she ever complained.'

'An uncomplaining wife, a real treasure,' he said with a grin.

'Yes, even towards the end when her cancer was at its worse, she never complained.'

'I'm sorry. When was it? Your father must have been devastated?'

'Well, he was – it was the year before university. I was immersed in my 'A' Levels – but he never complained either. Would just take the dog out for a walk. 'Get some fresh air,' he'd say. No trace of self-pity, just took it on the chin.'

'And you? Did you take it on the chin?'

She looked at him and said nothing.

'No packed lunch for you I'm afraid, but we've got water and fruit, so we'll be alright.' She leant closer towards him. 'Your hat's not straight, *Mister Explorer,*' she said, reaching over to make it straight.

A fragment of a memory he had carried with him down the years. *Mister Explorer*, a name she called him even when they set out to walk the short distance over the marshes towards the sea.

He buttered a slice of toast and refilled his coffee cup. Well, he was a real explorer now, on his own, striking out, unsure of where he was going or what he might find.

***

Five

T he hostel picked up immediately.

'My English is not good, but can I help?'

He told him who he was. 'My son Adam's phone was left with you. For him to collect when he discovered it missing. By a young woman called Cristina. She found it and left it with you.'

There was a silence and what sounded to him like papers being shuffled.

'I am sorry, senor. I have nothing of the phone. I have a bag with some cream for the sun but no phone. I have looked in our book and have no record of the phone.' He asked him to check the register for arrivals. 'Yes, a Mister Adam, stayed here for one night, three days ago. But no Cristina. I am sorry.'

He ended the call and thanked the receptionist, Roberto, of the Marriott who'd offered to be on hand to help with the Spanish if need be. He'd planned to call the Embassy but decided not to. 'Wild goose chase' or worse 'Helicopter parent' would be what they thought if they didn't say it. It didn't make sense. First, it was clear that Adam had checked in for one not two nights at the hostel. Second, if he was to believe Cristina, whoever she was, that his phone had been lost and found – how else had she called him? – but why had the trail gone cold? And why had she reneged on her promise to leave the phone at the hostel and be willing to talk with him? Second, something had happened to Adam to prompt him to cut off all contact. If he had lost his phone, he had enough funds to buy another. Adam had left some of his things in his room which meant he intended to return. It didn't make sense and was out of character.

And what about work? His phone was his lifeline to the paper. Something had happened, perhaps to both of them?

Roberto gave him detailed instructions of where he could pick up a luxury coach that would take him from the centre of Lima to Huacachina, the oasis town. From there it would be a stone's throw to the handful of hostels that ringed the lagoon. If it helped, he could leave most of his luggage in the hotel's box room. Just take a backpack with enough clothes to last a few days. A good suggestion.

Half an hour later he was walking out of the hotel and up the broad *Avenida Benavides* in the direction of *PeruHop*, a reliable coach company – or so Roberto assured him - that sold him a flexible return, but if he wished, could take him further up into the Andes. *Flexible, adventurous, and safe* was printed on the side of the bus. There was one leaving at two that afternoon. He would be in Huacachina in just over four hours. He accepted the complimentary bottle of water and declined the tee shirt. In different circumstances this would indeed be an adventure. As he settled into his seat, his only thought was of Adam – *Where are you? Why haven't you called?* – and of Sarah sitting in the empty seat next to him, sharing his bottle of water and telling him not to worry. If only he believed her.

***

During the first hour of the journey the coach crawled through the suburbs of the capital until it reached the Pan American Highway that runs south down the coastal spine of the country. This was the route the Hernando Pizarro and the conquistadores took after the execution of the Inca at Cajamarca in 1533. Turning south, they reached the sea and then hugged the shore until they arrived at the ancient citadel of Pachacamac. Here the Spanish had plundered more than a hundred thousand pounds of gold, most of it spirited away to Spain. He looked out of the window as the coach rumbled pass huge chicken sheds interspersed with half-built housing, most plastered with the names of political hopefuls. It was a dry and unforgiving landscape, the only relief coming from the sea which seemed completely devoid of life.

The flight and time difference were beginning to catch up on him. Luxury coach. They were right about that. So very different from the bone-shattering bus he'd taken up into the mountains in the mid-80s. Now he could recline his VIP seat and empty his mind of the anxieties and uncertainties that made him feel anything but adventurous. He tried to remember what it had been like in the '80s. *Flexible, adventurous, and safe* too?

Soon they took a sharp turn inland driving through large vineyards in the centre of which sat the impressive haciendas. Clearly the arrival of the Spanish had contributed something, though he wondered how much of the industry was in the hands of the locals. After an hour motoring slowly through the wine country, the driver announced their imminent arrival into Huacachina, *the only oasis town in Latin America*. This was greeted by an enthusiastic round of applause. As the coach slowed, he looked over to his right and saw they were descending towards an emerald-green lake surrounded by three-hundred-foot dunes. They came to an abrupt stop next to what appeared to be the town hall.

Flexible, yes – he remembered the casual attitude the bus driver had taken to when they'd begin their journey. *Adventurous?* Of course, he was in South America, the land of the conquistadors and Hiram Bingham, and he still had the leather bushwhacker hat his father had given him on the day he left. *Safe?* More difficult to judge but then England under Thatcher was hardly a model of security, the IRA Brighton bombing, the miners' strike, the Heysel tragedy. Safe was elsewhere, safe was South America, safe was adventurous.

He was awoken by the driver shouting something rapidly in Spanish. The coach had stopped outside what looked like a large primary school. Passengers were already dragging suitcases from the bowels of the coach watched by a small group of local women offering bottles of water, chewing gum, and small posies of bright yellow flowers. He waited until everyone had descended and then climbed stiffly out of the front door. He had kept his backpack at his feet and now slung it over his shoulder and took out the instructions Roberto from the Marriott had written down for him. *Keep the lagoon on your left and at the top end take a sharp right, walk one block, turn right and you will see the best hotel, El Huacachinero on your left. You cannot miss it.*

To his left he could see the olive-green waters of the lagoon fringed by a line of palm trees, a few dinghies moored to a rotting post. This place had clearly seen better days, but it possessed a sense of tranquillity he found refreshing after his journey. It was quiet too, no sound of the sand buggies either but it was too early to venture up the dunes. That he knew from the guidebook was timed for sunset. *El Huacachinero* was quiet too, the young woman at the front desk taking down his details, photocopying his passport and asking him if there was anything he needed. If there was, he must be certain to ask. He said he would. The hotel consisted of two floors with a small dining room opening out onto a swimming pool.

Behind, the dunes soared up almost blotting out the sun. It was a strange place, ethereal almost. He could see why Adam had chosen to start his journey here, but given it was more of a village than a town, he could see why he hadn't stayed long. There wasn't much to do, apart from sand-buggy up on the dunes or get wasted in one of the bars which he noticed were offering free pisco sours with every round of drinks. He had a shower and changed. Perhaps the hostel owner could tell him more, anything he might have heard Adam say, any new information about the phone, or where he might have said he was moving on to. For a moment, he wondered about the police. But what would he say? Tell them about a lost and found and then lost again phone? About no news from his son or from a woman called Cristina who had called him. They would smile, write out a report, and tell him not to worry. Young people, adventure, flexibility. And safety? They'd tell him not to worry on that count too.

The hostel was a few hundred yards or so from the coach stop. A small two-story building fronted by a few tables shaded from the sun by an awning that had seen better days. A street dog lay beneath one of the tables. It was mid-afternoon and still very hot. He ordered a beer and marshalled his thoughts. He'd forgotten to write down the receptionist's name – Jose, Juan? – the young woman who brought over his beer would know. Her name was Luciana and the owner, Diego. He was due back in an hour, so why didn't he take a seat and enjoy a beer. He ordered a *cusquena* and a bottle of water. The only photo he had of Adam had been taken a few years ago but it still looked like him, beard, smiling, his arm around his mother. The waitress took it from him and examined it closely.

'He looks like you, senor, but has his mother's eyes.'

'Do you recognise him? Diego is certain he stayed here three or maybe four nights ago. When he returns, I'd would like to check the register if possible.'

She handed back the photo. 'No, I don't recognise him, but then I'm only part-time, and I started working here very recently – and no disrespect, senor, but the travellers who stay here all look much the same.'

'And a Cristina? Do you remember a young woman with that name? Maybe with Adam?' He told her about the phone.

'No, the name is not known to me – and the phone – I don't think we have anything left here. The other receptionist, Lourdes, is no longer here, but if it was handed to her, she would write in the book. It is true they sometimes leave a phone or something in their room and then we send it on to a hostel in Cusco or to Lima or wherever. It is costly for us, but it is good, not so? For the TripAdvisor.' She pointed to the logo above the fridge behind the counter. 'But please excuse my English which is not good...another?'

He asked for just another bottle of water and returned to his table. He would wait for Diego. Hugh checked his phone. There was a text from Avril hoping he'd arrived safely, and that he was making progress. Nothing from Adam or Cristina. He resisted the temptation to call Max.

He stood up and stretched his legs. The hostel was unremarkable. A small two storey building – rooms above – downstairs the reception and bar area and perhaps a restaurant at the back. An external spiral staircase gave access to the first and second floors. The front had been turned into an attractive patio area with a handful of round tables and chairs interspersed with pots of red and orange bougainvillea. It gave off an atmosphere of calm and appeared to be well managed. As he returned to his table, two backpackers arrived and walked directly to a table next to the spiral staircase. From their accents they sounded American or maybe Canadian, and were clearly staying at the hostel. Mid-30s, she was carrying an expensive rucksack, he a leather-bound book that looked out of place. She said something to him and then walked up the stairs leaving her friend – husband? – to order the drinks.

After about ten minutes she returned with a large sketch book. Luciana brought over the drinks and began a conversation about sandboarding. If they fancied it, she knew a guy...on her way back to the bar, she stopped at his table. 'Diego just called from Ica, the next town, to say he has to stay there today. His mother is unwell, but he hopes you can meet with him tomorrow at, say, ten in the morning. He remembers your call and looks forward to talking with you. Oh, and if you need a room, he tells me to give you the nice one at the back that looks over the lagoon.' He thanked her and asked her to tell Diego, he looked forward to the meeting, but that he had a room nearby. He finished his drink and made to leave. On an impulse, he walked over to the couple sitting to his right. She had set out several coloured pencils and he was immersed in a book.

'Sorry, to disturb you but could I take up five minutes of your time?' On the long coach journey, he had rehearsed what to say in this situation, though it now sounded stilted and overly formal.

'Sure, please join us' she said motioning towards a chair. She held out her hand. 'I'm Mindy and Mister Bookworm here is Joe.'

'Hello, I'm Hugh, Hugh Wilson.'

Joe slipped a small piece of paper into the book and closed it. His smile was like hers and he wondered if they were brother and sister. 'Can I buy you both a drink?' he said.

'Thanks, but no. But don't let us stop you,' she said. They were from the United States. 'Des Moines, though you wouldn't know it from our accents.' There was no answer to that, not helped by him having no idea what a Des Moines accent sounded like. Whatever, he was sure it wasn't attractive. 'In case you're wondering, I'm the *struggling* artist, and Joe here is the *struggling* investment banker who finds it a real *struggle* to take time out and when he does want go anywhere, he won't go without sis here to show him the ropes.'

'And who has absolutely no problem picking up the tab,' he said with a grin. 'And she's right, if she didn't force me to leave the delights of downtown Des Moines, I'd never do anything worthwhile with my ill-gotten gains'.

He immediately liked them. They had an easy way with each other, the banter and the teasing which reminded him of himself and Sarah, especially in the early days. They shared another trait too, something he'd noticed in other couples, the woman leading the conversation, often talking directly to the other woman, whilst the men looked on waiting for an opportunity to add something. It suited him, as he often had little to add to what Sarah was saying. After five minutes of polite conversation, Joe asked him how they might help. He withdrew the photograph from his wallet and pushed it across the table. 'My son, Adam, who may or may not have gone missing, at least has gone off grid. He stayed here a couple of nights ago for one or two nights – I need to check with Diego tomorrow – but since then I've heard nothing except for a strange message from a woman called Cristina who said she'd found his phone and had left it here at reception…'

Mindy interrupted him. '… and you've heard nothing from him?'

'Well, the phone?'

'Two things spring to mind. First, that he still has retrieved his phone but for some reason has decided – as you say – to go off-grid; and second that this Cristina might be part of some scam, she found your number – maybe from your son's phone – and aims to get you to transfer funds into an account. Happens all the time in the States.'

It was Joe's turn to speak. He picked up the photograph and looked at it for a second or two. 'I think I do recognise him. Seeing you reminds me of him. We've been here ten days, love the place, and…' He turned to his sister. 'Remember, Mind, the guy with the notebook, asking questions, always on his phone. A Brit.'

She took the photo again and looked more closely at it. 'I don't want to give you false hope. A lot of guys swing by this place but maybe Joe is right, maybe he was the guy we saw a few days back.'

'Do you remember anything he said, anything about where he was going? And was he alone or with someone else, a young woman?'

'Not much, and no, I don't remember any young woman, but if he is the guy, I do remember him asking Diego about who he might talk to, something about a book he was writing…'

Mindy broke in again. 'If Joe is right, then Diego would have sent him over to the library, a couple of blocks from here. The librarian and Diego are old school friends, and what he doesn't know about this place isn't worth knowing.'

The library. It surprised him the place still had one. He'd go tomorrow after meeting with Diego. Joe had visited once and told him it opened from eleven until two and was about half-way between the hostel and his hotel. A plan. He felt better, more optimistic. Luciana came over and asked if they'd like another round.

'And pizzas – we do very good pizzas,' she said with a smile. 'See TripAdvisor.'

***

Six

Thank you for visiting. My granddaughter, Cristina, told me a little about your enquiries, senor Adam, and I hope I can assist you in some small way. Before we talk, may I humbly request, you give me sight of what you write, when it is complete. There will be no problems, I can assure you, but in this country, it is easy in my position to make friends, and I regret to say, others who do not wish you well or to hear what you have to say. And I must apologise, too if I talk of things you have already read about or know, perhaps from my granddaughter here? Still, as they say, it is good to hear it from the horse's mouth, not so.

First you must realise a number of things. Although many – some of my colleagues in the military included – claimed victory against Sendero Luminoso, the Shining Path, these terrorists remain, though nothing like the force they once were, in the coca growing regions such as the valleys of the Apurimac, Ene and Mantaro rivers – and the Upper Huallaga valley or VRAEM for short. For the past ten years or so, they have consolidated their power in this area killing dozens of our soldiers, attacking military bases and forming close alliances with the farmers – not an easy thing considering the distrust engendered by the war in the 80s and 90s – with the one aim to control the transportation routes of the coca and protect the traffickers or mochileros who are recruited to carry the coca from the VRAEM to the Bolivian border.

Cristina here will have heard me talk often about one 'Camarada Jose,' who now leads the group. The Civil Defence forces killed his father, an active Sendero member, and he shows no mercy to any who resist his efforts to control the trade.

And I have to say, that he has been successful. We fly low over the VRAEM and on our last reconnaissance we counted an estimated 120 improvised airstrips, and a number of river jetties which are used to transport the drugs by river to Brazil. Of course, the mochileros who transport the cargoes on their backs are invariably caught and sentenced to lengthy prison terms, but we estimate that many earn as much as 500 United States dollars a month, which is a great deal more than that earnt by the humble farmer.

Poverty and little hope for advancement fuelled the original rise of Sendero in the early 80s and it is the same thing now, except that instead of talk of a Maoist revolution, the motivation is money pure and simple, though of course, nothing in this country is pure or simple.

I should add that as a military officer involved in the rounding up and interrogation of the revolutionaries during those years, I have no regrets for any excesses that might have occurred. Extraordinary times call for extraordinary measures. I was happy to give testimony to the Commission looking into these things, and my conscience is clear. The sinchies? You ask about them. They were a specialised anti-terrorism unit within the national police service. Unorthodox and tough. But they got the job done. If you wish, I can introduce you one who had the honour to serve with them. With distinction I might add.

But I have talked enough. I hear from Chrissie you wish to travel into the VRAEM, to see for yourself. I can of course only warn you of the risks, less so if you stick to the tourist routes but far more so if you stray into areas even my soldiers would regard as unwise.

Yes, I will ask my colleagues about transport, many of us prefer to use unofficial means to get there and back – and I have reliable contacts I can help you with. Cristina here knows more about suitable accommodation. Perhaps two of my trusted associates, Majors Salazar and Cortes can accompany you to ensure you are kept safe and well?

May I commend you, senor, for wishing to write about this dark side of our country. You will be fair and just; I know in how you tell our story. I wish you well. And again, I ask both of you to be careful.

Great first interview. Just proves my point that you need to be an insider to make for a good story – thank you Cristina. Bit of a creepy guy but clearly someone in the know when it comes to the Sendero years and what's going on now. The offer of a lift to VRAEM might be useful too. And protection if things turn nasty? Good to be away from Dad's stifling presence too. He means well but ...I want to think just about Mum. Just glad Cristina found the phone and asked me to move in with her. Bit of a rush but it's all paying off. Eat your heart out, Max!

***

$\mathbf{H}$is room at the hotel was well away from the road and the roaring of the sand buggies. It meant he slept well, helped by the cooler, less humid air. After breakfast, he decided to walk around the far side of the lagoon which should take him eventually to the hostel. Huacachina had once been the preserve of the rich with its pleasant climate and tranquillity. Luciana looked up from polishing glasses as he arrived.

'You enjoyed the pizza, *senor*, it was good?'

He nodded. '*Café con leche, por favor.*' A language he hadn't spoken in decades, seemed to be coming back. A short, stocky man strode towards him, his eyes darting here and there, as if this was his first time of visiting the place. Hugh extended his hand. Diego grasped it firmly.

'My mother, senor, she says she is ill, but the doctors can find nothing. She is alone now, my father Eduardo passed two years ago, and she what I think is called a broken heart.' He invited Hugh to sit and asked Luciana to bring more coffee. 'You have eaten breakfast?' He told him he had. 'I do what I can, but you know, there is no cure except for time, something she has a great deal of.'

Hugh found himself warming to the man. This was a man who understood the illness visited upon his mother and the responsibility it brought to those nearby. He thought of Sarah. During the final weeks he felt he had become two people, one the rationale, objective, evidence-based academic concerned with her and himself, the other, a desperate, irrational soul clutching at straws, receptive to the charms of the snake-oil salesmen. He remembered a brief conversation they'd had in the hospital during what would be his final visit.

'So, *Mister Explorer,* what have you discovered today? What new route are you going to take me down?' She was lying propped up in bed waiting for the nurse to bring the meds. He had laughed, reaching for her hand that lay open next to his. He reminded her of their walks along the sewer pipe and that it was always she who did the leading. 'But on this occasion, it is me who is lagging behind, me who is in danger of falling off.' He reminded her that she had always been there to help him back up when he had fallen. She leaning down, he reaching up, a metaphor he told her for a marriage well-lived, a life well-shared. They both knew what lay ahead, knowledge, she told him, that brought her some peace, clutching his hand, the only occasion he saw her cry.

'But I must not neglect the purpose of our meeting,' he said. With the coffee Luciana had also brought over the hostel register. It was neat and tidy with date, name of guest, and details of their ID. The hostel owner pointed a stubby finger at an entry. Adam had stayed one night – which would have been his second in the country – just under a week ago.

'Senor Hugh, you asked about the phone, which I think you said a young woman found and said she would leave it at with us? We keep a record of lost things, but I know that I or Luciana or Lourdes, would have remembered such a thing being given to us for safe keeping. She must have been mistaken, senor.'

'Lourdes, your part-time receptionist, might I speak with her?'

'She is no longer here I am afraid. A small matter of a disagreement between myself and her family. Unfortunate, but I understand, she has returned to her home in Lima.'

'And Adam's things that were left in his room?'

'Of course, you would like to see?' He stood up and said something quickly to Luciana. 'Come, follow me.' Hugh followed Diego towards the back of the building. The room was small but pleasantly furnished with a single bed, desk under the window and a table pushed against the far wall. On the table was a pile of things: a neatly folded shirt he recognised, a packet of gum, and an old copy of *El Commercio* he must have picked up at the airport. Hugh walked over to the bed and ran his hand over the pillow. This was where his son had lain his head.

'Was there anything else in the room?'

'No, senor. We left these things here to assure you that he stayed here. Now I will ask Luciana to place them for safekeeping behind the bar, even the old newspaper in case it is of importance.' The owner moved towards the door. He asked the Englishman how long he intended to stay in the town. As he spoke, a huge dune buggy roared by.

'You could try the hotels and coach offices. They keep records like I do of their customers.' He waved a hand in the direction of the lagoon. 'And please return to me if you wish to talk more. I am here to help, as I know Luciana is too.'

When he told him he would visit the library, have dinner with Mindy and Joe, and then catch a night bus back to the capital the following day, Diego smiled.

'A pisco sour, senor, we make the best,' he said as he pointed him in the direction of the library. 'And please greet Jorge, the librarian, for me. We go back many years. Too many,' he said with a chuckle, adding, 'we don't agree on all things, but we are brothers.'

***

He decided to return to the lagoon. It was a bewitching place, the emerald-green water dwarfed by the huge rising walls of sand that encircled the town. Diego had suggested he walk along the Malecon, the attractive promenade, until he came to the old library. He was about halfway when he saw the library on his left sandwiched between a pizza restaurant and another hostel. Like most of the buildings constructed during the colonial period, it was grand in an understated way, wooden-framed glass doors set back from a veranda that housed a leather sofa and three small chairs arranged around a small table. He climbed up three steps and walked towards the main door. It was partly open.

The room he entered was cool and peaceful, furnished with rows of books and a quiet sense of indifference to the roar of sand-buggies outside. A white-haired figure was seated at a desk in the corner peering at an opened tome with the help of a large magnifying glass. Hugh coughed quietly, preparing to answer as best he could about why he had entered.

The old man seemed unaware of him until he put down his glass and spoke softly.

'We close in an hour, senor.' His English was faultless with that perfection rarely found in a native speaker.

Hugh walked over to his desk.

'I apologise. You seem very busy with your book.'

'The Gettysburg Address. Marvellous don't you think? And reprinted here in this magnificent volume, so kindly donated to us by the United States consul on his last visit to the town. So very generous.'

He looked down at the page the librarian was reading. The print was indeed small.

'Do you work here, senor?' A polite but somewhat redundant question.

'Of course. I'm the librarian.' The old man held out a hand, almost as pale as his pressed shirt, its sleeves held up by two black leather armbands. Hugh grasped his hand which was as cool as the interior of the room. 'Please sit, join me for a while, I like to hear your language as much as read it from these American books written so long ago.'

'I'm not American, I'm afraid.'

'Ah *Ingles*? Such a marvellous country. Shakespeare, Sherlock Holmes, Harry Potter...' The librarian laughed quietly.

He had never read any of the Rowling books – Adam hadn't shown much interest in the wizards of Hogwarts – preferring instead to immerse himself in the shipwrecks and pirates that had once plied the Norfolk coast.

The librarian rose slowly and fetched a small collapsible chair which he placed next to his own. He gestured a pale hand towards his thermos. 'It's all I can offer, I'm afraid, and it's not as hot as it was, but if you would like to join me?' Hugh helped him unfold the chair and waited whilst the old man went into a small room at the back to fetch another cup and saucer. 'What brings you to our lovely library, senor?'

There was something about the demeanour of the librarian that encouraged a restfulness he hadn't experienced since Sarah's death. The librarian listened intently as he told his story. Every now and then, out of habit, he twirled the magnifying glass in his left hand. When he had finished, they picked up their coffee cups and sipped the lukewarm contents.

'Thank you for the coffee, and the opportunity to unburden myself. I'm sorry to disturb your reading of such a magnificent text but...'

'Please, don't apologise. Do you have a photograph of your son?' He looked at it closely with the help of his glass. 'Yes, he came here, three days ago. Now I see the likeness between you and him. Diego – you know Diego? He suggested I might be able to help him, with a story, a newspaper article he was writing. I did as best as I could. My job of course is to act as a repository.'

'What was he looking for?'

'He seemed interested in the calamity that befell our country forty something years ago – I'm sure you know of this – but in particular one of the legacies of this, the production and shipment of illegal drugs – and I'm talking about cocaine – and who is involved. He seemed to think the remnants of the rebels and rogue elements of the military lay behind it all. I told him it was likely but ...'

'Was he alone when he came?'

'No, there was a young woman. I forget her name. Her family are from these parts, but I did not know her. Your son told me she was helping with the translation, transport arrangements, that kind of thing.'

'And when he left, did he give any indication of his plans, where he was headed?'

'No, he didn't but he did seem interested in meeting my sister Julia. Perhaps he went there? She lives alone in Ayacucho – it is eight hours by road from here - and has her own stories to tell. But then we Peruvians, we all have stories to tell.' He smiled and offered more coffee. 'But I have said a lot. Please, it's good for me to listen to a native speaker too – and one from the home of the great William Shakespeare – and as for your reason for coming to my country, my library, may I just say that, of course, I wish you well, and, if I may also add, that I too have experienced something of what you are going through, the compressed feeling in your chest, the shortness of breath, the inability to sleep, even rest...?' He put down his cup '...Please forgive me, it is not my place to intrude, to weigh one man's grief against another...'

'No please, I would like to hear what you have to say.' Hugh raised his cup and drank what was left of the coffee.

'I thank you. And who knows perhaps what I have to say can bring both of us some comfort... you no doubt have heard about the calamity that befell our country in the '80s and '90s, the devastation wrought by the Maoist revolutionaries, and the even more terrible retribution visited upon us by the State and its paramilitaries, call them what you will...'He removed a large white handkerchief from his pocket and began cleaning the magnifying glass. 'Well, to be brief, my son Juan got caught up in all the rhetoric of Professor Guzman, the architect of the *Shining Path*, you know the kind of thing , and before he knew what had happened – or had realised what he'd got himself into – he was seized, along with others, in a small village not far from the epicentre of it all, the city of Ayacucho, a place I associate with learning, where I studied at the university before the calamity that befell us all. He'd had been visiting his aunt…we learnt this from a girlfriend who was with him and who managed to escape.'

'Who took him? The police?'

'I do so wish it had been, but it seems they were *sinchis*, a unit of the Civil Guard, doing the dirty work of the state, which is what we know now, of course…' He swept his arm around the books that lined the shelves. '… and there have been enquiries, a Commission to apportion blame, even an apology from the President himself, but of course it changes nothing…' He put down the glass and returned his handkerchief to his pocket. '… My son officially remains missing – one of the disappeared – what in my language we call, *los desaparecidos* – the vanished – the men and women, teachers, writers, humble farmers, forcibly taken against their will, murdered and then their bodies thrown into some make-shift grave, or worse never found.'

Hugh said nothing. The library was empty, approaching the time when the old man would lock up and go home. 'I'm sorry to hear of all this. You looked – you still look – for your son?'

'Oh yes, we haven't stopped looking. It is, after all, the least we can do, but it is of course a hopeless task. Our great writer, Mario Vargas Llosa once said that it is impossible to know what is really happening, so we Peruvians take refuge in lying, dreaming, and in illusion. For me and my wife, the illusion is that he will be found. For certain he lies buried somewhere probably in a field close to the barracks in Ayacucho, and I expect we will hear, in the not-too-distant future, that he has been found and identified. We now have DNA database which is a wonderful thing...but forgive me, I have taken up enough of your time. Do indeed leave me a card and I will display it here in the library. I cannot guarantee many young people will see it, but it is the least I can do. I gave your son the address of my sister, Julia. Maybe he went to see her'.

He shook the pale hand and placed his chair against the wall.

'Goodbye, senor, and good luck. I'm sure he'll be found; they almost always are.'

Hugh closed the library door behind him and stepped out onto the terrace that looked towards the lagoon. On an impulse he decided to walk around the lagoon once again. It was small and would only add thirty minutes or so to his journey. He stepped off the Malecon towards the sandy edge of the water. It was possible to continue towards a row of dilapidated beach huts on the northern side of the lagoon, after which he'd have to climb up the steps and re-join the Malecon. It was late afternoon, the oasis slumbering as if in a siesta. One or two tourists were rowing small dinghies back and forth across the water. It was peaceful, the kind of place Sarah would consider too quiet, but it suited his mood.

When he reached the beach huts, he climbed up and re-joined the Malecon. Discarded plastic water bottles had collected under the small verandas of the huts increasing the sense of neglect and melancholy. He looked around him. He would continue walking until he reached the Italian restaurant at the far end. Then he would walk away from the lagoon and towards his hotel which should be on his left. Immediately in front of him, he saw a low stone wall. On closer inspection he noticed that it was a mural of some kind, figures and an inscription carved into the rock. It was understated and perfectly suited to the calmness of the setting. The carved figure was of a young girl sitting beside the lagoon, her gaze directed up towards the towering dunes. In both Spanish and English, the inscription said that Huacachina, in Quechua meant, *where a young woman cries*, an Inca princess shedding tears for her lost paramour, staring into her mirror until it broke into a thousand pieces, some of which became the lagoon at the centre of the town.

He continued walking until he reached the steps of the Italian restaurant. A group of noisy local men were huddled around a mobile phone, their huge sand-buggies parked alongside them. He resisted the temptation to approach and show them a photograph. It was late, the jet lag was catching up on him, though the conversation with the librarian, in some way calming him. The librarian had told him a bus left for Ayacucho each evening at around eight, arriving in the early hours. From what the librarian had told him, Adam was very much alive and for whatever reason had decided to cut all ties with home. The Lima bus left for the capital a few hours after the other headed towards Ayacucho. Perhaps he should do what Avril would advise and return the way he had come?

The following day he returned to the library. The librarian was sitting reading. He smiled as he entered.

'I wondered if I'd see you again. Please join me. I can assure you the coffee will be warmer this time.'

He told him of his plans. He had decided he would continue to Ayacucho. He had no choice. He had started looking for his son and wouldn't stop until he had definitive proof he was alive and well. And there was *El Flamenco*, their old haunt. If there was anything he could take to his sister, he would be delighted.

'And when will you stop, senor...?' Jorge asked, pouring some of the rich dark coffee into their cups. '... perhaps never?'

Hugh said nothing.

'Have you stopped looking, for Juan? After so many years?' The librarian laid his cup delicately on the table and put his hand upon the Englishman's sleeve.

'I have hope – *esperanza* we say in my language – that you will find your son, perhaps in one of the more popular places such as Cusco, and then discover from him the reasons for his sudden disappearance. Perhaps it was not of his own choosing but as fathers we know so little of our sons.' He spread out his hands towards the book-lined shelves. 'So much wisdom in these books, so many words about so much, but how little we know of the children we bring into this world, why they do what they do, why they bring so much pain and sorrow to those who love them so much... but let us not dwell upon such sad things. Go, my friend and continue your search. I am sure yours will be more successful than mine.' He smiled and offered his hand. 'And I ask a small favour, that when you find your son, you will contact me. *Esperanza*, something we all need in the search for *los desaparecidos*, not so?'

Hugh stepped out of the library and walked over to an elegant iron bench that faced the lagoon. For a moment and thought about what Jorge had told him. He was sure Adam, and most likely Cristina, had taken the night bus or possibly a taxi to Ayacucho, to talk with Julia. Of that he was certain. Where Adam went after that only Julia might know. The business of the phone and no word from Adam made no sense. From what Joe and the librarian had told him, Adam didn't seem particularly distressed, and was clearly with Cristina, who must be acting as some sort of interpreter. In her phone call to him – was it before or after their visit to the library? – she had presented herself as some kind of good Samaritan, who'd found a stranger's phone and was trying to locate its owner. This was clearly untrue, as there was no reason to dispute what Diego and Luciana had said about not receiving the phone. Something was missing in all this, perhaps a small detail he was overlooking. It was clear that Adam and Cristina had visited the library together and that the woman who Jorge thought he knew was Cristina and no-one else.

He looked back at the library. The veranda at the front was in shade. He looked at the sofa and the three chairs. The chair on the left was occupied. He could make out a figure, seated, who then stood up as if by command. It was a woman, slightly scooped, wearing a brown mid-length skirt. As he stared, she slowly raised a left hand in greeting. In the other she seemed to be holding a small bunch of flowers.

He raised a hand, and as he did so, her image began to fade, shimmering at first in the haze and then disappearing completely.

***

Eight

T*ranscription of Interview*: Panco- member of
paramilitary force, the sinchies.

*So, you want to know, gringo, what I did back then?
Maybe why we sinchies were packed off to Ayacucho? You
really want to know why? Or maybe you want to know what it
is like to waste your first 'cholo', eh? Sometimes we lit up
some dope. It was the tension. Look, when the terrorists
attack, they send in the cholos first. The cannon-fodder. So,
we waste them first. You look surprised, gringo? You maybe
think, well so Peruvians are killing each other, taking down
our own people? But what can we do, buddy? They are going
to take us down, no question. It is the ideology they have; you
know they don't understand the meaning of democracy. The
only thing they know is communism and the Shining Path,
nothing more. That is why we waste them.*

*But now it's different, now we're on the same side. Funny
isn't it, now we see that instead of fighting each other, we
work together. There are gains to be had in the 'white city' –
you've heard of that, senor, the 'white city', in the VRAEM?
The place of purity. The land of the coca. You've heard of
that. But wait...*

*I see you are recording this, gringo. You need to be
careful my friend, careful. One day you are here with your
beautiful senora, and then the next day you are not. You are
disappeared.*

*So be careful senor, senora. Some who are disappeared
return. That is good. But some of them, they are disappeared
forever, which is how it is, how it must be. So be careful senor,
senora.*

---

*He's right, we both need to be careful. Cortes said as
much before we met Panco. But – and it's a big but – they'll
be watching over us as Salas said they would. Next stop*

Ayacucho where the whole Shining Path thing kicked off. Cortes says I should talk with the Ricardo, the owner of El Flamenco – wasn't that the bar where Dad and Mum met? – strange coincidence – maybe I can weave it into the article, you known, the human touch?

***

Nine

'So, senor, this is your first pisco sour?' Hugh sipped the drink, in a tall glass and ice cold. Joe was drinking a *cusquena* from a bottle.

'I had my first way back in the '80s during my first visit to the country. It was at a bar, *El Flamenco*, where my wife was working – well, she was my girlfriend then - but it was nothing like as good as this.' Diego was clearly delighted at the praise.

'*El Flamenco?* I think I know it. You should visit the place when you go to Ayacucho. Check out their pisco and compare it with mine.' He took a mouthful of his drink. 'When Mindy arrives, I'll make us another. And as she's not here, I'll tell you that we Peruvians – the men anyway – have an expression about our national drink, 'Pisco sour is like a woman's breasts – one is insufficient but two is enough!'

Joe laughed. 'I'll drink to that, not that it's my poison. I prefer a beer.'

The hostel owner motioned them towards one of the bigger tables. In the centre was a small crystal vase containing a small bunch of purple flowers. Hugh took another sip of his drink and looked towards Diego.

'You, OK? For a moment it looks like you've seen a ghost,' Joe said as they sat down.

Diego had retreated into the back of the hostel where Luciana was preparing the pizzas.

'Not quite, though it's funny you should say that as early today when I left the library, I thought I recognised someone, a woman, who I had seen once before, on some saltmarshes, in England, where we used to holiday just before I came out here.' He told him something of the few days he'd spent in Norfolk, and the landscape that was both wild and unforgiving. Joe listened without interrupting.

'Sounds like the kind of place Mindy and I would enjoy, open skies, a chance to be alone, nature as it was intended.'

'Yes, it was one of the things we liked, and the fact that Adam could run free, be himself.'

'And the woman you saw today – or thought you saw – you think she's the same woman you saw on the marshes and at the grave of your wife?'

'No, I don't think so, that wouldn't make sense, but...' He hesitated. '...I've had a rough few months – and what with Adam disappearing – I think the mind is playing tricks.'

Joe swigged from his bottle. 'And this woman - if you don't mind me asking - did she in any way look like Sarah?'

Since her death he hadn't had a conversation like this with anyone. Everyone tiptoed around him being careful not to offend. It was a relief to offload some of his thoughts with an almost total stranger.

'Yes, a little, and yes, I'm familiar enough with the literature on grieving to know that if you look hard enough for something, or someone, you'll eventually see them. Whether they actually exist of course is another thing, and there is a very rational part of me that knows Sarah has gone and I'll never see her again.'

'And the other part, the irrational part?'

'That something I am only beginning to learn about, which would be fine, but given Adam's disappearance, I feel a bit overwhelmed...'

'...which is one good reason for getting Diego here to provide you with that second pisco sour.' He took a long swig from his beer as Mindy arrived clutching her notebook and an impressive-looking camera.

'I see you guys have started without me,' she said running upstairs with her things. 'When Diego reappears tell him I'll have one of those mean concoctions,' she called down. 'Any luck at the library, Hugh?'

'Yes and no. Yes, in that Adam and the woman who I think is Cristina, did visit and both of them may well have gone to Ayacucho to visit Jorge's sister – she knows a lot about the Shining Path and all that – but no, in that I'm no further in knowing why she told me she'd found Adam's phone, why she said she was going to leave it at Reception, and then nothing.' Jorge thought that Cristina – if it was her – was acting as some sort of interpreter, not that Adam needed it when he visited Jorge at the library.

Mindy had been silent up to this point. 'So, it's likely that nothing serious has befallen Adam – or his friend, Cristina – apart from the disappearance of his phone?'

He nodded.

'You think I might be worrying over nothing?'

'Not necessarily, as you haven't heard from him since he arrived in the country which does seem a little unlike him from your description.'

He thought for a moment about what she was saying. If he were asked to describe Adam, he would paint a picture of a kind and thoughtful person, particularly at a time when both of them were coming to terms with Sarah's death. But then, perhaps Adam saw things differently, perhaps his response to his mother's death was very different from his, more private and not to be shared with his father?

Mindy smiled at him. 'It's easy for folk like us to question your motives. We've no children of our own but now you're here, I'd recommend you take the next bus to Ayacucho which leaves mid-morning tomorrow and see what Julia might have to say?'

He agreed, at least he had some kind of plan. Before they ate, he checked his phone. Nothing from Adam.

Nothing from Cristina. Nothing from Max. Nothing. The pizzas were good, and he agreed to sharing a bottle of good Argentinian wine with these new friends. Joe and Mindy were leaving at the end of the week, but he promised he'd keep in touch. Diego joined them at the end of the meal.

'And you, senor, we are family now, you must return here from Ayacucho with news. Understand?' Hugh agreed.

He walked back to his hotel, the emerald-green lagoon to his left. The restaurants were filling up with those who'd sand-boarded down the dunes and were now ready to continue to party late into the night.

Ayacucho, Sarah, where I'll find good news of him. Promise. And I'll then take him to El Flamenco – if it's still there – and we'll raise a glass to you ... to us.'

He looked towards the water which was still and black. There was no moon, the dark sky and the towering dunes blotting out all light. A row of Victorian streetlights illuminated the Malecon as he made his way back to his hotel to pack his bags and check out.

***

Sleep when it came took him back. He was on the pier in the town where they had moved, ready to take up his post at the university. He and Sarah were excited, and Adam was thrilled to be by the sea. Sitting on the shingle beach, he was never happier when he could throw stones of every size towards the ocean. Sometimes they would pack a picnic of egg sandwiches and fruit, and sit with him, the city's main pier looming beside them.

For as long as he could remember Adam was in wonder of this cast iron monument to sea-side pleasure, its fruit machines within a mysterious, covered cavern called the 'Palace of Fun,' a misnomer if there ever was one. Towards the end of the pier were the rides and a helter-skelter. Beyond stretched the Channel.

They had enjoyed their sandwiches and were now standing at the far end of the pier looking out towards the horizon. The sea was flat. Adam was just over seven-years-old, the visit to the pier a delayed birthday present, the weather fine if a little chilly. He was wearing a purple and white scarf, his birthday dungarees and a knitted bobble hat of the same colour as his scarf.

'Desperate for a pee,' she said heading in the direction of the large ornate bar and restaurant that was connected by a short walkway to the 'Palace of Fun.' 'Ten minutes. Keep an eye on the little monster.' He took his son's hand and walked towards the entrance of the pier. The chilly wind kept most visitors to the shore-end of the pier where you could buy doughnuts and popcorn. Maybe they'd buy him something sweet before they went home, a late birthday treat. Adam was kneeling just behind him, squinting through the cracks in the boards at the sea below. His ability to concentrate for a sustained period of time was one of the things he admired about his son. If only some of his students had such an ability. He looked left beyond the pier towards the famous chalk cliffs. Peaceful. Quiet.

'Where's Adam?' His wife was standing just behind him.

He spun round. 'He was here, a minute ago, kneeling here, looking at the sea through the wooden floorboards.' There was no sign of him.

'I told you to keep an eye on him,' she shouted as she ran from one side of the pier to the other. 'You look around here, and I'll check the fruit machines.'

He ran quickly back towards the restaurant, which was empty and then into the 'Palace of Fun.' It was dark apart from the illumination provided by the whirring machines. A bored-looking attendant asked if he could help. 'Small boy, Adam, my son. Was at the end of the pier. Five minutes ago. Have you...'

'Hasn't come this way.'

'Adam!' he shouted above the din of the machines. He ran through the hall to the door at the other end. Two leather-jacketed young men were walking towards him.

'Are you looking for a young boy about this height?' the taller of the two asked. 'Well, I think if you look at the clairvoyant kiosk up by the entrance, you'll find him, not that he seems very interested in being found.'

Sarah had walked around the left-hand side of the hall and was talking animatedly to an electrician who was fixing a series of fairy lights at the entrance to the 'Palace of Fun.'

'I know where he is. There. Behind the kiosk.'

Sarah gave a small cry and ran towards the kiosk that proclaimed itself to be the home of the world's greatest clairvoyant. It was closed. Adam was crouching down, tucked away behind its entrance, seemingly oblivious to his parents' calls and distress. They decided not to make a big thing of it but to talk to him quietly just before he went to bed. How he had managed to get from the end of the pier to the kiosk in such a short time, was the question Hugh wanted to ask him. Perhaps he'd been admiring the chalk cliffs for longer than he thought? She came down the stairs after putting him to bed.

'He says he's glad we found him because he loves me and is sorry if he scared us.'

'He said he loves *you*, not *us*?'

'Yes, and said he ran away because you don't like him. Told me you never talk to him and when you do it's to tell him off.' She put her hand on his arm. 'It could have been worse, couldn't it? And he's seven, an age when he's beginning to share his feelings. We'll both need to pay him more attention from now on. And watch him like a hawk.'

Which he thought he did, though perhaps on his part there was more watching than talking, something he considered a part of their relationship. He admired his son rather than interacted with him. Sarah on the other hand, threw herself into every activity that took his fancy from building a telescope to participating in a skimming stones competition. He admired her for that, preferring to sit and watch his bright, inquisitive son engage with his energetic, loving mother. She knew how to be close to him. He sat on the side-lines, a paler version of the parent he would like to be. It was almost as he had disappeared, both from them and from himself.

He was woken by the sound of a sand-buggy revving its engine outside the hotel. He lay for a moment and focussed upon the day ahead. At eleven a coach would take him to Ayacucho. It left, not far from the hostel, time to drop by and say goodbye to Diego and Luciana; and the Canadian couple if they were in.

***

Ten

H e stood for a moment on the threshold of her house. Her small apartment was on the second floor of a small block not far from the main square and opposite a large tourist hotel. Once inside however it was quiet, a little like the atmosphere of the library in Huacachina.

After the bright sunshine, his eyes took some time to adjust to the gloom inside. It was a pleasant enough room though simply furnished. The woman who opened the door was younger than he expected, her dark hair drawn back in the traditional style with two long braids reaching down to her waist. Her face was lined with a filigree of faded beauty turned to fragile charm. She was wearing a dark woollen jacket over a wide, bright, multi-coloured skirt. She smiled and offered her hand.

'You must be Senor Wilson? Please come in. You will be tired after your journey. My brother told me to expect you.' She guided him into a sparsely but pleasantly furnished front parlour. 'Please sit, and I'll make us some tea. Or would you prefer some home-made lemonade?'

'Lemonade would be lovely. Thank you.' He sat in an old leather chair at right angles to a small sofa. 'I asked your brother, Jorge, for your telephone number but he told me he could never remember it, but when he did, he would call you.' Hugh laughed. 'He did remember your address though and so it wasn't difficult to get a taxi here from the bus station.'

She smiled broadly and moved towards the door.

'Let me fetch the lemonade.'

As she turned to go, she said with a shrill but muted laugh that sounded to him like a wind chime, 'Jorge knows a great deal about many things. Shakespeare, the American Constitution, our fight for Independence, but I'm afraid he is not so knowledgeable of some of the important details of day-to-day life, such as my telephone number, or come to that the birthdays of his nieces and nephews,'

Ayacucho, the small town where he had met Sarah. Little had altered since his first visit. He remembered it had changed its name from *Huamanga* in the middle of the nineteenth century to the old Quechua name, *Ayacucho* which meant *corner of the dead*, commemorating an important battle between the Spanish Royalist forces and the revolutionaries. The cathedral, a scattering of peach-and-pastel-coloured restaurants and bars that fringed the main square, the bus and taxi stop. He thought *El Flamenco* might be off the square opposite where the coach dropped him, but he couldn't be sure. It had been a bone-shaking long journey from Huacachina.

Whilst she busied herself in the kitchen, he looked around the room. There was a bookshelf behind a small desk. On the top shelf were three framed photographs, the central one of two children, a girl who looked about eight, holding the hand of a slightly older boy. Both were looking with the same slightly quizzical air towards the camera. The other two photographs were of a couple on their wedding day, one of the bride smiling directly towards the camera, the other of the couple, his protective arm around her waist.

'My parents, who passed many years ago, and me and Jorge. He must have told you about Juan and his disappearance. He tells everyone his story which helps him a little, I think. In the early days, they were willing to listen, but now there are many in our county who want us to forgive and forget. Which is not easy if your son is one of the disappeared,' she said as she re-appeared with the tea and a plate of biscuits.

'You're both a lover of books I see,' he said, as she put down the tray. She laughed.

'Yes, I share my brother's love of the written word. Our father was a teacher and he encouraged us to read, mostly books in Spanish, but also the occasional English book, given to him by our American friends.' Next to the bookshelves was a large grandfather clock and what looked like a record player. There was no television or radio, creating an impression of a room that had changed little since she'd moved in. 'I like my peace and quiet,' is all she said when he helped her unload the tray of lemonade and what looked like lemon drizzle cake. He reached into his bag and took out a book.

'Your brother asked me to give you this.' He handed over the book. 'Jorge said you'd been keen to read *Moby Dick*, and he had found a good edition on a visit to Lima.' He drank some of the lemonade. It complemented the drizzle cake. 'Lovely cake, Julia. May I call you that?'

He put down his plate. 'There is a question that has been on my mind all the way from Huacachina. Did Adam visit you here? Have you seen him?' He reached into his inner pocket to retrieve the photo.'

'Hugh – and may I call you that? – no, he hasn't been here, which does surprise me given what my brother told me.'

'Could he have come here, to Ayacucho anyway?'

'Yes, it is possible he came to visit other contacts and to visit the museum, but it does surprise me he hasn't called, given the contact Jorge gave him.' She looked at him, and smiled. 'Not the answer you were hoping to hear, Hugh, but rest assured I will help as much as I can.'

He paused. He was tired from the coach journey but felt in some way he had met an ally.

'Thank you, Julia, for agreeing to help me. I'm most grateful,', he said. 'Please, now tell me something of yourself.'

She put down her cup and looked up at him.

'I have only one story to tell, one that I have told many times.'

'I would be honoured to hear it, senora.'

'It concerns my husband, Martin. And I take you back to the mid-80s. She drank a little of her lemonade, and then placed the glass delicately back on the tray. 'It was in November 1989 when they arrived. They took him at eleven in the evening while I was asleep with Martin in the small bedroom at the back of the house. They woke us, hammering at the front door and yelling, 'Perez! Perez!' We'd spent a peaceful afternoon at home, talking about our niece, Ana Maria, who had just turned five, who lived with her mother in the next village,' she said, speaking quietly, as she poured tea for him. My husband, barefoot and wearing a tee-shirt and pyjama pants, went into the front room. He switched on the light before opening the door. I heard what sounded like a thudding noise and when I got into the living room, I saw two soldiers both wearing balaclavas beating him with the butts of their guns. One was holding him by his arms whilst the other hit him. Martin was saying nothing, just groaning. Three other soldiers stood behind him in a semi-circle, pointing their machine guns at us, blocking the front door. They were dressed in black ski masks and army uniforms, black sweaters, dark combat boots, and green trousers. The biggest of the three pointed his gun at me when I tried to go to my husband. He seemed to be the leader of the group, tall – about six foot three – and very broad across the chest.

The soldiers stopped beating Martin and bundled him out of the front door to a yellow pick-up truck where I could see more soldiers in masks and army uniforms. I stood looking at the truck, holding my husband's shoes and wanting to go to him. The truck drove away leaving behind the big Army commander who pushed back inside. I didn't know what to do and asked him if he'd like some water. He switched off the light in the living room and told me to go and get my husband's papers. His voice was slurred, and his breath smelt of alcohol. I told him the ID was in the bedroom and that I'd fetch them and some water too. I also told him that they had got the wrong man, that my husband was just a teacher, a good man. He didn't listen. Instead, he followed me into the bedroom and pushed me down on the bed. Then he raped me on the bed where I had been sleeping with my husband.'

He listened in silence as she spoke, every now and then, taking a sip of the coca tea she had provided. He looked at the elegant and dignified woman sitting opposite him, and thought of the events of the night in November 1989 when the soldiers came, took away her husband and assaulted her; and with a casualness, as if it was their right to take what they wanted.

'We were humble teachers remember, which meant we had to be supporters of the rebels, people who had to be crushed at all costs.'

'I'm so sorry, Julia, it must have been so terrible. What did you do?'

'Well, I waited until dawn, about six I think, and then I walked to my neighbour's house about half a kilometre away. Roberto and Milagros were also teachers though they taught in different schools to me. When I arrived, they were both getting ready for work.

'They didn't hear or see anything?'

'No, they were shocked of course, but said that all they heard was the truck leaving some time after midnight. What you must remember, senor, is that in those days if you heard the sound of a lorry in the night or soldiers shouting, you stayed quiet in your home. After Roberto had left for school, Milagros agreed to come with me to the police station in Ayacucho which was about thirty minutes away by taxi. We could ask where they had taken my husband and then go to the army barracks at *Los Cabitos* which is on the other side of town.'

She turned and faced him, tucking a loose strand of hair behind her ear. 'Imagine that several years ago they detained you, accused you of terrorism, and took you to a military barracks where they subjected you to brutal tortures. Imagine that after a while they realised that you were not a terrorist and they let you go. You know you were lucky, but you still feel bad because the same thing did not happen to many people. You know that others were killed and others more, disappeared forever. But the knowledge of your luck does not alleviate the memory of the pain and humiliation your suffered. Imagine having to go back to the barracks where these things happened to you, to verify before the judicial authorities what you lived through. To revisit the 'pink house,' places of detention, torture, execution, forced disappearances in the initial years of the conflict Peru lived between 1980 and 2000.' She paused and glanced at the wedding photograph on the top shelf of herself and Martin on their wedding day. 'You know, sometimes I think I have disappeared too, that we are nothing but images of images, that we are nothing but a thin and fragile veil beyond which there is nothing.' She walked over to the framed photographs on the top of the bookcase. 'Here is a picture of me and Martin, the only photograph I have of him.'

He took the black and white photograph and looked at the young couple. It had faded a little over the years. She was right. It was as if they were both gradually disappearing from view.

'Would you like a glass of water? You must be tired, and I shouldn't keep you.'

He thanked her and agreed he was a little weary from the journey. The clock in the living room struck four mournful chimes, outside he could hear the laughter of school children making their way home. Julia returned from the kitchen with two glasses of water and two slices of panettone.

'We Peruvians have a sweet tooth, I'm afraid.'

'I think we English do too.' He broke off a piece of cake. It was indeed very sweet. 'But I must ask you, Julia. Did you find Martin? Did you discover what had happened to him?' She hadn't touched her cake.

'Of course, no, we never found him. The police directed us to the barracks of *Los Cabitos* and they told us he was not there. They wrote down his name and ID and told us they were sorry.'

'And you continue to look, of course?' The same question he remembered asking her brother.

'Yes, my brother and me, and Roberto and Milagros and the others, we continue to look for him, for them all.' She suddenly looked tired. 'You know during the first few days after he had been taken, the sensation you have is that the outside world has disappeared, that you have left the world, that the language you speak – that you could trust – has disappeared too.'

'How do you mean?'

'Oh, when I went to the police station or the barracks, they would talk about *transfers* and *operations*. One even told me that the *subversives* deserved the *treatment* they had received.' She sighed. 'The officers seemed impatient, annoyed that someone such as me had the temerity to search for my husband.' She turned and looked directly at him. 'You know, one of them, a captain I think, told me they called the children taken, *perejil*, parsley. It is so abundant here, so cheap, greengrocers give it away. That's what they thought of our children – cheap little leaves made for throwing away.'

'A new lexicon of terror.' She said nothing but picked up the plates. 'Do you and Martin have children, Julia?'

She nodded her head slightly in his direction and stood up to collect their plates and glasses. 'Sadly, not. We tried but without success. Sometimes I wish we had produced a son. He would remind me of what I have...' She paused and smiled sadly, '...but also of course, of what I have lost.' He helped her carry the plates and glasses into the kitchen. 'But, senor, you must rest now. I will take you to your hotel and we can meet tomorrow to talk some more. What matters for you is to find your son...and his friend if she is with him. Thank you for coming and for listening to my story. I will take a taxi with you to your hotel. No, I insist. It is the way we do things here. It can drop me back after I have seen you are safe and sound. My story is an old one, but yours is new and just beginning. And we must have hope, not so. For both of us.'

***

Eleven

T*ranscription of interview: Marco Alverez, combatant with the Shining Path*

I guess you'd call me a child soldier. Must have been twelve or thirteen when I followed my brother, Juan, into the cause. And, my friend, it was a cause, something we believed in. Juan told me; we were no longer brothers. We were now comrades-in-arms, fighters for the Revolution, on the shining path to victory! It was quite something I can tell you, but it had its tough times.

Companera Maria was the one I remember, maybe because she was the first, who we had to kill. She was making some food when the leaders told her to come and see them. We were there in a circle when she came and sat in the middle, on a chair brought over by Juan. They tied her to the chair. She was a good person, her food was very nice, and she treated us like her children, like she was our mother.

But she was condemned to death. What had she done? Without permission she had stayed away for an extra week, telling the leaders her mother was sick, but in truth had met up with a soldier in the next town. The leader had found a small piece of paper beneath her mattress. It was from him, the soldier telling her he loved her. She cried in front of us. We left her tied to the chair all of the afternoon. None of us said anything to her. We felt bad for her, but she had done wrong, and we were told obedience and loyalty to the leaders was the most important thing.

Juan and I and another boy were told to hang her in the night. She was a big woman, and it took us more than twenty minutes because she was so strong. In the early hours of the morning, we buried her. The next day, we were called to the place where we had buried her and she was gone, just a hole and some earth. The leaders were very angry and told us that for this we could be shot. We told them we had hanged her, for sure. Later we found her body further down by the river. She must have been unconscious or something and climbed out of the grave until she fell.

The leaders told us we would be excused this time. One of them, a man called Ricardo Flores who owns a bar in town, El Flamenco, told us, 'Bad plants never die, they are disappeared.' We laughed at that, but we felt bad for Maria.

Child soldiers could be an important angle for the article? Great to find El Flamenco – I'm sure that's Dad's bar. Odd coincidence, wonder if Flores owned it back then? Will have to ask Cristina, she seems to know everything and everyone. Really getting to like Cristina. Shame Mum will never meet her. If we get time must call in on the librarian's sister. Maybe she'll be up for an interview?

***

Twelve

Hugh woke late. The long journey and two nightcaps in the deserted hotel bar had helped him sleep but had left him muggy-headed and tired. His room, which was on the top floor, was larger than it needed to be, furnished with huge pieces of dark furniture that might once have graced a Scottish baronial hall. Opened in the early '80s, the hotel had lost most of its custom when the town was engulfed by the troubles. He wondered how it had managed to keep afloat.

The restaurant was empty. A strong black coffee would help him clear his head. He was certain Adam – with or without Cristina – was not in Ayacucho – he would surely have gone to Julia's place first? This confirmed the view he'd formed between his second and third whisky, that he really was on a wild goose chase. He checked his phone again, no messages from anyone.

Julia had promised to take him around the hostels and taxi offices to see if anyone might have seen them but he knew it would yield nothing. He would thank her when she called to collect him from the hotel and then return to Huacachina on the next coach which was likely to be tomorrow at about eight in the morning. Unless she could suggest anything else he might try, he'd take a walk down memory lane and try and find *El Flamenco*.

She was punctual.

'I know, we Peruvians are known to operate our own time schedules, but I want to make the most of the day.'

'Julia, do you think we'll find any trace of them here? After thinking about it last night, I'm not convinced they ever came here. If they did, they would surely have come to see you.'

She sat quietly for a moment. 'I agree, it seems unlikely, but I had another thought after you left yesterday, that if Adam was coming here, he would indeed want to come and see me, but also he would want to visit the museum here, set up by the women of the disappeared.'

'A museum?'

'Yes, a museum for those who vanished, were forcibly disappeared. The German people supported its establishment in 1983, and for years now the women – mothers, grandmothers, sisters of those taken by both sides – have devoted their energy and time to remembering those lost, and educating the young ones, so that they know about what happened.' She gave him the sort of determined look he imagined she would give a pupil arriving late for class. 'So yes, let us go there first and ask about Adam or Cristina, then, if we have to, we can do the rounds of the hotels and hostels.'

***

'I see him, of course, every day. Sometimes, rascal that he is, he catches me unawares and appears just when I'm taking a shower or talking to my friend Angela here.' She patted the arm of her friend who was sitting beside her. Both women were wearing identical clothes: thick stockings beneath a heavy, brightly coloured skirt, on their heads the traditional brown bowler hat. Upon arrival they had led their visitors into the small dining area, the *Adolfo Perez Esquerel Room*, where for almost for decades two hot meals a day had been prepared for the orphans they had taken under their wing.

Julia turned to Angela. 'Do you see him too, Angela?

'Of course, not. It is for the one who loves – the mother – who is blessed with the sight of the son or brother or father. Sometimes, in the early morning –if I am awake – I do not see Manuel, my son, I will never see him again – but I do feel his presence, as if he is standing at the foot of my bed watching me, looking at me, just as he used to when he was very small.'

Julia said something to the two women in Quechua. 'They have asked me if you have the photograph of your son?' First Angela and then her friend looked closely at the photograph, glancing up at him, checking for similarities.

'Yes, he is like you, senor,' but I am sorry to say I have not seen anyone who looks like him here.'

Faviana looked at the photograph again, as if she was searching for something out of sight, perhaps hidden from whoever took it. She pointed to line upon line of black and white photographs on the wall behind them. 'Who took the photographs of our disappeared is of great importance to us. Often the photographs here were taken by those they loved, a mother, brother or friend, snapshots taken on a birthday or at a wedding. But sometimes the photographs that you see here were taken elsewhere, in a police station or military barracks; or those taken by Sendero, a basement in some provincial house or occasionally in a field just before execution.'

Faviana turned to Julia and spoke quickly. 'She says that she cannot be sure, but she remembers the director talking of a young man coming here a few days ago with a woman, a Peruvian, who asked lots of questions. Perhaps this is your son.'

'But let me take you to our director, Mama Maria Mendoza. She is always happy to meet with people like yourself.' said Angela.

The three women then turned to him, raised their hands, and clapped together in unison. Julia turned to Hugh.

'Faviana says she claps because if he is found, your sorrow will have ended. Our director will know. She will help. She is our mother.'

Faviana guided Hugh and Julia towards the director's office which was at the far end of the building. She rose from behind her desk to greet them as they entered.

'Thank you, Faviana. Could you bring us some water, please?'

'Thank you very much, Mama Maria, for agreeing to meet with me,' he said slowly.

She smiled and resumed her seat. 'Please, you can speak normally. We are fortunate in receiving a number of visitors from your country and the United States, and so I'm told my English is much better than it was.' Her voice was high-pitched like a small bird. 'Faviana has told me of the reason for your visit, and whether I might have met your son recently.'

Hugh handed over the photograph. She glanced quickly at it and looked up to the man sitting opposite her. 'I am sorry, but he is not the young man I met a few days ago, though I can see why Faviana and Angela might have thought otherwise. He has the same questioning look common amongst those who come here,'

He liked this woman who spoke directly and honestly. 'My friend Julia, here, thought that Adam would have come here – maybe he will come here – given his interest in what you have achieved here.' He told her a little of Adam's plans to write an article on the legacy of the violence and its relationship with the cocaine trade.

Faviana entered with three small bottles of water.

'Thank you, senora, for giving me some of your time. But if I may, could you tell me a little of your story and how you came to establish this place?'

Mama Maria twisted open the bottles of water and took three glasses from a shelf behind her. Placing the glasses on the desk, she pointed to a large map on the wall. 'This is a map of Huamanga Province of which Ayacucho is the capital city. As you know, we were at the epicentre of the violence that befell us for some twenty years or so. The large red circles you can see are the sites of places where violence occurred, usually at an outlying village or gathering of farmers in a field. Many of those who were taken, who were disappeared, may be found close by. The DNA database we now have is of course a great help but there are still many waiting to be found.' She paused and looked directly at him. 'Of course, this is just part of the story. We know from the relatives of those taken – and from witness testimonies of those responsible – that many of the crimes committed were against single individuals, a brother taken here, a mother there, usually at night, usually for no reason, always by small groups of armed militias or the terrorists.'

'On both sides of the conflict?'

'Yes, here we do not discriminate. A *disappeared* is a *disappeared*, ripped from a family unjustly. It matters not the reason for the crime. A grandmother remains crying, a father bewildered at the loss of his son.' For a moment he felt a sense of guilt. Nothing he was experiencing could come close to what these people had suffered, were continually suffering. 'But, if I can, now I can tell you a little of my story which may throw a little light on why I am here and the work of this place.' He took a sip of water. 'It was July 12th, 1983, when Aquila, my only son, was taken. He was nineteen and asleep in his bedroom at the back of the house. Shortly after midnight, we were woken by the sound of loud banging on the door. Eight military men and two policemen broke in. They said they were looking for something but did not tell me what. They took my son with them, pointing their weapons at us as they took him towards the door. You must come with us,' they said. 'Why do you want to take my son with you?' I asked. 'Be quiet, old woman,' the officer in charge said. I held onto Aquiles, but they kicked my legs, twisting my ankle. As they pushed him into their vehicle, the officer said, 'Tomorrow, old woman, come to the airport and I will return your son.'

The next day, when I went to the airport to look for him, they said, 'He is not here.' I didn't know what to do. Then I went to the army barracks and a soldier at the gate told me to wait. After about two hours he handed me a paper. It was a note from my son. He had written, *Mom, please get me a lawyer and leave no stone unturned for me, so that they will bring me to Court, because my situation is very complicated. When you go to the military base tell them you have money to bring me to see somebody or to take me to the Court. I am fine. Do not worry about me. Bye, Aquiles.* And then he disappeared. Forever'.

'Did you hear anything more from him? Any other letter?'

'No, I received nothing from him but over the years I have pieced together what I think might have happened, and who was responsible.' She paused for a moment. 'He was taken that night to *Los Cabitos*, the barracks – the same place where they took Julia's husband, Martin. My trip to the airport was just a ruse to get me out of the way. The barracks are to the west of the city. We have since learnt from the Truth and Reconciliation Commission that those who were abducted were taken to the pink house – *casa rosada* – just inside the entrance of the base. Here they were interrogated and then killed. Their bodies were then thrown into a grave in the cemetery outside the base or cremated in the oven – *El Horno* – near the cemetery. Though they destroyed this oven, in 2005, pieces of it were found and excavations nearby led to the mass graves of many who were taken. With the help of the DNA database, we can now match some of those discovered with their relatives. It brings us some comfort.'

Julia was sitting quietly listening to the director describe the mechanics of abduction, torture, and the disposal of people like her husband. He wondered what she was thinking. During the brief time he had known her, he hadn't seen any emotion, just a quiet, pensive quality that seemed to define her. The museum director extracted a large folder from the top drawer of her desk.

'Here is the list of those we have identified. Aquiles is not among them, but I am sure we will find him soon.'

'And who do you think was responsible? The army officer who took him away?'

'This is not an easy task. In many ways it is much easier to identify the dead. The living, those responsible for these crimes, are much more elusive.' She opened the folder and gently ran a hand over the first page. 'Though some of the guilty have admitted their crimes, the majority remain silent, they deny any responsibility. In fact, a number are unrepentant. On the night my son was taken, we know that a team of men – a snatch squad, I think you call them – was operational in the part of the city where I live under the command of a Captain Alejandro Salas....'

He interrupted her.

'...this Captain Salas, has he been, was he questioned by the Commission?'

'Oh yes, in fact he volunteered to talk to them. Said he was proud of the duty he had shown his country in its time of need. Of course, he regretted some of the excesses but wasn't it true that, *extraordinary times call for extraordinary measures*? These were his exact words. When questioned on what had happened to those taken, he said they were either charged and taken before a court or released, which we know is not true. Why else the hidden graves and *El Horno*?'

'And where is he now, this Captain Salas?'

'He is retired, at the rank of colonel and living in comfort on his farm just outside the wine-growing area of Ica, not far from Huacachina, where Julia's brother is the librarian.' She closed the folder and smiled grimly. 'A decorated and respected military officer enjoying his golden years, the years that so many of the disappeared had taken from them.'

'He is untouchable?'

'He is – though there are rumours he is involved in the trade.'

'The trade?'

'Yes, in the coca growing regions such as the valleys of the Apurimac, Ene and Mantaro rivers and in the Upper Huallanga valley or what we call VRAEM for short. Using his friends in the military to traffic the drugs from there to the border and beyond.'

He looked up at the row upon row of photographs of the disappeared.

'Do you think he'll ever get to court?'

'Maybe. I hear rumours a prosecution is being put together but...' She spread her hands.

'...these things take a very long time in this country.' On their way out, he accepted a supporter application form from the director. 'Goodbye, senor. If I learn more about your son, I will of course contact you.'

Julia offered to take a taxi with him back to his hotel. It was a bright day with hardly a cloud in the sky. He decided to walk. He needed to clear his head and work out what he should do. Adam clearly had not reached Ayacucho, alone or with Cristina. He was certain of that. Which meant that either he had never left Huacachina or had gone elsewhere? To the VRAEM? This seemed a possibility but why not travel to Ayacucho first and meet with Julia as he had promised? And Hugh felt sure he would have known about the museum as a good source for his article. Nothing made sense. He'd call Max later and see if he had any news. He promised Julia they would meet for dinner at a fashionable restaurant that overlooked the main square.

An older man in a faded brown suit watched him enter the hotel. Finding the room of the foreigner had been easy. Killing him would be more problematic. He waited a few more minutes and then walked back towards the square and his battered brown sedan.

***

Thirteen

M ax's answerphone kicked in after the third ring. He kept his message brief and to the point.

Hi, Max. This is Hugh Wilson. It's about Adam. Nothing to worry about but wondering if he's called? He's not picking up so it's possible he's lost his mobile or is off grid. If he makes contact, could you ask him to call. A small family matter. Thanks.

Just leaving a message made him feel more at ease. Julia wasn't due for a couple of hours, so he had time to kill. The receptionist on the front desk of his hotel knew the bar.

'*El Flamenco*? Oh yes, it is not far. Left from the hotel, cross over the *Plaza de Armas* where you will see Avenida Julio 28. Halfway up on the left you will see your bar.'

Hugh thanked him and set off. He walked the length of the Avenida without seeing it. Nothing was familiar. At the end of the street, he retraced his steps. About a third of the way down he saw the bar. It was much smaller and grubbier than he remembered, wedged between an art gallery in what would once have been a grand colonial residence, and a small clothing shop selling baby alpaca sweaters and scarves. Above the narrow entrance to the bar was a faded drawing of a flamenco dancer, her left hand lifting the edge of her colourful skirt. He stopped for a moment and crossed over the street to get a proper look. To his left, a line of taxis was disgorging passengers into the main square, to his right a solitary black saloon had stopped to let out a passenger from the rear of the car. The passenger door nearest the pavement opened and a woman climbed out. He could make out her deep red blouse and long brown skirt that reached almost to her feet. She stopped and looked towards him; her left hand raised as if in a greeting. In her other hand she seemed to be holding a small bunch of light-purple flowers. When he looked again, she had disappeared.

***

It was hot and he felt tired. The meeting with the museum director and the call to Max had drained him of energy. Perhaps a drink wasn't a good idea, but now he was here he wanted to look inside and see what had changed. The image of the woman alighting from the car had disturbed him. He couldn't be certain, but she looked very much like the woman on the marshes and in the shadows of the old library. The long skirt, the hair drawn back, the posy of purple flowers. He pushed open the door and entered the cool interior of the bar.

He looked around, half-expecting to see the old woman sitting in the corner. It was empty, that hour between the end of lunch and the arrival of dinner. No-one appeared to be serving which gave him the opportunity to examine more closely what had become of the place. He recognised nothing. It looked like a number of similar watering holes that had fallen on hard times. He stood at the bar and waited for the bartender to emerge. Then it was quite a watering hole, he remembered ordering a beer for himself and a small glass of white wine for Sarah.

'Let's sit over there by the window,' she said. 'Oh, and ask if they have any snacks. I'm famished.' He carried the drinks over to the table. 'Well, here's to us, 'she said clinking his bottle against her glass.

'To us,' he said, leaning back in his chair to get a good look at the woman he was getting to know. She reminded him of someone he'd seen on the screen, but he was hopeless with names. The woman who played opposite Glenda Jackson in *Sons and Lovers*. Jennie Lyndon, wasn't it? He laughed quietly to himself.

'Share the joke.'

'Just thinking, you remind me of the actor who played opposite Glenda Jackson in *Sons and Lovers*.'

'Neither were particularly attractive if I remember right? Thank you very much! And in case you're thinking you don't look at all like Oliver Reed or Alan Bates.' He laughed again. He *was* too serious, she'd told him that early on, and that it was her job to get him to lighten up. 'And I'll have a another one if you're thinking of making an afternoon of it.' He returned to the bar smiling at his good fortune. He'd only known her for a few days, yet he felt invigorated, happy even. Perhaps she was *the one*? If she was, he was certain of one thing, he wasn't about to spill the beans. Any revelations of that sort could come later.

His recollections were interrupted by an old man in a grubby collarless shirt and dark brown waistcoat who had emerged from somewhere out back.

'Senor?'

Hugh ordered a beer and took it over to the small table by the window. Some of it was coming back. This was surely the table at which he and Sarah had sat, looking out at the street, laughing at the sight of an old woman pushing an alpaca into the back of a taxi. The bartender started wiping down the tables, stopping occasionally to draw on a small cigar.

'*Senor, por favor*? Is it Ricardo?'

He stopped his cleaning. 'Yes, I am Ricardo. And you? Have we met?' The old man looked at him shrewdly. 'Ah it's you,' he said in English. He lent forward and extended his hand. 'Many foreigners have come to this place over the years, none of whom I can remember, but if you say we have met... still, you look a little familiar.' He scratched his chin.

'We – my wife and I – we came here – in the mid-1980s – to eat and drink, maybe three or four times. I remember it a little, but as you say, things have changed.'

'And it is only now you have returned, without your wife?'

'Yes, I am alone now. We always said we would return but you know how it is, the years go by...'

'...indeed. The years go by.'

Ricardo stopped at his table and asked if he'd like another drink. On the house. Then he squeezed out the cloth on the floor, and returned to the bar. 'Middle of the 1980s, you say. Things were indeed different then. Then we had hope.'

'Hope, for what?'

'For change. That our society might see that the path it was taking, might see the injustices all around...' He raised his voice. '...might see that change only comes to the courageous, to those willing to act.'

'And did you act, senor?' He spread his arms wide. 'I – or rather – we did and for that I have no regrets. We did what we could do, what we had to do with the resources at our disposal but, as you know, senor, it all came to nothing. We were defeated. We lost hope, and without hope you have nothing. Oh, we made mistakes, of that I am sure but the sacrifice, senor, it was a heavy price to pay.'

'But you have your bar. You still have that.'

He laughed and lit up another cigar. 'Yes, I have this, and I am one of the lucky ones. I avoided what the moneymen and the corrupt in the capital call *reconciliation*.'

'How was that?'

'By obeying the golden rule, *senor*, drilled into us in those days of struggle.'

'Obedience? Faith?'

'No, senor. Keeping your goddam mouth shut, which is something I am beginning to forget.' He stopped for a moment. 'I think perhaps that I have seen you more recently, *senor*. But who knows, time is a cruel mistress, and my memory is not as it was.' He laughed and reminded him that the evening menu was on offer from six. 'The drink, my friend, is on the house. For old time's sake.'

Hugh left the bar and headed back to the hotel. The air was cooler, and he felt refreshed despite the beer. Julia had texted to say she would be late, and for a moment he wondered about returning to the bar and asking if Ricardo had seen Adam. It seemed unlikely. As he walked across the main plaza, he ran over the conversation again in his mind. Ricardo's English was good, though clearly, he had said more than he should. From what he had read, Ricardo was right, despite all the fine words about truth and reconciliation there had been little reconciling in terms of the huge disparities in wealth and opportunity. The poor were as poor as they had always been, and the moneymen in the capital remained untouched and untouchable.

He stopped for a moment. What had he said early in the conversation?

'Ah, it's you.'

Perhaps it was a direct translation from the Spanish. On the other hand, he seemed to recognise him, something that seemed unlikely after more than thirty years, and the *more recently* didn't make sense. A slight breeze ruffled the collar of his shirt. He had crossed the square in the direction of his hotel. There were things he needed to discuss with Julia. And the bar he needed to return to.

In the lobby of the hotel an old man in a grubby suit lit a cigarette and watched the Englishman walk upstairs. Hugh opened the door of his room. The bed had been turned down and a blood-red flower left on his pillow. He sat on the bed and removed his shoes.

He cast his mind back to the first time he and Sarah had gone to *El Flamenco*. It was such a long time ago and he could remember nothing of the owner. No wonder, Ricardo had said the same about him. But the *Ah it's you*, was odd. He tucked his shoes into the wardrobe and padded into the bathroom. He was looking forward to meeting Julia for dinner, a feeling tinged with expectation and a little guilt.

***

Fourteen

Julia seemed genuinely pleased to see him. She'd made an effort, a crimson silk blouse over a long pleated grey skirt. 'We Peruvians like to dress up, especially in the evening,' she said with a smile when he complimented her on her dress. He was wearing his crumpled linen suit and the last of his clean white shirts. He had rested a little and felt better. He decided to go easy on the beer. For one thing, he wanted to talk which called for a clear head.

She had suggested a fashionable restaurant that overlooked the main square. Downstairs was a small bar that served light meals, upstairs a more formal dining room. It was early evening, time before locals and tourists even considered dinner, and they easily found an empty table at the bar. He started by asking her if she'd been in touch with her brother. 'I have and he sends his greetings. No news I'm afraid, no responses to the notice he put up on the library notice board. Oh, and he did say one thing, that you should take extra care if you are thinking of straying off the recognised tourist routes. Jorge says it's the same thing he said to your son.'

Does he mean the VRAEM?'

'Most especially there, but also places a foreigner should be careful if visiting army barracks, military airfields and the like.' A young waitress who looked European brought over two glasses of home-made lemonade and a small bowl of dried nuts.

'Do you think, Julia, that he and Cristina might have gone to the VRAEM?'

'I'm not sure Hugh, perhaps we should start by reviewing what we know. He and the woman called Cristina visited my brother at the library four or five days after he arrived in the country. That is the last sighting we have of him.' She paused. 'Huacachina is a small place and it's clear that they are not there, that they've moved on... but where? Jorge said Adam was interested in Ayacucho and meeting you.'

'Yes, I agree, it is strange they didn't come here, and we know they didn't visit Mama Maria at the museum, a place he'd be sure to visit if he was coming here.'

'Where else could they have gone, the VRAEM? He was interested in the cocaine links with Sendero and all that.'

'Did he tell you that was his main reason for coming here?'

'No, he just said he wanted to write something about Peru but not the usual touristy stuff, something 'off the beaten track'.'

'The legacy of the violence and the drugs trade?'

'He didn't elaborate but I know from other pieces he's written that he's interested – passionate even – about drugs and their impact on those caught up in the business.'

'We also know that he lost his phone – it was found by someone called Cristina, the same woman we can assume, who visited Jorge in the library with Adam, that she called you and promised to return the mobile to Diego's hostel but for some reason didn't.'

'And what I can't understand is why Adam didn't buy another phone and then call me, if only to say he'd arrived safely? He must have known, I'd be worried sick, especially after all that's happened at home.'

She leant forward and touched him gently on the arm. 'Would he expect you to come looking for him?'

He stopped and looked out across the square. It was close to sunset, the square bathed in an orange glow. The beauty of the country amidst such striking levels of poverty never ceased to surprise him. 'A good question, Julia. I don't think he would, thinking I'm all wrapped up in grieving for Sarah. Finding he'd lost his phone; he'd probably think it wasn't worth worrying about.'

'But you worried about him, don't you, like any father does?' No-one had asked him such a question for a long time. Even he took the view that worrying about Adam was Sarah's responsibility. And now she had gone, had he assumed that task without being aware of it?

'I'm sorry, it must look like I'm interrogating you.'

The waitress came over to their table and she ordered another lemonade for herself and a beer for him. 'And two plates of local trout,' she said. 'It's not just the guinea pig we eat,' she added, which helped lighten the mood.

'And you, Julia, know so much more about what it means to have someone you love taken from you. It's just that when I had that first phone call from Cristina telling me she'd found his phone, and then nothing more, I felt something was wrong, intuition perhaps, a feeling that something has befallen him, that he has disappeared, even if it was by his own volition.'

After the waitress had cleared away the plates, they stayed on for a coffee and a plate of *churros*. The square below was beginning to fill up with revellers spilling out of a large backpacker's hostel next to the Peace Corps office.

'So many young people come here from the United States and from your country,' she said. 'What draws them here is a desire to do good. We are, as you know, a very poor country or do you think it's more, a thirst for adventure, a need to flee the nest?'

'Probably a bit of both,' he said.

'You came all those years ago, what was your motivation then? Given it was at a time when no-one in their right mind would come to my country, particularly given the escalating levels of violence we were inflicting on ourselves.'

He looked at this small, perceptive woman, her jet-black hair, her eyes darting here and there, a little like a bird, inquisitive but wary. She must have been a great teacher. 'You are right, for me it was a bit of both but also the need to get away. In the 1980s England was not a good place to be – Thatcher, austerity, the Irish troubles. We knew nothing about the violence you were experiencing, and even if we had, I think I had that feeling of invincibility that only the young possess.'

She nodded. 'I felt the same you know, protected by our family and friends. The government, and all that, belonged in the capital. Here in Ayacucho, we carried on much as we always had.'. Across the square he noticed two police officers were walking towards the backpacker's hostel. 'That is until the soldiers broke into our house and violated us.'

'Again, I'm sorry for you, Julia, for Martin too.'

She turned her eyes back to him. 'But why Peru? You could have gone anywhere – and forgive me for saying this – but your Spanish is not so good.'

He laughed, and for a moment considered asking her if she'd teach him. Even thinking of such a thing meant he was considering staying longer. 'To be honest, I didn't think about language problems. I just wanted to get away, and like most people in England, assumed everybody spoke English. And if they didn't, well, I'd speak slower and louder.'

It was her time to laugh. 'Well, you are lucky I do, or you'd be in a big pickle. Is that correct, *a big pickle*?' The waitress returned and asked if they'd like a nightcap. She ordered another lemonade, and despite his good intentions, he a shot of pisco.

'It was one of the reasons I became so interested in cultural history, realising that people are in many ways so similar, seeking love or the connection with someone special, wanting the best for their children, but remembering too that it's the differences that are so important, the uniqueness that resides in each of us.'

She turned her head and looked the square and the mountains beyond. 'I share your vision, Hugh. It's what took me into teaching, believing each individual child is unique, special, even if we all share a common culture, language, memories...' She paused and for a moment seemed lost to him. 'There were many young teachers like me who looked at the huge inequalities between the rich city folk and us poor farmers, and decided to join the struggle. At the time we thought we had nothing to lose, seduced by the fiery words of Guzman with his talk of the shining path to a better, more just society.' She tucked a stray lock of hair behind her ear. 'But it was something else that motivated me. It was the fact that we were invisible, Hugh, invisible to all those rich and powerful in the capital who knew nothing of our lives, and if they did, they cared even less. We were of no consequence to them, just *cholos* useful for pulling a cart or cleaning a house. It was as if we had all disappeared from view.'

'And you feel more visible now?'

'Yes, I think we do. But what happened taught us a lesson, a very painful one, the need for education, for healthcare in places like this, for social justice. In that sense the Shining Path were right. Where they were wrong was in the way they believed they could achieve those aims.' She sat back in her chair. 'Here's me now giving the lecture... but things are a little better now, though...'

'...though?'

'I was going to say, the cocaine business is a very big battle for us and one that we cannot afford to lose.'

As she spoke, he thought of Adam. And the real possibility that he had strayed into the field of battle, a terrain he knew so little about. It was getting late. 'It's been a lovely evening, Julia. I'm not sure I'm any clearer about what I should do next, but it's been good to talk. Thank you.'

Hugh entered his hotel and looked at his watch. Was it too late to return to *El Flamenco* for a quick nightcap? Perhaps Adam would be there with Cristina enjoying a drink like he and Sarah had. A foolish idea. He nodded towards the receptionist who was talking to an old man. His bed had been turned down and a new bottle of water left on the bedside table. Thoughtful. Outside he thought he could hear the solitary chimes of a bell coming from the church in the square. He counted the chimes, something he and Adam liked to do whenever they heard church bells.

***

Fifteen

H e dreamt heavily, perhaps it was the pisco or the discussion with Julia. He was back on the marshes walking along the pipe to the sea, a dark-haired, short woman walking slowly behind him, her gentle, mournful singing mixing with the cries of the brent geese. Ahead he could see the shore and the slowly turning wind turbines on the horizon. A solitary figure was standing on the shoreline. He turned and looked towards him, an arm raised in greeting, a gaping mouth open in a grimace, a scream he was unable to hear.

The sound of an electric drill woke him. The room was twice as large as it needed to be, his bed occupying the centre with a small chest of drawers and a heavy mahogany wardrobe pushed together to the left of a window. On the adjacent wall was a large painting of bougainvillea with a hummingbird hovering above the red flowers.

He checked his phone, something of a habit at the start of every day. Nothing from Adam. No call back from Max. Just a text from Julia to say she would be a little late. And why didn't he meet her mid-morning at the restaurant overlooking the square. He looked into the mirror above the sink, half-expecting Sarah to be glowering back at him. On his way into the dining room, a receptionist he hadn't seen before, approached him.

'Senor, for you.'

He handed him a small white envelope. Adam? Once inside, he sat at his table overlooking the street and opened it. It had been delivered by hand. His name and room number written in an old-fashioned italic script on the front. Inside was a single folded sheet of plain white paper, the kind once used for thank-you letters and the like. On the sheet of paper was one word written in English, *quota*. Nothing else. Written in large italics. He took his time over his breakfast, the single sheet of paper open in front of him. *Quota*. What on earth could it mean?

On his way out to meet Julia, he stopped at reception. 'I am sorry to disturb you, but did you see who delivered this envelope for me?'

'Sorry, senor, no. When I came on shift at six this morning, I found it here. We have a night guard who watches the desk but sometimes he sleeps, just there,' he said pointing to an old leather sofa pushed up against the wall.

'Thank you. If you receive any further letters for me, could you ask for the person's name?' He agreed and returned to checking his mobile phone.

Quota? Did it mean the same thing in Spanish? He would ask Julia.

At the restaurant there was no sign of her. For a moment he wondered if he should have called last night just to check she had arrived home safely. He looked up and saw her running across the square in his direction. She kissed him on each cheek.

'*Por favor*, Hugh. Even for a Peruvian, I must apologise.'

'Lovely to see you. As we say in England, better late than never.'

She looked perplexed. 'I will never be *never*, but thank you. Nothing serious I assure you, but there is something I wanted to discuss with you, but please after a large expresso. We Peruvians need our coffee.'

The waitress who had served them the previous evening took their order. They were sitting at the same table – *their table* – overlooking the square. Down below he could hear a brass band warming up with what sounded like Colonel Bogie. He ordered a *cortado* which came with a small almond biscuit.

'You wanted to discuss something?'

'Yes, I did. But first we should talk about your plans.'

He sipped his coffee and thought about *his* plans. What he would prefer to talk about was *their* plans, and whether she would accompany him wherever he decided to go. But he held back. She had gone beyond the call to support him so far. She had her own life, and her own quest to find what had happened to Martin and Jorge's son all those years ago.

'You are lost in thought, Hugh. Have you thought about what you plan to do? And of course, if I can help you in any way.'

Was she the woman walking slowly behind him on the pipe across the marshes? Walking with him towards the spectre screaming something he could not hear.

'Yes, I predicted your question, and thought about it a lot this morning. I'm certain of one thing, that Adam is not here in Ayacucho. It's possible that for whatever reason he has returned to London, but I think Max would have told me if he had. The other, and I think a more likely possibility, is that he and Cristina have decided to press on into the VRAEM and get some sort of first-hand view of the trade that originates there.'

'I agree. I think he is still in the country but not here. But if he was thinking of travelling from Huacachina to the VRAEM, it would take him through Ayacucho. It is possible of course he's stopped somewhere on route'.

He nodded. 'Before we talk about where I might go, and what you wanted to discuss with me, can I show you something strange I was given this morning.'

He handed her the envelope and single sheet of paper. She put the envelope down on the table and looked closely at the paper.

Quota

She was silent and placed the paper next to the envelope. '*La Cuota* in Spanish. It is many years since I heard this word and it is fearful, Hugh.' She looked at him closely. 'This is no accident, senor. This message is a warning – the fact it is written in your language – tells me that. And that you would ask someone like me to explain.'

'The *quota*? What does it mean?'

'Well, much has been written about it, and a great deal was discussed in the Truth and Reconciliation Commission but in essence it was something dreamt up by Abimael Guzman. He talked of the violence that would be unleashed – the *rupture* – as he called it and the dozens, hundreds, and thousands of dead that would pay the ultimate price, what he said in one of his speeches, the necessary crossing of the river of blood for the ultimate victory to be achieved. A bloody Sinai, as inevitable as it was historically necessary. On the other side lay the Promised Land.'

'And the *quota*? How did that fit in?'

'The *quota* was the willingness – indeed an expectation – of offering one's life when the party asked for it. From making this solemn announcement, preparing for death, became a central preoccupation for each militant as well as a way of indoctrinating newcomers. After agreeing to the *quota*, militants no longer owned their lives. If you have given everything to the party, then your life is not your own. And of course, when the party owns your life, they can decide when to dispense with it whenever they see fit.'

He picked up the single piece of paper. 'So, is this a warning or what?'

'In the early days, before we knew what we were getting into, we used to sing a sad ballad at the end of a meeting or when we were walking through the fields.' She leant closer and sang in a voice just above a whisper,

'On the way out of Aucayacu
There's a body, who could it be?
Surely, it's a peasant.

Who gave his life for the struggle?

Today the quota must be filled.

If we have to give our blood

For revolution, how good it will be.'

She stopped singing and looked shyly up at him.

'Whose blood is it that has to be given, Julia, for the quota to be filled?'

'I think in this case, I am sorry to say, it is yours. But remember the taker of the blood has to be ready to shed some of his own. It is a pact signed in blood.' She placed her hand over his. 'This is clearly a warning, and one we must take seriously. The fact that it was written in English and was intended for you, is clear that you are being warned.' She paused for a moment. The band below were now playing at full volume. 'One good sign, I think, is that it indicates that Adam must be alive. That they are hoping to scare you off.'

'Or follow up with a ransom?'

'Yes, we cannot rule that out. And if that happens then everything will change, with decisions that we would need to take concerning the police – if we can trust them – your Embassy, and the like.'

'But you don't think it is from a kidnapper?'

'No, I don't. If they had taken him – and possibly Cristina – they could have made their demand with the first contact. No, I think this is a warning directed specifically at you. It means we have to take particular care, especially in what we plan to do and where we intend to go.'

We, where we intend to go. His hopes rose. 'Perhaps two very large expressos might help?'

'You English reveal your sense of humour at times of stress. I have read about that.'

Strangely, he felt invigorated as if the warning had opened a window of opportunity. To find Adam at whatever the cost. Something *they* would do together.

***

Sixteen

Transcription of interview: *Ricardo Flores, owner of El flamenco bar, Ayacucho*

So, my brother tells me you are interested in the old days? How things happened. On the ground, in the field? Much of what I tell you I told the counter-intelligence people, so my conscience is clear. I have made my peace. But still, we all love lies and half-truths, even now.

Yes, it was hard, but we were young, and we had faith. Presidente Gonzalo made sure of that. And we were courageous and brave. I remember the first time I joined one of the squads in action. We met in the farmhouse of the commander, Julio. He came from the city and there were stories he knew the leader. That's what we heard but you never spoke about the leadership.

It was raining the night before the action. In the farmhouse we assembled, the four squads of about fourteen of us. Julio put me in the first squad, the 'annihilation detachment'. We would arrive first, near the target, which in this case was a large police station not far from where we are talking. There were four of us in each squad. Our job was to arrive and pose as innocent civilians, passers-by, street vendors. Our guns were hidden beneath our clothing of course.

The second squad was also of four of us, and was the 'assault squad'. Two of the guys who working in my bar were in that group. They would create a diversion. On this occasion one of them threw a stick of dynamite into the store behind the station. In the confusion the annihilation squad would attack. When the dynamite exploded, the policemen came running out of the station, two were firing pistols, one I remember shouting that we were bastards. I think they knew who we were.

This is where the third squad, the 'containment detachment' comes in. The four in that group are ready to neutralise any counterattack. My friend, Alejandro shot the two officers with guns. It was all over in about twenty minutes.

The fourth squad? The 'razing detachment' was made up usually of one or two fighters, usually women like my girlfriend. She was with us, and her job was to finish the job, a shot to the head or the heart or to leave a placard behind telling the peasants the reasons for our actions. Our razing detachment were the bravest, the most dedicated to the cause, the comrades most eager to fill the quota.

What have I done since? After the troubles ended do you mean? The time of truth and reconciliation? Well, of course, I still have my humble bar here, but I think you are not interested to hear about that. Perhaps more about how an ex-combatant survives? How I manage to scrape a living from a distasteful trade? As my brother Diego says, means justify the ends. For him it is easy, his conscience is clear. For me it is harder.

But you look worried, amigo? Please rest assured senor, it is good to talk with you. Our story needs to be told. For that we are grateful. Gracias, muchas gracias.

Cristina has clammed up. She came with me to the bar but says the place gave her the creeps and she doesn't want to talk about it. I don't blame her as Ricardo is a pretty nasty piece of work. She's adamant we should finish up here and head out to VRAEM with Cortes and Salazar. That's where the action is. 'Quick and dirty', as Max was fond of saying. Getting in should be ok; it's the getting out that worries me.

***

Seventeen

T hey would leave the following morning for the VRAEM.

'Come to my house tonight, Hugh and we can plan away from prying eyes and ears.'

'Are you thinking of whoever wrote that note?'

'Not only him but clearly people know who you are and when they see you with me, they will realise you're not just a tourist, that you know about things their people would prefer to keep hidden.'

'Like what? Your search for Martin or your nephew, Juan?'

They were walking back to his hotel. The late afternoon sun had lost most of its strength and the city walls were cast in a soft glow, shadows beginning to lengthen. On one corner he could see two old women standing with four alpacas, their faces immobile.

'No, searching for the disappeared, sadly is no longer news here. When a mass grave is found, a journalist from Lima may think the story is worth a visit but for most people they want to put what has happened behind them and then move on. It's hard enough making a living these days without worrying about the dead. No, it is the connection Adam wanted to explore between the remnants of Sendero and the cocaine trade. It is that which puts him and you in danger but it also means that he is alive, perhaps being held somewhere, but alive.' They had arrived at his hotel entrance. For the first time, he had the feeling he was being watched. 'One of my friends, Freddy, owns a car. I'll ask him to come over at eight to pick you up. He will tell you he is a friend of Jorge, the librarian of Huacachina.'

His room had been cleaned. On the pillow the maid had left a solitary chocolate wrapped in silver foil. He checked the bedside cabinet. The room had no safe and a faded notice above the door told guests to deposit valuables in the hotel safe at reception. This he considered unsafe and had taken to hiding his passport, air ticket and extra photographs of Adam between the covers of paperbacks he had picked up at Gatwick. Everything was in its place, but something was wrong. His possessions were exactly where he'd placed them, yet he had the feeling they had been moved and then put back exactly as they'd been found. He was convinced his room had been searched and by someone who knew how to do such a thing without leaving a trace. Julia was right, he had to be careful. *They* had to be careful. He was glad he was moving on. Perhaps he could stay at her house tonight and collect his bag just before they set off for the VRAEM? At about eight he checked his phone. No new messages or missed calls. On his way out he popped the chocolate in his pocket. Julia had a sweet tooth and would enjoy it with her coffee.

Coffee liqueur had also been Sarah's thing. 'Tia Maria over ice,' she'd said when they ordered coffee. They'd been back from South America a few days when she'd called and asked if he'd like to go with her to a concert at the Festival Hall.

'Carl Nielson, his flute concerto,' she'd said brimming with enthusiasm. For the life of him he had no idea who she was talking about but agreed to go. An hour or so of an obscure Danish composer seemed a worthwhile price to pay for the company of an intriguing woman. And to see her on her home turf seemed important. A little voice told him it was nothing, just a holiday romance, an exotic woman way out of his league. After the concert, they wandered over the road to the *Archdukes* for a coffee and brandy. Spirits weren't really his thing but then neither was listening to Carl Nielsen in the company of a beautiful woman.

She had dressed up for the evening in a pink silk blouse and long brown skirt. In her hair she'd pinned a small purple ceramic broach in the shape of a posy of flowers. Cornflower blue to match her eyes. My goodness, he thought, I'm falling in love. When she'd asked what he was smiling about, he'd said something about the concerto and that he'd have to listen to it again to really appreciate its quality.

'And try and keep awake, that helps,' she said, leaning forward to kiss him gently on the lips. 'My buttoned-up Englishman, what are we going to do with you?' The waiter brought over two coffees and two glasses of Tia Maria. There were also two chocolates wrapped in silver foil.

Sarah, his Sarah.

He was standing on the pavement outside his hotel. He saw a large black BMW cruising towards him. As it approached the driver slowly lowered his window.

'I'm Freddy, a friend of Jorge from Huacachina.'

He climbed into the front passenger seat and shook hands with the driver.

'I'll be your driver tomorrow, too, when we go to Pichari. It is my hometown,' he said proudly. Freddy parked the car a short distance from Julia's house. She ushered him into her small front parlour.

'First, we will eat. I have decided you must eat one of our national dishes, *lomo saltado*. Freddy knows a fine butcher and they say my recipe is one of the best.' She placed a bottle of local beer on the placemat next to his chair. As she bustled off to the kitchen, he looked up at the photographs on the wall. It seemed such a long time since he'd arrived in this small house and had met this remarkable woman. The beef stew was delicious, served with potatoes rice and an array of vegetables. He was glad he'd skipped lunch.

'The wine is from Ica, Hugh, from Jorge's small vineyard. He doesn't drink but is very proud of his grapes.'

He declined coffee but with a grand flourish presented her with the chocolate.

'Thank you. I will save it for later but now let us plan for tomorrow and our journey north.'

***

After dinner he helped clear away the dishes and then unfolded his map onto the large dining room table.

'Don't know about you, but you can't beat an old-fashioned map.'

She smiled at his enthusiasm and pointed to where they were. 'I think we both agree, he's not in Ayacucho and from what Mama Angela told us at the museum, he's not been here. Which means that if he is anywhere, he's up in the VRAEM.'

'The Apurimac and Ene Rivers? The VRAEM?'

'Yes.' She ran her finger up from Ayacucho. 'See here, the two rivers and the small towns of San Francisco, Pichari and Sylvia. I'm sure this is where they are and as no one speaks English – and many little Spanish – he'll be relying on Cristina to help him.'

He looked at her, this earnest, short woman with piercing blue eyes.

'Like you are helping me?'

'You need more coffee, senor! Not quite in the same way. Perhaps more so. But now we are sitting and talking I can tell you my news.' He nodded. 'When we first met, I told you I was from this town, Ayacucho, but that is not quite correct. I trained as a teacher here and have spent most of my life here, but my real home is here in Pichari. It is where I was born and raised. My father, like everyone else grew coca and my mother worked hard to make sure we didn't struggle like they did. She brought us books from the

American missionaries – it is where Jorge gets his love of literature from – and made sure we did well. Which we did, me at the Teachers' College, Jorge at the university here in Ayacucho. Some of my cousins still remain. You will meet them tomorrow when we travel.'

'You said you had some news?'

'Last night after I returned from our meeting, I called Pepe, the cousin we will stay with to tell him of our plans. He told me three days ago, that Nelson who manages the local hotel, the *El Dorado,* had recently served drinks to a young white man and a slim Peruvian woman. asking lots of questions.'

It had to be Adam and Cristina.

'Did Nelson say anything else? Where they might have gone? Where were they staying?'

'No, he didn't, but he did say that they were with two other strangers, Peruvian men who looked military. Sunglasses, and a certain way about them. He said the two men didn't talk much and after they finished their drinks, they all left in the men's car, in the direction of Silvia which is on the other side of the river.'

'It's got to be them. I know it is. It means Adam is alive.'

'Yes, I think the same, but it doesn't mean he is safe. In fact, the description of the two men isn't good. Pichari is a small place, we all know everyone, even who is being violent to whom, but it is not wise for a stranger to ask questions.'

It was unlike Adam with all his journalistic experience to take risks.

'Perhaps he felt safe with Cristina and the men?'

'Maybe, I hope so.' She moved her finger across the map. 'My parents and their parents lived here, eking a living by growing coca and selling it to the highest bidder. The illegal buyers paid up to four times what the government could offer and so they complied. Their neighbours were the parents of Martin and together they vowed to support me and Jorge and Martin and his sister through school. Growing coca was – and still is – the only way to make an honest living. When we go, I will introduce you to Reyvit who can tell you more, and who knows, he might have met Adam. He's a *cocalero*...'

'A *cocalero*? Yes, one who farms the coca and organises the maceration and addition of the ammonia, potassium permanganate and sulphuric acid. Not a nice business...'

'What happens to it then?'

'After three days in the maceration pit, the chemicals are added. It is then mashed into tight balls of coca paste and given to the *mochileros* who carry their backpacks through the jungle to the Bolivian border. When they arrive at the border – and remember many are found shot in the river or never found – they return home with one hundred, maybe two hundred dollars in their hand.'

'And the paste is then manufactured into cocaine? I hear that in Lima it sells for eleven thousand dollars a kilo, and on the streets of Miami, and other destinations, ten times that amount.'

He thought for a moment of the quiet librarian bent over his books. 'You and Jorge have done your parents proud, as have Martin and his sister.'

She looked up at the photograph on the wall, taken on her wedding day. 'Yes, until that night when the soldiers broke in and took away everything I had. Everything we had fought for was taken and disappeared. Just like my marriage and my hopes for the future.'

They sat in silence.

'They did not take everything, Julia. They did not take your courage and determination, or your concern for justice and helping people like me, they didn't take that. They never can.'

She stood and moved towards the kitchen. Outside he could hear the faint sound of a car engine starting up.

'If he and Cristina are in Pichari or somewhere close, Hugh, we will find them. I am sure we will. It makes sense too for Adam to go there despite the risks. What you say about journalists going with their nose?'

'Even if the smell is of sulphuric acid?'

'And the smell of corruption and death. This is my hometown, and the place I live, but I cannot stress too much that it is no longer the El Dorado the Spanish considered it to be. It is now a lawless place, a place where the ideals of *Sendero* – if you can call them that – have been traded for the American dollar.'

He smiled grimly. 'Not a place for the tourist, but a great destination for the investigative journalist?'

'Yes, which confirms Nelson's sighting. But this is the lion's den, my hometown.' She showed him to the spare room.

'Good night, Senor Hugh. *Duerma bien.* Tomorrow the VRAEM and the lion's den. Tomorrow Freddy will take you early to the hotel to collect your things. Then you'll return here where I will be waiting'.

I will be waiting.

He thought of this as he climbed into the small bed at the back of the house.

Duerma bien, Julia, duerma bien.'

***

Eighteen

Transcription of interview: *Jorge Noriega, 83 years old, Father of a disappeared*

Thank you for asking to meet with me. The past few months have not been easy. We have been searching for almost 19 years for our son, Jesus, one of nine peasant farmers from Santa in the north of my country, and we have now found him and his friends. For years we have searched the slopes and scoured the hills ... and now, only 20 minutes away from our homes, our children have reappeared. We had almost given up hope, but at the beginning of August, the police found a skull, bones, and some scraps of clothing near the Pan-American Highway, and then they told us these were from the farmers taken in 1990 by the Grupo Colina.

Grupo Colina was a death squad set up by President Fujimori to eliminate the left-wing terrorists belonging to the Shining Path and Tupac Amaru. They targeted trade unionists and political activists who opposed the government or got in the way of influential figures, as was the case in Santa where a businessman was in open conflict with the farmers. My son was the head of the Landless Peasants organisation, that's the only crime he committed. I was 39 years at that time with four children. Four hooded men took him from his home one night in May 1992, along with eight other residents. I tried to publicise his disappearance, but the police did little to help. But we continued to look and to press for justice. In 2010 leading members of Colina were brought to trial and were sentenced to 15 to 25 years in prison. One of the accused admitted that the farmers had been murdered the day they were kidnapped and buried near Santa. Now we have found them. It is a relief for us to know our children are not lying in some unknown place. You know, until they were found, several mothers were convinced that their sons were being held prisoner in the jungle or even in another continent. And until the bodies were found, the parents keep on hoping they would find their children alive.

You know, we, the relatives of the disappeared became devoured by the idea that we ourselves were lost. Many of us are still unable to believe it, many parents of children taken, dwell on the disjunction between the disappearance of their loved ones and that life went on around them. One of my friends, her son was taken at 2 am, yet a few hours later, the neighbourhood awoke, children were going to school, buses were running. She told me that she would stare down at the street from her window as though it were a telescope and the street below a faraway planet.

Of course, those responsible – Fujimori and the others who led the death squads – are where they belong, in jail, but there are many who remain at large with their fingers in other pies. I am old, and they care nothing of me, but for those who seek justice, those who seek the truth, they must take care. There are many who are new to this country who think it is all about the past, but they are wrong. The disappeared remain with us. The perpetrators remain with us.

I ask Cristina if her father would search in the same way as Jorge has looked for his son. She seems surprised at my question, indignant almost. Well, it can work the other way round, a son seeking detachment, an opportunity to breathe. An opportunity to recalibrate the relationship or perhaps just the chance to jump ship and get away? Mum understood that. But to be fair – aren't we journos supposed to display a little of that? Fairness? – I'll give him a call when the time is right.

Cristina overheard Cortes talking to Salazar last night. Something about disposing of the cargo. She's going to call her grandfather to check everything's OK.

***

Nineteen

T he night guard was sound asleep on a battered leather sofa in the lobby when Hugh returned to pick up his bag. They'd decided he'd hang on to his room whilst he was away to avert any suspicion. Julia and Freddy were waiting in a small street just off the main square. Freddy insisted he sit in the back with Julia, joking he was their private chauffeur.

'If the road is good and there are no landslips, we should make Pichari by sunset. We'll arrive unnoticed, which is good,' she said as he climbed into the back. In all the planning he'd forgotten to ask where they'd be staying. She laughed and tapped Freddy on the shoulder. 'He reminds me of Martin, Freddy, always thinking of something else.' They would be lodging with her cousin Pepe and his wife Elizabeth who lived north of the town.

'You'll like them, Hugh, they love all things British: *Jewel in the Crown, Benny Hill*...'

'*Benny Hill*...?'

'Yes, and Tony Hancock too! Remember, we're talking about the '80s and '90s, when we were at our lowest. These programmes made us laugh.'

He thought for a moment about Benny Hill's views of women but wisely decided to say nothing. Just as long as Freddy didn't start singing, *The Fastest Milkman in the West*.

Soon they had left the city behind and were climbing north towards route 28B which would take them the 180 kilometres to Pichari. Six hours? Surely at this rate they'd do it in three. An hour out of Ayacucho he revised his opinion. Heavy rain during the night had washed away part of the road. Freddy stopped the car and got out to inspect the way forward. Hugh and Julia used the opportunity to stretch their legs.

'Reminds me of something out of Jurassic Park,' Hugh said.

Julia shielded her eyes and pointed towards a few dilapidated buildings at the end of a path that snaked away from the highway.

'The only monsters that roam these valleys I'm afraid are poverty and malnutrition. But you are right, Hugh, there is something ancient about these lands even with the planting of those trees below.'

Freddy edged the car around a fallen boulder and the remains of a tree that had crashed down during the storm. Once they resumed, Julia reminded Freddy there was no need to increase his speed. They were happy to get there when they got there.

Julia lent a little closer and whispered, 'He also likes watching Formula One, which is not so good for a driver?'

They decided to push on for another hour and then stop for a refreshment break at a place Freddy knew well. Hugh thought of Adam. Every summer they would pack up the car and head towards the North Norfolk coast, the boy sitting in the back with his favourite toys to keep him company. But instead, he preferred to hum quietly to himself and gaze out of the window. He once asked him why.

'Oh, I don't know, Dad, perhaps it's coz I'm happy in my own head.'

He mentioned this later to Sarah when they were snuggled up together in their tent. Adam was fast asleep in his pop-up next door.

'He's not always happy you know, Hugh. School, teasing, the usual things.'

'Are there other things that make him unhappy? Maybe things to do with us?'

She turned her head towards him. 'Nothing particular, but sometimes I think he is worried we expect too much of him. Your job, my work. Don't get me wrong, it is good, I think, he sees us as successful, though sometimes I think that can be a weight he carries around.'

'Never good enough for your parents, you mean?'

'Possibly. But remember you can never win. Just try and love them and hope that'll do.'

And had it? He looked out of the window and began to hum quietly to himself. Julia was dozing next to him. His thoughts returned to Adam. *Perhaps his disappearance was not as sudden as he thought but an opportunity to get away made more urgent by the death of his mother. Or to get away from him? Heavens, he often wanted to get away from himself...*

Julia stirred and looked at him.

'You look troubled, Hugh. Everything alright? Thoughts about Adam or maybe its Freddy's driving?'

He smiled. This woman knew more about him as each day passed. 'Being an academic means, you're taught to think clearly and with focus. But for me I've always found I'm thinking about the wrong things. Like you said earlier.'

It was her turn to smile. 'Better than not thinking about anything at all. I've taught many a child during my time, mostly boys, who never had a thought in their head.'

'Did they keep in touch? Any of your past pupils?'

'One or two did, usually funnily enough, the ones you had the most trouble with. Some just wanted to thank me, not for any love I might have shown them, but for paying them attention. Something their parents rarely did.'

He thought of Adam once more. Perhaps that was it. He'd told him many times that he and his mother loved him but how much attention had he actually given him? Perhaps if he had given him more, things might have turned out differently.

They pulled over next to a small row of shacks selling snacks and drinks. He was directed towards a spotless toilet around the back. When he returned, Julia was sitting at one of the small metal tables eating a huge plate of rice and chicken.

'Join me, Hugh, before I embarrass myself.'

A young girl who must have been of primary school age brought him a plate and cutlery. The food was delicious, far nicer than anything he'd eaten at the hotel. Ten minutes after resuming the journey he settled down and closed his eyes for just a minute, and then for the rest of the journey.

***

Elizabeth opened the door. She kissed Julia on both cheeks and then shook Hugh by the hand.

'Come in, come in, you must be exhausted. Freddy, you know where to go, Julia and senor please follow me.' She led them into a spacious open-plan living room with French doors at one end that opened out onto a veranda. 'Pepe is held up at the office, but he's promised he'll join us for dinner.' She exchanged a glance with her cousin and they both laughed. 'But, Hugh, I am remiss, let me show you to your room and the bathroom. You must be tired.' His room was furnished simply, like the living room, but enlivened by a Rothko-like abstract above the bed. A large picture window to the left overlooked the street below. The sun was sliding down casting its dying rays over a scene he was beginning to recognise, stragglers hurrying to get home, an old woman waiting to cross the road with a huge bag of groceries, two elderly men sitting together on a bench. His eye returned to the old woman waiting to cross. As he watched, she turned and looked towards him, as if aware of his presence, her upturned face cast in shadow. She was wearing the traditional brown bowler, her hair drawn back. But it was the bright crimson shirt and long dark skirt that caught his attention. Then she turned back and made her way slowly across the road, her right hand holding her bag of shopping, the other clutching a small posy of pale-purple flowers.

Pepe was a criminal lawyer and possessed of a huge sense of humour that matched his wide girth and big smile. Apart from an exhaustive, and exhausting, repertoire of Tony Hancock and Benny Hill impersonations, he was a fount of knowledge on British comedians Hugh had completely forgotten about, *Harry Worth, Charlie Drake* and *Tommy Cooper* being his favourites. After several glasses of Malbec, he entertained them with his favourites, even persuading Hugh to 'help him out' with a rendition of the Python's *Cheese Shop* sketch.

'You must excuse my husband, Hugh but when he finds a genuine Englishman, he just can't hold back.'

Her husband kissed her on the cheek.

'Cross-examination, Hugh. What wives are good at. And now, a top-up.'

Elizabeth and Julia suddenly stood up together and made their way towards the kitchen.

'So, now we can talk, Hugh,' he said, his tone suddenly more serious. 'I apologise for my destruction of your comic heroes but Elizabeth is correct. When I return home and find our home blessed with a *bona fide* Englishman, I can't contain myself. But I digress, what I wanted to ask you is easy. What do you hope to achieve here in Pichari, and perhaps more importantly, how might I assist you?'

He looked at the large man sitting next to him. Clearly, he wasn't to be underestimated.

'Well first, thank you and Elizabeth for being so hospitable...'

'Thank you, senor, but let's cut to the chase as I think you say. What do you hope to do here in our humble town? Of course, I know from Julia you are searching for your son, and from what she has told me, I think he may have been here, but I'd like to hear more from you, if I may ask.' Before he could answer, Julia and Elizabeth returned with a tray of drinks and an ominous looking bottle of pisco.

'Stop interrogating the poor man, Pepe. You could do that in the morning after he's had a decent night's sleep.'

'Apologies, counsel for the defence, let me offer our trapped guest a night cap and indeed an opportunity to get a good rest.' The two women got up and wished them both a good night's sleep. After they had gone, Pepe poured two measures of the spirit into the small crystal glasses.

'There is one other thing, Pepe, I thought you should see.' He handed him the note left for him in his hotel room. The lawyer looked at it and smiled.

'*Quota.*' He stood up and walked towards his bookshelf.

'You should read this, Hugh. *The Shining Path* by the very brave journalist Gustavo Gorriti. Chapter eight is devoted to the concept and practice of the *quota*.' He rifled quickly through the book. 'Listen to this. It's from the man himself, Presidente Gonzalo, leader of the Shining Path, and it tells you a great deal about the mindset – fanaticism if you like – of the individual who left this note for you.' He found what he was looking for and began to read, as if he was addressing the jury. 'This is a summary of Guzman's proclamation on the quota, written down by a Shining Path leader in 1984 near Ayacucho: *Blood makes us stronger and if it's this blood bath that the armed forces have made for us, the blood is flowing, it's not harming us but making us stronger.* It has always been a strength of communist warriors, Hugh, the willingness to sacrifice yourself for the common good, for the Party, and for whoever is leading it, even if that happens to be, in this case, the narcissist Abimael Guzman.'

'Julia thinks the note was meant as some kind of warning?'

'Yes, I think she's right, and it was intended for you, but let me ask you one further question. Do you still have the envelope it came in?'

'Yes, it's here.'

'Senor Wilson, nothing else, no room number...'

'...But clearly meant for me.'

'Of course, it's just my devious mind always seeking an alternative explanation...'

Hugh stared at him. 'But what other explanation is there?'

'It is just that at the moment, we have two senor Wilsons in our delightful country, one looking for the other'.

'You think this note might have been intended for Adam?'

'As a lawyer, you quickly learn that the most obvious explanation is usually the right one. The truth, in other words, is looking at you in the face. But let's imagine for a moment that whoever wrote this warning intended it, not for you, but for Adam, who may well have booked to stay in your hotel after you left, and unwittingly the receptionist gave it to you. Not impossible, though I grant you, unlikely.'

'But if it *was* intended for me, I need to be on my guard?'

'Yes, you do. Julia has made that clear, and though you are much safer here than in Ayacucho, this is a very small place – everyone knows everyone – and so it's much harder to get up to mischief.' At this he topped up their glasses and lent back in his chair. 'But as long as you are here, under my protection, you are safe. Of that I can assure you. But nevertheless, we must all take care. The VRAEM is a lawless place, and I say that as one who knows the kind of people who live in such a place. But to bed.'

Despite the long journey – or because of it – he found it difficult to sleep. Pepe, a friend and someone he could trust. He went over to the large window to lower the blind. The woman in the long brown skirt had gone. The street was quiet. He spotted a couple of cars parked up on the pavement, in one, a brown sedan, he could just make out the driver asleep at the wheel. A pie dog was rummaging around some bins. The threatening clouds had gone. It was clear night. He opened the window a fraction and looked out.

The night air was cool, welcoming after the fug of the car. It cleared his head. He would sleep with the window and blinds open. There was no moon to disturb him.

Adam, where are you? Are you somewhere in this strange town? He lowered the blind carefully and made his way to the bed.

***

Twenty

H *e leaves the pipe behind him and walks slowly towards the shore. His eyes are firmly fixed on the beach and the large sperm whale, beached, its body slowly breaking down, its organs failing, dying slowly in a pool of its own blood. He stops a few feet from the animal. Ahead a figure is standing to one side looking on, dressed in a brown cowl. As he approaches, it turns, its face translucent, its mouth open in a scream he cannot hear.*

'Coffee, Hugh?' Pepe asked. 'I must say you look much better after a good night's sleep.' They were seated in the lawyer's office in the centre of town. The building was Spanish colonial but had been extensively renovated inside, all white paint and polished wooden furniture.

'Lovely place, Pepe, looks something out of an upmarket office in New York.'

'Which is where I used to practice, Hugh, before I decided to return home.' He picked up a photograph of Elizabeth on his desk. 'And I'm glad I did, or I'd have missed out on the opportunity of making an honest woman out of her, not that criminal lawyers, in my opinion, know much about honesty.' A young woman entered with a pot of coffee and a plate of biscuits. 'So, Hugh, before we start, let me answer the question most people ask, namely what is a hot shot ex-Manhattan attorney doing here in lovely Pichari, home of my dear wife, but not exactly the epicentre of the Peruvian legal world.' He poured out two cups of coffee. 'First, let me be honest – here I go again with my honesty – my main office is in Miraflores, heartland of Lima's money, and I have another subsidiary practice in Cusco – we're working on the new airport contract – but it's here in Pichari where I like to spend as much time as I can.' Hugh hadn't seen much of the town, but it did look like little had changed since the Spanish had built the place. 'We've been here a couple of years now, which suits Elizabeth just fine, most of the work I do just about covers government taxes, running the office, that kind of thing.' He laughed. 'And employing most of Elizabeth's extended family but that's what we Peruvians are expected to do.'

'What sort of work do you do here, Pepe?'

'Good question. Pichari is indeed off the beaten track when it comes to legitimate economic activity but it's very much *on* the beaten track when it comes to what we criminal lawyers like to call the shady, illegal, and downright criminal. In fact, I'd go as far as to say that dear old Pichari has enough work to keep a law firm like mine in business for quite a long time!'

He laughed loudly and rubbed his hands together. Clearly this was a joke he'd told many times before. 'I think it was our friends in the *New York Times* who recently told their readership that Pichari lies at the epicentre of the VRAEM, and that the VRAEM lies at the epicentre of the trade in cocaine – they like the word *epicentre* – aided and abetted by the US Drug Enforcement Agency that went as far as describing this place as the axis of evil...' He laughed even louder, getting into his stride. '...the axis being, not the two beautiful rivers that frame this VRAEM but the two groups of really bad guys that give us good guys quite a lot of work.' There was a gentle knock at the door. He hopped off his desk and shouted something in Spanish. The young woman came in to collect the cups. 'When I say really bad guys, I mean two well-established criminal enterprises and where there is crime, sadly, there are lawyers, if only to defend the guilty and prosecute the innocent.' Hugh had to laugh at this huge character of a man. 'Don't be deceived by the *El Dorado* appearance of the landscape, Hugh, you know there were many Spanish who thought they'd found it when they arrived here, but this place is actually the battleground of a war that started in the early '80s and continues. Though we've moved on from an ideological struggle to persuade the peasants that Mao was right to a much more straightforward contest, namely who has control of that lucrative white substance so popular amongst those who can afford it in your civilized West.' This time he didn't laugh. 'Personally, my poison of choice is a good bottle of Malbec from a particular vineyard in the Mendoza country but each to his own.'

'And the two enterprises, Pepe?'

'For argument's sake, let's call them *left* and *right*. On the left you've got the remnants of Shining Path, some two to three hundred fighters broadly organised into two or three clans headed up by hombres such as Jorge Quisepe. They are based here in Pichari and also in Lima where they handle most of the logistics, getting the drugs out of the country, that kind of thing.'

'And what do they do here?'

'Here they do everything from signing up the farmers who plant the coca, recruiting guards to watch over the maceration pits, where the leaves are mixed with some pretty mean chemicals, to organising and protecting the *mochileros*, the backpackers, who transport the coca paste through the jungle to the Bolivian border.' He paused for a moment, clearly an effective strategy he had used in court. 'And when I say, *organising* and *protecting*, I mean the settling of family feuds and the shooting of any *mochileros* who might think about defecting to another clan or going solo.' Hugh still couldn't see what kind of work Pepe was engaged in unless he was part of one of these enterprises. 'To give you some idea of what we're talking about here, Hugh...' He pointed to a large map on his wall. 'Approximately 20,000 acres are given over here to the production of coca, six percent of which is legal. At the last count there were some two hundred clandestine maceration pits in the valleys, so we have ninety-six percent of coca to fight over.'

'And the other side?'

He sighed theatrically. 'Ok, so you remember what Julia said about 80,000 of our countrymen dying or being disappeared in the early '80s and '90s? Well, the Truth and Reconciliation Commission estimated that just over half of these crimes were committed by *Sendero Luminoso*, the Shining Path.'

'The other half committed by the army?'

'Indeed, the regular army, the paramilitary *sinchies,* and the local village militia given guns by our friend in the Presidential Palace, Alberto Fujimori. And we all know what happened to him, now sharing splendid isolation with his nemesis Professor Guzman, both languishing for a very long time in the Callao Maximum Security prison in Lima.'

'And the military are involved here?'

'Indeed, they are. Ostensibly, of course to eradicate the trade, encourage farmers to turn to legitimate crops, but in reality, to grab a slice of the action themselves.' He lent backwards and extracted a newspaper clipping from his desk. 'See here is a cutting from *El Comercio,* our respected newspaper, reporting on the discovery of two army helicopters chock full of coca paste destined no doubt to a freighter awaiting its cargo at Callao.' He paused again. 'Please, I must make a quick call, something I've just remembered.'

Hugh got up to stretch his legs and walked over to the window that overlooked the main square. It had rained heavily during the night and the cobblestones glistened in the sunshine. To all intents and purposes, it looked like a very ordinary Andean town, peaceful even.

'So, Hugh, enough from me. Please tell me what you know and how you think I might help.'

He had expected this question. In brief he told him the bare bones of what had happened since the night on the marshes when he'd received the message from Cristina to what he had learnt from Jorge in Huacachina and then Julia in Ayacucho. Pepe was particularly interested in his conversation with Ricardo at *El Flamenco*.

'I know the place. Very down at heel. Been like that since the early 80s.'

'Yes, it's where Sarah and I met.'

The lawyer paused. 'And Adam knew that?'

'Yes, I told him just before he set out but I'm sure he didn't get as far as Ayacucho. Though Ricardo did say something strange, as if he recognised me in some way, and I can't believe that dates from thirty odd years before.'

'But he told you he hadn't met Adam?'

'I didn't ask him but by that time I was convinced Adam had never made it to Ayacucho. If he had, he'd have called in on Julia and the museum.'

He nodded. 'Which brings us onto the possible sighting here. That call I just took was from a cousin of Freddy's who works at the *El Dorado*, the place where he served drinks to a young gringo and his Peruvian girlfriend.'

'And the two heavies?'

'Yes, without doubt military and I'm sure they're less interested in protecting Adam and Cristina – if it is them – and more concerned in ensuring that the prying journalistic eyes only see what they're supposed to see.' He replaced the newspaper cutting into the file and looked at his watch. 'I suggest we walk over to the *El Dorado* and take an early lunch. Freddy's cousin will be there, and you can show him the photograph of your son.'

***

They walked briskly in the direction of the hotel. 'Don't raise your hopes, Hugh, the *El Dorado* is at best, cosy and clean...'

'And at worst?'

He laughed. 'Well, no disrespect to Freddy' cousin, Nelson, but let's just say it's not the place to be later on in the evening.' As they crossed the main square several people stopped to shake the lawyer's hand.

'You know a lot of people.'

'Marry a Peruvian and you marry a community,' he said as they approached a modest three-storey building above which two flags fluttered in the breeze. He recognised the Peruvian but wasn't sure about the other one, a blue globe on a yellow rhombus.

'The owner, who lives in Lima, is married to a German who supports Brazil. Traitor!' He pushed open the door and ushered Hugh inside.

'But what I can assure you is that the food is excellent, the best in town. Look there's a recommendation from TripAdvisor.' There was no sign of a receptionist or Nelson the manager. In fact, the place seemed empty. 'Let's wait in the restaurant and I'll call Nelson.' After a few minutes, a young man approached them, tentative and worried. 'Ah, Maurice, you old rogue. I wondered where you were hiding.' Maurice wasn't sure whether to smile or retreat to the safety of the kitchen. 'Maurice here is the chef and wizard behind what we are going to enjoy today, *lomo saltado,* one of our national favourites,' said Pepe, which seemed to increase the chef's nervousness. 'Bring us a couple of bottles of water first, please, Maurice while we wait for Nelson.' They didn't have to wait long. The screech of a motorbike and the loud crash of the main door announced the arrival of the manager.

'Sorry I'm late, Pepe. And pleased to meet you, *senor*. You are most welcome to the *El Dorado* Hotel. I hope Maurice has taken your order.' While they waited for the food, Nelson pulled up a chair.

'To business, gentlemen. Hugh, please show Nelson the photograph of Adam.' Clearly, Pepe was used to being in charge. Hugh placed the photograph on the table and bent low over it.

'He looks like you, senor, but...' He said something rapidly in Spanish.

'He asks if he may speak in Spanish.' The two men spoke for several minutes, at one-point Nelson pointing to the photograph and frowning. He then pointed to the bar on the other side of the reception area. 'Ok, Hugh. First let me say that you can trust Nelson here. I have known him since his schooldays and his mother is a close friend of Elizabeth. Second, Nelson has an excellent eye for detail, a first-rate memory which for one thing stands him in good stead when it comes to remembering who has paid and who needs reminding.' He laughed and translated for Nelson. 'The other thing is that despite the TripAdvisor recommendation we don't see many gringos here, so Nelson would certainly remember any that visited. He said something rapidly to the hotel manager. 'In a word, Hugh, yes. He recognises the man and says that he was here last week with a young Peruvian woman who did most of the talking. They were with two men who said nothing but sat and looked at their phones.'

He was alive. He had disappeared and now he had reappeared. But where was he and why hadn't he made contact?

'Did they say anything about where they were staying or where they were going?' Pepe translated.

'They didn't stay here but he did overhear one of the men say something about getting there before dark.'

'And Adam, how did he look? Can he remember if he looked worried or under threat?'

'He says, no he seemed like any other tourist, though he was surprised at the questions he asked. Pepe turned to Nelson. 'I've asked him to call Maurice who was also here that afternoon. He might have overheard something or can corroborate what Nelson heard.' The chef returned wiping his hands on a dishcloth that had seen better days. Maurice and Nelson immediately entered into what sounded to Hugh like a ferocious argument. Pepe raised his hand.

'OK, so this is good. Maurice agrees that when the *gringo* asked a question the woman translated. He also says the white man first asked Nelson some questions, then when he left to attend to reception, he talked some more with him when he came to take the order.'

'And the two men with them, did they say anything?'

'No, they said nothing apart from wanting to get to where they were going before dark. Maurice specifically remembers them saying that.'

'And the questions, Adam talked to both of you?' This provoked further intense conversation. Pepe turned to Hugh.

'This is interesting, Hugh, and proves a point I've often advocated that no two people can ever agree on anything they've heard, or come to that witnessed, but no problem. It seems Nelson here was asked a couple of questions about employment, what sort of work existed, that kind of thing – he told him the truth that the coca trade was the most lucrative, and Maurice was asked if he knew people – the *mochileros* – the guys who carry the coca paste to the border – who might be willing to meet up and talk.'

And what did Maurice say?' Pepe turned to the chef and spoke rapidly.

'He says, of course, he knows friends who do many jobs and maybe some involve transportation.'

'What did Adam say? Can he remember?'

'All he remembers is that he wrote down what he had said and said he would be interested to meet some of these friends.'

'Did he leave a contact phone number?'

'No, he didn't but the woman with him said she would call the hotel later that evening to arrange a meeting – which before you ask – she didn't do.'

Hugh tried to get a sense of what had happened. Adam had rocked up in Pichari with Cristina and the two men, possibly some sort of security, and had made preliminary enquiries about the cocaine trade, in particular the role of the *mochileros,* the backpackers, a perspective he could see would bring the story to life. He was clearly going later on that evening to a pre-arranged lodging – if the aim was to arrive there before nightfall - clearly it couldn't be more than a hundred kilometres away. But where and why not stay at the *El Dorado*?

He turned to Pepe. 'Can you thank Maurice and Nelson – the *lomo saltado* was excellent by the way – and ask them if there is anything that struck them as unusual.' Nelson said nothing he could remember other than the fact that the two heavies seemed very unfriendly.

'And Maurice?' The chef had heard what his manager had said and agreed that the white man and the girlfriend were like many he'd met before, a journalist with an interpreter coming to write a story, but the two men he didn't like.

'Can you ask him why?'

Maurice paused and looked at Nelson and Pepe. The criminal lawyer broke the silence. 'Don't worry, Maurice, nothing will happen. Just tell us what you think.' He sighed and said something rapidly in Spanish. Pepe smiled and told him he was grateful and that he could now return to his kitchen. When he left, Nelson excused himself and disappeared towards the back of the hotel.

'What did he say, Pepe?'

'Interesting, Hugh. He said that before he came to the hotel as a chef, he'd worked for the army, catering, that kind of thing. Said, he recognised one of the men, an old timer, possibly connected with the *Grupo Colina*. And that he thought they were both carrying guns.' Pepe stood up and wandered over to the door.

'Excuse me, but I'd like a coffee. I'll order two. Sorry ... yes *Grupo Colina* is the assassination unit set up by President Fujimori and his head of intelligence, Vladimir Montesinos. He, by the way, is enjoying the comforts of a cell down the corridor from Fujimori, and next door to his nemesis Guzman. Most of *Grupo Colina* have been apprehended and put behind bars, but there are some – and I talk from a professional point of view here – who are not only free but are more than free to offer their services to the highest bidder.'

'Could that be a coincidence?'

'I doubt it. My take on this is that Adam and Cristina made it clear to someone they met – maybe in Huacachina – that they were headed for the VRAEM, and then those with, shall we say, *an interest*, decided the best way was to facilitate an eager – and if you'll excuse me – naïve, young journalist, was to provide him with some protection - our two heavies - who'll not only assist with opening a few doors but make damned sure that quite a few others remain closed.'

This made sense. Three years before, just after he'd joined the newspaper, Adam had been cock-a-hoop at the chance to go to Afghanistan and write a backstory on a certain General Dostum, warlord-cum-possible-president who was keen to present himself to the West as a benevolent successor to the Taliban, something he more or less achieved with the help of a number of pieces written by young journalists like Adam.

But one thing was certain, Adam was here in the VRAEM with Cristina and the two minders. Clearly, he was out of his depth and possibly in danger. *But the lack of contact? Did he think it was best to go silent or was there something else?* A mosquito disturbed his thoughts. Pepe had gone to speak with Nelson, his coffee now cold. He sat and thought about Julia. She had decided to spend the day with Elizabeth visiting a sick aunt and then going to a market where she told him they sold the world's best trout.

He sat and waited for Pepe to return and tried to make sense of what Maurice and Nelson had said. It was good news but it was troubling. Adam was in the VRAEM, that was clear. He'd hold onto that. It was progress. His thoughts turned to Julia. Where did she fit in? He looked down at his coffee cup. For the first time, he wasn't thinking about Sarah, but another woman.

You'd like her, Sarah. She's like you, feisty and quick to get the measure of me.

He looked up to see Pepe emerging with two glasses.

'Pisco sours, dear boy, on the house!' This was about the last thing he wanted, but when in Rome ... and wasn't he supposed to be a cultural historian, well versed in adapting and adjusting?

'Thank you, Pepe, and I hope you've told Maurice and Nelson that I'm grateful for what they've told me?'

'Yes, I have, and more so, told Maurice that what he revealed about *Grupo Colina* stays between the two of us.' He took a sip of the pisco which was ice-cold and refreshing. 'Yes, that's what makes it lethal,' said Pepe, laughing loudly.

'But where could they have gone, after leaving here? You know the landscape, are there any hotels or lodges further on into the VRAEM?'

'Good question. No, there aren't. If Adam wanted to interview coca farmers and *mochileros* he'd be better off staying here in Pichari.' He smiled and looked morosely at his coffee.

'Do you have an idea where he might be?'

'Maybe a private house or a small hostel. I'm guessing somewhere suggested by the boss of the two heavies. Our best bet is that he or Cristina break cover and call you on your mobile. What do we know about her, her connections?' Before he could answer Pepe's mobile uttered a macaw-like screech. 'My father, God bless him, was a naturalist who did research in the Amazon. He loved the macaws, and this ringtone helps me remember how irritating he could be!'

Hugh looked around at the dining room. There was a faded poster of David Beckham alongside the Peruvian Football team. During their second visit to *El Flamenco*, Sarah had said something about the posters on the wall. A few years before she'd trekked up through Vietnam and had seen pictures of Ho Chi Min gradually losing ground to football stars, personalities linked to the Vietnamese love of gambling. They'd won the gamble during the war, now it was riskier – and a more exciting game – guessing whether the nimble Englishman would score against his rivals. He thought about the odds of finding Adam and more importantly, alive. *Alive, that had to be the most important. The odds seemed to have tilted in his favour.*

***

Twenty-One

T*ranscription of interview*: *Major Enrique Salazar, ex-member of the Grupo Colina*

The colonel said you might ask. I am pleased to talk. I have nothing to hide, nothing to be ashamed of. None of us have. I have paid my price. What you must remember, senor, is that the country was a very different place then. Sure, there were excesses, but on both sides.

Did you visit the Tarata statue in Miraflores, in the heart of our capital's banking and commercial district? You haven't? OK, so when we return you must take a visit. Then you can see what we were up against, what the Shining Path could do. Tons of high explosive packed into two lorries off Avenida Larco at a busy time in our capital city. Boof! Twenty-five innocent people killed, more than a hundred badly wounded. So much for advancing the cause of the poor!

To understand you must realise it is not like what you read in the newspapers. We had intelligence that something was planned. I was young, a junior office with the Army Intelligence, seconded to the Colina. Some have called us a death squad, but we saw ourselves as the last bastion of democracy, doing the dirty work in a dirty war. We had read about Shining Path and knew what they'd done in Ayacucho and what they wanted to do here. No way were they going to kill my family.

It was 3rd November 1991, and we had learned of a BBQ planned at a Sendero safehouse on Jiron Huanta in the district of Barrios Altos. They were raising money to renovate the building. There you will find the poor Peruvians and the bourgeoise university types living cheek-by-jowl. There were six of us armed with semi-automatic machine guns fitted with silencers. They would show no mercy to us, so we had to be prepared. At half past eleven in the evening we switched off our sirens and lights and stormed the building.

We wore balaclavas. Important if we failed and they recognised us and came after us or our families.

Two minutes that's all it took. Fifteen terrucos dead, including a boy of eight years. I feel bad about the boy, which is why I am telling you this and why we are sitting here in this bar with you. One of us starting shooting and the boss shouted, 'he will grow up and when he is big, he will take revenge,' but it was wrong, and I am sorry, but now I can make amends.

You know, senor, a prison sentence cannot heal. We here in this country must atone for our sins in our own way. We must support the families of those we have harmed. We must pray for forgiveness. That is what I have done, and that is what I will continue to do.

And I've had time – plenty of time – to think about how I can do this. So, when the colonel talked to me about you and your mission, I suggested – I volunteered - that I could accompany you and Cristina, with Santiago here, and protect you, make sure you see the truth and write well about it. I know this place from the old days. My father owned a big coca farm here and before the army I used to come and play. Now I can – how do you say it – kill two birds with one stone (he laughs).

The boy you see, the eight-year-old child, he had cousins, some from Barrios Altos, some from the VRAEM, scraping a living like they have always done here. So, it was easy for me to do a little research – an old army intelligence officer never dies! – and find the small village, on the banks of the Urubamba village where his relatives live. We are on our way there now. A cousin works as boatmen, taking tourists down the river to the rapids. Perhaps you can talk to him as well?

And you will discover, too, how the poor of our country really live, what they have to do to make a living. We will take you there. It will be my pleasure. But we must be careful, senor. Memories from the old days never die. And for some revenge is more important than forgiveness. Truth and

Reconciliation, but not in a stuffy courtroom but here on the ground, where the tears have been shed. Maybe you can write about that for your English newspaper, not so?

It's clearer now why Salazar and Cortes are with us. Make sure you see the truth and write about it. And if I don't? Or worse, see a different kind of truth and write about that? Cristina just smiles and says that her grandfather, Salas, would never put her in harm's way. She's family, and that counts for a lot here. But does her protection extend to me or am I just feeling out of my depth? We seem to be following the river. No signal and no damn idea where we are. Salazar's keen we get to experience the famous Pongo de Mainique rapids further ahead. Says it'll be the trip of a lifetime.

***

Twenty-Two

I t was Julia who asked the question on everybody's mind.

'So where do we think Adam and Cristina might be, assuming they are still together?' They were at the end of dinner, a feast of locally caught trout and garden vegetables washed down with several bottles of dry white wine from the *Intipalka* vineyard in Ica. 'They produce wine that is beginning to get noticed', said Pepe, as he helped Elizabeth clear away the plates. She returned carrying a large map of the area which she unfolded across the table. Elizabeth pointed at the map.

'Here is where we are, Hugh – Pichari – on the northern side of the Urubamba. Now, from what Nelson has said we know that they were keen to reach their destination before nightfall, which is always at about 6.45. He said this at two o'clock so that means they had in mind a four-hour journey assuming they weren't going off-road.' Hugh lent over the map and watched Elizabeth draw a faint circle around Pichari with a pencil. 'For once, geography is on our side. If we head north there is nothing in terms of villages or significant habitation, and the river here has no crossing points. If, however, we look south-east we can see the road from Ayacucho to here continues towards Cusco and Kiteni.'

Julia interrupted. 'Kiteni? The petrogas boom town? I had the misfortune to go there once. Dreadful place. The end of the road, and full of get-rich-quick types, a magnet for those in search of a fast buck.'

It was Pepe's turn to join in the discussion. 'And can you remember how long it took you to get there, cousin Julia?'

She laughed and looked up at the ceiling. 'Yes, I do. I travelled by local bus from the main square here and it took just over five hours, two of which were spent waiting by the roadside for a replacement distributor cap whatever that is!'

'And the return journey?'

'We were lucky. Apart from starting an hour late, the journey took about four hours, with a fifteen-minute stopover at the half-way point.' Hugh leaned over to get a better look at the map.

'And is there anywhere else they could have gone?'

Elizabeth traced a finger down the 28A highway towards Ayacucho. 'It's not inconceivable they returned the way they'd come and headed for Ayacucho on the 28B. That would take about five hours and there are one or two small settlements just off the highway, but it would make no sense. Why travel all the way from Huacachina, give Ayacucho a miss, and then spend just a few hours here before turning tail?'

Pepe turned to Hugh. 'If they were headed back to Ayacucho, it would increase the possibility that the *quota* warning was intended for him and not you, but I still think that's unlikely.' He looked hard at the map, tracing his stubby finger along the road from Pichari to Kiteni. 'I think Elizabeth is right, and if Kiteni, was their ultimate destination – and it is the end of the road literally – they might see Pichari as a good spot to break off for lunch.'

'And for Adam to get the opportunity to ask a few questions about the VRAEM and the trade? And to set up a few interviews on the return journey?' said Hugh.

Julia touched the Englishman on the arm. 'We know from Nelson and Maurice that he was interested in talking with coca farmers and *mocheleros*. Yes, it's possible he did arrange to meet people here on the way back. They'd have to return this way.'

They were all silent for a moment. Pepe had wandered towards the sideboard and returned with a bottle of pisco and four small glasses.

'I feel like I'm summing up the case for the defence,' he said with a laugh, '...but I think Elizabeth is right. Kiteni makes sense, particularly given there are so few other options. As I said, Hugh, we are at the end of the world here.' He poured the clear liquid into the glasses. 'The next question – the one-million-soles question – is why were they going to Kiteni? Adam, we know is interested in everything and anything to do with the VRAEM, but what could he hope to achieve in the one-time boom town of Kiteni? Oh, and as a criminal lawyer, I can assure you there are no shortage of bad *hombres* in that fine place but from what I know it is mostly all the shenanigans associated with mining contracts and the like, though now I think of it, perhaps I should open a sub-office there.' He sipped his pisco. 'In my line of business, it is not only about evidence but also motivation. In other words, what is Adam's motivation for going to Kiteni? If we can answer that we may have an idea of what his plans are.'

Julia stood up from the table. 'We need a clear head for this, so let me make some coffee.' Pepe quickly topped up his and Hugh's glass and handed over the bottle. 'Good idea, Julia. And thank you. I'm with Elizabeth on this, Kiteni is just about the only sizeable place he could have gone to. Let's think about what he's looking for, the opportunity to talk with some *mochileros*. Well, that is possible given the transient nature of the place, young men who've drifted in from the countryside in search of work. And maybe he hoped to meet with some of the coca farmers, something I would have thought was easier from here, but there will be people in Kiteni who do both; manage a coca farm as well as work in one of the petrogas offshoots. So, he could be persuaded by Cristina or one of the heavies that it's a good place to visit'.

Julia returned with the coffee. 'And any other reasons to visit?'

'A good question, Julia. There is another which might be attractive to him. The other day, Hugh, you mentioned that Adam had a real fondness for the sea and all things water.'

'Yes, he did. Once we arrived at the Norfolk marshes, we couldn't keep him away from the sea and the creeks. But what's this to do with a Peruvian boom town?'

'Well, let me show you something.' He walked over to his bureau and brought his laptop back to the table. 'Do the words, *Pongo de Mainique* mean anything to you?' Hugh shook his head. Elizabeth and Julia answered together.

'The rapids on the Upper Urubamba?'

'Yes, ladies, you remember your geography well. If you take the road north out of Kiteni you'll eventually reach Ivochote where you can hire a boat to carry you down river towards the rapids. I should say, I've done it once with a visiting American oilman who wanted to see the *real Peru*, wherever that is. Anyway, after you pass Idriato, another small village, you'll see the rapids ahead, two kilometres of barely navigable, quite awe-inspiring. The *pongo* or canyon is 45 meters wide and three kilometres long, surrounded by cliffs between 900 and 300 metres high. It constitutes the only passage in the entire Cordillera Vilcabamba and divides the Urubamba, the source of the Amazon, between the upper and lower branches of the river. Some would go as far as saying, it is the most dangerous stretch of water in the Amazonian system. The town's Machiguenga name is *Kiteriari*, which means blood-coloured river. It was named after a turn-of-the-century battle between the Yine and Machiguenga Indians that turned the river red. The place is special and has attracted no less than Werner Herzog who made a film there about the rubber-baron, Fitzcarraldo there, and my Python hero, Michael Palin who made a TV documentary - and I should add - said it was his *favourite place in the world*. And some say, there was once a secret Inca bridge that gives you access across the river to the fabled city of Cusco, more like the real *El Dorado*.' Pepe drank the final drops of his pisco and picked up his coffee. Julia turned to Hugh. 'I'm thinking Adam could have been persuaded to go to Kiteni for work, maybe interviewing *mocheleros* or coca farmers who have relocated there, with the added attraction of a chance to shoot the rapids.'

'Yes, it would appeal. Do you think Cristina set this up or one of the two minders?'

'Another good question,' said Pepe. 'But there is another less pleasant scenario we have to consider.' Elizabeth shot Pepe a quick glance, as if warning him to be careful with what he might say. 'Ten years ago, a colleague of mine. One of the best criminal lawyers I've had the good fortune to know, acted for the prosecution of an ex-military officer who'd moved into real estate in Kiteni and during the building of the gas plant, there was some good pickings to be had. Anyway, it seems he fell out with a competitor and decided that the best way to resolve the matter was to arrange for *a little accident* to occur on the stretch of water just before it descends into the maelstrom that is the Pongo. Of course, the best laid plans and all that, soon fell apart once the boatmen realised, they might also take the rap.'

Hugh looked towards the two women who both sat with their hands in their lap. 'Are you suggesting, Pepe, that another motivation for luring Adam and Cristina to Kiteni and the Pongo is to kill them?'

The criminal attorney looked pained.

'It's in my nature to try and explore all possible motivations. I hope, of course, that I'm wrong, but we need to know what might have happened and the risks involved. I'm sure Adam is well aware of the risks as well'. He looked mournfully at his empty glass. Elizabeth took the hint and returned with the bottle of pisco. Hugh declined but Pepe and Julia both said that a small glass would help them sleep. It took Pepe to wrap up the discussion. 'It is clear *where* we are going to go next. I know that Elizabeth has commitments here and that Julia had plans for you to meet Reyvit our friendly *cocalero* in town but if you are willing, I suggest you both accompany me tomorrow to Kiteni.

Freddy can drive. And who knows, Hugh, you might get the chance to experience our Python's *favourite place in the world*.'

***

Twenty-Three

Once again, he woke early. It was becoming a habit. They'd agreed to leave mid-morning. Pepe had things to do at the office and Elizabeth had decided to cook enough food to last for the journey, and for the two or three days they planned to spend in Kiteni. He closed his eyes for a moment, his thoughts drifting back to his arrival at the airport and everything that had occurred since. In many ways his search was over. Adam had been found if not located. He was clearly alive, just unwilling for whatever reason to get in touch. So, their search was over, and he could return home. Whether he was in danger – and there was some evidence he might be – that was surely a matter for Adam, an accomplished journalist, and not a helicopter parent who had enough issues of his own to deal with. He raised himself up onto his elbows and looked towards the window. He'd go downstairs and inform Elizabeth and Julia of his decision. Then he would walk over to Pepe's office and tell him it was over.

Hugh reached over for his phone. There was one missed call. He recognised Max's number. The call had been made at midnight, UK time and he'd received it early evening shortly after he'd decided to switch the thing off and enjoy Pepe's pisco. Midnight suggested it was urgent. He called him. It would be early afternoon, a good time to catch him in. The answerphone began its message before Max broke in.

'Hugh, it's Max. Glad you've returned the call.' He got straight to the point. 'I received an email from Adam late last night and wanted to bring you up to speed, but first, where are you?'

'I'm in the VRAEM, Max, the cocaine-growing area, and about to leave with some Peruvian friends, towards a place called Kiteni where we think Adam is headed.'

'OK, great Hugh, but let me share Adam's email with you. It's brief but there's something that troubles me about it, a few words that are very un-Adam...'

'Fire away.'

Quick heads up, Max. Things are going well. Lots of great interviews, good support from my local PA and interpreter, Cristina. Doors being opened. Pulitzer Prize awaiting! One or two tricky things but rest assured Kurtz is looking after us well. Off-grid for a week. Best, Adam.

'When did you receive this, Max?'

'Yesterday at about ten in the evening. I fired off a reply to Adam and then tried calling you about midnight, I guess. But the thing is, Hugh, there's something not right about this. First, Adam never uses email – he's welded to his mobile like we all are – which means he's using email instead of a replacement phone – because it is the safest way of getting a message out...'

'...emailing from a borrowed laptop silently?'

'Yes, not unusual for journalists to do it this way, because he doesn't want to be overheard. And second, there's something coded here.'

'The, *but rest assured Kurtz is looking after us well*?'

'Yes. Saying one thing and meaning something else. It's all part of the journalist protocols when you think you're in some kind of danger.'

'Kurtz? The Colonel Kurtz from *Apocalypse Now*, the crazy colonel living up-river?'

'Yes, though I'm thinking he's drawing our attention to the source of the movie, Joseph Conrad's *Heart of Darkness*. But whatever, my reading of this is Adam trying to tell us something about where he is or where he's going, and that he is in some sort of danger. The *looking after us well* is ominous, written I think in case whoever's holding him gets sight of the message before it is sent.'

Hugh told him of their plans and that he'd be out of touch for a few days but would make contact when he had signal. He washed and dressed quickly and went downstairs. The search wasn't off. In many ways it had only just begun.

***

It was mid-day before they finally left. As they swung out onto the road, a battered brown sedan moved away from the kerb and drove slowly behind them. Pepe turned round and pointed out the car that was keeping its distance between them.

'We've been joined by your friend in the shabby brown suit, Hugh. I'm not surprised. He's been watching the house since you arrived. My guess is that he'll follow us all the way to Kiteni. Perhaps then I'll get an opportunity to ask him a few questions.'

'You knew he was watching the house, Pepe?' said Julia.

'Yes, I didn't want to alarm you, but it was one of my security boys who told me.'

'Security boys?' said Hugh.

'Much as I would love to sleep peacefully in my bed knowing I was being guarded over by the noble police forces of this country, I prefer to arrange my own security.'

Julia said nothing but glared at her cousin. For a few miles nobody said anything, Pepe appearing to have decided to catch up on his sleep. Hugh turned to Julia who was looking straight ahead. He spoke softly.

'I meant to ask you, Julia why you first went to Kiteni? Was it to look for Martin? You said you had the 'misfortune to go there once?'

She leant back in her seat and spoke in a low voice. 'It was a year or so after Martin had been taken and, though it wasn't safe to travel anywhere outside your home place, I was desperate to follow up any leads I had.' She stopped for a moment as Freddy negotiated a sharp bend. 'One of the children in my school had an uncle who worked as a security guard for a geo-physics company in Kiteni – this was in the days before they struck big – and he sent a message that some soldiers had been seen offloading a group of prisoners late one night.'

'Did the contact say where?'

'Yes, it was on the bank of the river not far from the rapids, though he said he couldn't be sure exactly. Worried for his safety he returned to Kiteni and through word of mouth, the information came to me.'

'How did they know one of the prisoners might have been Martin?'

'Yes, that was my first thought. The uncle, Julian, said he heard one of the soldiers shout the name *Martin* ordering him to stay behind with the lorry until they returned.'

'It is a common name here in Peru?'

'Not particularly but the description he gave of the man fitted my husband in terms of age and height.' She paused again. 'Of course, I had to go, even though I was worried I might be followed. Here, if a family member is accused – or worse – arrested, then all the immediate family are regarded as suspect.'

'And I'm guessing you found nothing?'

She said nothing but gave him a small smile.

'Even if he was amongst those poor men, Hugh, it is likely their bodies were thrown into the river up from the rapids.' Pepe had begun to snore quietly. 'When I returned from Kiteni, a strange thing happened. I decided to break the journey back to Ayacucho by staying with Pepe and Elizabeth. Pepe was out at the office and Elizabeth visiting her mother, who was not well, so I had the house to myself. I was in the kitchen preparing supper. I had decided to cook a dish Martin loved *Pollo a la Brasa* – roasted chicken – when I heard a sharp intake of breath behind me. I turned and saw him standing in the doorway. My Martin, his clothes dusty, wearing no shoes, saying nothing, just his arms outstretched. I dropped the knife and ran towards him.' Hugh took hold of her left hand as she stifled a sob. 'As I ran, he slowly faded, leaving behind just a faint aroma I recognised, his favourite brand of cigarettes.' She squeezed his hand and then let it go. 'It was the only time he reappeared to me. Even in my dreams, he is absent. And you, Hugh, do you ever see Sarah?'

He told her of the woman by the grave on the marshes and in the doorway of the library in Huacachina. 'I think it might be Sarah returning to me in some sort of way.'

'In what way?'

'Well, my head knows she has gone, of course, but I guess the heart can play tricks.'

Julia nodded. 'In the first few days, weeks even, after Martin had been disappeared, I was frantic, looking everywhere, closets in the house, even under the car. Then I calmed down and tried to stand outside myself.' She shifted in her seat. 'I began to consider things differently, that Martin hadn't actually disappeared but rather he was out of view for a while, and that we were both together in some way but just separated. It worked for a while but as the months and years went by, I began to accept that he really had gone, really had disappeared, and the best I could hope for would be the discovery of his remains. I remember the moment – I wasn't doing anything in particular – when I realised that I would never see him again. *I'm sorry, Martin*, I said to him. *I will not meet with you again, but I will fight for you, for the justice you deserve.* She pushed back a strand of hair that had fallen over her left eye. 'It was a terrible moment, *senor*, but a liberating one, and one I felt sure my husband would concur wherever he was.' She leant forward and said something to Freddy. 'I have asked him to stop at the next place so we can get some coffee or Inka Cola, the best coffee, by the way, this side of the Andes.'

He couldn't help but laugh at this extraordinary woman. 'I'm sure it is, Julia, though you say that about almost everything.'

She said something quickly in Spanish and settled back into her seat. Hugh swivelled round to look out of the rear window. He could see a large lorry full of fruit. Behind that he caught sight of the right front fender of the brown sedan that had clearly seen better days.

**

Twenty-Four

Transcription of interview: Major Santiago Cortes, *sometime commander, military counter-insurgency unit, Ayacucho*

You have spoken with my colleague Major Enrique, and now you wish to speak with me? We travel together, and so I will of course comply. Besides, I have nothing to hide. In fact, I welcome the opportunity to explain the reasons for accompanying you and Major Enrique to the VRAEM.

I apologise that I am not so good with the words of your language, but I am sure Cristina here will help me out.

Major Enrique has reasons of his own for coming here, whereas my own reasons are very different. I know he wishes to find the family of the boy who was killed in the barrio in Lima and for that I respect him. For me it is different though I am sure you will see some similarities in the two of us. To understand, I must describe something that happened to me during La Violencia. It was November 1989, at the height of the troubles. I was a young officer, the lieutenant's pips newly minted on my shoulder flashes. For reasons I never understood, I was drafted into the military counter-insurgency unit and posted to Ayacucho, which you will remember was at the heart of the insurrection. My job was simple. I would liaise with the local police, who would provide me with a list of names – often supplied to them by disgruntled neighbours – and then our unit – a snatch squad – would locate, arrest and interrogate the identified terrorists. Sometimes we would take a family member, particularly if the intended target was not at home. We soon discovered that they would hand themselves in once they knew we had someone dear to them. I was second in command to a captain from the district. He was very different from me, a brutal man, who thought nothing of taking whatever came his way.

I forget most of the operations, but one stays with me. The target was a local teacher activist called Martin Perez. He had led a demonstration against the poor salaries and was known to be a sympathiser of the crazy Professor Guzman. On the night in question, we raided his house and took him to the barracks on the other side of town. Like most, he complained and said he was innocent, but what I remember most was his wife, Julia, who did her best to protect him. Perhaps it was her resistance or her display of spirit that drove the captain to do what he did? I think it was simply an opportunity he could not pass up on, a spoil of war, a chance for a little pleasure.

After leaving the house with Perez in the truck we drove to Los Cabitos, the barracks where Perez and four others were interrogated. I had nothing to do with that but was tasked with transporting the prisoners the following day. We were just a few men including a sinchi called Panco and a Corporal Nicholas. We were to drive them towards Kiteni and finish the job. I was told there was a favourite location for this kind of operation. Why to that place I am not sure, but you must remember that in those days our orders were never to be questioned.

Panco drove and I sat in the back with Perez and two of the others. Normally I would have sat in the front, but I wanted to talk with the prisoners, to find out a little more their motivation for what they did, what they intended to achieve. It is a whole day journey from Ayacucho and so we had time for what I liked to consider was a philosophical discussion of revolution, the politics of the Shining Path, that kind of thing. And I learnt a lot from Perez. The other said nothing, for which I don't blame him.

We arrived just before dusk and drove to the execution site on the banks of the Urubamba. I remember it was very beautiful. We handcuffed the two men and ordered them out of the car. I had my orders and told them that I had no choice but to follow them. The quiet one looked down at his feet and said nothing. Perez shuffled close to me and asked if he might say something. We are not brutes and I said, 'of course.'

He then told me the name of his wife, Julia, and asked if I could tell her what had happened, that he loved her and would carry her image with him to his grave. I told him it was not possible as we had strict instructions to conduct our work in utmost secrecy. He said nothing.

Before I could say anything else, Panco looked at me and seeing my firmness of purpose shot the two men in quick succession. We then tipped their bodies into the river and made our way back to our barracks.

I am telling you this because I have carried with me a deep regret and shame about my conduct that evening. Not that we killed the two men but the fact that I could not honour the request of Martin Perez. I do not seek forgiveness or sympathy – these men had allied themselves to the communists – but I would like to meet with her and tell her of the bravery of her husband, the love he expressed for her, and show her the place where his life ended.

During the past few days, I have learnt that she is making plans to visit Kiteni and so I will use this opportunity to arrange a meeting. It will not be without its risks, but I am prepared.

So, senor, we all travel for different reasons. I need not remind you of course, that what I have just told you – though true— is not to be used by you in anything you might write. I have told you because you need to know, to understand the complexities of the events you seek to describe.

And the guilt some still carry around with us.

So, Cortes is responsible for at least one murder. Something he seems proud of and happy to tell me, a journalist. If Max hears about this, he'll tell me to go straight to the authorities. But why did Cortes tell me this? Is it to keep me onside and to keep my trap shut? Cristina has called her grandfather again and he's told her we are in safe hands. Nothing to worry about. But I'm not sure I believe her. Cortes and Salazar are both armed – they're forever cleaning their guns, and have changed in their attitude to us. We need to be careful, and when we reach Kiteni we must do all we can to find a way out. Take our chances. Shit.

***

Twenty-Five

T hey pulled over and stopped in front of a ramshackle row of zinc-roof shacks. Pepe bounded out of the car and commenced shaking hands and laughing with everyone he met. 'He knows everyone, and if he doesn't, within five minutes it'll look like he has known them all his life,' said Julia. Pint cups of dark black coffee were dispensed from a huge urn and served with small dough balls drenched in sugar. Pepe offered the plate to Freddy.

'Peru has a real problem with obesity and type-2 diabetes,' said Pepe laughing. 'These don't help but I think we all need cheering up,' pausing for a moment to point towards the road. 'Our friend in the battered sedan has just passed. He'll re-join us again further up.'

Julia sipped her coffee having declined the snacks. 'Will he follow us to the hotel, Pepe? What do you think is his plan?'

'He'll certainly tail us to the hotel, but then I'm guessing he'll call it a night, report back to whoever is paying him, and re-join his watch after sunrise...which is why I am proposing that we get an early night and head off from the hotel before he returns.'

'And where will we be heading off too?' asked Julia.

'Ivochote, a small community just before the rapids. An old friend from my law school days has a house there which has enough room for all of us. More importantly, everything that happens in Kiteni will be on his radar. If Adam and Cristina have arrived, Alfredo will know about it.'

An hour later they arrived at the *Hotel Amazonas*. It was built close to the river and claimed to have excellent air conditioning, that is when the electricity was working. Pepe had booked a twin for himself and Hugh, and two single rooms for Freddy and Julia. An elderly porter carried their bags up to their rooms.

'I've asked him to let me know if he sees anyone acting suspiciously,' said Pepe, 'though given this is Kiteni, that rules in a lot of people! Still, he might spot something or someone before we check out.' Freddy and Pepe decided to relax in the bar.

'I'm not sure about you, Hugh,' said Julia, 'but I've had enough sitting for one day, why don't we leave these gentlemen to their drinks, and walk down to the river?'

As they left, Pepe gave them a wave of his huge right hand. 'Take care, *senor*, most Peruvians are incapable of lasting five minutes in the water!'

The roaring of the river increased as they made their way across the road and through a small estate of half-completed apartments. Most had no roofs.

'Did they stop construction because they'd run out of money?'

'Not always, Hugh. Usually, it is because of our antiquated laws we've inherited from the Spanish.' They were now picking their way around discarded cola bottles and piles of twisted metal discarded by the builders. 'Yes, it drives Pepe mad. When the last surviving parent dies, all the descendants have to agree on how the inheritance will be spent. For a while there are no problems but soon enough one sibling wants out and so the idea of investing in a home for one or some of them collapses.' She pointed towards a large three-storey house lacking a roof. 'And it's not helped by our taxation system that applies construction tax when the building is finally completed, hence many like this one lacking a roof. When they add the finishing piece, they'll be liable for tax, and most cannot afford that.'

The afternoon sun had lost some of its intensity, but it was still humid. The path between the apartments soon joined a similar track that ran along the riverbank. To the left it was slightly less overgrown and ran past a row of eucalyptus, between which was an old wooden bench.

'Let's sit there. I'm sure it can take our weight,' said Julia. She was wearing a simple white blouse above a bright, full skirt of red and black stripes. 'It'll keep us out of the sun too.'

They lowered themselves gingerly onto the bench. Julia was right, it was good to walk even if they were once again sitting. The river swirled and eddied in front of them. He thought of the creeks on the Norfolk marshes, and the rushing and gurgling as the tide roared in. For a moment he wondered what to say. It seemed enough to be just sitting with Julia and watching the river.

'Are you optimistic, Hugh, about finding Adam?' She paused. 'Your mood seems to have lifted.'

'Yes, I do feel optimistic particularly given what we know so far. I know some of it seems flimsy but it all points to Adam being alive, and more importantly in this part of the country.'

She nodded and spoke quietly, 'There's still a lot we don't know, of course. Why he decided to come here instead of staying in Pichari – if he did decide – and when he arrived. We still have no way of knowing when he left Pichari though it is reasonable to think it was shortly after the meeting in the *El Dorado*.'

She was right, and there was another more fundamental unanswered question. *Why did he to cut me off? Maybe it has something to do with Sarah, or me? Who knows, I haven't been myself since her diagnosis, and after her death I did fold in on myself when I should have been thinking of him.* He shared his thoughts with Julia.

She placed a hand over his. 'Don't be too hard on yourself, Hugh. Yes, I'm sure you weren't always the perfect father – as I was not always the perfect wife – but when it comes to grief, there is no textbook answer on how to behave. What matters is that by coming here and looking for him, you have demonstrated your love, something he will realise when you meet.'

'And there has been another good thing to come out of all this?'

'What?'

'Meeting you, Julia.'

She laughed and squeezed his hand. 'My mother would call you a silly old romantic fool!'

'And what would you call me?'

'*A silly old romantic fool*, but one who I happen to like very much.' She removed her hand and continued to look at him, her face suddenly serious. 'A more important question is what you intend to do when you find him. Make up and then return to your country?'

It was a question he had thought about a great deal. In one scenario they would say nothing, just give each other a hug like they used to when he was a small boy. In another they would be sitting in the pub on the Norfolk coast, talking man-to-man about what had happened, and importantly what had to happen for their relationship to recover.

Julia seemed to sense his thoughts.

'Whatever prompted his distancing from you, he will appreciate your love and concern for him, of that, I am sure.'

He wasn't quite so sure.

'And you, Julia, what lies ahead for you? Continuing the search for Martin, of course, but can you ever see an end to that?'

'Settling back into my old life in Ayacucho, do you mean? Returning to my school, tending my garden, establishing new friends who will accompany me into my old age?'

'Actually, Julia, I can't image you settling back into anything. You are driven by a desire to see justice done. If for whatever reason the search for your husband ended, you would find other causes to champion, other battles to fight.'

She laughed. 'You think too highly of me, Hugh, and you sound like Martin, God bless him. He was always telling me to put my feet up and to be honest there are many times when I want to do just that, put it all to one side, and return to some kind of normality.'

He thought about his own life at home. After Sarah's death, a Macmillan nurse had taken him to one side and had offered him some advice. 'It sounds cliched, Hugh but my advice is to take each day as it comes. Don't even begin to think about the long or medium term. You need time. It really is the great healer. When the time is right for you to begin to think about tomorrow or the day after, you will know it. 'Grief is a many feathered bird' someone once said. One day it will fly away, and you'll be able to make your own journey into what life has left to offer.'

He looked at the river and the woman sitting beside him. Something had changed, he felt lighter, more at peace. He would find Adam, and they would repair what damage had been done. And maybe Julia had a part to play in that?

Six months after their return from South America, he and Sarah had hiked to the top of a hill that overlooked the South Downs. From the top hang gliders would leap and be lifted up over the Sussex countryside. There was an old wooden bench at the summit and they both sat quietly enjoying the moment. Then she had turned to him and had said, 'You wanted to ask me something?' He turned to her and blushed. As with so many times in his life words failed him, a surprising thing for a university teacher. 'Yes, I did, do...'

She laughed. 'Well, the answer is yes, Mr. Decisive!'

They were married three months later.

Julia touched him gently on the arm. 'We should return to the hotel, Hugh, or Pepe will send a search party after us.'

They turned away from the river and made their way back. A street dog followed them up to the steps of the hotel. Before they entered, Julia turned and kissed him lightly on each cheek.

'Thank you, my silly old romantic friend, I have enjoyed it.'

He blushed. Inside they found Freddy waiting at the reception desk.

'Good to see you both.' He looked worried. 'After you left, we finished our drinks and Pepe said he wanted to take a siesta but that I should call him at five, about half an hour ago. Well, I have called his room but he's not answering. You are sharing a room, senor, and so I think we must go up and look.

Inside the room looked much as Hugh had left it. There were two bags at the foot of their respective beds and clearly Pepe's bed had not been slept in. Nothing seemed out of place.

As they turned to leave, Julia saw a piece of paper stuck to the back of the door. She raised a hand to her mouth. On it, written in red ink, was one-word: *quota.*

***

Freddy carefully detached the note from the door and handed it to Hugh. 'Does this look similar to the one you received, senor?'

'Yes, it does, similar paper and I'd swear it was written by the same hand.'

They were huddled together in front of the closed door. Freddy was taking photographs of the room and several of Pepe's wallet and mobile phone on the bedside table.

'I think we should take these with us in case he calls,' he said.

Julia spoke next.

'Yes, and we should move down to my room. Then I can call Elizabeth and we can work out what we should do.'

Julia's room was on the floor below. Before they entered Freddy said, 'I also think I should find the duty manager and talk to any of the staff who might have seen anyone suspicious entering or leaving the hotel. It's unlikely but I'll check if they have CCTV. If they do – and it's working – we'll be able to see if Pepe left the building alone or with the intruder. There's always an outside chance he went for a long walk or that some harm has come to him outside the hotel.'

'Good idea, Freddy, and let's not say any more than we have to at this stage.'

'Do you include the police in that, Julia?'

She sat down on the bed. 'Please sit, Hugh. Yes, if we do contact the police, it might make things worse, but let me call Elizabeth.'

He walked over to the window while she made the call, her voice low and urgent. The room overlooked the carpark which was almost empty except for their car and a rusting VW beetle that had seen better days. Behind him, Julia had stopped talking.

'Elizabeth is arranging for one of Pepe's security men to drive her here. She hopes to get here by midnight. I told her we'll stay up. I imagine none of us will get much sleep tonight. Oh, and she agrees with us that at this stage we shouldn't contact the police. Pepe had quite a number of enemies, one or two might be working in the local force here.'

He pulled the chair under the desk nearer where she was sitting. 'Well, there are two things that have happened which may not be as interconnected as we think. First, there is the *quota* note, clearly intended for me, a reminder if you like. We were sharing a room and it wouldn't be difficult to discover this from the hotel register on the reception desk. Second, it is possible - likely even - that the intruder had expected to find the room empty and, in a panic, forced Pepe to go with him. If he did that – and given Pepe's size – he must have been armed with a gun or a knife…'

'…if Freddy discovers anything from the cameras, we will know that at least…'

'Perhaps, Julia, but I haven't noticed any cameras and even if there was one, it's unlikely to be working.'

Julia nodded. She suddenly looked her age, and it took a great deal of willpower for him to resist the desire to scoop her up in his arms. 'There is another thing you should know, Hugh. This isn't the first time Pepe has been threatened, although it is the first time he has disappeared. About six months ago two men on a motorcycle shot at his car as he was about to park near his offices in Lima. The police tried to reassure him that it was just a carjacking, but Pepe had one of the bullets that had embedded itself in the rear upholstery examined by some friends in forensics and they said it was regular army issue. At the time he was prosecuting a high up in the Callao Port Authority accused of colluding with a well-known businessman to import large quantities of sodium nitrate into the country, an essential ingredient in coca paste production.'

'It's possible then, Julia, that the delivery of the note – which was intended for me– is separate from the disappearance of Pepe. But I think it's more likely the two are connected and that Pepe was in the wrong place at the wrong time. If he has been taken by whoever is behind the notes, then we might expect to hear from them either in the form of a ransom of some kind or further instructions about what to do.'

She leant forward, her dark hair falling over her face. 'You are correct, Hugh, that might be what happens. But we must prepare for the worst outcome too, that Pepe saw who left the note and was either killed and his body dumped or has disappeared, and we will never see him again.'

'What would Pepe do, Julia?'

'To be certain he would not sit and wait. He would argue for a course of action: utilising all the resources at his disposal, money, contacts, police officers he could trust, local leaders ... but we must wait for Elizabeth to arrive before we decide what to do.'

He nodded. There was a soft knock on the door and Freddy entered.

'I've spoken with the manager and the old porter who was on duty behind the desk. The manager confirmed what we thought, the CCTV isn't working and that he saw no-one enter or leave the hotel since our arrival. The porter was more helpful saying he saw Pepe go up to his room after we left the bar and that he looked worried.'

'How did he know that?' said Julia.

'Just before he went up to his room, he took a call on his mobile and he overheard him say something like, 'are you sure?' then 'OK, I will come.'

'But he didn't see him come down later and leave the hotel?'

'No, though he did say that sometimes he takes a break late afternoon so it wouldn't be difficult for anyone to arrive or leave without his knowledge.'

'Which means it's possible for Pepe to have left shortly after being seen by the porter and then the note being delivered later?' said Freddy.

'Yes, though it doesn't explain why Pepe left his wallet and phone in his room, unless he thought it safer to meet whoever he was meeting without means of identification.'

'I think that's unlikely. I can imagine him leaving his wallet behind, and as you say just taking some cash, but his phone. It seems unlikely somehow.' Freddy had been standing waiting for further instructions. 'I'm sorry, Freddy you must be tired. May I suggest you go and eat, and Hugh and I will join you in a minute?'

After he had gone, Julia turned to Hugh. 'There is one other thing you should know and it's important only you and Elizabeth know.' Below the room he heard the wail of a police siren getting closer. 'It's the old porter who helped us with our luggage. I may be wrong, but I am sure I have seen him before. I cannot be sure, and I would not want to accuse someone unjustly, but I think he was with the soldiers when they came to my house and took Martin. In fact, I am sure he was.'

***

Elizabeth arrived shortly after midnight.

'No traffic and Pedro drove faster than Pepe, which says a lot!'

She looked tired but otherwise had lost none of her spirit. After a brief summing up for Elizabeth, Hugh headed for his room and Freddy to his. Pedro had agreed to share with him, and Elizabeth with Julia.

'We'll meet early at breakfast and decide what to do,' said Julia.

He wished them a goodnight, wondering if any of them would sleep much. Before he turned in, he wandered over to the window and looked down on the carpark. Pedro had parked his car next to Freddy's and apart from the old VW it was empty. He checked his phone. As he did so a text arrived from Max asking for any news. He'd call him the following day. Clearly, the editor had no news.

Surprisingly, he slept well. He was the first down and found the table set for breakfast. The elderly porter was pushing a broom across the floor of the reception area. He seemed frail and innocuous. Had he really been part of the squad that had raped Julia and abducted Martin?

Julia arrived next. 'Elizabeth is on her way down. She's just checking Pepe's phone for unusual calls. She doesn't recognise the call he received yesterday just before he went up to his room but then he receives a lot of calls every day, and not all of them are friendly. But it's best Elizabeth explains.'

They ordered fresh orange juice and coffee. Elizabeth smiled as she joined them. 'Hello, Hugh. I've asked Freddy to check the car. Pedro has relatives nearby and I've suggested he takes the day off. We can all squeeze into one car, and anyway, it'll be less noticeable than if we travel around in a convoy.'

Julia then described the events of the previous day in detail, apart from the walk to the river. 'Freddy has already told me what happened after you went for your walk, a couple of drinks at the bar, and then Pepe's decision to take a nap. We also know from the porter that he received a troubling call just before he went upstairs.' Julia turned to Hugh. 'There's another thing, Elizabeth.' She then told her of her suspicions.

'I'm sure you are right, Julia, it's not something you'd get wrong. Do you think he might be connected to Pepe's disappearance?'

'Well, he knows who we are from the register, but I don't know, it seems it might be a coincidence. What do you think, Hugh?'

Up to now he'd let the women hold the floor. 'Well, the *quota* note is clearly linked to the previous one, and I'm sure that Pepe's disappearance is connected to it in some way. Your recognition of the porter muddies the water, but I tend to agree with Elizabeth that it might be just a coincidence.'

They agreed to leave what to do about the porter until after they'd found Pepe. He would know what to do about him.

'But how do we start looking for him?' asked Julia. He wondered about going to the police with Pepe's phone. If they could trace the last call, it might lead them to the lawyer. 'I know what you're thinking, Hugh, but I think we should do that as a last resort. The problem here, is that law enforcement is not as straightforward as in your own country. Salaries are low, and in an area like this, it takes a great deal of principle to keep off a drug lord's payroll.'

'Julia is right, Hugh', said Elizabeth, 'and Pepe wasn't universally popular, but my suggestion is that we stick to Pepe's plan, take the road to Ivochote and meet up with Alfredo. I called him before breakfast to tell him about Pepe. He's obviously worried but agrees. He says he'll expect us after lunch sometime. It's just under fifty kilometres so it should take about an hour. Freddy tells me they've graded the road which means they'll have cleared any landslides.' That left the morning. The two women said something quickly in Spanish. 'Julia suggests we do a quick drive around the town. It'll take our minds off Pepe and who knows, we might see something useful.'

Freddy's response to the idea of a tour of the town was laughter. 'Ok, with me, but there isn't much to see in daylight hours anyway.' As they pulled out onto the road into town, he turned to them. 'Keep your windows up and doors locked.'

A road off to the left was signed to the airport. Julia was staring out of the window. 'Strange, I know for such a small place, but it's grown from 600 to more than 10,000 inhabitants, mostly incomers working for the petrogas companies, and the consultants writing environmental impact studies or growth monitoring studies. You can guess which gets priority.'

The road had now become the town's high street, opening into the main plaza. At one end was a white-washed church, at the other a row of small cafes and grocery shops. Beyond the square could be seen the sides of a thickly wooded hillside that ran down to the Urubamba.

'This is more or less it, so let's park here and take a coffee and a snack in one of the cafes. We can sit outside,' said Julia.

Café Dick was next to *Video Dick*. They ordered coffee and *empanadas*.

'Don't tell me, Julia, but these are the best *empanadas* this side of the Urubamba?!'They laughed but when they arrived, they were surprisingly good, the pastry crisp and fresh. In different circumstances, it might almost be relaxing. The occasional minibus hurtled around the main square.

Julia pointed towards the church. 'The road carries on past the church, Hugh, where it then divides, the right fork continuing to Quillabamba which is very much like here, and then onto Cusco. The left road, which we'll take this afternoon goes as far as Ivochote. There it ends.'

'If everyone has seen enough, let's go back to the hotel and check out,' said Elizabeth.

'And the porter, should we talk to him?' said Julia.

'No, let's tell him we'll be away for two or three nights, which may be the case once we've found Pepe, and made progress on the whereabouts of Adam and Cristina. Whatever, we're likely to spend one night here before we drive back to Pichari,' she replied.

Freddy went inside to pay and came out almost immediately, his phone clamped firmly to his right ear. 'The manager of the hotel says a certain Senor Pepe is sitting in the restaurant enjoying a late breakfast and he wondered if we'd like to join him. Apparently, he has something to tell us.'

***

E lizabeth ran ahead into the dining room. 'Pepe, you old fool, you've had us worried sick!'

'My dear Elizabeth, I apologise, and for subjecting you to a very uncomfortable car journey here.' He kissed her lightly on both cheeks. 'But sit everyone and I'll order more coffee. I've got quite a story to tell. And hello to you, Hugh. You were at least spared my notorious snoring!' Coffee and glasses of water were brought to the table. 'Well, let's start with the good news, Hugh. I have evidence from the horse's mouth as they say that Adam and Cristina are safe. *Where* they are is another matter, but we'll come to that. Enough to say they aren't far, Ivochote perhaps.' Julia looked at Hugh and smiled. 'But let me tell you what I know before we decide next steps.' Pepe was clearly in his element. As he spoke, Hugh marvelled at his ability to marshal the facts so effectively into an engrossing narrative. If only he had done the same with his lectures. 'So, let me sum up the salient events since I left Freddy after a very pleasant drink. First the phone call. It was from one of the heavies, a certain ex-Major Santiago Cortes, who said he had some urgent business with me and that I was to meet a car outside the hotel, but that I was to come with no ID or phone, hence you finding those things in my room. I also reasoned that even leaving you a note might be dangerous.' He paused, as he would have done in court, and took a swig of water. 'I was met by a car I hadn't seen before. It looked like it might once have been a taxi. The driver was mid-twenties, the kind of guy you can ask to do anything for a hundred bucks. He told me I had to wear a blindfold. We must have driven about forty minutes north. Once or twice, I heard the river to our right. When we stopped, I was met by Cortes who apologised for the theatrics but assured me he meant no harm. He led me into a small bungalow off the main road surrounded on three sides by thick woodland. I'm guessing we were somewhere near Ivochote.' He paused again and said something in Spanish to Julia. 'I have just told Julia that what he told me primarily concerns her and that it might be painful to hear.' Julia said nothing, her hands folded neatly in her lap. 'Major Cortes's main reason for coming here is to meet with you, Julia. To make amends, he says, for a crime which has hung heavy on him, and now he's seeking some sort of absolution. He told me with a great deal of repetition that he *was* one of the officers – second in command in fact – of the snatch-squad that abused you and disappeared Martin all those years ago. He is insistent that though that the taking of Martin was planned, what happened to you, was not. Something he calls an *unfortunate result of war*. As if we were at war!' He was speaking quietly now, all the courtroom theatrics put to one side. 'He told me that what happened to you lies heavy with him and it's what has brought him here. He wants to arrange a private meeting, to apologise to you personally, and to seek, what he calls an *atonement*.'

Elizabeth turned to her husband. 'But why all the secrecy? Couldn't he just come to the hotel and say what he has to say, assuming that Julia is willing to meet with him?'

'A good question, Elizabeth. When I put that to him, he said he was now a married man and keen to avoid any stain on his character, any likelihood of any of this getting out. Perhaps he was thinking of Adam and his enquiries, who knows?' He laughed grimly. 'I told him he should have thought of that years ago.'

Julia leant towards Pepe and spoke to him quietly. She turned towards Hugh. 'I've just said, why should I meet with this man, what do I gain from all this?'

'He seems to have thought about that eventuality and told me that if you agree to meet him, he will take you – and only you – to the place where Martin was killed and disposed of, a place by the river some distance from here but easy to find, particularly for those who visited many times. He told me it was a kind of killing field where the disappeared were taken after interrogation and thrown into the river.'

Hugh looked over at Julia who glanced in his direction. 'I see. A deal. He wants me to hear his confession and in return he will end my suffering. No sense, that I might also be seeking something more - not atonement for him - but justice for Martin and all the other *desaparecidos?*'

Pepe moved closer to Julia and gently laid a hand on her head. 'These people know or care little for justice, Julia. Talk of atonement for these people is like saying a few Hail Marys after you've sinned. What we need to remember is that these were soldiers acting under orders of the State, carrying out extra-judicial abductions and executions. For this alone they must be brought to account. They may be motivated primarily by their own feelings and desires but always it's about their own survival. Everyone else can go to hell. It is the problem of this country, no sense of nation and responsibility at that level.'

'How did he know I was here?'

'It seems that someone in the hotel tipped him off. My money is on the old porter – whose name is Nicholas by the way – who might well have passed on copies of our ID documents when we checked in. If you remember, he went into the back room to copy them. My guess, he could be one of Cortes's men, maybe even involved in Martin's death.'

'And Adam, how does he fit into all of this?' said Hugh.

'Well, we need to remember we are in the midst of a hornet's nest, Hugh. It seems that Cortes and his friend, Salazar – who like him is an ex-Army officer – were asked - ordered maybe - to accompany Adam and Cristina here. Why, isn't clear but Cortes did tell me that they were working for a Colonel Salas who runs a profitable vineyard just outside Ica and who just happens to be Cristina's grandfather. Seems he has a soft spot for her. Cortes also said that Adam was interviewing anyone who knew anything about the drug business, the Shining Path, the military, you name it, for his article.'

'Did he say where they were?'

'No, he was careful about giving anything away, but he hinted that if Julia agreed to meet him, he'd talk with Salazar and arrange for Adam and Cristina to be dropped off wherever we wanted. I didn't say anything about our plans to stay in Ivochote.'

And would Adam agree to see me?

Pepe drained his cup and looked benevolently towards his wife and cousin. 'I think that's just about it, but I'm a little disappointed that none of you asked about where I spent the night.'

Elizabeth rose and kissed him on the check. 'With Cortes?' she said.

'Indeed. He was insistent he tell me all about his exemplary military record and the various good deeds he's been involved in since he left the army. He promised me he'd call his driver early in the morning and take me back to the hotel. If it means anything, I think he is genuinely remorseful about the crimes he and his men committed but as Julia says, it's nothing to do with justice, it's all about saving his own skin and reputation. Leopards, never change their spots and he's no exception.'

Elizabeth spoke quietly to Julia.

'And if I agree to meet with this Cortes, how do we get in touch with him?'

'He told me we should leave a message with Nicholas the porter and he'd then call me on my mobile to arrange a meeting.'

Julia said nothing. Beyond the dining room it was possible to hear the rushing of the Urubamba. The same river that had consumed the body of her husband.

'If you do agree to meet with Cortes – and there's no reason why you should – then we need to think carefully about your safety, Julia, and whether we involve the police – you can guess what I think about that – but we must consider everything, including the unpleasant possibility that the actual reason he wants to meet with you is to eliminate all those who witnessed what happened to Martin.' Pepe raised a hand. 'Let's go to our respective rooms and pack. After lunch I think we should stick to our original plan and head out to Ivochote, in my car. Freddy can drive and Pedro can take the other to his relatives, which will distract anyone watching us leave. But before that, I'd like to suggest we have a brief chat with our friend Nicholas here, to confirm Julia's suspicions that he was indeed part of the squad but also to rule out the possibility he knows who attached the *quota* note to our door. If he really doesn't know anything about that, we still need to be on our guard. As I said, it's a hornet's nest.'

***

They agreed that only Pepe and Julia would meet with Nicholas. 'We'll be speaking in Spanish, and Julia can brief you later, Hugh.'

Julia can brief you later. Were they beginning to see us as a couple? And Sarah, is she now consigned to the past, was she disappearing too. Does love appear, reappear, and then when it's run its course, disappear for ever?

Hugh went up to his room and packed. For a moment he thought about walking down to the river. Moving his bag off the bed, he lay down and stretched out. Suddenly he felt very tired. A lot had happened in the hours since they'd arrived in this one-horse town. He closed his eyes and listened to the river rushing endlessly beyond the hotel. The phone next to the bed rang. It was Pepe.

'I've spoken with the manager, and he's told me a little about our porter friend Nicholas. Apparently, he's an old timer here in terms of employment. Ten, maybe fifteen years, long before the current manager took up his post. The previous manager did tell him, however, that he was reliable, if a little slow. He'd been in the army and had been discharged for some kind of misdemeanour. Didn't say what kind but did say that he worked to the satisfaction of the manager and the owners, and as far as he was concerned that was that. We've arranged to meet him in half an hour just after he comes on duty. The important question will be if Julia recognises him as a member of the squad, and if we can get him to tell us who was in command.'

Hugh lay back on the bed and sighed. *How simple life was on a summer's day on the marshes with Adam and Sarah and not a care in the world. Walking together along the pipe, one foot carefully placed in front of the other, a skein of brent geese flying overhead...*

He was interrupted by a sharp knock on the door. Pepe walked in and eased his large frame into the chair beside the bed.

'Sorry to disturb you, *senor*, but let me brief you.' He was carrying two opened bottles of *cerveza*. 'Don't tell Elizabeth, but I need a drink, and anyway, it's past midday.'

'How did it go?'

He took a large swig from the bottle.

'Well, Nicholas is not the sharpest mind on the block, but we made some progress. I'll leave Julia to tell you what she made of it, but suffice to say, she's pretty certain he was one of the soldiers who broke into the house. After a little of – shall we say *persuasive interrogation* – he admitted he was part of an army snatch-unit made up of regular army, local police and *sinchies* who operated in Ayacucho at the height of the troubles. Said he didn't recognise Julia but then why would he? What he *did* say, was that the officers came and went and there was one, a Captain Santiago Cortes, who was second in command for about nine months which corresponds with the time of the attack on Julia and Martin's disappearance.' He raised the bottle to his mouth and finished it off in one gulp. 'Julia then asked him about his other duties. It was then he became shifty, saying he was just given his orders which he carried out. I'm afraid he wouldn't budge on information about what happened to those who were disappeared. For that Julia will need to speak with Cortes. She's agreed to meet him by the way.' He got up and made his way to the door. 'Oh, we didn't mention the note on our door, but I did ask him if he saw a stranger enter or leave the hotel after I'd left. Of course, he said 'no' but to be honest, I don't think we can believe a word he says, though what he's told us about Cortes rings true'. He rubbed a big hand against his trousers. 'But I'm still convinced that the same person was responsible for both notes, which means they must have followed us here, probably in the beat-up brown sedan, or in another car we haven't spotted.' He stopped at the door, as if he'd forgotten something. 'Oh, Elizabeth is out buying one or two things for the journey, so Julia is in her room alone and packing if you want to call by.' He rubbed his hands together and chuckled. 'She's someone special, Hugh.' He paused and shook the empty beer bottle. 'But then so are you.' With that he collected the empty bottles and closed the door softly behind him.

***

'Why don't we walk down to the river again? We've got time. And it's easier to talk as we walk.' He agreed. 'I'll send Pepe a text in case he gets worried and starts looking for us.'

For a moment he felt like a recalcitrant schoolboy bunking off from last lesson. When they arrived at the river it was quieter, sombre almost. They found their seat and sat together.

'Well, Julia, how did it go? Pepe gave me a summary but …' He paused for a moment unsure of how to continue '… but maybe you're prefer to let it rest?'

She turned her head towards him.

'You are very kind, senor Hugh. *Muchos gracias*. Well, the disappointing thing is that I don't recognise him as a member of the squad but maybe he was a part of the unit but outside, waiting in the vehicles. Whatever, I'm convinced he played a part in what happened to us and more than likely other, similar operations. When we asked him about what happened to people like Martin after they were taken, he looked shifty. She paused and looked out at the river. 'Hugh, I am convinced he played some role, maybe in his interrogation or worse.'

They sat together and watched the river.

'And Pepe says you've agreed to meet Cortes?'

'Yes, I have. I told Nicholas to tell Major Cortes I will give him details of where we will meet soon.'

'That's very brave of you.'

'Not really. I know Pepe raised the possibility he may want to do harm to me but I do think he is looking for some kind of forgiveness, and as a good Catholic, who am I to refuse, even if he *is* one of the men who took my Martin?' She turned back and looked down at her lap. 'And I need to know what happened to him and where his body lies. I think I can persuade Cortes to tell me that.' She turned towards him. 'And, Hugh, in doing so we may also solve a few more puzzles, where Adam is and why he wishes to remain away from you. We in this country find such a wish a very strange thing.'

'Thank you again, Julia.' He squeezed her hand. 'The least I can do is accompany you to the meeting.'

She laughed. 'We'll see, but Pepe will be thinking we've eloped once again! We must head back.'

When they arrived back at the hotel, Freddy was loading their bags into the boot. 'Pepe is talking with the manager about reservations for two days' time. Even if we don't keep to the meetings, it's good to keep those watching us on their toes.'

Pepe emerged from the hotel smiling. 'We've got most of what we need but the journey shouldn't take more than an hour. Even so, I'd like to start soon as possible, just in case we encounter trouble on the way. The rain may have caused some landslips, so it's important we arrive well before sunset.' He climbed into the front passenger seat and patted Freddy on the back. 'I have spoken with the porter as we agreed. I didn't tell him of our destination, but my feeling is it won't be difficult to find us. Ivochote is even smaller than here, which isn't saying much. Still, it should be an easy journey, about fifty kilometres and who knows, Hugh, you may get your chance to see our Pongo de Mainique, the rapids you *gringos* seem so taken with.'

***

Twenty-Seven

T ranscription of interview: Daniel, a 'mochilero,' or cocaine smuggler.

He doesn't smile much and looks older than his years. His face is quite immobile when he speaks, though his right foot switches constantly during the interview.

My name is Daniel Jesus Hermoso. I am from Ayacucho which is where I attended primary school. I dropped out of secondary for many reasons, the most important being the health of my father and my poor examination grades. My father could no longer work at the mine and so we had nothing. My mother has passed and there is just my father and my younger brother, Herbert.

Yes, the reason I became a mochilero was for my family. My plan is to return to my school one day and complete my education. Then I will go to the university in Ayacucho to study law. My ambition is to be a lawyer and to defend the young boys like me who are apprehended and put in jail.

When I began – which was eighteen months ago – I first was put with a group of twenty mochileros. We each carried fifteen kilos of the cocaine from the VRAEM, down to Ayacucho and then on to Ica where it was taken by lorry to the capital. For this journey we would receive two thousand dollars.

We took the small roads alongside the rivers and through the dense forest. I remember the first time I made this journey. We had four guards each with machine guns, two at the front and two at the back. They never spoke to us, but sometimes when we would stop to rest, they would shout at us to get moving. One of my friends in the group told me they were there to stop other gangs from taking our loads and to prevent us from running away with our packs. I remember the guard at the front. His name was Marco, and he was the guard in charge. Unlike the others he liked to talk. He would give us water when we stopped at midday. One day we stopped and sat, off the track, hidden by the dense forest. We sat around Marco, drinking our water and smoking cigarettes. He had grown up in Ayacucho, was one of us, he knew our families.

The other guards were sitting some way off and sleeping. Marco told us to remain sitting. He said he wanted to tell us something. I remember his voice which was high like a girl. He spoke fast.

'When I was younger than any of you, I joined Sendero Luminoso and went into the field. We did many brave things and I learnt a great deal about comradeship, loyalty and obeying orders. One time, we had to kill one of the women who used to cook for us. It was a terrible thing but, on that day, I learned what it means to be a comrade, to obey orders.'

He also told us about the quota and what it means to make a vow to kill enough, for the cause, to get the job done. He told us that for him the quota is his guiding light...and that he will kill not just the Westerners – and those who stand in the way of the poor – but also those like us, who betray the Revolution. He said that once the Americans with their army came to the VRAEM, he decided to carry the struggle forwards, on behalf of the poor coca farmers, like his father.

We sat and listened to him, and we believed him. Always believe a man with a gun. And he finished by telling us that we were now brothers, comrades, and that if we betrayed each other, we would be added to the quota.

It was then I decided to go by myself. I have my own gun, a Mauser, and am strong if I meet some bad men or maybe the police.

It was very hard work. When I walked with the long line of mochileros, one time one boy fell off the path into the ravine. No one stopped to help him. You are all together, but you are alone. Another time, my feet became swollen and the left one changed colour. I had to continue until Ica. Then I went to a pharmacy.

I feel I am safer going solo. The people who pay you know that we are fit and know which paths to take. We are better than transporting the goods by car or plane. We can avoid the checkpoints and the attacks by other gangs. But sometimes it can go wrong. One of my friends from my first time with the big group, is now in the central prison serving fifteen years. He was captured just outside of Kiteni here. The police and soldiers were hiding at the start of the path. They told him he had been betrayed by the men who employed him. What happens is that a big assignment is planned to be sent by road or air and on that day, the police are tipped-off by the gang leader. We then act as a decoy for the other consignment which arrives safely.

Being a mochilero is good for only a short time but if you want to retire, you become indispensable, sometimes a boss will betray you or inform a rival gang of where you live. For me it is a problem, but I am strong, I have my faith and I will survive.

Now I have left, I do sometimes miss those days, but I have money enough now for my family and schooling. I will complete the secondary and then apply to the university.

Yes, I am fearful of Marco and his boss Ricardo, but I am careful and keep a good look out for him in case he learns of my departure. Two weeks ago, for example, I was visiting my aunt who works in a small shop just off the main square in Ayacucho when I saw him walking out from a restaurant, El Flamenco which is near the main square. I followed him to one of the big hotels. He is old but he is strong.

Salazar says we're not prisoners, just that we can't leave. They've taken Cristina's phone for safekeeping, leaving me with the laptop but without Wi-Fi there's no way we can get a message out.

Arrived the day before yesterday, and from what Cristina says we are somewhere near Cusco in one of her grandfather's properties. She thinks it's all a bit of a misunderstanding, something to do with one of my interviews that has created a problem, maybe put us in a tight spot. When she spoke with Salazar, he said he'd check with her grandfather and then it should all be fine. I'm not so sure. Cortes refuses to talk with either of us, grunting if Cristina asks him anything. And anyway, why are we here miles from the valley and the final interviews Cortes had told me were easy to arrange?

While Cristina was sleeping, I walked back into the sitting room to see Cortes sitting by the door cleaning his revolver. He looked up, and for the first time in days, smiled. Just the kind of smile a snake gives to its prey.

***

Twenty-Eight

T he journey to Ivochote was uneventful. Every ten minutes or so, Pepe would turn around and peer out of the rear window. 'No-one on our tail, which is good,' he said grimly.

They took the road through the town, past the church and then Freddy branched left. Pedro beeped once, and continued on towards his relatives.

'Do you think we're following the same route you took with Cortes's driver?' Julia asked.

'Yes, I think so, which means that in about twenty minutes we should start looking for a track off to the right.'

Fifteen minutes later, Pepe asked Freddy to slow down. On their right was a large advertising hoarding behind which was a narrow road which ran down towards a group of buildings. The track looked overgrown and uncared for.

'Slow, Freddy, I am sure this is it. Listen, can you hear the river about two hundred yards away?' Freddy drove a few yards and parked up on the hard shoulder. He spoke to Pepe. 'It's best I go and take a look as it is unlikely they'll recognise me. Wait here, I'll be ten minutes. If I can I'll take some photos to see if you recognise the place.'

'Good. But Freddy, take great care not to be seen. Even if they don't recognise you, we've no idea if any of Cortes's heavies are still there.' After twenty minutes he returned. 'No-one there, I'm certain. Have a look at the photos, Pepe.'

The lawyer peered at Freddy's phone. 'Yes, I'm sure this is where I was taken. They put the blindfold on only after I had walked out of the front door which gave me a chance to see the immediate surroundings. I remember the low wall just beyond to the left of the door, the orange bougainvillea, and the broken wheelbarrow lying against it.' He patted Freddy on the shoulder. 'Let's drive on. I'll show Alfredo these later. He knows every inhabitation between here and Ivochote and should know about this place.' They drove another twenty minutes and Pepe called Alfredo for precise instructions for getting to his house. 'If you think Kiteni was a one-horse town, wait till you see Ivochote,' said Pepe.

'Blink and you'll miss the main street which is like hundreds of other dirt-poor places. A couple of restaurants, one or two hostels, and some tourist places where you can hire boats and crew to take you through the rapids, and that's Ivochote for you.' They drove slowly up the main street where the road appeared to grind to a halt. Freddy manoeuvred around a line of oil drums where the road gradually narrowed until it became a grassy track. 'To the right is the river but we carry on towards those trees on the left where Alfredo says we'll see another dirt road leading up to his place. Just over a mile he says.'

They bounced along the track until they approached a set of modern metal gates beyond which the track was tarred. Ahead of them were several low-lying buildings, the central one being an impressive hacienda-style house.

'Well, this is a surprise, Pepe. Remind me what your old law school friend does. And more interestingly, why he lives out here?'

Pepe laughed as Freddy drove the car under a canopy to the right of the buildings. 'I'll let Alfredo tell you all, but first let's arrive and meet. If I know my old friend, he'll have a feast and a few beers waiting for us!'

Alfredo Martinez and Pepe could have been brothers. Bearded, with a shock of white hair, he grasped Hugh and Pepe firmly by the hand, kissing Maria and Elizabeth lightly on each cheek.

'I know what you are thinking, Hugh, that we lawyers all look alike!' Pepe laughed as Alfredo directed the visitors into the house. Freddy remained outside to check and clean the car. The house had been designed with an open-plan ranch style in mind. In the centre of the room was a huge wood-burning stove around which were two brown leather sofas and several wooden, Shaker-style chairs. The ceiling was low, but the room was bathed in late afternoon sun that flooded in through the floor-to-ceiling windows at each end of the room. On one of the walls was a watercolour of a young woman wearing traditional dress.

'That beautiful woman, Hugh, lived an exemplary life until she made the fateful decision to marry a young law student....'

'...And it's been downhill ever since!' interrupted Pepe as an elegantly dressed woman came into the room with a tray of tea and a jug of water.

'Talk of the devil,' said Alfredo. 'Our English friend was just admiring your portrait, and I was about to tell him about the long-suffering artist who painted it.'

She put down the tray and came over to each of them, smiling and offering her cheek to each.

'For a judge he can be very economical with the truth', she said.

'It is what I was telling, Hugh, earlier,' said Pepe. 'Listening to crooks and liars for a lifetime eventually rubs off, and before you know it you find yourself lying to your nearest and dearest.'

'And lying to yourself if you're not careful,' said Alfredo.

'But let's get down to business,' said Pepe who stood and addressed the room. 'First, Alfredo, it might help Hugh here, if you could tell him a little of your circumstances, particularly why a retired judge of a Provincial Superior Court is living in this beautiful but isolated house.'

'Indeed, but first, thank you all for coming. It is indeed isolated here and it is rare for me to be able to welcome people into my home. I have Patricia of course, but it is not easy living here. This was once the home of my uncle and I used to spend family holidays here. Our children are now studying in the United States and so there are just the two of us, and I would be dishonest if I didn't admit to missing colleagues and friends.' He paused. 'And come to that everything the city offers.'

He was a short man but of stature. As he talked, he ensured he caught everyone's eye in the room. It was easy to see how he had risen through the ranks.

'When my good friend, Pepe, suggested bringing you here, Hugh – I hope I may call you that – it was for a purpose. He was convinced that your son – and the young woman he is travelling with – were in the vicinity, perhaps in harm's way, and that I would be able to help. As you can imagine, it is in my own interests to know of everything that occurs in this district, from comings and goings to the usual crimes and misdemeanours that are day-to-day occurrences here. For example, when Pepe described the property where he thinks he was held, I had no need to see Freddy's photographs. I know of the place, a part-abandoned property owned by a family of three brothers living in the capital who all agree upon one thing, namely that they will not permit either of them to inherit or buy out the other. And so, it remains empty, available for rent, which is how our friend Santiago Cortes found it. And from what Pepe tells me, his invitation to Pepe to visit the place was entirely consensual.'

Pepe laughed at this. 'Yes, your honour. And the blindfold?'

'Theatrical of course, but in fact, not illegal. He was careful to stay just within the bounds of the law, promising you his driver would return you to your hotel the following morning. Which he did.' Pepe smiled widely and held out his arms as if in surrender, 'But, let me briefly explain my situation, Hugh, as I think it may throw light on yours.'

Before he could start, Freddy arrived looking worried. 'Sorry to disturb but it looks like we've a problem with the car. Distributor cap, I think.'

Alfredo picked up his mobile on the table next to him. 'It may surprise you, but we have a good, if intermittent, signal here. Let me call a good friend and neighbour. If it has four wheels, he will be able to fix it.'

Whilst he made the call, Patricia said something quietly to Elizabeth and Julia. 'While he makes the call, let us prepare some snacks and something more refreshing than tea.' At this, Pepe gave a slow handclap, at the same time offering to help.

Alfredo turned to Freddy. 'He should be here in about half an hour. You deserve something to drink and if you want to freshen up, Hugh, the bathroom is on the first floor.'

Pepe took the opportunity to talk. 'While we wait, why don't you bring Alfredo up to date on what we know so far of Adam's whereabouts. He knows a lot of the background from our previous calls, but it would be good to hear things from your perspective.'

Hugh spoke quietly for ten minutes, aware that he was addressing a leading criminal lawyer and one-time Superior Court judge. 'Thank you, Hugh', said Alfredo. 'There are two things that intrigue me. One, the reasons why your son has remained silent from you – if he had lost his phone, it's not difficult in this country to replace it with another – and second, the business of the *quota* notes. I share Pepe's view that they were written and delivered by the same hand but it seems out of place if it was the work of Salas and his military friends. The *quota*, as you know, was at the heart of the guerrilla mindset and their insane desire to accrue blood. My view – for what it's worth – is that your son, in his desire to talk with whoever he could find, might have inadvertently met with an ex- or current combatant who said something, or rather gave something away, which he now regrets. And, more importantly, wants to make amends by threatening you. What is odd is why he directed the note at you rather than Adam. Perhaps Cortes and Salazar have at least been successful in keeping Adam and Cristina safe. What I am sure of is that someone wants you to stop searching for Adam. Why, is more difficult to deduce, but I'd lay a bet that it has something to do with Colonel Salas and his business partner, Major Santiago Cortes. So, now Julia has returned, let me continue with my story. Oh, and thank you, Hugh, for briefing me on your perspective. It was most illuminating if puzzling. But we can come to that. I said I would elaborate further on my own situation, and why I am living the life of a semi-recluse, enlivened of course by Patricia here. Well, three years ago, as President of the Superior Court of Ayacucho, I began to receive word that my life was at risk. This is not an unusual thing in this country, or come to that, any South American country, especially those facing the challengers of a growing cocaine trade. Though most of my Court's work involved hearing appeals from the lower courts, there were times when we could proceed with our own prosecutions. As Pepe knows, before moving into the judiciary I - like him - practiced as a human rights lawyer, with a particular interest in the rights of those affected by the events of the '80's and '90's.'

Pepe interrupted. 'Hugh, he is being modest. Judge Alfredo, here, was our leading advocate in bringing to trial senior *Sendero* leaders who slipped away at the end of the conflict and more importantly, ex-military personnel, like Salas, Cortes and Salazar, who not only considered themselves absolved of any wrong doing during their military careers but thought nothing of carving out new opportunities in politics, our lucrative mining business, or real estate.' He paused for effect. 'Businesses, by the way, that bring you many friends, apart from judges, like Alfredo here, who can't be bought.'

'Thank you, Pepe. Yes, I do like to see the guilty where they belong – behind bars – but three years ago information came to me that a certain Colonel Salas – our vineyard owning friend in Ica – was chief suspect in the disappearance and subsequent murder of at least twenty-three people abducted by his men from the mid-1980s to about the end of the following decade. Our *Truth and Reconciliation Commission* did a superb job, but since its report, evidence has come to light – not least in the discovery of mass graves around *Los Cabitos* in Ayacucho – that implicate a number of individuals, one of whom is Colonel Salas.' Alfredo's phone rang. It was his mechanic announcing his arrival in five minutes. 'I must be honest and say that I had been considering retirement. The lack of resources, manipulation from the Executive, threats to our staff and the local police force, all were persuading me that it was time to hang up my wig so to speak.' He paused and refilled his cup. 'It seemed to me the judicial system wasn't working, and when it was, it wasn't doing the job for which it was designed. It wasn't unusual for example, for known terrorists or drug traffickers to be released for 'insufficient evidence' by judges with no protection whatsoever but with responsibility for trying those suspected of terrorism. Largely because of corruption or inefficiency in the system, only five percent of those detained for terrorism had been sentenced by 1991. We who were responsible for administering justice were under threat from all sides of the political spectrum: guerrilla movements, drug traffickers, and military-linked paramilitary squads. Notable cases included the murder of the defence attorney for *Sendero's* number two man, Osmán Morote Barrionuevo, by an APRA-linked death squad, the Rodrigo Franco Command; the self-exile of a public attorney after repeated death threats during his investigation of the military's role in the massacre of at least twenty-nine peasants in Cayara, Ayacucho Department, on May 14, 1988; a bloody letter-bomb explosion at the headquarters of the Lima-based Pro-Human Rights Association; and the March 1991 resignation of an attorney general of the military court martial, after he received death threats for denouncing police aid and abetment of the rescue by the Túpac Amaru Revolutionary Movement or MRTA of one of its leaders, María Lucero Cumpa Miranda.

The lack of protection for judges dealing with terrorism cases; many of them normally rode the bus daily to work, totally unprotected, didn't help of course'. He placed his cup on the table. 'Sorry it turned into a lecture but after talking with Patricia here, I decided to bow out, but not before I could bring Colonel Salas to trial. The dossier we had was damning with first-hand evidence from people, such as you Julia, who witnessed the crimes of the men under his command.' He paused for a moment. Outside Freddy was explaining what was wrong with the car. 'The most damning evidence we had concerned the practice of *false positives*. Essentially, it concerns the practice by the military of inflating the numbers of terrorists captured, such as the Shining Path here, or the FARC in Colombia. To do so, innocent young men mostly are killed and passed off by the army as rebels to keep up with the quota.' He paused for a moment. 'Ah, I have just had a thought.'

Pepe looked at Hugh.

'A different quota to the one on the two notes?'

'Yes, different but not dissimilar. *Quota* we need to remember is specifically part of *Sendero's* ideology, but an interesting link, nonetheless. But let me wrap up. Three years ago, I took the decision that we had enough evidence to indict Colonel Salas and several senior officers who served with him in the Fifth Brigade. It was then, that I received information from colleagues in national intelligence, that if I proceeded a price would be put on my head.'

Patricia had said nothing up to this point. 'And he has a fine head which we would like to see remain on the rest of his body.'

Pepe laughed. 'So, what did you do?'

'I submitted the file to the Supreme Court in Lima which oversees the work of the lower Superior Courts and met with two or three of our top justices. Things move very slowly here, and they advised me to retire – and more importantly – to disappear until the Salas case comes to court and then to emerge when those charged were safely behind bars. Even then, they warned that people like Salas have long memories and friends in high places. At first, I assumed that with the file submitted, I no longer posed a threat, but sources close to the prosecution told me that Salas is convinced that I know more than the evidence presented in the file, and importantly that I will be the leading witness for the prosecution.

'And do you know more?' said Elizabeth.

'Yes, I do, a lot more, some of which does not concern Salas but would implicate those business associates close to him. So, I decided that if I really wanted to be safe, I would need a bolt hole, a secure place where I could tend my garden, enjoy the river, but keep alert, which is what I do.' He swept and arm around the room. 'After the death of my uncle the house remained empty, so I set about making sure I could live here with the appropriate level of security. You won't have noticed it, but behind the property is a helicopter landing strip. If need be, one of my friends who runs a successful helicopter taxi service for the rich and famous, assured me that if things heat up, he'll airlift Patricia and I to safety.'

Hugh looked at the grey-haired justice sitting bolt upright next to him, a cup of tea balanced in one hand. 'You said that you thought my situation is in some way linked to yours? And I'm guessing it has to do with Adam meeting Salas on his estate in Ica?'

'Correct. My guess is – and we judges are loathe to acknowledge guesswork – is that Adam discovered something early on during his first few days in Huacachina, maybe at the hostel where he was staying or from meeting Cristina who of course introduced him to Salas, her grandfather. By the way, I think she is likely to be an innocent in all this but as Adam collected more and more information for his article, Salas began to realise that Adam posed no real threat – who would believe a naïve gringo? – but that he might play a useful role in leading him to me.'

Julia had been listening intently to the judge. 'And what about when Hugh joined the search?'

'That increased the threat to Salas. He was happy for Adam to discover all he could in the VRAEM but wouldn't welcome the added attention of a full-scale hunt for him. The last thing Salas wants is publicity but once you arrived in Ayacucho, Hugh – and met Julia here – he saw an advantage. It wouldn't take much to realise Pepe was an old friend of Alfredo and had an office in Kiteni.'

'So, if Adam didn't lead us to Alfredo, we might?'

'Yes, Julia, my feeling is that both you and Hugh were under surveillance from the moment you met in Ayacucho. Maybe, the *quota* note is part of that? It's difficult to say.'

'And the proposed meeting between me and Cortes?'

'Cortes may well be telling the truth in his wish to receive some kind of redemption from you Julia, but I fear his major motivation – along with Salazar – is for you to lead him to me.'

'Which we've done!' said Pepe, in an exasperated tone.

'No, Pepe you haven't – yet. When you asked me if I could help in the search for Hugh's son Adam, I genuinely wanted to help, thinking that if he had ended up here, I might be able to ensure that he came to no harm. But when it became clear that he was accompanied by Salazar and Cortes, I realised that their purpose was to find me. And then to stage an accident, like the one a few years ago at the rapids.'

Pepe stood and refilled his glass. 'I see, Alfredo, what you are saying is that until Adam leads them here or Hugh and Julia lead them here, Adam remains of value?'

'Yes, I'm afraid to say, Hugh, that once I am discovered and eliminated, there will be no more need for them to hang on to Adam or Cristina. They will have become a liability, as I'm afraid will you and Elizabeth, Pepe.' He placed his cup on the tray and poured himself a glass of wine. 'At the moment, this is all conjecture, of course, but with powerful men like Salas anything is possible. Cortes and Salazar know on which side their bread is buttered and will do everything to save their own skins and reputations.'

Pepe nodded. 'What isn't clear to me is Salazar's role in all this. Maybe he's coming along to hold Cortes's hand but I don't think so. From my experience men like these prefer to work alone. I'm worried he may have an agenda of his own. A lone wolf if you like.'

Julia had been quiet for most of the discussion. 'And the two *quota* notes left at the hotel in Ayacucho and Kiteni? What part do they play in all this? Could Salazar have planted them?'

Alfredo scratched his head theatrically. 'As I said, it seems unlikely, he's ex-military and these are clearly wrapped up with Sendero symbolism. No, my guess is that they are some kind of warning, first to Hugh here and then a second reminder in Kiteni. But it doesn't make much sense as the *quota* was more about blood sacrifice on the part of the terrorists than a direct threat to the enemy, unless...'

'Unless...?' said Pepe.

'Unless our note-writing friend has in mind some sort of suicide mission, and I don't need to remind you of Shining Path's success in that particular strategy.'

No-one spoke for a moment.

'So, what do we do, Alfredo?'

'Well first, we enjoy the marvellous dinner that Patricia and I have prepared. Then I suggest we have an early night. I think Freddy should sleep here too and that he calls Pedro and advises he stays put. Then we plan.' Pepe topped up his friend's glass, and then his own. 'Thank you, Pepe. What I should like to propose comes with some risks but no more than we have faced so far. I also have resources at my disposal which will help. But enough! Dinner is served.'

***

After dinner they sat together around the woodburning stove while Alfredo and Pepe regaled their audience with stories of their legal career. As each tried to outdo the other on who was the meanest, ugliest, nastiest *hombre* they had managed to put away, even Elizabeth couldn't resist telling the story of the time the two lawyers tied red balloons onto the roof of the university law building the evening before graduation. 'As misdemeanours go, this escapade pales into insignificance, particularly, when you consider the crimes some of these *hombres* have committed,' she said grimly. Outside the wind picked up and soon the house began to shake as the storm gathered in strength. Alfredo rose from his chair and went outside to secure the shutters.

Patricia turned to Hugh and touched him lightly on the arm. 'I hope, after we have made our plans, Hugh, Alfredo will be able to show you the rapids. Last year he bought a fine craft fitted with a state-of-the-art outboard motor, and he loves showing it off.'

'That depends on the weather and our plans of course, 'said Alfredo as he slammed the front door behind him. Hugh nodded, his eyes beginning to droop. Patricia must have seen him and soon commanded the men to let the poor Englishman get some rest. Alfredo nodded. 'Good thing, Patricia, as we all need clear heads tomorrow. Breakfast at eight.'

His room was on the first floor towards the back of the house. From his window he could see the large garden, half of which was given over to vegetables, the remainder laid to lawn. Beyond was a line of eucalyptus that marked the edge of the property. It was pitch black, the only illumination coming from the lights in the living room below. He could hear the muffled voices of the two lawyers who, despite the advice about an early night, were clearly set on a night cap.

Good men thought Hugh. *Men I can trust.* He wondered what Alfredo had in mind for tomorrow. Whatever, he felt sure it would be for the best. He wandered over to the window and looked out across the garden to the row of trees that marked the edge. Beyond was the river. Despite his earlier tiredness, the coolness of the room had revived him. He pressed his face to the pane and looked towards the trees. As his eyes grew accustomed to the darkness, he began to make out a small path that ran from the kitchen door through the line of eucalyptus and then branched sharply right, probably leading down to the river or perhaps the helicopter landing spot. He switched off the central light and moved back to the window. As a child he had been fearful of the dark, especially on stormy nights such as this, but on this occasion, he found the sight calming. It reminded him of the storms they had experienced once or twice while camping on the marshes, the wind roaring around their tent as they huddled inside. 'Let the elements do their worst, we're all snug inside,' he'd said to Adam. His thoughts returned to his son. *When all this is over, we'll return to the marshes* and *spend a few nights camping like we used to.*

And then he saw her. Walking slowly up the track between the trees was a figure, almost indistinguishable from the surroundings. It then stopped a few feet from the gap in the trees and raised its head in the direction of the house. Quietly he opened the window. All he could see was a pale, oval face, the hair pulled tightly back. It looked like a woman, but he couldn't be sure. After a minute or so standing there, she raised her right hand slowly, her palm facing outwards, as if in a salutation. And then she turned and walked back towards the trees, her dark hair and clothing disappearing into the blackness that surrounded her.

***

By the morning, the storm had burned itself out, leaving the sky clear and bright. Outside, he could hear Freddy stopping and starting the car engine. Patricia was cleaning out the woodburning stove as he walked into the room. The map they had scrutinised the night before lay neatly folded up in the centre of the table.

'Ah, Hugh, I hope you slept well in spite of the storm? But now, if you please, could you open the door for me. I like to put the ashes on the bougainvillea at the front. Alfredo says it makes no difference but he knows nothing,' she laughed, carrying the tray carefully towards the door. 'Breakfast is in the kitchen, where we normally eat. Help yourself to yogurt and fruit. When Pepe is down, I'll make us all some omelettes. Coffee and tea are by the sink.'

He ducked his head beneath the staircase and walked down a narrow corridor to the kitchen. Beyond the door he could make out the garden and the row of trees. He could see the narrow gap where the path headed towards the river. He thought about the woman with the dark hair and pale, oval face. *Who are you? And why do you never come nearer? Sarah, is it you?* He didn't hear Patricia come up behind him.

'Hugh, you look like you've seen a ghost.'

'Last night, Patricia, I thought I had. And it is not the first time...' He poured himself some coffee.

'Yes, Julia mentioned this to me yesterday. I hope it is not disrespectful, but we know of these things here, particularly people like myself who are descendants of the Inca, a noble people who had a particular way of seeing things.' She carried a bowl of fruit to the small table and sat down. He sat opposite her. 'We believe in three realms, you know. The *Hanan Pacha* or upper world, which is what you might understand as the heavens, but for us it is where the gods exist. Then there is *Kay Pacha*, the middle earth if you like, where we humans live, and lastly, *Ukhu Pacha* or the underworld, the realm of the dead, the dominion of *Supay* the Inca god of death.' She stirred the fruit in her bowl and looked across at him. 'But this underworld is not entirely a negative concept, for this world is also associated with the feminine, with mother earth, and with the bones of our ancestors. We can gain a glimpse into this world in the caves and rivers, even the sea with its rushing tides and churning waves.'

He interrupted her. 'And is it possible to move between one realm and the other?' He thought of the Norfolk marshes and the rapid tides reaching almost as far as the small churchyard where he had glimpsed the woman standing by the grave of his wife. Had she ridden up on a night tide, a messenger from a subterranean world? He shook his head. All his intellectual training and gut instincts told him otherwise. Grief, that's what it is, trying to see a loved one now disappeared forever.

'You seem lost in thought, Hugh? I hope my talk of *Ukhu Pasha* hasn't spooked you?'

'Not at all, fascinating stuff. No, I was thinking of Sarah. And of you and Julia, and how similar you look.'

'And let's not forget Elizabeth, she's dark haired too you know.' She laughed. 'I'm sorry, Hugh, here you are, a guest in my house and I'm teasing you.' She stood up and made her way towards the stove. 'Let me make you the closest I can to a *full English*, though it'll have to be without the bacon and black pudding, I'm afraid.'

Alfredo put his head round the door. 'Did I hear the words *full English*?'

'You did, Alfredo and I'm just apologising for our lack of essential ingredients.'

'Well, let's make it a full half-English then,' he said with a roar. 'And if I may make a request, could you, dear Patricia, bring the food into the dining room where I've laid out the map. Then I can show you where we are going to go, and more importantly, what we are going to do.'

Breakfast turned out to be a huge tomato and mushroom omelette with small fried potatoes. Once the plates had been cleared away, Alfredo took charge.

'Before we look at where I propose we go, let me just say that my two prime objectives are the safe return of Hugh's son – and his friend Cristina – and perhaps even more important, to ensure that no harm comes to any of us gathered here.' He cracked his knuckles and looked across at his wife.

'Hear, hear,' said Pepe theatrically. Alfredo raised a hand. He was clearly in his element.

'As I said last night, it is my belief that Colonel Salas has one ambition, to find me, and prevent me from testifying in court. I think he is also quite willing to eliminate anyone else who advertently or inadvertently – Adam for example – poses a threat to his business, and therefore, his survival.'

'What is his business, Alfredo?'

'A good question, Julia. To put it bluntly, drugs and money laundering. One of our old friends – Philippe, from our law class – is now a leading adviser to our national anti-narcotics police, DIRANDRO. They train police in the legal tools and procedures available to counter drug trafficking, particularly routes from the VRAEM, south to Chile and Bolivia, or north to Lima where the drugs are then freighted to Mexico and the US. There are two major players in all this. One is Victor Quispe Palomino, head of the remnants of *Sendero Luminoso* here...'

'...And don't tell me, the other is our friend Colonel Salas?'

'Correct, Pepe. It seems from Philippe's intelligence, that Salas controls a route from VRAEM to Ayacucho, then on to Ica, and from there along the coast to the capital. And remember Ica is close to Huacachina, the first port of call of Adam, the drug route pretty much mirroring the reverse journey Adam and Hugh made from Lima to here.' Alfredo stopped talking and bent his head closer towards the map. 'But remember we're not sure if Adam stopped in Ayacucho. On the one hand it would provide him with an opportunity to interview a number of different players in the game – ex-paramilitary, coca farmers, *mochileros* – but on the other, it would increase the risks.' Pepe looked towards his old friend. 'You look worried, Pepe.'

'Not worried, Alfredo, just a little anxious about what you might be proposing.'

'Don't be, as our safety and security are, as I said, my primary concern. What I propose, however, is that we have to take the initiative. The longer we wait for Cortes to contact us, the more likely it is that my hiding place will be discovered, and then we'll have a small army descend on the place.' Hugh sat looking at Julia who sat with her hands folded in her lap. She looked strong, but at the same time vulnerable. 'So, what I suggest, is that we contact Cortes. Or rather Julia does.'

'But we know he will have disposed of the phone he used to contact you, Pepe?'

'Yes, of that I'm certain. No, we won't contact him directly, but we know Nicholas at the hotel can.'

'And get him to phone, and say what?'

'He won't talk if we do that, Pepe, but what I'm suggesting is we play them at their own game, namely that we persuade Nicholas to give us Cortes's number.'

'And if he refuses?'

'Then, I'm sure Freddy and Pedro can persuade him.' Pepe muttered something in Spanish. 'Pepe has just said something interesting, Hugh, about this being a surprising thing to hear from the mouth of an ex-justice of the Superior Court! I agree, but then sometimes justice needs to bend the rules a little, not so?'

Julia smoothed back her hair. 'And so, is the plan that I call Cortes, Alfredo?'

'Yes. Once we have the number, you will call him and tell him that one of your close relatives has been taken seriously ill, has been transferred to a major hospital in Lima, and that you will be leaving for the capital in the next twenty-four hours.'

'And then what?'

'You will tell him about our choice of venue for the meeting, somewhere not far from here but far enough away to give them no idea of where we are.' Hugh rubbed his eyes. He'd slept well but still felt tired. Alfredo looked at Hugh. 'We are here, Hugh,' he said, pointing at the map. 'And you can see that there are few options for such a meeting. There is a decent hotel here in Ivochote just by the bridge that crosses the river, then there are one or two other places I know of along the Kiteni road, and some hostels and small hotels in the other direction towards Qillabamba.'

'You're thinking of a hotel or guest house?' said Julia.

'It needs to be a public place and therefore be safer in terms of anything they might try to spring. On the other hand, an empty house, a bit like the one you were taken to Pepe, has the advantages of being more under our control.'

'Alfredo, I have a question.'

'Yes, Pepe.'

'Once we've arranged the meeting, what will Salas do?'

'I think he'll realise that we will be on hand or hidden somewhere to protect sweet Julia her. If she was to meet him alone, he'd think nothing of extracting our whereabouts from her.'

Julia looked hurt. 'I'm tougher than you think, Judge!'

He leant towards her and gave her a kiss on the cheek.

'Yes, you are indeed, but Salas is one of those mean *hombres* Pepe and I were talking about last night and he'll use any means to get to me. No, we must always have the upper hand, which is why I suggest we find a suitable place, an empty or unused farmhouse, and entice Cortes to meet with you there.'

'And then what?' said Elizabeth. 'It sounds to me a little like *The Magnificent Seven* or one of those hostage films.'

'Indeed, Elizabeth, but we have no choice. The longer we wait, the greater the likelihood that Salas will discover this place, which will then put Adam and our lives life at risk. No, we must act. And soon.'

Pepe stood slightly and leaned over the map. 'And the local police and military based here, Alfredo? Do we contact them once the meeting is set up, if only for protection should a firefight ensue?'

'In normal circumstances, I'd agree we should work with them. But from what I know of Salas, he has more police on his payroll than those charged with trying to stop his evil trade.'

'The next question concerns the meeting. If Cortes agrees to meet with Julia – with us hidden somewhere nearby – what next? said Pepe.'

'Yes, I've thought about that. Let's see it from Cortes' point of view. He gets to meet with Julia. She gets to learn about Martin. He may not realise that we know he's got Adam and Cristina, so there is an opportunity for you, Julia, to try and discover more about where they are staying. It's got to be nearby, maybe somewhere on the road between here and Kiteni or down towards Quillabamba. Once we know that we can work out what to do next.'

Julia nodded. 'And what risks do I face, Alfredo?'

'I suspect the real reason why Cortes wants to meet with you alone is that he intends to eliminate all those who know of his crimes.' He cracked his knuckles. 'Which is why we will make sure to protect you, Julia. But at the moment, I think Cortes is on some sort of private mission. Finding me is his day job. That gives us an advantage in taking us one step nearer to Adam and Cristina.' Alfredo folded up the map while they waited for Patricia to bring coffee and *empanadas.* 'Marvellous, Patricia, now I know why I married you.'

'Alfredo, you know very well why you married me,' said, Elizabeth laughing

'Now, from the map I have two suggestions for the meeting. First, the hotel I mentioned just up from here by the bridge across the Urubamba. It's the season for tourists going to see the *Pongo de Mainique,* so there will be one or two guests there, which would make it harder for Cortes to do anything.' He then pointed further upriver. 'Here is possible too. He drew his finger slowly up the river until it reached a sharp bend to the right. 'If you cross over the river by the hotel, I just mentioned, and travel along route 120, after about half an hour you reach a small port, Centro Poblado Saniriato. It's popular with the more adventurous tourists. From there a motor canoe can take you up to the rapids in about forty or fifty minutes. There is nothing there except a few huts, shacks selling snacks, and some dwellings used by the boat guides during the season. When I was searching for a place to hide, I found an disused environmental research station set way back off the road. I've been up there a couple of times and it is still habitable. There's talk one of the tourist companies in Cusco rehabilitating it and turning it into some sort of luxury eco-lodge. A good idea and something I might well invest in once all this has blown over.' He put his hand into his waistcoat pocket and withdrew a key. He chuckled, 'which is why I have a spare key to this potential future investment.'.

Patricia put her hand on her husband's arm. 'Which, for the record, your honour, is the first I've ever heard of this.

I suppose you were thinking, Alfredo, of inviting me to its grand opening once we've drained all the funds from our retirement savings?'

Her husband pulled a long face and squeezed her hand. 'I married you for the *empanadas*…and for the hard time you give me.' He laughed. 'But seriously what do we think of the lodge?' Alfredo cast his eyes around the table. They all nodded. 'So, to conclude, ladies and gentlemen, I propose that Pepe goes with Freddy back to the *Amazonas Hotel* in Kiteni to meet with our friendly employee, Nicholas – Pedro can hook up with you – and the rest of us, apart from Patricia who I'd like to stay here, make the journey to Saniriato once we hear from Cortes.' For a moment he looked serious. 'And let us not forget our prime objective: to ensure that no harm comes to any of us.'

***

Thirty

Freddy and Pepe left shortly before lunch. 'When we arrive at the hotel, we should catch Nicholas on his lunch break. Will be a good time to persuade him to give us Cortes's number,' said Pepe grimly. 'Once we have that we can take the initiative and Julia can set up the meeting.' Elizabeth came out to see them off.

'Well, just take care and stop for lunch halfway. I've put some rice and chicken in your bag,' she said as Freddy backed the car out of its parking place. Hugh watched them drive slowly away. He tried to remember what Nicholas looked like but could only recall a wizened old man who shuffled along, his eyes firmly downcast. He didn't envy him meeting Pepe and Pedro.

Alfredo approached carrying a large military-style jerrycan. 'Follow me, Hugh, let me show you something.' He led the Englishman out of the kitchen door and across the garden towards the line of eucalyptus. For a moment Hugh half-expected to be ambushed by the mysterious woman with the oval face. The storm had moved on leaving behind a carpet of small branches and a scattering of large, intensely red flowers shaped in the form of an elongated bell. Alfredo crouched down and collected a handful of the flowers.

'Patricia loves these, Hugh, the shape and the colour, they mean so much to us.'

Hugh bent down and picked up one of the flowers.

'I've not seen them before. They are glorious.'

'Yes, they are our national flower, you know. The *cantuta*, though in Quechua we call them *qantu*. It is a sacred flower much venerated and loved by the Inca. I think it was the vibrant colours that appealed to them, colours you can see today in the bright skirts of the mountain women. Our ancestors promoted the cultivation of the flowers and dedicated them to the god of the sun, which is why we consider it a sacred flower. It provides a link to our past, something even the city dwellers recognise as important.' He put the jerrycan down and gathered another handful. 'Beautiful, aren't they?'

Hugh picked up the jerrycan and followed Alfredo towards the trees. The path then veered sharply to the right for about a hundred yards. He could hear the rushing water of the Urubamba but there was no sign of the river.

Alfredo had stopped beside a small garden that contained roses and *cantutas*. He picked a single red rose and gave it to his companion. 'For Julia, Hugh. I'm sure she will appreciate it.' He chuckled and continued along the path. 'I prefer the *cantuta*, of course, such a noble flower. You know the Incas liked to use the flower for funeral purposes.' He handed Hugh one of the flowers. 'They believed that the dead during their journey to the underworld could use the nectar to quench their thirst. Today householders make garlands from the flowers with which they adorn their doors as a sign of hospitality. I grow them for the same reason, though I assure you my hospitality doesn't extend to Salas and his cronies, who I am sure would be happy to send me off to the land of the dead'. He waited for Hugh to catch up with him. 'On Lake Titicaca young single women wear posies in their hair to signal to the young men that they are ready to be courted. Marvellous, don't you think?'

Hugh nodded but wasn't sure what he was driving at.

'And does that apply to the widow and widower?'

'Of course, we are never too old to find love, not so? If a woman catches your eye, senor, give her a flower. If she is young, may I suggest a small bunch of *cantuta* and if she is more mature, may I suggest a single red rose, a little like the one you are carrying.' He chuckled again. 'But I digress.'

The sound of the river soon drowned out their voices. Alfredo stepped closer and pointed towards a bank of bushes. 'Beyond there is our great Urubamba which flows from here to the sacred valley of the Incas, but it is not the river I wanted to show you.' He pointed to a low hut tucked a little upstream, painted green. Next to it was a narrow slipway. He removed a large key from his waistcoat pocket and with a flourish opened the door. There was just enough room inside for the boat, a sleek eighteen-foot wooden craft, attached to which was a new outboard motor.

'The motor was imported from Germany and delivered here by a trusted colleague. Have only used it once.' He stroked the wooden canopy above the seats.

'Built in the traditional way. What do you think of it? Not quite Oxford and Cambridge but a gem of a craft.' Hugh climbed inside and ran his hands over the polished wooden seats. 'I'm introducing you to my baby because she will be the one who'll transport us back from Saniriato after the meeting. I'll explain later. It's about forty minutes from here. The river is running fast which will be in our favour.'

'And the rapids, the *Pongo de Mainique*, where are they?'

'Beyond Saniriato, another hour or so, but only possible if the river allows. I was thinking that, depending on how the meeting with Cortes goes, we might take you and Julia to the rapids soon.' He patted the hull of the boat. 'None of the women have been to the *Pongo*. Patricia said she had no intention in joining her ancestors in the swirling maelstrom, and Elizabeth added something about being unable to swim.' He laughed and locked the boatshed. 'Women, strange creatures. They participate in birth, the greatest and riskiest adventure of their lives, but when it comes to navigating a few rapids, they cry off!' He spread out his hands. 'But I wanted to show you the boat, Hugh, for another reason. Last night, after we talked, I thought of an additional way we can ensure that we have the upper hand.'

'With the boat?'

'What I propose is that we will drive up by car but return by boat. My boatman, Antonio is completely trustworthy, as are all those who work for me. The river also tends to be quieter in the afternoon. 'Hugh handed him the jerrycan. 'Oh, I'd forgotten about that. Let's put it inside.' He unlocked the shed and tucked it back inside. 'What is important is to have the element of surprise. Cortes will arrive and depart by road, the 102 from Ivochote. He'll expect us to do the same. We Peruvians may love our rivers but it's our cars we love even more. He will never expect us to arrive or leave by boat.' Hugh looked towards the river which seemed close to overflowing its banks. Surely it wasn't safe to navigate the river even in a craft that looked top of the range. 'What I'm saying is, that if the meeting turns nasty and Cortes arrives with reinforcements, we can leave the lodge by road and then divert to the mooring place and escape back here in that little beauty which will be waiting for us. If they want to do Julia harm or believe we are with her, my guess is they'll try and waylay us on the main road back. There are a number of sections where the road narrows, ideal places for an ambush.'

'And when we arrive back here by boat?'

Alfredo pointed beyond the boatshed.

'Do you remember what I was talking about last night, my secret get-away plan? Just beyond that fencing over there is my helicopter landing spot, well-hidden but clearly visible from the air. Let me show you.'

Hugh had assumed the story of helicopters and secret landing strips was a flight of fancy. 'A helicopter, Alfredo? How on earth...?'

'Not my own, of course. But as I said, what matters in this country is your network of friends, many of whom, by the way, will be classmates. One of mine, a dear chap called Emilio-Jesus, runs a helicopter business showing tourists the Nazca Lines. If need be, he can be here in no time at all. And besides, he owes me a favour.'

'What kind of favour?'

He smiled. 'Let's walk back, senor, Patricia will be waiting for us, and Julia needs her rose.' The clouds had departed leaving a clear blue sky. 'Another classmate is the current Minister of Tourism. Emilio-Jesus was facing a great deal of bureaucratic nonsense in registering his firm, so I put in a good word. You know how these things work.' He laughed and rubbed his hands together like Pepe did.' The two men approached the kitchen door and could see Patricia bending over the work surface. 'But I must warn you, Hugh, Saniriato is like many places in our wonderful country, full of sound and fury, especially when the river is in full flow, but ultimately it is another forgotten dirt-poor settlement. Still, I have friends there who I trust and cherish. Which is what matters, not so?'

They entered the kitchen. Patricia looked up from her cooking.

'Ah, you two rogues. I wondered where you'd gone.' She saw the rose in Hugh's hand and smiled. 'She's sitting in the living room, senor!'

***

Julia looked up as he entered and smiled.

'Ah, the wanderer returns.' He handed her the rose. 'Thank you, Hugh. One of my favourite flowers. But you look worried. You think I might refuse your gift.' He sat next to her on the sofa. For a moment he wondered if he was betraying Sarah in some way. 'Actually, if I'm honest, it was Alfredo who picked the rose and suggested I give it to you.'

She looked at him sternly. 'And there's me thinking the handsome Englishman has romantic feelings for me. How wrong I was! But I accept the gift, even if it is from both of you.'

He sat next to her. 'Actually, if it was possible, I'd give you a bunch of roses.' He stopped for a moment unsure of what he was going to say. 'Since we met, you've been a real source of support for me. I also feel I've known you for much longer than I actually have, which I know sounds ridiculous.'

She placed the rose on the table and turned towards him. 'And to think an Englishman wrote *Romeo and Juliet*! But thank you, Hugh.'

He sat awkwardly. '*Romantic old fool* was the expression I think you used before.'

'Yes, and on a more serious note, Hugh, you know, of course, that when Martin was disappeared all those years ago, I made a promise – to him and to myself – that a day wouldn't go past when I didn't think of him or consider giving up my search for him. We made a vow on the day of our wedding, a vow I intend to keep.'

'And if, when you meet with Cortes, and you discover he was killed?'

'I expect to learn this but I will at least have the satisfaction of knowing more about his fate and seeing the place where he took his last breadth. That is important among my people.' She picked up the rose. 'Then, my search will be over.'

And what will you do then, Julia?'

'Oh, return to my home in Ayacucho and who knows, perhaps I'll start growing roses. They are very beautiful.' With that they stood up and walked towards the kitchen, 'Let's see if we can find a vase, a very slim one.'

As they entered Patricia motioned to where an empty vase stood. Alfredo was drinking coffee and seemed lost in thought. Hugh held the rose and raised it to his nose before putting it into the vase. Sarah had enjoyed filling the house with flowers and here he was here doing the same thing. *An act of betrayal, Sarah. I'm sorry.* He paused and said quietly to himself. 'It is just a flower, what matters is that we appreciate its beauty.

***

Thirty-One

Patricia had lit the woodburning stove and was busy preparing dinner.

'Any more news from Antonio or Pepe?' said Alfredo.

'Pepe rang an hour ago to say he's got the number from the porter, and they're now having dinner at a relative of Pedro's.'

'Did they give you any indication of when they'll be back?'

'He thought about ten tonight, assuming there's no problem with the road. Apparently, the storm has caused some damage.'

'And Antonio?' said Alfredo.

'Yes, he's just called and says he's safely home but he's coming over. Said it's a family matter, and he apologises. But says it's urgent he talks with you.'

'I hope it isn't serious?'

'No, he says everyone is well at home but while he was away his wife has received a message from someone who wants to meet with him. An ex-army officer said his name was Major Enrique Salazar.

Hugh took his things up to his room. On the bedside table, Patricia had placed a small bunch of *cantutas* in a delicate crystal vase. He looked out towards the line of trees.

Where are you? Will you reveal yourself to me again?

He checked his phone. Nothing. Tomorrow, he'd call Max to see if he'd heard anything. He thought about his son. *And will you reveal yourself to me?* He removed his shoes and lay down on the bed. He looked up at the ceiling and thought about Julia. It was important for her to learn the fate of Martin. To achieve that made it all worthwhile.

Adam's disappearance paled into insignificance compared to what she had suffered. He showered and changed. Below he could hear Alfredo laughing. The man was irrepressible. He wondered what he was like in court.

'Ah, Hugh. Please try a glass of our extremely sweet white wine. Ok, you can have something drier,' he said cheerily. 'No pisco I'm afraid.' They carried their glasses into the dining room.

'We aren't sure when Antonio will arrive, so let's tuck in and enjoy the meal,' said Alfredo.

Hugh turned to Alfredo who was sitting at the top of the table.

'Why do you think Salazar wants to meet with Antonio?'

'Well, we'll find out soon enough, but I can't think why, unless he has got wind of his work here, and thinks he can lead him to me which seems unlikely. Antonio is loyal and would never betray us. No, my guess is that Salazar, like Cortes, has some unfinished business he wants to deal with which has nothing to do with me.'

'What can you tell me about Antonio, Alfredo?' said Hugh.

'Not a great deal as he has only been working here the past few months. But so far, he's proved dependable, trustworthy and important for me, discreet.'

'If you don't mind me asking, how did you meet?'

'Not at all, Hugh. I've spent a lifetime listening to questions being posed, and questions – some of them - being answered.' He rose from his chair and walked over to the sideboard. 'More wine? I met Antonio through a friend, which is usually the way you get employment in this country. Either that way or through a relative's recommendation. Anyway, he has proved extremely useful. He grew up in these parts and is adept at all things mechanical. He knows the river too.'

'Where does he live?'

Patricia looked up from her phone.

'About five kilometres from here, in a small house just off the Quillibamba road. I visit sometimes to help the children with their homework.'

'You didn't realise that Patricia is a gifted teacher, Hugh?' He laughed and raised his glass in her direction. 'The thing is, that Antonio is scraping a living like most people in these parts. He told me once that his only ambition in life is to raise his family to be hardworking and honest, and to avoid having anything to do with politicians, narcos, and I hate to say it, any members of the legal profession.'

Patricia suggested they return to the living room, and she'd bring in coffee and a dessert. 'I'll give Antonio a call and let him know we've finished dinner, 'she said. As if on cue, they heard a car approaching. Alfredo got up and moved to the window,

'We need to be careful. Ah, it's Antonio's car.' He laughed. 'I'd recognise that rattle anywhere.'

For some reason, Hugh expected a short, reserved man to enter. He couldn't have been more different, tall and lanky, and full of life. He gave each of the women a kiss on each cheek and then shook hands vigorously with each of the men. When he reached Hugh, he stopped and smiled.

'Almost as tall as me! Pleased to meet you, senor. Apologies for my mangled English.' Alfredo went into the kitchen and returned with a beer. 'Just one, Antonio. As a judge I cannot be found encouraging drinking and driving but sit and talk, something I know you like to do.'

'Ok, and if I run into trouble, I'll ask Patricia here to translate.' He poured his beer carefully into his glass. A careful man despite his size, thought Hugh. 'Yesterday, early, I had a call from someone who called himself Salazar. Said he was staying at the hotel in Ivochote – the one by the bridge – and that he wanted to speak with me. Said, it was important. I asked him who he was, and how he got hold of my number. He said it would be better if I could meet him and suggested I came to his hotel. He also insisted I told nobody about the meeting but that he would guarantee my safety.'

'I think that would deter me for certain,' said Julia.

'Yes, I was a little worried but decided to go...'

Alfredo interrupted, '...the hotel by the bridge?'

'Yes, that green monstrosity. I'm not one for such places but it seemed a safe place to meet. I remembered what you said to me, Alfredo, about not trusting strangers who come to this place.'

'Wise man, Antonio, so what happened?'

'Well, turns out his full name is Major Enrique Salazar, and that he was here with some friends looking after a couple of tourists who wanted to see the rapids...' Julia looked at Hugh and smiled. '... He went on to say he had long retired from the military and now mostly did private security work but that way back in 1991 he said he was one of the soldiers of the *Grupo Colina* squad who was involved in the *Barrio Altos* massacre in down-town Lima...'

Alfredo raised a hand. 'In a nutshell, Hugh, *Colina* was a vigilante group set up by President Fujimori to combat what he and his intelligence chief, Montesinos, considered Maoist rebels and sympathisers. On this occasion, the fifteen poor souls enjoying a BBQ were entirely innocent.'

'...he then told me he had come to make amends for what had happened.'

'With you, Antonio, how come?' said Elizabeth.

'Well, the truth is that the youngest of those killed during the attack was an eight-year-old boy, the son of my uncle. My uncle had been visiting Lima on business – he was a teacher but had plans to start a small import-export business – and on the night in question had dropped his son off at the BBQ and told him he would return after a couple of hours. He knew he would be safe as one of his classmates from the Teachers' College said he'd look after the boy. It was the last time he saw him alive.'

Alfredo listened intently at what Antonio was saying. 'A number of the *Colina* group were prosecuted and sentenced to lengthy jail terms. Was Salazar one of those?'

'No, he said Santiago Martin Rivas, the operational head of the Group, and Fujimori and Montesinos are in jail, but that several junior officers and NCOs never stood trial. He was one of those, and as such, the guilt hangs heavy on him.'

'So,' interrupted Alfredo. 'We have this Major Cortes seeking some sort of redemption from Julia here, and Salazar - his partner-in-crime - wanting to make his peace with your family. All very nice, but I wonder why he hadn't thought of coming here before now?'

'Yes, I asked him that, and how he got my number. He said he had visited here twice before but nobody would talk to him. Recently – he didn't say when – he said he'd run into a young British journalist who had discovered more about the background of the massacre which had enabled him to discover where I lived. After that it wasn't difficult to call the house.'

Alfredo raised his hand, as if calling for silence.

'Did he say anything about where he'd met this British journalist or the manner of his peace-making?'

'No, he couldn't be drawn on where he met the British guy. When I asked him about making peace with my family, he said he knew that I had young children of my own and wanted to make a financial contribution to support my eldest through school. Said, if possible, he would like to visit my home, meet my family, and then arrange the bank transfer.'

'What about your uncle? Shouldn't it be him he talks with?'

'Yes, it is, but Salazar knew that he died last year and said that as I had a young family with a son about the same age as the boy who was killed, he felt it would be best if he made the offer to me.'

'What did you say, Alfredo?'

'Well, as you know Alfredo, my family wants nothing to do with these people, and we certainly have no intention of taking any of his blood money. I was also very worried, and so told Salazar I would meet with him in two days, at the hotel, after I have talked with my wife and son.'

'You did the right thing, Antonio. Thank you for what you have done. It can't have been easy. I hadn't realised your family suffered in this way.'

Julia came over to Antonio and rested a hand on his arm.

'It's a long time since I've seen Ana, please tell her I will come and see her soon.'

Antonio nodded and stood up.

'If I may, senor, I need to return home. Would you like me to come here tomorrow, judge?'

'Thank you, but no. We will need you to help with the boat, but I'll give you a call when we know when we will travel.'

After he'd gone, Alfredo spoke.

'Well, ladies and gentlemen, the cat – or rather cats – have certainly been thrown well and truly amongst the pigeons. I don't know about any of you, but I don't believe for a minute Enrique Salazar is on a mission of salvation. More likely, he knows Antonio works for me, and if he's patient, he'll rely upon Antonio to lead him here. This means we must be ultra-vigilant in our comings and goings. It wasn't difficult for him to get hold of Antonio's landline number; and it won't be hard for him to locate this place.' He turned and looked towards Hugh. 'What I do believe, however, is that he did indeed meet with your son. At least that confirms he is alive.'

Almost on cue, Elizabeth's mobile rang. She spoke quickly.

'That was Pepe. Seems there's a landslip just out of Kiteni, so they've turned back to Pedro's. Said they'll find an alternative route tomorrow morning and should be with us at midday at the latest.'

***

The events of the day, plus several glasses of wine, persuaded them all to get an early night. Once again, Hugh found himself standing and looking out of the window towards the line of eucalyptus. There was a new moon which cast a silvery light over the garden.

He opened the window. The coolness of the night air was invigorating. He wondered what it would be like to sleep in a small tent in the garden. When was the last time he had done that? There was an occasion when Adam was ten or eleven when he decided that it wasn't enough to camp by the marshes once a year, he had to pitch his popup in the back garden. On the first time, he didn't last the night, coming in at two in the morning complaining of strange noises he'd heard from the next door. But the following evening, armed with a torch, and an old boxing glove, he had proudly emerged at breakfast telling us about the ghosts he had frightened off and the strange growling sound he had taken to be a large brown bear. For several years, the boxing glove had hung on his bedroom wall, replaced eventually by that poster of the *Friends* stars sitting on a metal plank over New York. He closed the window and began to change into his pyjamas.

During Antonio's visit he had spent most of the time looking at Julia. She had listened to him intently, her hands folded neatly in her lap. It was how she often sat. Quiet and at rest, but determined. And Martin, what was he like, equally strong? His strength, of course, had eventually cost him his life. He wondered how Julia would react if Cortes lived up to his promise and told her what had happened and where her husband had been killed. During the first visit to her house, he remembered a small black and white photograph of Martin and Julia, perhaps taken on their honeymoon. He remembered how earnest he looked and the expression of love he showed for his young wife. Since his disappearance she had drawn upon that determination and tenacity to search for him. Like the mothers and grandmothers of the disappeared at the museum, quiet, resolute, women, unwilling to take no for an answer, determined to seek justice for their loved ones.

He thought of Sarah, as he often did, at the end of the day before crawling into bed alone. In the first few days he had found it impossible to get into bed, let alone fall asleep. He had developed a way of coping, sitting sometimes in the easy chair in their bedroom with a cup of ginger tea, thinking about her, trying to remember the way she spoke, the phrases she liked to use, the way she smiled. As each day passed, he found it harder to recollect these things, and berated himself at forgetting so quickly.

If I'd loved her more, I would remember more he would say as he woke from wherever he'd been sitting, angry at himself for letting the side down. He wondered how it had been for Julia. It must have been much worse, the violence of his abduction, the abuse she had suffered, and the not knowingness of his disappearance. Awful, unforgivable. For a moment he wondered if she was still up, perhaps making tea or chatting with Patricia. He opened his wallet next to his bed and took out a small photograph taken on their Scottish honeymoon. They'd decided to take just a handful of photos, enough to fill a small album. On their final day, they'd met a couple of walkers who'd kindly taken the photograph of them both in front of Dalmally station. It turned out to be the only one of them taken together. On their return from the honeymoon, he'd had it framed and it had stood on their bedroom chest of drawers, rarely looked at but reassuringly there. Now he carried it with him. His thoughts returned to the honeymoon.

They had taken the train from Dalmally to Glasgow and changed to another that would bring them into King's Cross late in the evening. They had played silly parlour games all the way to London. One, *Adam and Eve and Pinch Me went down to the river to bathe* had sparked a discussion about the large number of children they would have.

'The first boy will be named Adam and if it's a girl, Eve,' Sarah had said.

As it turned out they had just had Adam, and despite their efforts to have more, gradually accepted the fact that he would grow up a singleton.

'Singleton's, a funny word,' he remembered Sarah telling him one day. They'd just returned from seeing a fertility specialist who had told them of his low sperm count - they'd been lucky to have conceived Adam. She had put her arms around him later in the evening. 'Be thankful, Hugh, that we have him. There are so many couples I know who are desperate to have even one.'

He'd nodded, saying something about all the more reason to take special care of him.

He pulled back the covers and climbed into bed. He'd left the curtains open, allowing the room to be flooded with moonlight. 'Perhaps that was it, his *special care* turning into a constricting blanket of concern? At least Adam was alive, which was more than most fathers of the disappeared could ever hope for.

Oh, stop beating yourself up, she would have said. *You just loved him a great deal, which is more than can be said for a lot of fathers.*

He lay for a moment looking up at the moonlight reflected on the ceiling. Tomorrow they'd hear what Pepe had to say and then make plans for the meeting with Cortes. And Antonio's meeting with Salazar. Who knows, what these might bring, maybe him a little closer to his son? Sleep eluded him. He pulled back the covers and walked over to the window. Perhaps if he opened the curtains and slept in the moonlight, he might find some sort of rest. He looked out towards the river. It was then that he heard her voice, low and guttural, coming up from the garden below. He looked down expecting to see the pale face framed by the dark hair. But there was nothing. What had she said? He shook his head, trying to remember the few words he understood. Of one thing he was certain, when she returned, he would be prepared to ask her the one question he sought an answer to.

***

 P epe and Pedro arrived shortly after breakfast. 'No problem with the road. The landslip was cleared by the time we arrived. Nice to know a few things are improving in this neck of the woods,' said Pepe. Patricia made a new pot of coffee while they waited for Alfredo who was in the garden inspecting his roses. He soon arrived with a single red rose which he handed to Patricia. There was no sign of Julia.

'We can't be outdone in the romantic stakes by our Englishman here,' he said with a laugh.

'Ah, Pepe my dear friend. Good to see you. No problems on the way, clearly. And Pedro. Welcome.' He glanced around the room. 'Before you tell us your news, let me bring you up to date on what has happened here while you were away.'

'Now Pepe, it's your turn. Tell us your news, in particular your meeting with our good friend, Nicholas.'

Pepe rubbed his hands and described their arrival at the *Amazonas* and meeting with the porter. 'Freddy can be persuasive, but it was not necessary. He seemed more than happy to give us Cortes's number, scared I think, that we might haul him off to the police.'

Alfredo smiled. 'And you checked it was the correct number?'

'Yes, we asked him to call Cortes and tell him something inconsequential. His phone was on speaker, and it was clearly Cortes.'

'Excellent, so now we are able to surprise Major Santiago Cortes with a call of our own.'

'Won't Nicholas call him back and warn him off?'

'Oh, I'm sure he will. In fact, I hope he does, as it will ensure he takes the change of plan seriously. But let's pause for a moment and consider *our* plan. My suggestion is that Julia, if she is still in agreement, makes the call and explains her sudden dash to her ailing aunt etcetera. Assuming he agrees to meet with her soon, she can then discuss the proposed venue, and that she will attend the meeting with just Elizabeth here – likewise assuming she is willing – and Freddy who will be waiting in the car outside.'

'And if he rejects the venue?'

'He might, fearing some sort of trap, but my guess is that he will be willing to take the risk if he really does want to meet Julia, and get what he wants.'

'And remember, Alfredo, there are things I want out of this too,' said Julia entering with a jug of water and six glasses.

'I haven't forgotten, Julia, but of paramount importance is the safety of us all. And to ensure that this isn't part of some elaborate plot to uncover my whereabouts.'

'And let's not forget, Adam and Cristina in all this.'

'It's on Julia's agenda, Hugh.'

She turned to look in his direction. 'Your son is never far from my thoughts, Hugh.'

'So, let's make the call, Julia.'

'Before she calls, Alfredo, is there any way he could track this call?'

'Yes, if he wanted to, he could use a global positioning system, but I think that's unlikely, as there's no reason for him to think Julia has any contact with me or is calling from here. Thanks for reminding us to be vigilant, Pepe.'

Hugh went into the kitchen while she made the call. Patricia was preparing a simple lunch of chicken and rice. He helped carry the food into the dining room. When he returned to the living room, Julia was deep in conversation with Alfredo.

'I've made the call, Hugh. Sit here and let me tell what he said.' Alfredo walked over to his desk and started searching through a huge pile of papers. 'Like Alfredo said, he didn't seem surprised to get my call. I told him my aunt was ill and that she'd been transferred to a hospital in Lima and that I was going the day after tomorrow so if we were to meet it would have to be tomorrow.'

'He was all sweetness and light, agreeing that it was important I visit my aunt, and that he was happy to meet with me.'

'Did he suggest a venue?'

'No, but he did say he'd prefer somewhere quiet and private, and added that he was happy for Freddy to drive me to wherever it was but that he would have to remain outside in the car.'

'Did you tell him about the lodge?'

'No, I said that two hours before the meeting – which will be sometime after mid-day – I'd call him and give him instructions of where to go. That way, he'll have little time to round up the troops.'

'Beautiful *and* clever,' said Hugh.

'You are being foolish again, senor, watch your step,' she said laughing.

Alfredo looked up from his desk. 'He's just stating a fact, Julia!' They joined the others in the dining room. Alfredo piled his plate with rice and chicken. 'So, tomorrow it is. I'll speak with Antonio later about taking the boat up early tomorrow morning, then we'll all drive to the lodge. Pedro can stay here with the other car, in case...'

'In case of what, Alfredo?'

'In case things turn – shall we say —unexpected, then he'll then be able to drive and meet us. OK, Pedro? But let's eat. And then rest for the remainder of the day. I have some paperwork to attend to, but please treat this house as your own.'

Hugh decided he'd spend the remainder of the day alone, perhaps take a walk along the river. Julia seemed to sense his mood and left him to his own devices. Early in his marriage – before Adam had arrived – he had wanted to spend every waking moment with Sarah, not necessarily talking, just enjoying looking at her, the way she smiled, hummed while she was cooking, laughed at something he'd said. Then the demands of work - and if he was honest – a growing sense that he seemed to need her to validate his moods, his happiness. Staying later at the office, agreeing readily to an overseas conference, the occasional trip to the pub by himself; behaviour that seemed to raise no anxiety in his wife. In fact, she appeared happy he had found some sort of equilibrium in their marriage.

He sat on the bench and looked at the swirling river. He seemed to spend so much of his life looking out or at things rather than getting involved. But the movement of the river brought a moment of peace, tranquillity even. Then the sun began to slide down over the eucalyptus, bringing a chill to the air. He remained sitting.

Adam, be safe, be safe...

***

Thirty-Three

H e slept well. As he went down the stairs, he could hear Alfredo and Antonio in the kitchen, deep in conversation.

'Ah, Hugh. Good morning. I was just telling Antonio here that with the river nice and calm, he should have no trouble taking the boat downstream. We were also talking about Salazar's request to meet with him and Ana. But, let me not speak for him. Antonio, please share your thoughts with us.'

'Thank you, judge. I spoke to my wife last night, and at first, she agreed with me, that she wanted nothing to do with a snake like Salazar, but we have now come to a different conclusion. We are willing to meet with him in two- or three-days at the hotel by the bridge. If he is honest – and only wants to talk of the *Barrio Altos* killings and the money he wishes to give us – then we will hear him out, but won't take a cent from him. We also think arranging to meet with him soon will reduce the risk of things going wrong today. And for the safety of your son, *senor* Hugh, I have asked Ana to call him to arrange the meeting.'

'Thank you.'

Alfredo patted him on the shoulder. 'We'll talk later today about the meeting between you and Salazar, Antonio.'

'Breakfast, Hugh? We've had ours but there's coffee and pancakes in the dining room,' said Patricia.

Pancakes was one of Sarah's favourites. Loaded with honey and cinnamon she loved making them at the campsite. Adam, like his mother, had a love of sweet things. As for him, he'd always been a savoury man. Julia found him pouring coffee.

'Hugh, I was getting worried. For a moment I thought I'd have to come and wake you up.' She sat next to him and helped herself to a pancake. 'Remember what I told you about us Peruvians and our sweet tooth?'

He poured her a glass of orange juice. 'Remind me to sleep in again if that's your threat! But seriously, when will you call Cortes?'

'We are leaving after Antonio has set off in the boat, which will be soon. Once we've arrived at the lodge, which should be around mid-day, I'll call him. You'll all have plenty of time to make yourself comfortable in the back room. Then it's just a matter of waiting for Cortes to get to the lodge.' She had dressed in a pair of jeans and a simple white shirt. 'Good things to wear if I have to make a run for it, and ideal for the boat trip home,' she said with a laugh. She touched his arm. 'Patricia tells me she's going to ask you to join her for a walk along the river, the other way, beyond the boathouse and the landing strip in the direction of Antonia and Ana's place. Sounds like a good idea. Will take your mind off worrying about us.'

'Worrying about you?' he said quietly. 'And Elizabeth, Alfredo, and Freddy of course,' he added quickly.

'Of course, my foolish English friend,' she said, topping up his cup. 'Remember Patricia will keep in touch with us by phone, just in case Pedro needs to bring reinforcements, though I don't think it'll come to that.' She looked at him sternly. 'I know what you are thinking, Hugh, and that won't happen. I'm convinced that Santiago Cortes means what he says when he told me his motivation for meeting was to receive absolution for his sins.' She laughed. 'Well, that's what my parish priest would say.'

***

It was mid-morning when they gathered in the living room. Alfredo took the chair at the head of the table. His earlier jocularity had gone.

'I've spoken with Antonio and he's agreed to take the boat. He'll leave soon to ensure he arrives well before us. We will all go by road in the four-by-four. We should all squeeze in. The river is still high and fast, and it wouldn't be safe to overload the boat, but he knows the river like the back of his hand and will meet us at the jetty.'

Patricia came to see them off. 'Patricia, you know the drill. Any suspicious activity, call me immediately.' She nodded.

'And Alfredo, I'll lock up everything if I go into town. I have some shopping to do for tonight, but I should only be away for an hour at most.'

The four-by-four turned out to be an old long-wheel base Land Rover that had seen better days.

'You are right, Hugh. Antonio keeps telling me we should get something smarter, but I tell him, this old warhorse is ideal, inconspicuous, and unremarkable, just what we need.' They climbed in. Alfredo insisted Hugh took the front passenger seat.

'Riding shotgun, Hugh, just without the gun.' He laughed, drumming his hands on the wheel. His sense of humour seemed to have returned. They drove slowly up what passed for the main street of Ivochote before crossing the bridge that spanned the swirling Urubamba.

'See the large, green monstrosity there, Hugh, that's the hotel I mentioned. Great for a beer on a Friday afternoon, but I haven't heard anything good about the rooms.'

They then took the tarred road north. Soon the surface gave way to a mix of tarmac, sand and potholes. 'Is it safe, Alfredo, to leave the house and go to the hotel?'

'As you've probably guessed, Hugh, I'm not one to take risks, but Antonio always accompanies me, and so far, the pleasure of a cold beer and the chance to catch up with local gossip, outweighs the chances of running into one of

Salas's goons.' Soon the road became almost impassable with small gullies filled with water flowing in from the river.

'Your country gave us three great things, Hugh. William Shakespeare, the English language, and the noble Land Rover.'

'And let's not forget Tony Hancock or the other type of goons, Alfredo,' said Elizabeth.

'As a judge, I reserve judgment on those blessings, Elizabeth, but I do know Pepe's affection for your sense of humour, Hugh. Something, I confess, I have never quite appreciated.'

Just before Saniriato the road improved. 'They always do this, tar the road a few metres in and out of the place. Makes it look like the *Municipalidad* have done their bit. They parked close to the river. A small line of wooden canoes was hauled up out of the water. 'This is where Antonio will moor the boat. I've told him to wait here with it until we come back. As I said, some very fine people live here, but I would hate to see my new outboard motor carried off in the back of some pick up.'

Julia and Elizabeth suggested they stop for a few minutes to stretch their legs. The Urubamba had lost a little of its intensity but still rushed past carrying with it huge branches, and great clumps of rotting vegetation. Hugh looked downriver where it appeared to narrow,

'You need to go quite a long way further, Hugh, before it narrows into the gorge, and drops down into the rapids. Quite something I can tell you.'

'Have you ridden the *Pongo*, Alfredo?'

'Only once, ten or so years ago when Patricia and I were up here on holiday from Ayacucho. A good friend who has since passed kept an excellent boat moored not far from here. It was him who gave me the idea of getting my own.'

'And the rapids? Are they as fearsome as they say?'

'In those days, yes. But since then, boats have become stronger and with a good outboard, it isn't difficult, though you must always show the river the greatest respect. They say it is level one, if that means anything to you. There are still accidents, as I said, and some are more accidental than others.'

They soon arrived at the jetty where Antonio was waiting. Alfredo lent out of the window and exchanged a few words. The track leading up to the old eco-lodge was marked by a line of red-painted stones. They made their way through a small grove of trees before the path began to climb steeply up, thick forest obscuring any views on each side. At the top the track levelled off into a small clearing. There seemed to be nothing there.

'Look over to your left, Hugh. There in the shade is the building. When I first came last year, the entrance was completely overgrown but we've had a few men start clearing away some of the growth. Our plan is to improve the track up here too.'

He parked the Land Rover close to the building. 'While I show you around, Hugh, I suggest you make your call to Cortes, Julia. And call outside to ensure he doesn't overhear any of us. Try and get some idea, too, of when he might arrive.'

It had clearly been intended for hardy ecologists and the like, who gave little thought to creature comforts, yet inside it was perfectly habitable. A small inner hallway led off into two rooms at the front, a small kitchen and three small bedrooms at the rear. One of the bedrooms had bunk beds and the other had been turned into a storeroom. Alfredo took them back into one of the front rooms, which contained a large table, half a dozen wooden chairs, and what appeared to be various pieces of teaching equipment.

'Our plan is to extend out to the back and build a two-story accommodation block with a viewing platform on the roof. From up there you can see the river and if you're lucky spectacled bears, macaws the occasional jaguar or puma.'

Julia returned to the front room.

'He'll be here sometime in the afternoon. He said he's been to Saniriato once before and knows the jetty.' She sat at one of the two chairs Alfredo had arranged around the table.

'So, Alfredo, tell me what I am to do, and more importantly where you will be when Cortes arrives.' The judge pointed through the window. 'You will sit where you are with Cortes on the other chair. That'll keep both of you in sight of Freddy in the car outside and near enough for us to hear everything that's going on from the back room. It's important, too, that Freddy watches him arrive – and more importantly – watches him leave. That's the plan!'

'And if it doesn't go to plan?', said Hugh.

'You mean, if Cortes brings Salazar and a few heavies with him, thinking this is a good opportunity either to take Julia hostage in return for me, or if they think I'll be here – which of course, I will be – he might use the opportunity to get rid of all of us?' Before anyone could respond, Alfredo raised a hand. 'Fear not, my plucky band of brothers, it is how we manage the meeting, particularly when it's clear he's got what he wants, and he's told you all he knows about Martin that will decide the success of our plan.' He paused and marched over to the window. 'Then we need him to depart first, after which we can then leave and take the boat back to the house. He won't expect us to leave by boat, which rules out the risk of a hijack on the road back or simply being followed home. Once Freddy has dropped us off at the jetty, he can take a roundabout way back. He's a master at losing a tail.'

'And what about you, Alfredo? After all it's you they're after.' The judge smiled.

'If I worried about all the mean hombres who'd like to see me dead, then I should never have taken the oath of office all those years ago.'

Hugh looked at his watch. It was more than an hour since Julia had made the call, but they had no idea where Cortes was coming from. They made their way into the room at the back, Pepe and Alfredo on one side, Elizabeth next to Hugh on the other. The door into the front room was left slightly ajar, enough to allow Hugh to see a little of Julia but not of the major who would sit facing her.

Hugh listened for the sound of a vehicle. In the distance he thought he could hear the sound of the river and nearer what sounded like a flight of macaws, their shrill call fading as they made their way upriver. Then he heard the familiar sound of a vehicle coming closer. Alfredo put a finger to his lips. Hugh closed one eye and looked into the room. Julia was sitting bolt upright, both her hands laid flat on the table in front of her. He heard the front door open and caught a glimpse of a large man in a dark suit and white shirt.

With a quick movement Cortes pulled his chair around the table, so he was sitting at a forty-five-degree angle to Julia. Hugh watched as he lent his head closer to hers, almost as if he found it difficult hear. When he spoke, it was a low voice, more like a growl, slow and deliberate. Not understanding what they were saying, Hugh focused on the sound of their voices. She sounded forceful, indignant even; he equally so but his voice deliberate and measured, used to brooking no dissent.

Hugh watched Cortes. Suddenly, with a swift movement of his right hand, he reached into the inside pocket of his jacket and took out a short, stubby service revolver. Julia raised her hands to her face and gave a sharp cry, moving her head further back, away from the line of fire. Before Hugh could move, Alfredo laid a heavy hand on his arm and raised a finger to his lips. Cortes then let out a loud guffaw, put the gun back into his pocket. He then rose stiffly and bowed at Julia.

'Just to demonstrate, my dear, that if I had intended you harm, I could have done so. But thank you. And *adios*.' Julia continued sitting, her hands resting on the table, her gaze fixed upon the front door.

They waited until Freddy gave the all-clear and then crowded into the front room. Elizabeth pulled Julia to her and gave her a long hug. She turned to Hugh. 'If you all agree, I will tell Hugh here what happened in his own tongue.'

'But the gun first, Julia, what was all that about? Frightened the life out of me, and if Alfredo hadn't held me back, I'd have charged in...' Alfredo raised his hands in mock surrender.

She laughed. '...And rescued me like, what's his name, your St. George and the dragon?'

'But you ask about the gun. As he said, he could have shot me there and then and no-one would know...'

'Julia!'

'Yes, I think his purpose in coming was to honour his word, to receive absolution in return for revealing where Martin was killed.'

'And he told you?'

'Yes, he said he was a member of the squad that took Martin but that he remained outside during their attack on me. It was only later, back at the barracks, that he discovered what had happened ...'

They were interrupted by Freddy who told them it was time to leave for the jetty.

'Sorry to interrupt, senora, but I think I can hear a car's engine on the road. Perhaps Cortes is returning...'

'Let me finish my story in the car, Hugh.' There was no sign of Cortes as they made their way to the jetty. Hugh and

Julia squeezed onto the front passenger seat. 'And when he discovered what had happened to you, Julia, what then? said Hugh.

'He said he felt great shame, and that it was at that time he made the decision to find me one day and ask for my forgiveness.'

'But it didn't stop him killing Martin?'

'Yes, Martin was taken to *Los Cabitos* where he was kept for three or four days in a place called the *casa roja* or *red house*. Then Cortes was commanded to take a lorry of two or three prisoners to the special place near the river.' She paused. 'All the prisoners were shot, and their bodies tipped into the Urubamba.'

'I'm so sorry, Julia, 'said Hugh.

'He also told me that the driver of the lorry was Nicholas the porter at the hotel, and like all of them saying they were just following orders.'

'From whom, I wonder?' said Alfredo.

''Cortes said that what happened to Martin has lain heavy on his conscience, and he thanked me again for agreeing to meet with him.' She paused for a moment before continuing, 'When they arrived at the river, Martin must have realised what was going to happen and asked Cortes to do one last favour for him.' Julia raised a hand and tucked an errant strand of hair behind her ear. 'Martin told him to pass on a message from him that he loved me and would always be looking over me. It seems this request prompted him to find me and seek out a meeting'.

'A bit late in the day,' said Alfredo, adding 'he asked for your forgiveness, are you willing to grant him that?'

'But let me continue. I'll try and be quick, but I can continue as we travel home. After a few pleasantries Cortes got straight to the point. He was seeking forgiveness. I was equally sharp. I told him that forgiveness can only come after justice has been served.'

'And what did he say?' said Hugh.

'He said nothing at first but then said that if I wished he would show me where Martin and the others were killed. But on one condition.'

'Which was that you wouldn't take things further?'

'Yes, those were his exact words.'

'In other words, you would lose the opportunity to seek justice?'

'Yes, but what he forgets is that, on this occasion, I have no intention of keeping my word. Once he has shown me where Martin was killed, I will take every step to prosecute him and all those involved. And even if he reneges on his promise, he has told me enough for me to find the place myself.'

Alfredo clapped his hands.

'Bravo, Julia! If only our judiciary was composed of more people like you.'

'I prefer being a humble schoolteacher, thank you, judge. But I will bear that in mind when you fully retire.'

Hugh looked at Julia sitting quietly beside him, her hands folded neatly in her lap. An extraordinary woman.

'Did you ask him about Adam, Julia?'

'Of course. I asked if he had seen an Englishman and his Peruvian girlfriend, and he said he had some days ago, but now they had moved on.'

'Did he say where?'

'He thought towards Cusco, but I'm sure he was lying, through his teeth, I am sure.'

'I agree,' said Alfredo.

'And you'll meet him at the killing site, Julia?'

'Yes, I will. I said once I was ready, I would call him. Only then.'

She leant forward and spoke directly to Alfredo.

'I realise this increases the risk of Cortes and Salazar tracking you down, judge, but I have no choice. I actually believe Cortes when he says he is seeking some kind of forgiveness, but I still believe he and Salazar are here to find you, before you have a chance to testify against Salas.'

The car drew up alongside the jetty. Antonio hustled them quickly into the boat. The river was flowing fast. Freddy turned the car ready for the drive back to the house.

'Keep a firm look out for Cortes, though something tells me there'll be no ambush. See you at the house!' The journey home was uneventful. Julia sat next to Hugh at the front of the boat. The river seemed to be guiding them home.

Home, Sarah, is that where it is now? A place in which I feel I belong.

While Alfredo and Pepe stowed the boat safely into its house, Elizabeth and Julia walked ahead of Hugh towards the kitchen door. Patricia came out to welcome them, a broad smile on her face.

'Welcome home, travellers. I want to hear all about it from Julia and then we'll celebrate your safe arrival with my best *lomo saltado* and a bottle of the judge's best red.'

While everyone changed into fresh clothes, Freddy arrived with the car. At the end of the meal, Alfredo rose and lifted his glass in the direction of Julia.

'To our brave princess!'

Antonio then stood and joined Freddy who was sitting by the window. 'And my meeting with Salazar, the day after tomorrow. Should we go ahead?'

Alfredo put down his empty glass and rubbed his hands together.

'Yes, let's turn our attention to our other major and how we will deal with him. My view is that we go ahead, and you meet with him as planned in the bar of the hotel. You can take the car but I'd advise that Freddy or Pedro goes with you.'

Both men nodded. Alfredo pointed towards Freddy.

'Given the speed at which Freddy here demolished his plate of *lomo*, I'd suggest he accompanies you. If it comes to it, I'm sure he can pack a punch.' He refilled his glass. But please excuse me, I've some work to do outside.'

Elizabeth and Patricia cleared away the things. Freddy and Antonio followed Alfredo out into the back garden leaving Hugh alone with Julia. She came and sat by him.

'He's right, Julia, you are brave and resourceful.'

She thought for a moment.

'Oh, I'm not so sure. It's just that my search for Martin has gone on for so long, I'm just happy to see an end to all this.'

'And getting justice means an end for you?'

'Yes, it does. Not just for me but for Jorge and all those formidable women at the memory museum.'

'So, after Cortes shows you the place by the river, you'll turn him in?'

'Yes, but only after I can be assured it won't put any of us in danger, particularly Adam of course, and Alfredo.' She stood up and moved towards the kitchen. 'Cortes thinks he holds all the cards, and he does for now, but he forgets one thing...' She turned and smiled at the Englishman, '...he underestimates the strength and resolve of humble women like me. But it has been a good day.' She kissed him lightly on the cheek and left him sitting alone.

***

Thirty-Four

Hugh woke early. He changed into a clean pair of jeans and a fresh shirt. His phone was fully charged. Max picked up immediately.

'Hi Max, it's Hugh. You're up early?'

'Yes, big editorial meeting at lunchtime and, well I won't bore you, but any news of Adam?' There was a long pause. He quickly told him most of what he knew, leaving out Adam meeting with Cortes. In the background he could hear the editor talking to a young woman. 'Just checking, Hugh, he hasn't left me a message, but no, nothing.' He paused. '…and I should tell you, Hugh, that we— the paper – are concerned. To be brutal, we haven't the resources, financial or otherwise, to get involved in any hostage situation. And besides, he is a well-respected, hardworking journalist. Much liked here, I should add.'

'What do you propose?'

'Well, part of me thinks we should at least contact the Embassy, the other that we give him until the end of the week. If there's no news, let's talk again and take it from there.'

They agreed Max would call him at the end of the week. Clearly Max knew more than he was letting on. *Any hostage situation*? Not like a cynical editor to be quite so dramatic.

Julia was wearing a bright red and black sweater. She crossed her arms over her chest. 'Alpaca and ideal for this changeable weather.' She made to climb the stairs, and then paused. 'If you'd like a change of scene, how about we walk down to the river and on to Antonio and Ana's? You can show me the roses? But if you'd prefer to read…'

'Hold on a sec and I'll go fetch a warmer jumper.'

They walked out through the kitchen door and towards the line of eucalyptus. Once through the trees they turned towards the boathouse.

'From the boathouse we can walk along the riverbank away from the house, and then it's not far to their place,' she said.

Hugh agreed, remembering a walk he and Sarah liked to take along the Thames towpath.

'You get on so well with Elizabeth and Patricia, Julia. Have you known them long?'

They arrived at the river and began walking along the river leaving the boathouse behind them.

'Patricia not so much. He married late you know which is one reason they never had a family.'

'And the other reasons?'

'Well, work. As he rose up the ranks to become Chief Justice of the Superior Court in Ayacucho, many said was destined for great things, maybe to sit on the Supreme Court or even enter politics…'

'…But he decided against it?'

'Alfredo is an unusual man, particularly for this country, in that he is motivated by more than personal or financial advancement.'

'For him it's all about justice?'

'Yes, which makes him unusual, even among fellow judges, many of whom are mired in corruption.'

They were out of sight of the house. He took her right hand in his. For a moment they walked on together in silence.

'And Elizabeth? You seem as thick as thieves?'

She laughed. 'Yes, she is family, so in this country that means a great deal.' She let go of his hand and stopped. 'Hugh, you are very kind, but you must know that what preoccupies me from the moment I wake until when I lie down and close my eyes, is Martin. Where he is and what happened to him.'

For a moment he was silent. The river to their right turned sharply right, away from the path.

'My apologies...'

'No, please, there is no reason to apologise. I like being with you. You are calm, which is unusual in men here.'

He looked ahead. The path seemed to move further away from the river towards a thickly forested hill. Beyond the landing strip, the path ran along the river before branching right towards Ivochote. The air was cool, though was warming up.

'After a storm it is always like this,' she said hastening her step. She waited for him to catch up. 'I wanted to ask you about Adam, Hugh. Elizabeth told me a little about why you are here, but I wanted to ask you why you think he disappeared?'

'I wish I knew the answer, Julia. Sometimes I think it is a reaction to Sarah's death, at other times it has more to do with our relationship, or lack of it.' They had arrived on the outskirts of the town. Ahead was a small row of small kiosks. 'The one at the end, with the flags outside sells coffee. Why don't we stop. Oh, and don't ask for sugar in your coffee. They use condensed milk which you may find takes some getting used to.' Outside was a small table and chairs. The sat with their backs to the river. 'You think he cut off from you because of something bad in your relationship?'

'Yes, I do. There's no other reason I can think of. He loved Sarah – as I did – and up to her death, I thought we were happy as a family. He'd landed the dream job, no permanent girlfriends but it was his decision to focus on his career, the occasional flying visit home, sometimes a call from somewhere exotic, but nothing to prepare me for this.'

'And nothing to prepare you for Sarah's death?'

'Not really. We knew the diagnosis wasn't good, but the doctors said if the first round of chemo didn't work, there could be a second, and I guess we were hopeful...'

'You were right to be hopeful.'

She paused and asked if he wanted anything to eat.

'No thanks.'

'You know, Hugh, it might not be anything to do with you. Maybe the death of his mother hit him much harder than you think? When our children do something such as this, not talking to us, or retreating into themselves, we tend to think it must be a result of something we've done, or maybe haven't done'. She stopped. 'I apologise, as I don't know you very well and haven't met Adam, but my advice would be to be patient, keep the door open. It's the best you can do.'

'And when I meet him again. How do I ensure the door remains open?'

'Which you will, of that I can be sure. Don't ask for explanations. Express what you feel. That you were worried but that you are happy he is back. Leave the rest to him. If he wants to say more, he will. In other words, give him time. Take the emotion out of what is of course very emotional. A paradox I know but one also experienced by Alfredo and Patricia.'

'In what way?'

'Well, shortly after they were married – and I'm sure Patricia doesn't mind me telling you all this - Alfredo received word that his life was at risk. You must remember that these were the dark days of the early '90s. He was a senior prosecutor at the time, like Pepe is today, and was involved in a high-profile corruption case. Fujimori had just won a landslide victory, and it was made clear to him that the new government wouldn't cooperate with the prosecution. No witnesses, no access to evidence, nothing.'

'What happened?'

'Perhaps unwisely, Alfredo threatened to approach the judges trying the case, and if necessary, contact the media, both at home and abroad. You can imagine how this was received. Some jumped up lawyer having the audacity to investigate above his paygrade.'

'He was threatened?'

'At first, money was offered. Discreetly of course. Then when that didn't work, a phone call at night, reminding him of the care he needed when crossing the road, that kind of thing. When he told Patricia about the phone call, and the case he was involved in, she became very emotional, telling him he was stupid, a pig-headed principled fool, and he wasn't to expect her to attend his funeral.' She laughed. 'You can imagine what he said. That he *thanked her for her concern*, but that he would of course carry on. What Patricia remembers most were his words. *Take the emotion out of it. It doesn't help.*

'And did it help?'

'In a way it did. She was patient and listened to him each evening when he came in from the court. Some days he didn't say anything, other days he would just sigh and tell her it would be the death of him. Eventually, he changed a little. One day, over breakfast, he told her that he had given a lot of thought to her words and that he had decided to withdraw from the case. The court had adjourned – something that is common here – and it looked like the defendants would be acquitted for lack of evidence.'

'He must have been disappointed?'

'Apparently, he just shrugged his shoulders. Patricia remembers him sitting quietly and rubbing his hands together like he and Pepe do, and saying, *'You may lose the battle, Patricia, but you can still win the war.'*

***

When they arrived at Ana's she was at the front of a small house deep in conversation with a woman who looked remarkably like her.

'Ah, Julia, so pleased to see you, long time. And this must be the Englishman who is looking for his son?' She extended her hand and introduced her sister. 'Everyone thinks we are twins, but I am a year older,' she said, smiling.

They walked into the house, where a table had been set for lunch. Julia apologised for being late.

'I'm apologising on your behalf, Hugh. Here we worry less about timekeeping and more about being thankful our guests have arrived. And grateful we have food on the table.'

The house was small but immaculately kept. He noticed a photograph of Antonio and an older man on the desk next to the window,

'My father-in-law who passed away this year. A good man, but one who enjoyed his food too much,' she said, running her finger along the frame.

They were sitting in the front room. It was sparsely furnished: a bookcase and a television, the desk next to the window, and the dining table and chairs.

'We usually eat in the kitchen but today is special. Visitors!' she beamed. When they were all seated, Ana rose from the table and spoke quickly to Julia. 'My English is not so good, but I was just telling her, I have something for you, senor.' She dug into her skirt pocket and withdrew a small white envelope. It was addressed to Senor Wilson. 'If you had been here, fifteen minutes ago you would have seen him. An old man. A stranger but friendly.'

Hugh opened the envelope. Inside was a single sheet of paper. On it was a short message written in English.

Senor Wilson, we will protect our business. We will eliminate those who betray us. We will destroy the foreign imperialists who misrepresent us. Viva the people! Viva the struggle! Viva Presidente Guzman! Oh, and tell your son, senor.

It ended with one word, *Quota*. He passed the note to Julia.

'Can you describe his car, Ana?'

'It was an old brown one, maybe a BMW. I am not so sure.'

'And him, apart from being old?'

'As I said, he was friendly – though he did not introduce himself which I thought was strange - maybe sixty years of age, and dressed in an old brown suit that looked like it had seen better days.' She turned to Julia. 'Is something wrong?' She then said something quickly in Spanish.

He turned to Julia for an explanation

'Ana was asking me if the letter comes from Major Salazar. I told her I thought not but that she must not worry. If he returns, she must call us immediately.'

Ana turned to Hugh.

'What I don't understand is how the man knew you would be here?'

'It is possible he saw you both walking here. The path we took is close to the road in several places...'

'Yes, Hugh,' said Julia, 'but why drop the letter here and not at our house? My guess is that he has been following you and he took the opportunity – and risk – to deliver the letter.' Julia asked Ana and her sister about her son and his progress in school.

'Maybe we should return? It's better we take the path back in the daylight.'

'I think we should,' said Hugh. They were soon back on the path home. 'And Martin, Julia. Do you think Cortes will tell you anything you don't know already?'

She picked up his hand again.

'I believe him when he says he was there when they took him and when the men attacked me. How much he knows about what happened to Martin later, I don't know.'

'And you *want* to know, don't you?'

'Part of me says no, tell me nothing of the terrible things they did; but another part of me wants to know the truth. To know what his last days were like, and of course to know where he is lying now.'

'You have no hopes he might still be alive?'

'People ask me this question, and I tell them I know in my heart he is dead. When I say this, they must think that in some way I am giving up on him, giving up on being reunited, but that is not true. Of course, I would love to return to what we were, but I know this will not happen. For me - and for Martin - it is best that I at least know the truth, and can then fight for justice on his behalf, on behalf of the countless other innocent victims who got caught up in our country's madness.' They reached the boathouse and turned towards the house. As they walked through the trees, she released his hand, and kissed him lightly on the cheek. 'You would have liked Martin.' She held the kitchen door open for him. 'And I think he would have liked you.'

***

Hugh decided to return to the river. He needed time to think, to clear his head. The sky was clear, not a cloud to be seen. Sarah would have enjoyed the river with its changing moods, one moment a raging torrent, the next a placid, meandering stretch of water.

He found an old tree stump and sat, watching the river. Max. A *hostage situation*. What did he know and why wasn't he telling him?

Alfredo would interrogate him about the note, the third one he had received if he accepted the reasonable view that the second, delivered to the *Amazonas*, was intended for him and not Pepe. He threw a stick into the river and watched it swirl away. The three notes had to be connected. The first one, dropped off at reception at his Ayacucho hotel, had been left when? He'd received it at breakfast, but it was likely it had been dropped at reception the night before, the day he'd met Ricardo at *El Flamingo* and later Julia for lunch. Where had he been before that? The Memory Museum. Was it possible he'd been followed from the moment he'd arrived in town?

And the second note? Left on the door of the *Amazonas* room he shared with Pepe. The old waiter, Nicolas, had probably played some part in it. Perhaps it was a warning, to take the first message more seriously. And what of the last note delivered to Ana and Antonio's house. Another warning, but different in the explicit threat directed at him and Adam. Adam he could understand. He had a nose – and a liking – for a good story, even if it meant putting his own life at risk. It had happened once in Libya when he'd been covering the death of the US Consul.

Were all the notes, in fact, intended for Adam, his role being the carrier of the warnings? Pepe mentioned the possibility the first note was intended for a Senor Wilson but maybe it was intended for Adam? If so, Adam must have planned to stay at the hotel. Had he booked and then cancelled, the note being left at reception for him to pick up when he checked in? But something was missing, something that linked the three notes. He was certain of one thing. Whatever Cortes and Salazar were involved in was connected to the notes. There had to be a connection.

***

Patricia and Elizabeth had conjured up a huge meal of spaghetti and a rich source which with several glasses of wine which made Hugh feel sleepy. Instead of going upstairs he wandered into Alfredo's study. Law books were stacked on a shelf above an old desk at one end. Framed photographs adorned the walls, one showing Alfredo in his legal robes. It was quiet. He could hear Alfredo saying something to Patricia in the rear garden. From the front, one of the car engines started up. Pedro laughed. He got up and walked over to the window next to the front door.

The first shot was followed in rapid succession by two more. There was a scream followed by a shout. Instinctively he ducked down behind the window. Alfredo ran past him and wrenched the door open. At the top of the drive, he could see the battered, brown sedan speeding through the gates. Alfredo was kneeling beside Freddy.

'Patricia. Quick. I think Freddy's been shot.'

***

T _ranscription of interview:_ Cristina Lopez, 28, _translator, and interpreter_

So, here we are, your final interview! Thank you for asking me, Adam, but I'm not sure there is much you don't know already. Perhaps there are one or two things – background things – I can help you with.

Let me start by saying thank you, again for inviting me to accompany you. Your Spanish has improved 'un poco' but you still have to work harder at it! What you need is a good teacher.

Why I decided to come with you, is easy to answer. I know for tourists and visitors like yourself, my hometown – with its vineyards and the dunes – is all very lovely, but once you've experienced the city lights, it's all very dull, so when I found your phone where you'd thrown it, and started talking with you about your investigation, I thought, maybe this is my big chance to learn about writing and what better place to start than with a proper journalist?

No, honestly, that's what I thought. And an opportunity to improve my terrible English.

If I'm honest, when you told me why you'd thrown away your phone, and your feelings about your father, I did wonder about what kind of man you were. As I said the second evening in that bar in Ica, just before we met with my grandfather, we in this country look up to our parents, we expect to speak with them many times, we respect them.

I am sorry for saying this but you did ask me to be honest. And my first lesson you told me was to be honest, to be true to yourself, and true to the truth. I remember that.

About myself? Well, as I say, it is to my father and grandfather, I must thank. My father was a humble businessman who saved and saved, enough for me and Maria to attend the Pontifical University of Peru. Can you imagine how much he and my mother had to save to send us there? Which is why there is no way I could not speak or talk with them. Or talk badly of them. He is my father.

Perhaps you do not want to hear these things, but if you ask me to tell you something about myself, I must tell you about the people who are important to me, who shaped me, who made me what I am. Who I am.

My father, yes, is the most important. After mama became ill, he took centre stage, supporting me in my studies, finding a relative with whom I could lodge near the university business school. Asking my grandfather if he would allow me to stay.

So, my grandfather in Ica is important. In this country, Adam, your grandfather, your abuelo plays an important role in guiding you. My grandpapa is such a man, a man I look up to. Yes, you are correct, he helped me too, during my final year at CENTRUM, at the Business School, permitting me to spend my final year placement at the winery. It was there I learnt so much about what makes a successful enterprise in this country.

You know what makes something work here? Be a success? There are three things. First, you need strength and determination – grandpapa has so much of that. Second, you must be very well-connected. You know that now, from the people you have met, from those who you interviewed. Not all are strong. Major Cortes and Major Salazar are strong. Others like Ricardo Flores, the owner of the restaurant in Ayacucho or Panco, the sinchi are weak, men who just follow others with no regards for anyone else. Or for the truth. And the third thing is luck. You might laugh but just think for a moment about how we met, at Diego's bar in Huacachina. If you remember, I had found your phone and had left it at reception. When I saw you later, walking around the lagoon, I thought it must be yours and told you where it was. At the hostel when I returned with you, no-one could find it. You *shrugged your shoulders and said, 'good riddance' or something like that. You seemed very angry, upset perhaps, something I had not seen in a man before.*

For a woman here, such a thing is intriguing. Unusual. Perhaps a kind of strength I hadn't seen before?

Luck for me played a part when we met again later and you told me something about your reason for coming to my country, your ambition to write something great, to stand out, apart from your father. It was at that moment, I should have told you, I had called senor Hugh and that I would call him back, but when I discovered who you were, I realised I could not do that. You had to go your own way. If I wanted to get to know you further, I would have to play by your rules. Which is what I have done. That is how it is in this country.

And what I think of your ambition? Well, perhaps this is not what you want me to talk about, but it seems important to me, perhaps for you too.

But, back to luck for a moment. We have been fortunate, lucky perhaps, to have the guidance of Enrique and Santiago, men who I would trust with my life. You know enough of where we have been, Adam, to know that while we are safe in grandpapa's residence here, the VRAEM is a very unsafe place, and the photographs you have taken and the discussions you have had, will tell people what is happening here. Good men, like grandpapa, know about this place but there are many in the capital and outside this country who know nothing of all this. I think what you write will open people's eyes. That has to be a good thing, doesn't it?

But it is late. Let's pause and when we return to Ica, let's continue, do a 'wrap up'. I like that phrase.

She says she'd entrust Salazar and Cortes with her life. I think she's wrong. Maybe they appeared like that at the beginning, but both are behaving differently now, as if something has changed, something has happened out of their control, or their orders have changed?

Last night I wandered into the living room and Cortes was engrossed in cleaning his old service revolver. When I asked him why he carried a gun, he laughed and said something about always having the upper hand, always ready to defend yourself when the occasion demanded it.

He then regaled me with a story about guiding a rich businessman through some rapids not far from here and how the boat tipped and the guy was lost over the side. As he was talking, he continued to polish his gun. The businessman was never found. When I asked the major about that, he just looked up at me, smiled and said, 'good riddance.'

Cristina thinks we're fine, her grandfather wouldn't entrust us with anyone he couldn't trust. 'We're safe' she says. But if we're so safe, why are they forbidding us to leave the house alone? And they say there's no signal. Our phones won't connect, but I'm sure I could hear Salazar talking on his mobile last night. Something's not right. Of that, I am sure.

***

Thirty-Six

T hey were sitting in the living room. Pedro was keeping guard outside. Alfredo had given him a shotgun.

'If you see him return, you have my explicit permission to fire. Freddy was propped up on the sofa. 'The first shot missed you by an inch, Freddy and you took a splinter from the door frame.'

'I guess I am lucky, no?' he said with a smile. Patricia had cleaned the wound and had applied a bandage.

'You are, senor, but I'm still not sure if we should take him to the clinic? For a tetanus jab?' said Patricia.

'Normally I would of course, agree, but on this occasion,' said Alfredo, 'I wouldn't put it past whoever fired the shot to be waiting for us do just that. If you don't object, Freddy, lets forgo the clinic.' Freddy nodded. 'Pedro tells me you got a good glimpse of the car?'

'Yes, judge. An old brown sedan, like the one Hugh said he saw in Ayacucho.'

'So, it's our writer of the *quota*. Clearly the notes were not enough.' He stopped and scratched his head. 'I'm not sure what you all think but I'm convinced this isn't the work of Cortes or Salazar, unless Cortes arranged the shooter before the meeting with Julia. Same with Salazar. But that doesn't make sense, particularly given the meeting with Antonio tomorrow'. Alfredo stood up and walked towards the door. One of the shots had torn out a small strip of wood just above the lock. He ran his hand up and down the frame.

'Three shots. From the long barrel Pedro saw, I'd say it was an old M16 semi-automatic with a three-round burst fire selector, popular with the anti-narcotics force and more than likely stolen or sold on by one of their men.' He sighed. 'If only we could declare some sort of firearms amnesty in this country, we might start to make some progress in reducing the general level of violence, and the more specific crimes such as this.'

He turned to Julia.

'And not helped by Fujimori arming the village militias, who then conveniently forgot to hand back their weapons later.' Hugh asked if there was anything he could do. 'At the moment, no, but thank you.' The judge scratched his head.

'My feeling is that this was just another warning – albeit a more serious one – but I don't think he'll return today.' He continued to scratch. 'My worry is that this will escalate, particularly if he doesn't get what he wants.'

'Which is?' said Julia

'I think he wants – or whoever is employing him - is for Adam, and by extension Hugh here, to back off in terms of anything young Adam might have found and is considering publishing.'

Patricia spoke. She looked tired.

'Do you think we should move?'

'No, at least not yet. Let's try and get some sleep. Pedro and Antonio can take turns guarding the front, and I'll keep lookout at the back.'

'And me, how can I help?' said Hugh. 'I can split the watch with you, Alfredo. Then at least we'll both manage a few hours' sleep.'

'Good idea. Thank you, Hugh.' The judge walked over to Patricia and spoke quietly to her. 'I've asked if she can make us a simple meal before we break up. For now, let's just think about tomorrow. Freddy clearly is not going anywhere, but Pedro here can drive you to the meeting with Salazar at the hotel. Midday, isn't it?' Antonio nodded. 'I think we'll also need to be alert to the shooter too, but this is a small place and a car like the brown sedan isn't easily hidden.'

Julia turned to Alfredo.

'What do you make of it, judge. The notes and now the shooting?'

'Well, clearly somebody is very, *very* annoyed with Hugh and possibly his son, hence the notes. Being annoyed is one thing, being armed is quite another. My guess is that he might have hoped Hugh was sitting out on the terrace, and when he wasn't, decided to fire off a warning shot anyway. Probably frustrated too. The third note had something of that in it.'

'And you think he won't stop until he's killed one or both of us, Alfredo?' said Hugh.

'Certainly, it looks like it, but what perplexes me is what is it that has so incensed him? Searching for a son is hardly a crime, though some of these old terrorists contend that all *gringos* are legitimate targets, which makes me think that it's Adam who is most at risk – and you are just an extension of him, a conduit, if you like.' He paused and held his breath in his best courtroom manner. 'In my considered view, Adam must have discovered something, interviewed someone who's spilled the beans about some aspect of the organisation, a drug route perhaps, something that must not – and cannot – come out. And God knows there must be a lot of that.' He paused. 'And let's not forget what the third note said: *We will protect our business. We will eliminate those who betray us. We will destroy the foreign imperialists who misrepresent us.* The foreign imperialists business is easy. A justification for killing meddling foreigners. No, it's the reference to killing those who *betray us* that is interesting. Suggests that Adam has uncovered something from a member of the cartel, something they see as a kind of betrayal, something that will have an adverse effect on the *business*. The kind of thing you see every day in Mexico or on the streets of Chicago.'

Hugh nodded. 'And our friend in the brown sedan has been tasked with delivery of a series of warnings, and if that doesn't work, an assassination?'

'There is another explanation, Alfredo?'

'Yes, Elizabeth?'

'It's possible isn't it that the warnings are linked in some way to Cortes and Salazar? In other words, the shots were aimed, not at Hugh, but at you, Alfredo?'

'You'd make a first-rate advocate, Elizabeth. I agree that is a possibility, but I still think we've got one very angry ex-member of *Sendero Luminoso* on the one side, and Colonel Salas and his thugs on the other. What they both have in common, of course, is the protection of their business, which seems to rely upon the death of either Hugh, Adam, or myself, or possibly the three of us, or four, if you include Cristina.'

'And I'm sorry to say that in either, or both scenarios, the safety of Adam and Cristina, looks to be increasingly in doubt.'

Julia was sitting alongside Hugh and leant towards him.

'Don't scare the poor man, Alfredo.' She turned to Hugh.

'He's spent too long mixing with some of the worst *hombres* ever to set foot on the planet. Take my word for it, we'll find them safe and sound. You have my word on that.'

Alfredo stood up and yawned theatrically.

'I'm going to talk with Pedro and Antonio. It's getting late. I suggest we rest. Patricia will no doubt welcome an extra hand in the kitchen. For the rest of you, my advice would be to try and get some sleep.' He turned to Freddy and patted him on the head. 'In an hour or so, let's meet for a drink before supper. And a very large one for our hero here!'

***

Hugh decided to follow Alfredo's advice and get some rest. It had become a habit to stand by the window and look out towards the line of eucalyptus. The wind had picked up a little, scattering leaves across the garden. From where he was standing, he could just about make out the small rose garden. He turned away from the window and sat in the chair in the corner of the room. The house was quiet, apart from Alfredo's rich voice coming from somewhere near the carport at the front. He checked his phone, something he hadn't done for a while. There was a missed call from Max. He glanced at his watch. Just after midday, and if he was lucky, he'd catch him on his lunch break. Max answered immediately.

'Hugh, thanks very much for calling back. Not sure where you are exactly but if we're cut off, I'll call you back.' In the background he thought could hear what sounded like traffic.

'I'm out in a park near the office. Meetings all morning. Have to get some air.'

'Have you heard from Adam?'

'Yes and no. Received a very brief voice mail from his friend Cristina about an hour ago which prompted my call. Tried to return her call but the phone is blocked. It came through on Adam's phone by the way, which is a bit odd…' There was a pause. '…sorry, the line's breaking up, so I'll be quick. She said, quote, *'Kurtz is looking after us well. See you on Sunday.'*

'Just that?'

'Yes, I tried calling back. Sent her a text too but the phone's blocked.'

'Thanks, for passing it on. What's your take on it?'

'Well, as I said last time, I'm not by nature a worrier – I wouldn't last long in this business if I was – but I'm still uneasy about things. Adam is something of a loose cannon, so I'm happy to give him his head, but…'

'...but you think he's in danger?'

'What do you think? Any news your end?' He decided to be noncommittal. This wasn't the time to call the cavalry in.

'And the message, Hugh, any thoughts? Kurtz is obviously a reference to *Apocalypse Now*. That's odd too.' He agreed. The line started to break up again, so he decided to draw the call to an end by agreeing to ring in a day or so. 'OK, Hugh. Please let me know if you hear of anything more. Just hope it all results in a blistering good copy!'

It was impossible to rest now. Alfredo had returned indoors, and he could hear his voice in the living room. He found Pepe and Alfredo hunched over the map which was spread out across the table. Pepe looked up.

'Ah, hope we didn't disturb you. Alfredo has a voice that could wake the dead. We've told Freddy to get a good rest in his room.' He walked over to the two lawyers. 'We are looking at various options if I have to hi-tail it out of here. I sincerely hope it doesn't come to that, if only because of the work we've done to this place. And the boat...' Alfredo looked at the Englishman. 'You look worried. Not bad news I hope?' He told them about the call from Max. Alfredo scratched his head. It seemed to have become a habit. 'My first reaction is that it sounds like a message sent under duress, some sort of code too to allay suspicions if overheard. What do you think, Pepe?'

'I agree. And Max is right. Why did she send it and not Adam? She was using his phone after all.' He continued to scratch his head. 'Adam referred to Kurtz before if you remember. In a call to Max. *Mr.* Kurtz from the Conrad novel, or the *colonel* from the movie.' Hugh moved over to the sofa. He was still feeling tired. The two men remained standing, looking at the map. 'My guess, is that she's trying to let us know where they are, where they're being held.' He got up and returned to the table. 'Look here, Hugh.' He used a stubby finger to trace the course of the river.

'The Urubamba is about 450 miles long from where it rises in the southern Andes, here, to where it joins the Apurimac not far north of here. So, my guess is that the reference to Kurtz is that they are somewhere down river from where we are which would fit too with their known sighting in Kiteni.' He pointed at the map. 'That would mean they are somewhere to the north of here which narrows things down a bit – but though there aren't many villages or isolated homesteads – we are still looking for a needle in a haystack.'

Pepe peered closely at the map. 'I think I've got it. Look here, gentlemen.'

He jabbed at the map. 'Here we are at Ivochote, and a little further downstream is the small community of Sanariate, where Julia met Cortes. From here the river flows on and through the rapids at the Pongo de Mainique. See just beyond the rapids here, it winds and then bends sharply to the left.' He took a large gulp of water. 'Here, on the bend of the river is that old mining community, *Campo Domingo*. That's where they are! Surprised, I hadn't thought of it before.' He rubbed his hands together.

Alfredo stared at his friend, and then laughed. 'And here's me thinking you are just a simple prosecutor!' He paused. 'Sorry, Hugh, we forget your Spanish is not so good. *See you on Sunday*. Campo Domingo - or in English - *Sunday field*, is a piece of land, often uncultivated, which is what this place is like. Or was, before the *petroleros* moved in. I'm sure this is where Cristina is directing us. Clearly a clever woman.'

Hugh looked closely at the map. *Was Adam really there? And safe?* 'Alfredo, Pepe, have you ever been there? Is it easy to get there? You mentioned the river but what about a road?'

'I've flown over it once with Emilio-Jesus when we were surveying this place from the helicopter, but as far as I know a boat, or a helicopter is the only way in or out. The only other way is by car to Sanariate, and then on by chopper from there to Campo Domingo.'

'A drug route?' said Hugh.

'Not necessarily. Our Major Kurtz will have fingers in a lot of pies: drugs, money laundering but also the digging of wells for oil, the clearing land for gold. What you can be certain of – if he's here – it's because there's a fortune to be made, and one well out of sight of the authorities.' He paused and said grimly, 'And let's not forget, his pursuit of yours truly, a judge who will testify against him in court.'

Patricia ushered them all into the dining room where she had laid out a simple buffet meal. 'Thank you, Patricia. And sorry for not helping as I said I would.' She smiled and blew him a kiss. Once they were seated, he took charge of the conversation. 'I think we have agreed that tomorrow – noon, isn't it? – Antonio will meet Salazar as planned at the hotel in town. I suggest Pedro and Hugh, you too Julia if you wish, drive Antonio to the hotel. On the other side of the road is that café that sells the marvellous *empanadas*. If you park just up the road from there, Antonio can walk over to the hotel for the meeting. The bar is on the terrace which is in sight of the café. If we keep in phone contact, should anything happen, we can take things from there.' He looked at his audience. 'Salazar, like Cortes, seems genuine in his wish to make amends. Let's give him the benefit of the doubt but let's not forget that his day job is searching for me, of that, I am sure. Also, we need more information on where they are holding Adam and Cristina.'

Antonio nodded.

'I will try and find out what I can, senor.'

Alfredo looked at his watch.

'We all need to rest now, but two of us must keep guard. I'll take the first watch, and I suggest Pedro the second. You, Antonio should go home. Please, arrive early tomorrow morning, in case things have changed.'

Hugh needed rest, too, if he was to be of any use in the morning but sleep evaded him. He opened the curtains and looked out towards the line of trees and the river beyond. No pale faced woman to beckon him, just the eucalyptus swaying rhythmically in the evening breeze. Adam. He remembered the first time he had held him in his arms at the hospital, promising silently to protect him to his dying breadth, but had he ever got to know him during their time on the Norfolk marshes or sitting on the pebbly beach nearer home? Occasions he had allowed to drift by whilst his son grew into an adult, silently and gradually disappearing from view.

He closed the curtains and made his way to bed. Was disappearing the only way Adam could free himself from the constraints of a constricting childhood? What would Sarah advise? *You were a loving father; you did your best.* Searching for Adam, was that part of it? He climbed into bed. Judgement would have to be delayed until Adam reappeared.

***

Thirty-Seven

I t had rained during the night. Hugh pulled back the curtains and looked out. The garden was covered in a fine dew. He looked towards the line of trees. On the path that ran between them he could just make out a scattering of rose petals that must have been blown there overnight. And then he saw her emerging from behind one of the larger trees to the left of the path. She moved to stand in the usual place wearing the familiar long dark skirt that reached down to her shoes. Her face was partially obscured by a cowl. He could see, however, that she had a single rose tucked behind her left ear. Carefully, he opened the window. She must have sensed the movement or perhaps she had heard the latch. She looked up in his direction. He wanted to call out but no sound came. Instead, he raised his hand. She moved two or three steps forward, away from the line of trees. She must have seen him, for she lifted a hand, palm facing outwards. In her left hand she was holding a posy of bright-blue flowers, cornflowers perhaps.

He woke once more, for a moment disorientated, and looked across at the window. The latch was firmly shut. *Sarah, what is happening to me? Adam...* he said softly to himself. He picked up his watch and padded over to the window. It was early but not enough to warrant a return to bed. He thought about Pedro downstairs. He had missed his turn at keeping watch and, as no-one had woken him, he assumed all was well. The least he could do was to go down and make a huge pot of coffee. Sarah had been the early bird. He preferred a late night, watching a movie long after she had turned in. It was one of the few things that divided them. Before her illness, she'd talked of what they'd do together, just the two of them. Adam was more or less established, the job at the paper taking him further and further away, and his own retirement was looming.

Go part-time so you get used to it, she'd said one day, *and then you'll be ready for the big break, and we can do all the things we've never had the time for.*

The illness robbed them of more than just her life, it had snatched away future time, leaving him to look forever backwards. He sighed. Being maudlin wouldn't help. He dressed quickly and made his way downstairs. Pedro was curled up in a chair by one of the front windows. The shotgun lay across his lap.

'Good morning, senor,' he said sleepily. 'All is quiet, which is good, not so?'

Hugh agreed and went into the kitchen to make the coffee. After ten minutes, he heard Alfredo's rich voice.

'Ah, Hugh. I need a very strong coffee if you please. You will be delighted to know that I did catch some sleep and equally delighted to know that we were not troubled by any intruders, which is why we let you sleep. But staying up half the night is not something I intend to make a habit of.' He chuckled and started rooting around in one of the cupboards.

'She never puts anything where I can find it,' he said under his breath. On cue, Patricia arrived and pushed past him.

'You, Alfredo, can stop your search. I know what you're looking for and you know only too well what the doctor said about obesity and carbohydrates. And for the record, I have put the pasta somewhere even a judge of your calibre can't find.'

'Ok, ok, I plead guilty,' he said with a laugh. 'I happen to enjoy a plate of spaghetti with tomato sauce for breakfast. Unorthodox I know, but it is clear that this dragon here is intent on depriving me of this pleasure.' He kissed his wife on the cheek. 'If coffee and toast are allowed, I'll bring mine into the living room.'

***

They arrived at the café shortly before midday. Pedro carefully reversed the car into a narrow parking place around the corner. Alfredo had reminded them to keep the hotel in sight but to make sure they weren't seen.

'And call me if anything untoward happens or you notice anything suspicious.'

Julia went inside and ordered coffee for all of them. Antonio stood against the outside wall of the café, keeping a careful eye on the terrace on the first floor of the hotel. It overlooked the bridge where the road joined Route 102.

Two cars were parked on the hotel forecourt. After a few minutes, a small group of workmen carrying ladders and buckets walked into the building. Antonio continued to look at the terrace. Nothing unusual. He lit a cigarette.

'I can't see any sign of Salazar. If he is up there waiting, he's keeping himself well out of sight.' He glanced at his watch. 11.50. It was important Antonio entered the building exactly at twelve. It was Hugh who first saw the car driving slowly across the bridge in the direction of the hotel. It was the brown sedan. They all watched as it reversed into a space at the front of the hotel and parked next to the builders' pick up.

'Hang back,' said Pedro 'and I'll try and see who they are.' Two men, one the old man. Hugh was sure was the person he'd seen near his hotel in Ayacucho, climbed out of the car at the same time. 'Younger one is carrying a small shoulder bag.'

Hugh watched the men walking quickly into the hotel. Julia had Alfredo on the line and was talking quietly into her phone.

They waited. The day was heating up. Cloudless. It offered good visibility. Twenty minutes passed before the men re-emerged, walking more urgently this time. Slowly the sedan inched its way out of the forecourt and turned immediately onto the bridge. They watched the car as it joined the main road where it turned north in the direction of Sanariate.

'Alfredo says wait five minutes just to check they aren't returning. And he suggests Pedro goes in with Antonio.'

The two men nodded to each other and walked towards the hotel entrance. The terrace looked deserted. Julia turned to Hugh. 'We might be here an hour, depending on Salazar not smelling a rat,' she said. He nodded and smiled at her. She was about to say something when her face froze. Pedro and Antonio were running out of the hotel entrance.

'Go quick!' Pedro shouted. 'I'll explain as we drive.'

Antonio jumped into the front passenger seat. He was breathless, his hands shaking. Julia reached over and put a hand on his shoulder. They pulled out from the side street and made their way home.

'Keep your eye on the road, Pedro. I'll explain.' He turned in his seat to face them. 'There was no-one at reception, so we climbed up the stairs towards the entrance to the terrace. We saw no one. At the top, Pedro held back, and I looked quickly into the bar expecting to see Salazar waiting for me. There was no one there. Suddenly, Pedro pushed pass me and pointed to a figure lying on the floor next to the bar. It was as if he'd fallen off a bar stood, like a drunk.'

'Salazar?' said Hugh.

'Yes, he was lying on his side, his face away from us but we could see he'd been shot twice in the head from a range of about six or seven feet. Maybe the shooter had fired from the doorway.'

'And using a silencer,' said Pedro as they approached the house, 'which would explain why we heard nothing.'

He parked the car into the carport. Alfredo met them just inside the door.

'Inside, please. You all look shaken. Tell me what happened.,

Patricia and Pepe were sitting around the large table. Antonio repeated what he had told them in the car. When he had finished, he looked around the table. Alfredo spoke first.

'Was that all, Antonio?'

'No, there is one more thing.' He reached into his pocket and withdrew a small white envelope. 'This was in Salazar's left hand. It looks like it was placed there after he was shot.'

Alfredo took the envelop and opened it. Inside was a single sheet of paper on which was written one word.

Quota

***

Alfredo took charge. He'd laid the map out on the living room table. Patricia, Elizabeth, and Julia sat on one side, Hugh, Pepe, and Antonio on the other. Pedro had decided to remain by the window. Freddy was propped up on the sofa.

'So, we first have a number of questions to address before we decide what we are going to do.' He looked at his watch. 'And we must be quick, as I fear that those who killed Salazar are on their way to do the same to Adam and Cristina.'

Patricia half-raised her hand.

'But how would they know where to go?'

'Good question. But let's think for a moment. Antonio thought it likely Salazar was shot from the doorway to the bar, but it's quite possible he was killed after he'd been forced to tell them where Salas and Cortes are holding Adam and Cristina at Campo Domingo.'

'Which would explain why they branched right once over the bridge?'

'Yes, in the direction of Saniriato and from there by some unofficial track or being picked up by Salas in his helicopter.' Alfredo traced a stubby finger along the river. 'The question is one of motivation. Why was Salazar killed? Was it just to get to Adam and Cristina, their real targets, or did they have another reason to kill Salazar?'

Julia raised her hand again.

'The *quota* notes and the shooting here suggest that they have something against Adam. First his father was warned, and when that didn't work, they shoot.'

Alfredo nodded. 'As Pepe knows, sometimes the obvious is the most likely. It is obvious that we're caught up in some kind of turf war between the *Sendero Luminoso* cartel and Salas. I think it is also most likely that Adam, unknowingly, has discovered something a number of people wish to remain uncovered, and more importantly, unpublished.' He laughed grimly. 'Salas, on the other hand, knows full well that unless he can prevent me from testifying, not only does he face a long prison sentence for human rights abuses, but his business empire is finished as well. Adam, as I've said before, is the one card he holds to ensure I break cover.' He drummed his fingers on the table. 'I'm sorry to sound alarmist, but it seems that young Adam is the link.'

'And the killing of Salazar?' said Julia

'Once he'd served his purpose and told them where Adam is being held, he was of no further use. And remember he was meeting with Antonio to compensate his family for the *Barrio Altos* crime.' He paused and looked at Antonio. 'These *Sendero* men are not interested in compensation, for them it is a matter of revenge. Another reason for killing Salazar.'

Adam, where are you and are you safe? Hugh raised a hand to his forehead.

'You look troubled, Hugh? I'm sorry to sound alarmist.'

'I am troubled, Alfredo, and I'm thinking we should…'

'…do something? I agree, now is the time to act.' He pointed to the map. 'I think Pedro and Freddy should take the car to your relative's place outside Kiteni. And Patricia and Elizabeth should accompany him.' Freddy started to complain.

'You are in no state to travel down river through the rapids to Campo Domingo, Freddy, and you can play an important role if something seriously goes wrong, and we need the cavalry.'

Patricia turned to her husband.

'And what about you, Alfredo? Shouldn't you join us in Kiteni? It's you after all Salas and his men want to flush out?'

'Sensible advice, Patricia, but for once I'm not going to take it.' She said nothing. 'If Salas is holding Adam – as I'm convinced, he is – then it is another piece of evidence to be presented to the court. And I intend to present it.' He walked over to the cabinet above the sideboard and took out the shotgun and a rifle. 'We'll take these, just to be on the safe side. And if you are wondering,' he said with a chuckle, 'I hold certificates for both of them.' He handed the shotgun to Antonio. 'I'll hang onto the rifle but Hugh, you must join us. Your chance to ride the Pongo de Mainique!' Patricia and Elizabeth stood and quickly exchanged a few words. Alfredo spoke. 'OK, we are agreed. Pedro and Freddy will take you both via a back route to avoid the police who'll be swarming around the hotel, and Antonio, you go and prepare the boat.' He rested the rifle against the table. 'If all goes well, we'll be back here tonight. I've called Emilio-Jesus whose helicopter will be ready to pick us up this evening at the sports field in Campo Domingo. Antonio can return with the boat. Oh, and please talk to Ana, Antonio, but pledge her to total secrecy, OK?'

Patricia turned to walk back into the kitchen.

'And if it doesn't go well...?'

Alfredo raised a hand.

'Fear not, Patricia. Our course is set, and all will be well.'

***

O nce they were on the boat, Antonio took charge. Alfredo kept watch from the front with the others sitting on the rudimentary benches on either side.

'Up till the rapids we should have no difficulty, said Alfredo, as they cast off. 'It's when we reach the *Pongo* that we will have to be prepared.'

'And pray,' said Antonio with a grin.

The river was broad and fast-flowing. They kept to the centre to avoid the propellor being snagged on fallen branches and foliage. On any other occasion, Hugh would have marvelled at the brown, swirling mass of water and the vegetation that tumbled down to the river's edge. After an hour they reached Saniriato where the river made a series of meandering turns. Antonio pointed ahead.

'Look, about twenty meters ahead, see the whirlpools?' If small, the whirlpools were capable of being skated over, but as they approached a sharp bend, they saw five-foot waves converging from all directions, filling the boat with a constant stream of spray.

'Keep to the central current!' Alfredo shouted, as Antonio guided the boat through the water.

'This is just a foretaste of what's to come when we hit the *Pongo*,' said Pepe. 'I've only done this once, a few years back, and that was when the river was slower and calmer.'

He wiped the spray off his glasses his glasses and grinned. 'You OK, Hugh?' He nodded and shifted closer to Julia. They were all drenched, the spray a continuous sheet of water. At the next bend, the river quietened, and Antonio steered the craft towards the farthest bank.

'We're not going to get out,' said Alfredo, 'but let's pause and take some hot coffee and snacks. Antonio will tell us of the joys that lie ahead.' The boat rested, prow first, against the bank. Julia handed round small cups of coffee and tiny almond biscuits.

'Before we enter the rapids, we will navigate a series of smaller rapids. You'll see two or three large boulders in the centre of the river. You can see the top of these but below they are five or six feet deep which causes a build-up of water and big waves. It is not the waves that are the problem but the deep hole behind the rock, four or five times as high as the wave.' He gave a sign of the cross. 'But fear not, comrades. I know this river like it is my naughty child.' Julia refilled his cup. 'After the smaller rapids, the river narrows by half as we enter the gorge. You will see beautiful waterfalls cascading down in graceful veils. Look out for the famous Tonquini waterfall on our right just before we enter the gorge. It is very beautiful. But again, fear not, God has entrusted you to me and I am entrusted to Him.'

Julia squeezed Hugh's hand. 'He likes to joke, does Antonio.' He does indeed, Hugh thought, but he felt he was getting closer to Adam. That was all that mattered. They pushed off and continued downstream. To their right, he saw a group of macaws and what he thought were green parrots halfway up the rock face.

'It's a saltlick,' said Julia, 'they say at night you might see spectacled bears or even a jaguar. And keep an eye out for any capybara, the strange rodent some say are the friendliest wild animals on the planet.'

He smiled at her. She was wearing jeans tucked into leather boots over which she'd added a light waterproof. On her head she wore a bright yellow sou'wester, her dark braids tucked underneath. They continued for half of an hour until Antonio guided the boat towards a small wooden jetty. He jumped out and tied the boat to a wooden tree stump. Alfredo followed.

'A short break, for Antonio to perform a small ritual.' He pointed downstream. 'The rapids are just ahead. Here tourists sometimes camp for the night.'

He held the boat as they climbed out. There was a small path that ran through a clearing.

'The camping area is through there,' said Antonio. 'When I was a guide, I enjoyed staying here. Very quiet. Beautiful.' He took a small bottle from an inside pocket and walked down to the river. 'My people believe the Pongo is like a door – the *door of the bear* we call it – into which our ancestors have passed when their time in this realm is finished.' He poured the water into the river and spoke a few words in Quechua. 'Now we can continue. We are protected.' He held onto the boat as they returned. Alfredo carefully tucked his phone back into its waterproof bag.

'Trying to see if we had a signal. Emilio-Jesus should be taking off about now,' he said, resuming his seat at the front.

The entrance to the rapids was deceptive, marked by a series of mini whirlpools, the cliffs, six or seven hundred feet high suddenly narrowing. The river descended fast, squeezed between two huge shoulders of rock. Then the door of the bear opened, the water shrieking and growling like an animal in distress. The boat tipped forward, rocking from side to side as Antonio swung first to the left and then sharply right, avoiding a massive boulder that reared up. They could see nothing except spray. And then they were through. Within minutes the river opened out, resuming its leisurely pace. Antonio turned and raised a thumb.

'The door of the bear has closed,' he said with a smile on his face.

Alfredo was smiling too.

'An adventure, Hugh! Not an ideal time, but an adventure nonetheless.' His expression then changed. 'In twenty minutes or so, the river will turn sharply to the left and you will see Campo Domingo on the right. Manuel will be waiting at the small jetty to take us to a safe place.' He moved up to join Antonio at the front of the boat. He must have guessed what Hugh was thinking. 'Manuel has done many things in his life, Hugh, some not quite as legal as they might be, but I trust him, and that is important.

Julia whispered, 'I think he is the Manuel, Alfredo once helped after a wrongful arrest.'

'What was he arrested for?'

'Receiving a car stolen outside a particularly expensive hotel in Cusco, and then re-selling it to an American mining engineer.' She laughed. 'Most of us thought he got a good deal, apart from the owner of course!'

The boat glided slowly towards a small wooden jetty. The river meandered on towards its final destination, the Sacred Valley of the Incas. Hugh followed Pepe out of the boat. A small, wiry man with both front teeth missing held out a hand as they each clambered out. He couldn't see anything that resembled a camp. The terrain was flat, the once-dense forest ripped out to reveal the red earth beneath. Manuel had parked his white combi a short distance from the river. It didn't seem to bother him to have a car full of soaking wet passengers dripping water all over his seats and floor. Hugh was squeezed in the back with Pepe and Antonio. He wondered about the boat. As they left, he watched two young men hauling the craft up onto the bank.

'They'll keep an eye on it, fear not,' said Alfredo as they drove away. 'Manuel tells me there's a helicopter landing spot – a school playing field – about five hundred metres from his house.' He pointed to a huge complex surrounded by razor wire. 'One of several oil compounds that provide most of the employment in this place.'

Apart from a woman sitting next to the entrance of the compound, it looked deserted. If Salas had decided to base his operations here, he had clearly decided to do it out of sight. After about five minutes, they approached a scattering of squat, square buildings. One was a petrol station, another a school, its sign obscured by dust. Someone had painted 'Vote Castillo' in large letters on the side of the school building. This was clearly the centre of town, the road opening into a familiar main square, a small, whitewashed church at one end, a municipal building sporting a large flag at the other. The place looked shabby, but cared for. As they entered the square, Hugh saw a large lorry blocking one side of the road. A group of women were busy at the back of the vehicle buying fruit and vegetables. One of them raised a hand to Manuel as he passed. Just beyond the church, he turned sharply right and stopped.

'Please, this way. My wife is expecting us.' He led them across a forecourt towards a three-story building that looked as if it had once been an office block. 'We used to live above when it was a pharmacy, and when they moved to a new place, we were able to buy the whole building.' He was clearly pleased with his purchase. At the entrance sat an old woman in a plastic chair. Next to her stood a taller, younger version, spinning cotton in one hand. She ran forward as they entered. 'My wife, Laura,' he said, 'she will show you where you can go and change.'

They followed her up two flights of stairs to a floor made up of a wide corridor, off which were a set of identical doors. She spoke to Julia.

'She knows no English, Hugh, but says you are welcome. This is your home now, and she hopes she can make you welcome. Your room is here.'

He entered the first door. The room was larger than he expected with a large wrought-iron bed occupying most of it. Opposite was a huge, dark-stained wardrobe, next to which was a small desk and chair. Alfredo had mentioned the importance of a change of clothing but had said nothing about spending the night. Hugh changed quickly and bundled his wet clothing into a plastic bag. His room looked out onto the forecourt. Down below he could see the old woman unmoving in her chair. She was staring ahead, her lips moving as if she was reciting a prayer. She moved her hips slowly from side to side.

Are you somewhere here, Adam? In this run-down place?

He looked at his phone. No signal. He wondered how Alfredo would communicate with Emilio-Jesus.

'Ah, dry and respectable,' he said with a chuckle. 'We'll wait for the others. In the meantime, let's enjoy the coffee Laura is about to bring us, and I am sure some *empanadas*.'

'How did you meet, Manuel, Alfredo?'

He patted his arm. 'No doubt, Julia has regaled you with the story of how a new BMW found its way from the carpark of the Sheraton Hotel in Lima to the garage Manuel used to run in Pichari?' He laughed. 'Well, I managed to sort out a number of misunderstandings, and he was relieved and happy everything was resolved. In return, he introduced me to Antonio and then Laura – they are cousins – a fine woman who has kept him pretty much on the straight and narrow.'

'And why did he move here?'

'Kiteni, Pichari, Ivochote, and now here. As the mining companies shift operations, so humble workers like Manuel shift too. I think in your country you call them seasonal. Well here in my country the seasonal is always permanent.' He laughed again. 'A permanent state of temporary, that's what drives this multi-million-dollar business. Of course, the alternative is even more precarious.'

'Drugs?'

'Not just cocaine, but the enterprises that support and flow from it. As I said, Salas can take his pick from illegal land clearing, gold mining, prostitution, and good old-fashioned corruption of those we entrust to manage the affairs of state.'

Pepe had changed into a lightweight pale suit. He shook Hugh's hand.

'I'm glad at least we two are keep up appearances, senor.'

They were sitting around a large circular table. Though Hugh had changed into fresh clothes, he still felt the effects of the drenching from the rapids.

'Have some coffee, Hugh, it'll warm you up. This area is known for its quality.'

He also took an *empanada*. It was coated in fine white sugar. The coffee was bitter and reviving. Pepe spoke first. 'Do you have signal, Alfredo?'

He took a mobile from its protective plastic bag. 'Not for my usual mobile, but I have this.' From his brown leather backpack, he removed a bulky satellite phone....'this is another matter entirely.' He held it aloft. 'For the geeks amongst us, it's an iridium extreme 9575 linked up to an America company called "Ground Control". And very good it is too.' He laid the phone on the table. 'And its working. I'm in touch with Emilio-Jesus who aims to be at our landing ground at Ivochote soon. When we're ready he'll fly and pick us up.'

'When we're ready?' said Pepe.

He looked up. 'When we have located the whereabouts of Adam and Cristina and are ready to be picked up.' He placed both hands palm down on the table. 'I have spoken with Manuel who is a good friend of an official working as a liaison between the *municipalidad* and the oil industry. To put it bluntly, they know who comes and goes, who is dealing with whom, who is involved with what.' He clearly knew what he was talking about. 'My suggestion is that it would be unwise for me to meet with this official, but that Pepe and Antonio go with Manuel and talk with his friend.

He has told us where they like to eat, a restaurant called *Divina Rosa* popular with visiting engineers and contractors. And importantly, safe.'

Pepe rubbed his hands together and looked across at Hugh. 'Don't worry about the guns, Hugh. They're our last resort.'

Alfredo took another *empanada*. 'Take care, Pepe. Remember we have Salas and Cortes to consider – I'm assuming they'll have heard about Salazar – and our two friends in the brown sedan. If it comes to a firefight, I have no intention of being caught in the middle.'

Julia pushed the plate away from Alfredo.

'You think this official will know where they are? And if he does, he will tell us?' she asked.

'Manuel thinks he will. Apparently, he wants a transfer to somewhere – anywhere – just as long as it is away from here. Two teenage children needing proper schooling and employment opportunities that will keep them on the straight and narrow.' He looked at his watch. 'We have an hour or so until dusk.'

Julia rested her head on her arms.

'Which means a night here?'

'Yes, I think it does, but we have Manuel and Laura to thank for the hospitality. I suggest I talk a little with Pepe and Antonio, and then call Emilio-Jesus. He's agreed to come and pick us up. The question is when.'

***

The three men returned within the hour. Pepe patted Alfredo on the shoulder and sat down next to Julia.

'Well, that was interesting but not very productive.'

'Interesting, in what way?' said Alfredo who was patiently cleaning his glasses with a piece of silk.

'If you thought, Pichari or Ivochote was small, then you haven't seen anything of this place.' He laughed. 'The restaurant is about fifteen minutes' walk from here back to the square and then along a parallel street to this one. Small, friendly place, two tables outside, somewhat gloomy within but nice.' He turned to Julia. 'We were tempted to stay but decided in the end to talk to Juan, the friend of Manuel, and then hot-foot it back to here.'

'So, I'm guessing Juan knew nothing?'

'Correct, though he clearly knows everything about the comings and goings of this fine metropolis. Told us no-one of any interest had stayed since about ten days ago when a group of mining engineers had arrived by helicopter and had stayed for two or three days. As for *gringos*, no-one.'

Antonio was listening closely.

'Just to add to what Pepe is saying, Juan did say they'd been an interest in developing a second helicopter landing place by some army people, but as far as he knew it's still in the early stages. Perhaps Salas is behind that?'

Alfredo nodded.

'Thanks, Pepe and Antonio.' He cracked his knuckles.

'Looks like Campo Domingo is not Cristina's *Sunday camp* after all.' He rubbed a thick thumb over his forehead. 'At least you've had a chance to shoot the rapids, Hugh.' Alfredo looked up at Julia. 'I know what you're thinking - that we leave and regroup?'

'Yes, I think Juan is to be trusted,' said Julia.

Before she could continue, Alfredo spoke,

'I'll call Emilio-Jesus from my room and suggest that he can pick us up tomorrow morning. He can stop off for a break at our place and then make the quick hop to here. I'll suggest he gets here about nine.'

'And the boat, Alfredo?'

'I've already spoken to Manuel who is happy to arrange for it to be taken back to Ivochote tomorrow or the day after.'

After he had gone, Julia said, 'I should call Cortes too, to arrange our meeting. And who knows, maybe we'll learn from him where Adam and Cristina really are.'

Alfredo returned looking more cheerful.

'Well, I've spoken to Emilio-Jesus who will be with us mid-morning tomorrow. Said he'll land at our place for a pitstop and that we should be at the landing place ready to go. Manuel will accompany us.'

As if on cue, Manuel returned with huge plates of food and two large bottles of Inka Cola. As they ate, Alfredo and Pepe kept up a constant stream of discussion.

'The question, Pepe, is where are they?'

'Good question, judge, given that this is the only place called *Domingo* in these parts.' He turned to Julia. 'I think you're right, Julia. A call to Cortes can do us no harm and it might throw up a lead. It is late now. Call him early in the morning before we set off.'

After dinner, Hugh took Alfredo to one side, and asked if he thought it safe to take a short walk before bed.

'If there was any doubt Salas and his men or the thugs in the brown sedan were here, I'd warn you against it, but I think we can safely assume that the only strangers in town are us.' 'Do you want me to accompany you?'

'Thanks, but I just need to clear my head before I turn in. I'll only be gone twenty minutes, and I've got my mobile here, not that there's much signal.'

He laughed and patted his shoulder. 'Enjoy the walk but take care. Not of bandits or thieves but of potholes. It's a curse once you leave our civilized urban centres.'

'I'll take care. Thought I might head back to the river.'

'No midnight skinny-dipping, senor.'

He walked quickly towards the main square, crossing over towards the church. In about fifteen minutes he would be at the river. As he approached the building, the main doors were flung open and twenty or thirty people streamed out, women in bright skirts and the traditional brown bowler hats, men in dark suits and ties. Some of the men walked slowly away, a few helped by a walking stick, others stopped and gathered to talk. A bright orange glow shone from the interior of the church. On an impulse he entered. It was an unpretentious building with a row of ten wooden chairs on each side the nave, the altar a simple affair but behind which was an imposing Baroque painting, faded but impressive. He sat in the second row as the church emptied. Somewhere to the left, through a closed door he could hear the low murmur of voices. A door to the right of the altar opened and a tall, stooped figure dressed in clerical robes made its way to a small table upon which three candles flickered.

Hugh wasn't religious but took comfort in the buildings set aside for the faithful. After Sarah's death, he had spent time in his parish church, the vicar and congregation understanding he was someone who wanted to be left alone. He sat and looked at the painting behind the altar. He could make out the infant Jesus surrounded by a goat and what looked like a baby alpaca. Above the manger scene, the artist had added a bright yellow sun, its rays shining down on the scene below. He took a deep breath and looked around. Too late in the day to continue to the river and the short time in the church had given him what he was looking for,

He rose and turned to go. In the middle of the row behind him an old woman knelt, her face hidden from view. She seemed to be dressed in thick traditional dress, her head free of any hat, her hands holding onto the back of the seat in front of her. She was whispering something quietly.

He made his way towards the centre aisle. As he approached her row, she stopped whispering and looked up in his direction. Her pale, oval face was younger than he had expected. She seemed to be looking past him, in the direction of the altar. For a moment they stood, saying nothing. Then, she straightened her clothing and ran a hand through her hair. He stopped and nodded briefly towards her.

'*Buenos noches, senora,*' he said softly. She didn't answer but half-stood as if to curtsey, raising her left hand in greeting. In her right she held a small bunch of dark blue flowers.

***

Thirty-Nine

He walked back to the apartment. Only Manuel was up. 'Sleep well, senor. If you need anything, please ask.' He wished him a good night and climbed the stairs to his room. The bed was ancient but comfortable.

He was walking confidently along the pipe. When he looked up, he could see the waves breaking on the shore. Sarah was ahead and Adam behind. Stopping he turned to look at his son who was looking upwards. A skein of brent geese was swooping down, their wings flapping, their focus upon the small boy. He cried in terror, his arms flailing as he fought off the birds.

One of the shutters in his room was banging against the window. He lay wondering if the noise had woken the others. There was so much he had got so wrong, so many missed opportunities.

Adam, I'm so sorry. I screwed up and now it's too late.

Hugh continued to lie still, as if his stillness would shake off his feeling of self-pity. Below his room, he could hear the deep tones of Pepe. He looked at his watch and then his phone. If time allowed, he'd call Max after breakfast.

He woke, surprisingly refreshed. When he entered the dining room, Alfredo was deep in conversation with Pepe.

'Ah, Hugh. Good to see you nice and early. We have news.' Pepe was pouring coffee into three small cups. 'I've just had a call from Emilio-Jesus who is in the air and on his way. Tells me he's just flown over the house. He was going to land but decided not to when he saw the brown sedan parked in front of the house. No sign of life.'

'That sounds ominous, Pepe,' said Hugh.

'Yes, it's the sedan that worries me.' Pepe cracked his knuckles. 'They knew where Antonio lived, and so it was only a matter of time before they found your place, Alfredo.

My guess is that after they left the hotel they made as if to take the road to Campo Domingo, but then doubled back. The question is why? If they wanted to attack us or set an ambush, they'd have hidden the car from view. It doesn't make sense.' Pepe nodded and then stood up quickly. 'Alfredo, is it possible the sedan was followed by Cortes or Salas? In other words, they were at the hotel when Salazar was killed and then tracked them to our place?'

'For what purpose?'

'Well, first of course to find you, but secondly to settle the score with those responsible for killing Salazar. Two birds with one stone.'

'Which means they could be inside awaiting our return?'

'They could, Pepe, but again it makes no sense leaving the car in plain view.'

The three men sat in silence. Alfredo rubbed a fat finger across his temples.

'Julia will call Cortes before we're picked up. It may give us an idea of where he is at least.' He handed Julia his satellite phone.

Cortes picked up immediately. She moved quickly towards the window, putting a finger to her lips. Cortes had to believe she was making the call alone.

The call must have lasted thirty or forty seconds. She placed the phone back on the table and turned to face the men.

'He told me to listen very carefully and to obey his instructions to the letter.

Pepe drummed his fingers on the table.

'Instructions? About what?'

'He said it was simple. An exchange. Alfredo for Adam. He would tell us where the exchange was to be made later today when he would call. That was all.'

Alfredo leapt to his feet and spoke quietly and gravely.

'Well, this is not news, is it gentlemen? We have known all along that Cortes and Salazar's mission is to find and silence me. They are running out of time, and with Salazar killed, out of manpower.'

'There is one other thing,' said Julia. 'While he was talking, I could hear a church bell in the background. I think he was calling outside in a public place, perhaps so the call could not be traced.' She stopped and then continued. 'I have it! I know that bell.'

'Come on, Julia, what bell?' said Pepe.

'The Cathedral of Santo Domingo in the *Plaza de Armas* in Cusco. That's what I heard just now.' She looked at her watch. 'It was chiming nine o'clock. He was calling from Cusco; of that, I am sure.'

'Which means he's not at a house. There's a possibility that he and Salas have split up, but I don't think so. If he wants an exchange, you can be sure Salas will be there to ensure it succeeds.'

Alfredo gave a short laugh. '*See you on Sunday*. Obvious now I think of it. The Cathedral of Saint Dominic – *Domingo* – our word for Sunday. A clue staring us in the face.'

He growled, clearly angry. It was Pepe who asked the question preoccupying all of them.

'He'll set the terms of the exchange, maybe somewhere public like the main square in front of the cathedral. Do you think he seriously believes we will trade Alfredo for Adam?' He looked across at Hugh. 'I am talking frankly here, senor, having met many people like Cortes. They are ruthless but not stupid. For us to even contemplate such an exchange, they will have to threaten to kill their hostage – or hostages if Cristina is included – unless we agree to our side of the bargain. 'He paused. 'Of course, they can't control all eventualities, that we make the exchange and then engineer a way to prevent them leaving with Alfredo.'

Alfredo was saying nothing up to this point.

'I understand what my learned friend is saying - and just to be clear - we will of course comply with what Cortes is proposing. We will meet and make the exchange. But with one difference. It will be on our terms.' Julia's silence could be heard by all in the small dining room. Alfredo touched her lightly on the arm.

'There is a risk, but I believe the risks are greater, not only to Adam and Cristina but to ourselves if we do nothing. We need to nip this cancer in the bud, to end all of this once and for all.' He spread his arms out wide. 'And then Colonel Salas can have his day in court. He has a great deal to answer for, not least the games he and his men have been playing with us.' He looked around the room. 'We shall continue this conversation back at the house.' He looked at his watch. 'Patricia and Elizabeth should arrive an hour or so after us, so the house will be empty when we get there. Another reason for us to be cautious. Manuel is ready to direct us to the landing spot. Pepe you lead on, and Antonio and I will catch you up. I have a few things to sort out with Laura.'

***

The somewhat grand-sounding *helicopter landing place* turned out to be a large, deserted school playing field which had clearly seen better days. Manuel pointed to the centre circle of the football pitch.

'I used to play soccer here, but now they're more interested in watching the game on their phones,' he smiled ruefully. 'He'll put it down here,' he said pointing to a faint chalk mark.

They were standing in a small semi-circle as they watched the helicopter land. Hugh had never flown in such a thing and for a moment he wondered if they'd all squeeze in. Emilio-Jesus was older than he expected, tufts of grey hair poking out from beneath a red and white baseball cap. He jumped down and gave Manuel a huge hug.

'Good morning, all,' he said quickly.

He looked about for Alfredo, laughing when he saw him running towards them. He was carrying a rucksack on his back and had a large pink box in one hand. As he drew closer, he slowed to a more dignified walk.

'Laura insisted I carry a cool box, even though I assured her we'd be home before noon and could eat then but you know how it is....'

The pilot shook his hand.

'Indeed, we do, but from my point of view anything that reduces your waistline, and the weight of this aircraft has to be a good thing!'

He guided them to their seats pointing out where each of their packs was to be stowed. Alfredo called out to Manuel who was standing as close as he could to the helicopter.

'You know what to do about the boat, Manuel. If you run into any difficulty, call me or talk with Antonio.' Manuel nodded and raised a hand. They climbed up rapidly, the helicopter turning sharply as they made their way to the river. Pepe was sitting next to Emilio-Jesus and nodding as he explained the route home. 'He says we're basically going to retrace our journey here. If we keep a good look out on the right, we'll soon see the rapids below, then Sanatirino, and then we'll begin our descent towards Ivochote and the house. If you remember the landing spot, it is just beyond the boathouse.'

Occasionally the helicopter lurched from one side to the other. *God! I hope it doesn't end here,* Hugh thought, looking across at Julia who seemed unperturbed. Below he could see the *Pongo de Mainique*, the river rising and falling as it smashed into the granite rocks, white flecks of foam visible as the water screamed and swirled. The noise of the aircraft drowned out any attempts at conversation. He continued to gaze down at the meandering brown snake of a river. Julia tapped him on the arm and pointed to the left-hand side.

They were losing height and he could make out the rear of the house, even the rose garden and the line of eucalyptus. They circled to the left of the property, the boat house and landing place just beyond coming clearly into view. On his right he could see some of the front of the property. Half-way up the drive, the battered brown sedan had skidded to a halt, its right-hand front and rear wheels sunk into the lawn. There was no sign of movement from the car or the house. The helicopter lurched left and right before it settled down.

'Bravo, Emilio-Jesus! *Muchas gracias, senor!*' Alfredo said, as they clambered out of the craft. 'Please accompany us, my friend, at least until we've made sure all is well inside and more important, we've offered you something to eat.'

They walked towards the boathouse where he raised a hand.

'As Patricia knows, I am one who likes to be cautious. Though I'm sure whoever drove the sedan here has long gone. May I suggest, I, Emilio-Jesus and Antonio enter the house by the back entrance whilst Hugh and Pepe take a closer look at the car. Once I've given the all-clear from the house, you do the same Pepe from the car, and we can take it from there.'

As the three men walked slowly towards the kitchen door, he and Pepe made their way around the left of the house to where the car had come to a sudden stop. He followed just behind Pepe who motioned him to approach the vehicle from the passenger side. He noticed Pepe was holding a garden fork in his right hand. Perhaps he should have picked up something too.

They both stopped a few yards in front of the car. Pepe saw them first. The driver and the passenger next to him were sitting bolt upright, both looking straight ahead. Neither was moving. Pepe moved quickly to the driver's side. Both side windows had been pierced by a high-velocity bullet fired at close range. The driver and his passenger looked much as they had in life, except for their startled expression, and the two neat entry and exit holes on each side of their heads.

***

Forty

They assembled in the living room. Julia set out a tray of home-made lemonade and oatcakes.

Alfredo was standing by the main door, talking rapidly into his phone. 'Freddy has just called to say our two lovely women will be with us soon.'

Emilio-Jesus glanced at his watch.

Alfredo interrupted him, '...but you must go? I understand, Emilio-Jesus, and you've helped us a great deal. Thank you.'

'Yes, I've got an early pick-up tomorrow and will need to run all the checks on the bird later today.' Alfredo nodded towards the pilot.

'You know we don't need to ask you to stay, Emilio-Jesus. Work calls and we women know what that means.' Julia raised her hands in a mock salute.

'Thank you, but I need to get back.' He turned to Alfredo. 'And to be clear, judge, I'll keep quiet about what's occurred here until you tell me otherwise.'

'Thank you again, E-J. Rest assured you can leave us to contact the relevant authorities about the death of these two men. We know what has to be done. We'll talk later.'

He embraced Julia and formally shook the hand of Alfredo, Pepe, and Antonio.

'Senor Hugh, I wish you well in the safe return of your son. May God give you his blessing.' He gave a slight bow and extended his hand.

'I'll walk with you to the helicopter, Emilio,' said Alfredo.

At the helicopter, the two men shook hands. 'And I'll hear nothing about costs, Alfredo. This is for all you've done for me.' He waved him off and walked slowly back to the house. The brown sedan had tilted further during the night, rain softening the earth on the passenger side. He walked quickly to the driver's door. The tilting had caused the driver's body to fall sideways onto his passenger, his head resting on the other man's shoulder. It was almost as if they were asleep. Alfredo wrapped a handkerchief around his right hand and opened the door. A miasma of flies circulated around the heads of the two men.

The judge pulled the driver into an upright position. He knew what he was looking for and found it inside his inside coat pocket, an old brown leather wallet. With any luck his passenger would keep his in the same place. He closed the door and moved round to the passenger side. Nothing in his pockets, nothing in the glove compartment. Looking down at the man's lap he saw a cheap cotton wallet. It must have fallen into the footwell when the shooting started. He closed the door quietly. *No need to wake the dead* he said as he walked back towards the house. But he had what he wanted. Julia greeted him as he entered the living room.

'It's so awful, those two men out there, killed in that way. No-one, whatever crimes they might have committed, deserves to die like that.' She turned her head away. In a corner of the room, Antonio was speaking in a low voice into his phone.

'That was Ana. She's fine, but she says word has got round about the killing of Salazar. The local police have cordoned off the hotel but as far as she knows, nobody knows anything about the car here.'

'You should go home, Antonio. We can make plans and talk to you later.'

Alfredo had settled himself on the sofa.

'Friends, on my way back from seeing Emilio-Jesus off, I decided to take a cursory look at our unfortunate friends outside. And I found these.' He held up two credit card sized plastic cards. 'Hugh, these two things, are what we

Peruvians never leave home without: our *Documento Nacional de Identidad* or DNI.' He handed the two cards to Pepe. 'We inherited from our Spanish colonial masters a desire to keep very strong tabs on our potentially rebellious citizens hence the identity cards here which in this case tells us a great deal about who these unfortunates are, and more importantly where they were born, date of birth etc.' Pepe handed the cards to Julia. 'And in case any of you might be worried about my prints being left on these cards, as you all can attest, I have the perfect alibi once it is established when our two friends met their untimely demise.'

Pepe turned to the judge. 'You might not try to sound quite so jolly about it all, Alfredo.'

Antonio stood up. 'Senor Alfredo, I will go. There will be much to do so please call me if I can be of any help.'

'Indeed, please give my best regards to Ana. We will discuss what is to be done and let you know if we need your help.' Julia returned the cards to the judge.

'So, Julia and Hugh. The driver's ID tells us he is one Ricardo Flores. If I am not mistaken the owner of the *El Flamenco* bar, not so?'

Julia picked up the two cards again and looked closely at the photographs.

'Yes, it's him. And the other? I don't recognise him from his name or photo.'

'Marco Alverez. Have you seen him before, Hugh?' He passed the ID to Hugh.

'I don't think so. Maybe the hitman who killed Salazar?'

'Yes, I was thinking along the same lines,' said Alfredo. 'I am guessing they killed Salazar and then came here most likely to do the same to me, or possibly you, Hugh.'

'And they in turn were killed. By Cortes?' said Julia.

'Again, a likely train of events.' He paused and put the fingertips of each hand together. 'My take on all this is that Cortes was probably at the hotel when Salazar was killed – upstairs perhaps – and after the killing he – driven by Nicholas – followed Marco and Ricardo here. Once it was clear we were out, he used the opportunity to do a little payback on the death of Salazar.'

Julia moved over to where Hugh was sitting. 'So, Alfredo and Pepe, we have a link between Adam and Hugh and the death of these men?'

'We do indeed, Julia,' said Pepe. '*El Flamenco* in Ayacucho. We know that Hugh visited, possibly Adam too. We can also surmise that Ricardo and Marco killed Salazar and were on their way to kill either me or Hugh. Why – we can't be certain – but I would put my money on a cocaine turf war...'

'And the possibility Adam unearthed something?' said Julia.

'Yes, it has to be important enough to both sides to justify the killings...' He scratched his head. 'But let's not lose sight of the fact that what is most important to Salas is that I am removed before his case comes to trial. The turf war between the *sendero* cartel and Salas is important but of secondary concern.' He sat for a moment and looked out towards the battered sedan. 'Unless of course, the two things are connected...'

'What do you mean?' said Julia.

'That what connects the two is Adam.' She put her hand on Hugh's arm.

'Alfredo, it seems we must do two things. First, we must decide what we do about these two unfortunates, and second, I think I should call Cortes and set up the meeting he has asked for.'

Alfredo placed both his large hands on the table.

'Wait, that sounds like Freddy's car.'

Patricia and Elizabeth entered carrying bags and two large bunches of flowers. Alfredo rose and greeted them.

'The brown sedan outside?' said Patricia.

'I'm glad you didn't stop to look inside. It's not a pretty sight. Please go and freshen up and when you're ready, I'll tell you our news.'

'To address your question, Julia, first we must notify the local police and then we need to arrange the meeting as planned.' He paused and looked directly at Hugh. 'My worry is that once we have notified the police, any opportunity to meet with Cortes will be lost. Our police are particularly thorough when it comes to dragging their heels and requiring everybody to sit tight and do nothing...' He smiled and rubbed his hands together. 'Of course, an alternative is for Antonio to report the deaths of Ricardo and Marco early tomorrow morning, by which time we will be well on our way to our rendezvous.'

'Earlier you said it would be on our terms, Alfredo?'

'I did, Julia, and I am exercising my somewhat tired mind on that problem.' He stood and walked over to the door. 'I suggest, we leave these two unfortunates where they are until the early morning when Antonio can call the police telling them something about coming over to work on the garden, finding the car and the bodies inside, etcetera.' He turned to Julia. 'Yes, I think you should call Cortes, tell him your elderly aunt has now sadly died and you are returning to Lima very soon. Tell him the meeting must happen as soon as possible. I'm sure he'll respond.'

'And your plan for the exchange?'

'Rest assured I have a plan, but first let's hear what Major Cortes has to say about *his* plan.'

She put the phone on loudspeaker.

'I had to call you, Major, as I must return as soon as possible to attend the funeral of my aunt.'

'I am sorry to learn of that. My condolences.'

There was a pause.

'I apologise for my tardiness in calling you as I promised but events are moving fast...'

'Yes, the same for me...'

'So, let me be brief and let me be clear. We are willing to meet you and Senor Alfredo by the Inca statue in the centre of the main plaza in Cusco. This should take place tomorrow at six pm sharp. I will be accompanied by Senor Adam and his friend Senora Cristina. It is always busy with tourists and the like, which will suit our purposes very well.'

'Which are, Major?'

'A simple exchange. Senor Alfredo will join me, and we will walk back to my car which will be parked some metres away. You will return to your vehicle with the young English journalist and his lady friend.'

'And that will be that?'

'A good question, senora. I can give you my word that no harm will come to you or your family or Senor Wilson, who I am sure is listening in to this conversation. The recent unfortunate incidents involving our associates and those of a rival business organisation are of no consequence to him – or I would suggest to you.' He paused and uttered a quiet laugh. 'And, of course, Senora Julia, it is of the utmost importance to the welfare of the young Englishman and his friend that you are not accompanied by any members of our marvellous security services. Do I make myself clear?'

'I understand, Major. I will see you tomorrow.' The call ended. Alfredo raised a thumb.

'Well done, Julia. What I think you English would say as *cool as a cucumber*, not so?'

He got up from the sofa and moved towards the kitchen.

'We should eat. I will call Antonio later and explain our plans for tomorrow. I have an idea about what we will do tomorrow, but for my brain to work I need to eat some of Patricia's sublime cooking and to take a glass or two of my very special wine, reserved for occasions such as this.' He suddenly looked serious. 'At breakfast I will set out what we will do. And more importantly, achieve.'

'I'll help,' said Elizabeth. She stood and turned to Julia. 'You stay and keep Hugh company, Julia; I'll join Patricia in the kitchen and push Alfredo out. He thinks he can cook but he can't.' She laughed. 'I'll send him in with the wine, just a couple of glasses mind.'

Alfredo poured out three glasses of red wine. They raised their glasses. 'To our success tomorrow,' he said.

Hugh raised his glass, glancing at Julia as he did so. *Perhaps, tomorrow I will meet Adam*, he thought. And then what? *He reappears and we return to some kind of relationship?*

'You look worried, Hugh?' she said.

He put his glass down. Alfredo had wandered over to the window to make a call.

'Oh, just thinking about Adam and what happens after we meet.'

'I was thinking of that too. And, about Martin, and whether I will ever know where he is given that Cortes has shown his true hand.'

He reached over and took her hand.

'That is the question you must ask Cortes tomorrow before the exchange is made.'

He squeezed her hand. She gently removed his hand from hers.

'I am sure Alfredo has considered these things.'

'Yes, I am sure he has.'

He took a sip from his glass and put it on the table. And what was the question he had to ask Adam when, and if, they met? *Why did you disappear?* Or perhaps, *can you forgive me for being the one who disappeared from your life?* He looked over at Julia. And importantly, what would Adam make of her? A betrayal of his mother? Julia was looking back at him, as if expecting an answer.

'The glass is always half-full, Julia.'

She placed her glass next to his. She had drunk hardly any of the wine.

'It is, Hugh. It is.'

They sat for a moment saying nothing. The only sounds from outside were the gentle patter of the rain on the roof and the hollow, monotonous call of a nightjar.

***

Forty-One

S ince he had arrived in the country Hugh had been waking at dawn. Whether it was the birds or the sunlight that seemed brighter than at home, he couldn't be sure, but he was certain it would be one of the things he'd carry home with him. Being an early riser. They were leaving at six, but he felt refreshed, energised at the thought of the day ahead. During the night, as he had lain and listened to the gentle rain outside, he had resolved to return home whatever happened in Cusco. He would buy a flight to Lima and then on to London. He got up and walked over to the window. The line of eucalyptus was swaying slightly in the wind. For a moment he half-expected to see the old woman in the long brown dress beckoning to him, but he could make out nothing, just the rain and the distant sound of the river.

He'd go home, back to his house not far from the university, back to his garden with its unattended vegetable plot, back to his study with its shelves lined with books he would never read again, back to a cold, unwelcoming house that had once been a home. He had to laugh. As Sarah might have said, *when it comes to beating yourself up, Hugh, you're quite the real deal*.

He moved back from the window and began to pack his few clothes and belongings into his suitcase. He shook his head. *Maudlin thoughts won't be of any benefit to anyone*. He next thought of Julia. How did she fit into his plans?

Perhaps you should ask her, Mister repressed Englishman? Perhaps he should. *Ah, but then you'd be worried she might say 'no' and then what would you do?*

He finished packing and took his case down to the living room. Alfredo and Patricia were deep in conversation, his voice a soft growl, hers as light as a bird.

'Ah, good morning, Hugh, I hope you slept well. Grab a coffee and a pancake. We leave in twenty minutes.'

'I did, thank you, Alfredo.'

He helped himself to coffee and pancakes. Patricia had put out jars of her homemade honey and jam. Alfredo joined him at the table, loading his pancakes with honey and cream.

'Diabetes, obesity and cholesterol – my three constant companions.'

Patricia laughed.

'Well, perhaps you should change to a new set of friends?'

He waved a dismissive hand in her direction, and moved to the small kitchen table.

'So, you have a plan?' said Hugh.

'I do, but there are still a few fine details that need to be confirmed...'

Patricia interrupted.

'...Hugh, he tells me he is going ahead with the exchange but with back-up.'

Alfredo stopped eating for a moment and looked at his wife.

'Yes, what I propose – and I will elaborate when the others come down – is that we do indeed proceed with the exchange – we have no choice of course – but with sufficient back-up to ensure the outcome is in our favour and not theirs.'

'And in case you are wondering, Hugh, he won't tell me what this *back-up* involves...'

'You can be assured, my dear wife, that it will be robust and effective, of that, I am sure.' Antonio had arrived and had been briefed on his role: he would call the local police; explain how he had found the brown sedan, and that everyone else was away. 'And tell whoever is in charge, Antonio, that when I return, I will come to the station and help in any way I can.'

Freddy and Pedro backed the two cars out of the covered parking place. Alfredo, Pepe, and Patricia would travel in one car, Hugh, Julia and Elizabeth in the other. Hugh carried his case down and handed it to Freddy. Slowly the two drivers reversed the cars out. No-one ventured near the brown sedan or tried to imagine the insect feast within.

They decided not to drive in convoy but to meet at a roadside stopping point three hours into the journey. Then there would be a solid five hours of driving before they reached Ollantaytambo which was an hour or so before Cusco. With any luck they'd make the deadline with time to spare. Elizabeth climbed into the front passenger seat.

'Julia is bringing a couple of cushions from the house, Hugh, which will help when we hit a pothole or two.'

They soon joined the main 28B that led directly to Cusco. It was early and there was little traffic. As they sped away from Kiteni, he thought of Alfredo's plan outlined before they set off. He would make the exchange as planned. At the statue, Adam – and hopefully Cristina – would accompany Julia back to the car. Alfredo would then walk away with Cortes. They had all stared at him as he had told them of his plan.

'But then my back-up will intervene,' said Alfredo, infuriating Patricia when he refused to elaborate on who or what the back-up involved, and more importantly how they would *intervene*.

'They will call in an hour or so and then we'll know more,' was all he would say. To Hugh it seemed he was relishing the cloak and dagger of it all, something that exasperated his wife even more. After an hour, Julia, who had been staring out of her window, turned to him.

'Assuming it all goes to plan, and you meet Adam, what next, Hugh?'

'A lot will depend on what he tells me of his plans...' He paused. '...But I'm thinking of catching a flight to Lima and then on to England...'

'You *were* going to tell me?'

'Yes, of course. On the journey...' He hesitated. 'I've was waiting to tell you because I'm not sure in my own mind if it's the right thing to do.'

'I'm not sure if it it's about right or wrong,' she said softly.

'Shouldn't you be guided by your heart?' She moved closer to him 'And what does your heart tell you to do, senor?'

He took a deep breath and took her left hand in his.

'It tells me that whatever happens today, I want to be with you, Julia. Of that I am certain.'

She kissed him lightly on the cheek.

'Well, if that is your plan, then I would ask you to delay any idea of a flight home, at least until I have heard from Cortes the precise location of where Martin fell.'

He released her hand but stayed looking into her face. For the first time he noticed her left eye was a lighter shade of brown than the other.

'You have my word on that, Julia.'

For the remainder of the journey, they sat together. Every once in a while, they turned and looked at each other. If he smiled, she would look away. But something had changed between them, an invisible line had been crossed, some sort of pact had been entered into.

They arrived in the noble city of Cusco late afternoon. During a rest stop in Ollantaytambo Alfredo would only say that everything was arranged. The back-up – whoever they were – was in place. He also brought them up to date on events back at the house.

'I take back what I said about the speed and efficiency of our local police,' said Alfredo. 'It seems someone higher up has decided that the killing of Salazar is a priority. On hearing Antonio describe the sedan, they arrived within the hour followed by an ambulance which has taken the two bodies to the local morgue. Curiously, they seemed to be uninterested in where the owners of the house might be, telling Antonio – who gave them my number – that they would be in touch in due course. Suffice to say, I've heard nothing.'

Freddy parked the car within walking distance of the square. Within minutes Pedro pulled up behind. They assembled at the designated corner of the square. A few tourists were walking around the statue of the Inca in the centre. There was no sign of Cortes. Alfredo checked his watch. They were early by ten minutes. He smiled and looked up towards the heavens. At first Hugh could only see a rolling bank of rain clouds, an occasional shaft of sunlight breaking through.

'There, look Hugh, coming through the clouds,' said Julia. At first all he could see was just a smudge of red and white. Then it became distinct and familiar. A helicopter.

***

Forty-Two

I t was Julia who saw him first, striding out from one of the cafes that line the square, walking towards the statue of the Inka Pachacuti.

'It's Cortes,' she said in a low whisper.

When he reached the statue, he stopped and looked around, then lit a cigarette. Alfredo pulled Julia to one side.

'We will wait for the bell to ring on the hour, and then we go.'

Elizabeth pulled on her husband's sleeve.

'Is the helicopter your back-up, Alfredo? What good can that do?'

He stepped back and faced his wife.

'Look beyond the statue to the other side of the square. You see those four men standing in a small group?' They looked beyond where Cortes was standing. Four men were now standing in a semi-circle facing the statue. 'My friends from DIRCOTE, the special intelligence unit and all armed with 9mm lugers in case you are interested. I spoke with their commander late last night – called in a favour – and, well, here we are, back-up in front of us!'

He laughed.

'And the helicopter?'

'I'm surprised you don't recognise it, considering you travelled in it yesterday,' he said with a chuckle. 'Emilio-Jesus is in direct contact with the men in the square and just to be on the safe side, a further squad is waiting just out of sight of the café where Major Cortes took his lunch.' He rubbed his hands together. 'But we have a more immediate problem. Look.'

Cortes had reached the statue as the cathedral bell tolled three times. Alone.

'No Adam or Cristina. Perhaps he's caught sight of the helicopter or the four heavies over there. Whatever, I fear Major Cortes is about to betray his side of the deal.'

Julia moved back until she was level with Hugh.

'I'm sorry, Hugh, I'm so very sorry.' She then stepped forward and spoke quickly to Alfredo. 'I will go and speak with him, Alfredo. For all he knows we, too, have betrayed our side of the bargain.'

Pepe was training a pair of binoculars on the statue.

'I think Julia is right. The back-up will protect her, and we need to know why Cortes has showed up without Adam and Cristina, and what he intends to do now.' He turned to Alfredo. 'And we need to know about Martin and his whereabouts.'

Pepe glanced at Alfredo. Both knew it was futile to object. Julia walked slowly towards the major. As she approached, he dropped his cigarette and ground it under his foot. It was early evening, and the square was practically empty, the advancing rainclouds deterring tourists and locals from venturing out. The squad of four security agents shuffled closer, one detaching himself from the group and strolling towards the statue. Julia was a good twelve inches shorter than the major and he bent his head towards her as they spoke. They talked for about ten minutes before shaking hands. Hugh watched as she turned and walked back towards them. Cortes remained where he was, occasionally glancing towards the four men on his left who had inched nearer.

Julia walked quickly back to their corner of the square. Alfredo started to speak.

'Please, let me talk first, Alfredo.' He nodded. 'First of all, he wants to say that Adam and Cristina are safe and sound, and about to leave Colonel Salas's house which is about ten kilometres from here. One of his drivers is taking them to the airport in Cusco. They have a connecting flight to the UK. It has all been arranged.'

Pedro interjected.

'He's a rat...we would never have handed you over, Alfredo.'

'Thank you, Pedro, but please continue, Julia,' said Alfredo.

'I asked what he wanted, why he had agreed to the exchange and why he had now changed his mind.'

'Rats never change their mind...'

She patted Pedro's hand.

'Thank you, Pedro. I agree they don't, but he then told me that he intends to honour his side of the bargain...'

'Which is?' said Alfredo.

'To accompany us and show me where Martin was killed. He says he died on the banks of the Urubamba. It is between here and Ivochote. He must assume we are returning to your place, Alfredo. And after that he says he is more than willing to turn himself in. It seems he really has had a change of heart.'

'Well, I am sure the police will be interested in talking to him about many things, not least the murder of Ricardo and Marco,' said Pepe. They looked at Cortes who was staring in their direction.

Julia said, 'We need to decide quickly.'

'And what about Salas?' said Alfredo.

'It seems your nemesis has had a change of heart. If we are to believe Cortes, he is now on his way to Tel Aviv...'

'Tel Aviv?' said Pepe unable to disguise a note of incredulity. Alfredo slapped his thigh.

'Israel, one of the few counties that has no extradition treaty with ours.' He paused. 'It looks like I won't have my day in court after all, but if we are to believe – and trust –

Major Cortes – we should receive good news of Adam and Cristina soon, and then you, Julia, will learn the truth about Martin.'

They watched as she walked back towards the gilded statue of the Inca, Pachakuti. For a moment both Cortes and Julia looked up towards the helicopter that had descended towards the square. Alfredo was speaking rapidly into his phone.

'I've told the boys to wait until we have Cortes here and can vouchsafe for his intentions. They are in direct communication with Emilio-Jesus.' As if on cue, Cortes moved in their direction. He seemed genuinely surprised to see Alfredo.

'Ah, *senor*, so you *were* willing to make the exchange. I salute your bravery and principles.'

'Before I salute yours, Major, I must ask you to guarantee the safety of Adam and Cristina.'

The major reached into his pocket and withdrew his phone.

'They are both on their way to Lima right now. They have tickets for tonight's flight to Madrid where they can make the connection to Heathrow.' He punched a number into the phone and handed it to Alfredo. 'Cristina, senor.' Alfredo spoke quickly and then returned the phone.

'Thank you. She says they are both safe and well and about to check-in at the airport here in Cusco.' Hugh interrupted.

'And Adam? What did he say? Is he willing to talk to me?' Alfredo gently placed a hand on his sleeve.

'I asked Cristina if you could speak with him, Hugh, and she said he was tired but would get in touch with you soon.'

'I'm sorry, *senor* Hugh,' said Cortes, 'if our actions have caused your family grief. It is not something I take any pleasure from.'

They stood together, Pedro and Freddy standing back, waiting for the prosecutor or the judge to issue their orders. Pepe was standing next to Cortes. He said something quickly to Alfredo who nodded in agreement.

'Major Cortes, we accept your offer to return with us. Before you enter the car, we will of course ask you to hand over your mobile phone and any weapon you may be carrying.' They were interrupted by the member of the narcotics squad who had followed Cortes. He nodded towards Alfredo. 'It seems that as no crime was committed here, and so they are happy for the major to accompany us to Ivochote. I have given them my personal guarantee that I will deliver Major Cortes to the appropriate authorities Naturally they will want to question him about other matters, not least the murder of the two in the car. It seems that my status as a judge still carries some weight.'

The helicopter above them hovered for a moment, and then rose higher, turning away from the square. Cortes, Pepe, and Alfredo would travel in the lead car with the three women and Hugh following closely behind. As they approached the two cars, Cortes turned to Julia.

'Colonel Salas is not quite who you think he is, senora. Indeed, our plan was to exchange the young journalist and his friend – who happens to be the granddaughter of Colonel Salas – for the judge, but on reflection we considered the likelihood of you arriving with some kind of support was very likely; and so, he decided this morning to cut his losses...'

'We wouldn't have handed over Alfredo without sight of Adam and Cristina you know.'

A small smile played around his lips.

'Of course...' He hesitated. 'I can only speak for myself, but I have come to the conclusion – some time ago - that violence solves very little in this country, a conclusion that may seem strange coming from a military man...'

'By coming here, you were hardly cutting *your* losses?'

'Colonel Salas would no doubt disagree, but for me, my reason for coming here was to salvage…what?' He looked around. 'A semblance of honour perhaps or some form of redemption? I made a promise to you, senora, which I intend to keep. After that, I am quite happy to face the consequences of my past shortcomings…' He paused and looked directly at Julia '…and not before time.'

***

Forty-Three

Hugh sat up front with Freddy.

'We three sisters will be able to speak Spanish at the back,' said Julia, adding with a laugh, 'and knowing you won't understand a word.' He waved a hand in mock protest. With any luck he might manage a doze before they reached their destination. Freddy had told him it should take about four hours to reach Quillabamba and then another thirty minutes or so to find the place where Martin was killed. He stretched his legs out and lay back in his seat. Behind he could hear Julia talking in her light, high voice, the other two women laughing at whatever she was saying.

She was clearly in good spirits, the impending visit to where Martin died not plunging her into gloom. *But what do I know of how I would feel if faced with the same challenge*, he thought? In the West, friends would have talked about *closure* and needing to move on. He had heard such sentiments after Sarah's death, and had allowed them to wash over him. *Closure*? He would have liked to reply, *but what is there to close? My grief, our lives together, the future*? Whatever, he was sure of one thing. He would share his future with the remarkable woman sitting behind him. But it was one thing committing yourself to one person, quite another for them to feel the same way. He'd been lucky with Sarah. Could he be lucky a second time? Was it too soon? He closed his eyes. His mother used to say, *Let the future take care of itself*. For once he agreed with her.

He turned his thoughts to Adam and his rejection of the opportunity to talk. If he wanted to be kind to himself, he could summon up any number of reasons – he was tired, the ordeal of being held by Salas and his men, he had a plane to catch? No, he was convinced his refusal pre-dated Peru and everything that had happened here. It was bound up with Sarah's death and a realisation that the surviving parent – his father – was in some way responsible for the grief he now felt. Hadn't someone once said, grief is a thing with feathers? Either a small sparrow crushed by the gale swirling around it or the brent geese steering their own path to their nesting grounds high above the Norfolk marshes. Adam wanted to be detached. If that was the case then he had to respect that, acknowledge the anger his son seemed to harbour towards him. He looked out of the window. Adam's disappearance had clearly been a matter of choice. He had not *been disappeared*. Far from it, he had simply moved away, which meant it was quite possible that when he and Cristina arrived in England he would do so again. If that happened, and he took to trying to find him again, all would be lost. No, if Adam wanted to reconnect it would have to be on his own terms and at a time and place of his own choosing.

The three women had stopped talking. Freddy turned to Hugh.

'Kenny Rogers, OK with you, senor?'

He nodded.

Soon the slow seductive voice of the country and western singer began crooning, *Make no mistake, she's mine.*

Right. *Make no mistake, she's mine.* Absolutely, Kenny, absolutely.

***

The clash of gears woke him. Freddy was manoeuvring the car slowly up a narrow, boulder-strewn track. Hugh could see the other car parked beneath a tall tree. Cortes was leaning against the boot smoking a cigarette. They parked up close and got out. Julia took the hands of Elizabeth and Patricia and walked slowly to where Cortes was standing. He stubbed out his cigarette and stood before the three women. For a moment no one spoke. Pepe and Alfredo stood together; the two drivers sitting in their cars. Cortes broke the silence. He raised a hand and pointed a few metres up the track.

'Fifty metres or so is the river.' He walked around the car and stopped. Julia stayed where she was. The major crouched down and drew a cross in the dirt. He looked up in the direction of Julia. 'It is here, senora, here is the place where your husband was killed. This is the place. He bent down on his haunches and drew a cross in the sand with his finger.

Julia released her hands from Elizabeth and Patricia, and walked slowly to where Cortes was kneeling. She stopped and looked down.

'You are certain, this is the place?'

'I am certain. Corporal Nicholas Mendez – the old waiter at the hotel - was leading the men in a line along the track here. Another soldier, I forget his name, was following behind with myself.' He rose from where he was crouching. 'I ordered the prisoners to stop and then kneel.' He paused and looked at Julia. 'I remember two of them began to recite a prayer, but your husband said nothing, he just raised his eyes to the sky.'

'And what happened next Major, what happened next?' she said quietly.

'I motioned to one of my men, Panco, who moved quickly behind each man and shot them here, just behind the right ear. At most it took two minutes, and they were dead.'

'And then, Major?'

'Then, I ordered the bodies to be thrown into the river. He walked a little further up the track. 'If you wish, I can show you the place?' Julia crouched down and traced a finger around the cross. She scooped up a handful of dust and put it into the pocket of her skirt. 'Thank you, Major, but I have no need to see the river. What matters is to be here and to know this was the place where Matin died.' Cortes was about to say something but stopped. 'Our agreement was that in exchange for bringing me here, I would grant you some kind of redemption,' she said, 'Which from a personal point of view I can offer you, but there is something else that lies beyond me...' She stopped and looked towards Pepe and Alfredo. '...and that is what these two gentlemen spend their lives doing, namely the administration of justice and the punishment of those found guilty in a court of law.' She turned back to Cortes and raised her voice. 'Something you and your kind denied those you abducted and disappeared.'

Cortes said nothing. Pepe walked towards Julia and the major.

'She is right, Major, and let us not forget the prisoners who were murdered along with Martin, and of course the two men shot in the brown sedan.'

Cortes lit a cigarette. He took a lungful of smoke into his lungs and then exhaled it into the air.

'I must agree. And as I said, I am resigned to my fate.' He smiled at Pepe. 'And while we are on the subject of the administration of justice, I wonder if either of you gentlemen know of an advocate who might represent me, I would be most grateful.'

Pepe said nothing, but as they walked towards the car, he turned to Cortes.

'You will, of course be represented, Major, have no fear, but I am afraid I cannot help you on that score.'

Julia stood for a moment, her eyes staring down at the faint cross in the sand. When she was ready, the two women walked with her to their car. Hugh stood by the door. As she moved to climb in, she turned and gave him a kiss on his cheek.

'Thank you, Hugh,' she said softly.

The first shot ricocheted off the bonnet of Freddy's car, the second hit the ground in front of Alfredo. Walking slowly towards them from a line of trees to the right of the track came a tall, immaculately dressed man. Hugh recognised him immediately.

'Well, aren't you going to introduce me to your friends, Mister Wilson? And there's me thinking the English were possessed of good manners...'

Alfredo interrupted. '...Introductions are not necessary, Colonel Salas, we all are perfectly aware of who you are, just a little surprised at meeting you here, given that the major here had assured us you were well on your way to Tel Aviv.'

'Indeed, I will be but not until I have tied up one or two loose ends here. In case you are wondering my car is waiting just beyond the line of trees.' He paused. 'Once Major Cortes had confided in me his intention of meeting Julia here, I reasoned she would not attend alone. With any luck, I would then have the pleasure of meeting the honourable Superior Court judge, the thorn in my side.' He took a step towards Alfredo. 'It seems I have two courses of action. The first is that I persuade the judge to accompany me through the trees to my car where I can conclude our relationship. You, friends, would remain here for thirty minutes allowing me sufficient time to continue to my next destination...' He smiled.

'...And the alternative course of action? said Alfredo

'Well, a more radical and distasteful one in which I eliminate all of you and then dispose of your remains in the same manner as your late husband, Julia.' He raised his gun. 'Oh, and in case you were thinking, he has fired two rounds leaving only four, this trusty revolver is a .38 Magnum that holds eight rounds, quite sufficient to the task at hand ...'

Alfredo raised a hand. 'May I suggest a third option, Colonel, and one that would enable you to resume your flight out of the country but would leave us unharmed. I realise that abducting and killing me – let's not mince words – provides you with some sort of vengeance but you would leave behind a group of witnesses; something the state of Israel may take into consideration irrespective of current extradition arrangements. No state likes to have a murderer living amongst them. And, as for killing all of us, I don't think you are willing to go that far, a once-decorated veteran who does I believe still hold dear some notion of honour.' The judge took a step closer to the colonel. 'There is also the matter of your granddaughter and the close relationship we understand she has with Hugh Wilson's son. Are you really willing to let Cristina discover you murdered her friend?'

Salas bowed slightly, 'Splendid, judge, splendid, the kind of speech I expected from you. I am indeed a man of honour.' No one moved. A bright moon lit up the path to the river. 'Vengeance indeed can wait for another day, and I am persuaded by your suggestion concerning the love and regard I have for Cristina. I will now return to my car, and you will all remain here for thirty minutes, after which you may return home.'

With that he bowed once more, kept the gun trained on them, and walked briskly towards the trees and darkness.

'We do exactly as he says,' said Alfredo. They then moved towards the cars. Cortes said nothing, grinding a cigarette into the dust. 'May I suggest we talk about all this together later,' said Alfredo. 'We need to get home. It's been a long day and I am sure all our condolences are with Julia.'

The two cars moved slowly back towards the highway. Hugh thought not of Salas, but of Julia and the handful of dust in her pocket. *Was it enough for her to see the place? And after so long?*

He hoped so. Perhaps that is all you can ever ask for. *Enough.*

***

Forty-Four

N o-one felt like eating when they stopped for a break. Pedro volunteered to buy some food to take out. Only Cortes seemed happy to get out and stretch his legs. While they waited for Pedro to return with the food, he lent against the rear door of the car smoking. Hugh took the opportunity to look at him. *I wouldn't want to be in his shoes*, he thought, *if a long prison sentence doesn't kill him, the cigarettes will.*

Antonio was waiting for them when they arrived home. Everything looked much the same, apart from the brown sedan which had gone. Two deep tyre tracks in the mud were all that remained.

'The ambulance came first and took away the bodies and shortly after the police arrived and towed away the car,' he said as they unloaded their bags.

Alfredo ushered them all into the living room. Cortes held back as he approached the front door.

'Please enter, Major Cortes, though you won't be staying long. The bathroom is at your disposal. Then I will accompany you with Antonio to the police station. Though it is late, they are happy for me to deliver you into their custody. I will also make a short report on our meeting with Colonel Salas, though I suspect he'll be well on his way out of the country by now.'

Pedro handed Patricia the boxes of food.

'I'll wait until you return, judge, before I heat these up. Call me if it seems you'll be kept there.'

Alfredo nodded and pointed upstairs.

'The bathroom is up on your left, Major. You'll find a towel if you want to shower.'

Hugh sat on the sofa and looked around. *Wasn't expecting to see this place again.* Patricia emerged from the kitchen.

'You're back in your old room, Hugh. Give me a shout if you need anything.'

He went upstairs and dropped his bag at the foot of the bed. The room had been thoroughly cleaned. It was almost as if he had never stayed there. He walked over to the window and looked out. In the moonlight he could see the silhouette of a woman bending low near the rose garden. Was it the woman with the pale oval face in the long dark skirt? She turned, a bunch of roses in one hand. It was Julia. He showered and changed. Though it was late, nobody wanted to go to bed. Patricia was arranging the roses in a vase when he entered the living room.

'Alfredo and Antonio have left for the police station with the major.'

'How did he seem?'

'Resigned, I think. Possibly pleased it has come to this'

'Did he say anything to Julia?'

'No, she wisely went out to the garden to bring me these.' He resumed his seat on the sofa. 'Would you like a snack or a drink, Hugh?'

'Thanks, Patricia, but I'm not hungry. Maybe a drink when Alfredo returns.' She busied herself with rearranging the living room. An opportunity to ask her a question he'd been meaning to ask her since his arrival. 'Do you like living here, Patricia?'

She looked up and smiled.

'Well, it's where Alfredo enjoyed his summers as a child. His father owned the place, so it has good memories for him, but to be honest, I prefer somewhere with more a bit more life.'

'Ayacucho?'

'Yes, I had many friends during our time there, and it wasn't far to visit Elizabeth. But what about you, Hugh. Where is home for you?'

He stood up and stretched. After sitting for so long in the car, he felt he needed to get some exercise.

'I guess the family home in England, though I'm not sure I can call it that now that Sarah has gone, and Adam seems unlikely to return there...'

'...you could sell up and find a new place...?' She put the vase of roses onto the large table in the centre of the room. '...You could find somewhere here?' She paused and threw him a broad smile. 'I'm sure Julia would be delighted to welcome you as a neighbour...'

He laughed and asked if she needed any help.

'No, though you can help bring the plates and glasses in from the kitchen, if you need some exercise.' Patricia was about to suggest a drink when they heard the car drawing up outside. 'Well, you can be certain of one thing. If that's Alfredo, he'll be wanting a drink!'

She knew her husband well. Alfredo entered, took off his coat, and threw it onto the sofa.

'Where's Antonio?' said Patricia.

'I dropped him off at his place. Ana was delighted to have him back. He's going to come by tomorrow to see what needs to be done.' He looked at the tray of glasses on the table. 'I'm not sure about anyone else, but a stiff drink seems to be in order.' He rubbed his hands together, a habit Hugh now found endearing. 'There's quite a lot I need to share with you all, particularly what Cortes told us during the journey. Apologies to Pepe who's heard it all before. Where is he by the way?'

Elizabeth put her head round the kitchen door.

'I'll give him a shout. He's upstairs talking with a client who has been calling him all day. Something about bringing forward a hearing to this Friday.'

It was the early hours when they all sat around the table. Nobody wanted to eat but they all accepted a glass of wine. Pepe sat to the left of Alfredo. Pedro and Freddy had driven the cars to their respective homes, both promising to return the next day. Elizabeth and Patricia sat opposite Julia who was next to Hugh.

'Well,' said Alfredo, 'here we are all safe and sound.' He took a sip of his wine. 'First, Cortes. An old friend, Capitan Miguel from the Kiteni station was there to meet us. He took charge and said he would deliver him to Kiteni later today. There he would spend a night in the cells and be brought before a court in the next few days. Seems they have at least one witness who saw him leaving the hotel after Salazar was killed.'

Julia was sipping her wine and listening intently. 'He'll be charged with the murders of Ricardo and Marco?' she said.

'At first, yes, but then I expect if he confesses to the killing of Martin and the others, he'll be transferred to the Superior Court in Ayacucho. Or Lima.' Alfredo raised a hand in a dismissive gesture. 'You know as well as I do, Julia, that it could take weeks, months even, before a trial date is set. But the fact that he is willing to confess and enter a guilty plea should speed things up.' He topped up his glass. 'You can change that expression on your face, dear Patricia!' he said with a laugh. 'I have a lot to say and for that I need to be relaxed but sharp...'

'...but please allow a few hours for all of us to get some sleep,' she replied.

'As I said, Cortes was quite happy to spend his time in the car spilling the beans. What is clear is that Colonel Salas played a central role in all this. His major aim – if you'll excuse the pun – was to locate and silence yours truly.' He turned to Hugh. 'Apparently Salas calls me the *incorruptible judge*, which I take as a complement. Once the date was set for his trial – and it was clear I would be the chief prosecution witness – he increased his efforts to find me. Which was one of the reasons Patricia and I decided to retreat to the old family home here. Anyway, when Cristina unwittingly introduced Adam to Salas, he realised there was an opportunity for his granddaughter and this overly curious journalist to do the job for him, accompanied by Cortes and Salazar.' While he was talking, Patricia had gone into the kitchen and returned with a plate of chicken wings. 'Apparently, Adam mentioned to Salas that he also wanted to interview ex-*Sendero Luminoso* fighters now engaged in the cocaine trade. This suited Salas too who was always interested in gaining intelligence on his rivals up here in the VRAEM.'

Pepe raised a hand

'Sorry to interrupt, Judge. Salas knew that Adam and then Hugh had spoken with Jorge in the library at Huacachina and so it was likely at least one of you would meet with his sister. His thinking was that Julia would lead you to me, and I was likely to be in touch with my old law school friend, Alfredo. All roads, in other words, would lead to here. All he had to do was bide his time until Adam or his father led him to Alfredo. A clever plan, and one that kept him conveniently at arm's length.' He pushed the plate of chicken towards Alfredo. 'Of course, in the end, it was Cortes who led him to Alfredo once he knew of his plan to show Julia where Martin had been killed. Salas guessed rightly that I'd accompany her.' Pepe turned to Alfredo, 'I can understand why Sales decided not to kill all of us – as you said judge he wouldn't go that far – but what I don't understand is why he didn't abduct and kill you, leaving him free to have his day in court with no chief witness to his crimes?'

Alfredo tapped his fingers on the table. 'I think it was touch and go, but in the end his flight to Tel Aviv offered him the best chance of a new start. It will also present him with a good opportunity to transfer many of his business interests where few questions will be asked. In other words, a clean slate.'

'And Salazar and Cortes, what's their role in all this?' said Patricia.

Alfredo tore off a piece of chicken and wiped his hands on a napkin.

'They were in the employ of Salas of course. But as we know, each had their own reasons for wanting to come up here, Salazar to meet with Antonio's family and give them compensation for the *Bario Altos* killings, and Cortes to make amends, for the killing of Martin.' He turned to Julia. 'Your efforts to find Martin were well known in Ayacucho, and Cortes knew that sooner or later you would discover who was responsible for his death. I must say I believe him when he told us he had had some sort of Damascus conversion. But it put him in a very tricky situation. If he revealed to you who he was – and what he had done – he might find himself on the receiving end of Salas's ire. He needed to tread carefully, which was why he agreed to meet you at the eco-lodge.' What Pepe and Alfredo had said so far made sense, but it still left a lot of questions unanswered. 'You're deep in thought, Hugh,' said Alfredo.

'Yes, I can see what Salas and the two majors wanted to get out of all this, but what about Ricardo and Marco? What did they want?'

'It seems, from what Cortes told me, that Ricardo and Marco were leading lights in the Victor Quispe Palomino cartel – it's made up of old die-hard Shining Path *hombres* – transporting cocaine from the VRAEM across the country to Huacachina and then on into Lima where it was shipped out towards Colombia and eventually to the US.'

'Via Huacachina?' said Hugh.

'Yes – and this is where it gets interesting – do you remember when you met up with Ricardo at the *Flamingo* and he seemed to have seen you before? Well, apart from all those years ago when you visited the place with Sarah, in fact he had.'

'He had met me before?'

'Well, he thought he had, but it seems that when Ricardo visited his brother Diego in Huacachina, who runs the hostel where Adam stayed and which you visited Hugh, he must have met your son who had just lost his phone and had asked his brother if it had been found and handed in.'

He listened to Alfredo and tried to work out the sequence of events.

'So, when I turned up at *El Flamenco*, he confused me with Adam?'

'Yes, it's unlikely he remembered you from way back, but you were about the same age as Adam when you and Sarah visited, so perhaps it stirred a memory and added to the confusion?'

Julia raised a hand.

'But what links them with Adam and Hugh, apart from the hostel?'

'A good question. Cortes wasn't sure but it seems that Adam interviewed both Ricardo and Marco as part of his research. The major thinks that these interviews took place in Hucachina before Adam and Cristina came up here. Unwise of Adam but then a journalist needs a good nose for a story, and we Peruvians find it hard to resist talking about things that should remain unsaid. No doubt they also thought there might be something in it for themselves.' He looked over at Hugh. 'Not that for a moment would I suggest your son resorted to such methods,' he said with a laugh.

'Anyway, it seems that once the phone was lost – and it would appear that Adam had dropped it coming back to the hostel – it was found by Cristina who indeed handed it into reception. Of course, it was what was on the phone that was of great interest to Diego. Interviews and photographs of Ricardo and Marco. What he didn't know was that Adam had transcribed the interviews the afternoon after he recorded them, but he couldn't be sure.'

Hugh interjected. 'So, at some point Adam decided to cut off from me, before or after he lost his phone?'

'It seems so,' said Alfredo. 'Relying on a new phone to keep in touch with his office, record his interviews and presumably take photographs.' Julia touched his arm.

'To get a definitive answer to your question, Hugh, you will need to ask your son. Perhaps it is not as serious as you think. The death of your mother can produce such reactions, I am sure.' She looked around at the others. 'After Martin had been disappeared, I first accepted all the help I could get but after a few weeks I began to withdraw into myself. I am sure that if I had had a mobile phone at that time, I too would have cast it away. Grief is like a feathered bird; it can carry us to realms we have never ventured. It can also make us regret things.' She paused and stood up. 'Water or tea, anybody?'

Patricia rose and went into the kitchen with her. Alfredo stopped talking and stretched out his legs.

'It is almost dawn. Before we retire, let me finish by saying this. Once Adam had met Cristina, Diego must have realised that if he wasn't careful Adam might uncover more, digging up testimonies that would fall into the hands of Salas.'

'So, he had to silence Adam?' said Pepe.

'Not permanently but at least warn him off.'

'And his father, too, once he'd arrived in Ayacucho?' said Pepe.

'Yes, and Marco knew how to do that...'

'...by means of the *quota* notes?' said Julia.

Hugh rubbed his forehead.

'So, we have Salas searching for Alfredo and Diego and his men on the trail of Adam to make sure he keeps his mouth shut?'

'Indeed,' said Alfredo, 'and I suspect to destroy any evidence he had about the *Sendero* cartel. It seems from what Capitan Miguel told me at the station, Marco has form when it comes to eliminating rivals. He is also one of the few *Sendero* men who still believes in the concept of the *quota*. Death to the capitalist running dogs, that kind of thing.'

'And the shots fired towards the house? Was that Ricardo and Marco too?' said Patricia who had returned with water and glasses.

'Well almost certainly. Freddy caught a glimpse of the brown sedan, so we can assume it was them. I don't think they intended for anyone to get hurt. The *quota* notes had clearly had not worked, so they decided to up the ante. Poor old Freddy was what I think you might call *collateral damage.*'

Before he could say anymore, Patricia stood and announced sharply that they should all call it a day. Alfredo and Pepe remained seated.

'And that includes you two rogues,' she said loudly. 'Breakfast at ten.'

Hugh gave a small bow to Julia and Elizabeth who were standing at the foot of the stairs and went into his room. He didn't feel tired but knew that once his head hit the pillow he would be out for the count. He walked over to the window to draw the curtains. It was a clear night, the moon lighting up the garden. He opened the window to see if he could hear the river. He couldn't see anything but just as closed it something caught his eye.

Standing where she had stood before, in the gap between the line of trees, was the old woman in the dark skirt. As he watched, she crouched down and seemed to be tracing a cross on the path with her left hand. When she stood up, she raised her left hand towards the house, as if in a salute. In her left hand she was holding a small bunch of dark blue flowers.

***

Forty-Five

He looked beyond the old sewer pipe towards the distant shoreline. It was early evening, but dark storm clouds were coming in from the east giving the Norfolk saltmarshes a translucent sheen, bunches of purple sea lavender providing the only splashes of colour.

Coming towards him were two figures, dark, indistinct shapes, moving slowly across the creeks in a purposeful, almost solemn manner. They appeared to be walking side by side, but he couldn't be sure. They seemed unaware of his presence. He was distracted for a moment by the shriek of a corncrake. When he looked again, he saw a solitary figure now, a shapeless silhouette advancing and receding, appearing, and disappearing.

And then they were gone. For a moment he was certain the taller of the two was Adam, but then he had his doubts. Since his return he's heard nothing from him. Wisely, he had resisted the temptation to call Max. On good advice from Avril, he had decided to take himself off to the Norfolk marshes. At least they would provide some sense of predictability.

'What we psychologists call *processing,* Hugh,' said Avril when he'd run into her on his way to his office to pick up a dissertation he was supposed to be examining. 'Take some leave and lose yourself in the creeks of north Norfolk,' she said. 'If Adam wants to make contact you must leave it to him to make the first move. And from what you told me of his experiences I should imagine he has quite a lot of processing to do as well.'

He stuffed his hands into his windcheater pockets and turned back in the direction of the church. Julia had said she wanted to visit the place on her own and he wondered if the real reason was to visit Sarah's grave. He stopped for a moment and looked back towards the sea. There was no sign of the two figures. He went into the church and looked around. No sign of Julia either. It was cold and empty. Outside a breeze had whipped up. He walked quickly towards the churchyard and looked in the direction of the far corner where Sarah lay. At the foot of the grave, he could see a figure, pale, oval face, dark hair pulled back, her long brown skirt almost reaching the ground.

He stopped. Then she turned and raised a hand. In her other she was holding a bunch of blue flowers which she placed in the vase.

Julia. Was she the mysterious figure he had first seen on the marshes and who had dogged his footsteps in his search for Adam? A guardian angel from the future? He shook his head. She was indeed mysterious but was very much a part of the present. He returned her wave and walked towards the corner of the field.

'You look worried, Hugh?' she said with a laugh. 'I've thrown away the old flowers and put in these beautiful blue ones that are growing here. What do you call them in English?'

'Sea lavender, I think,' he said giving her a kiss on the top of her head.

She looped her arm around his and gave him a brief peck on the cheek.

'This is our twelfth day you know,' she said gaily.

'Since when, Julia?' he said as they made their way round the campsite.

'Since...' she punched him playfully on the arm, '...since your leaving party at my house, that's when.'

He slipped his hand into hers.

'Ah, now I remember. Since my reckless decision to ask you to marry me, and your even more reckless decision to accept,' she said. He wasn't sure what to say.

'And what's more my agreement to come to your wet and windy country. At least it is only a visit.'

'Well, I did warn you,' he said, 'and to be honest these marshes are not everyone's cup of tea.'

'Well, I prefer coffee. And nice and warm,' she said, gripping his hand more tightly.

They had almost reached the path that led up to the pub where they were staying.

'And to be serious for a moment, to hopefully meet up with your son. If only to tell him that in my country when two people fall in love, they fall in love with the whole family.' He said nothing, happy to just listen to her voice and feel the warmth of her hand in his. 'But I am happy I could come and see Sarah's resting place. It means a lot to me. Thank you.'

He stopped for a moment and cupped her hands around her face. 'I was with you when Cortes showed you the place where Martin fell, but there is a difference. Sarah died after a short illness, whereas Martin was disappeared and then murdered.'

'And I am at peace now that I know that Cortes will have his day in court sooner than he thinks.' She released her hand from his. 'And as for Colonel Salas, well, he showed a little of his earlier self before he allowed corruption and greed to enter his soul, and I think he'll find exile in Israel not quite the bed of roses he expects.' He said nothing. 'But the immediate task is to hope that Adam makes contact with you, and that you both can talk together. I do not want to talk out of turn, Hugh. I have never met him, but I look forward to that, if only to invite him as guest of honour at our wedding, whether it is here in your cold, damp country or back in my homeland. I hope I am not rushing things.'

He had to laugh at the woman who had given him a second chance. *You'd like her, Sarah; I know you would.* He fell in beside her as they made their way up the track to the pub.

'I hope he gets in touch too, Julia, but half of me is expecting to never see him again.' They arrived at the back door of the pub and scraped their boots on the mat. 'Let's have a quick drink and then go up to our room to change,' he said.

A narrow corridor led to a flight of stairs to the bedrooms and then on to the lounge bar and snug. They had been given his old room that looked out over the marsh. Julia patted her hair and straightened her skirt.

'You do so remind me of Martin, but fear not, I haven't fallen for a replacement. For one thing he wouldn't like this flat beer you drink here, and as for the marshes, he'd say, *where are all the people?!*'

Indeed. He didn't tell her it was the emptiness that most attracted him to the place. They walked down to the lounge bar.

'God, I hope they've lit the fire,' he said, glad of his fisherman's sweater he'd bought earlier in the day.

The lounge was empty apart from a couple sitting in the far corner nearest the fire. He was holding her hands in his across the table and they were deep in conversation. As they entered, the young man released her hands and turned to see who had come into the room. He looked at the older man with the dark-haired woman beside him, and then quickly back at the young woman sitting opposite.

'Dad?'

'Adam?'

Both men paused. Julia pushed past him quickly and walked towards the young woman.

'Cristina? *Buenos noches, como estas,*' she said quickly. They kissed each other on the cheek.

Adam seemed unsure of what to do, not helped by his father who was rooted to the spot. As men do, they walked over to the bar. Hugh looked back at the two women. If you didn't know otherwise, they might have been mother and daughter. Whatever Cristina had just said, Julia was laughing loudly. He looked quickly at his son. Adam appeared much the same even with a few days growth of stubble.

'She seems very nice, Dad,' said Adam.

'Major Cortes had mentioned you were looking for me with a Peruvian woman.'

'Are you staying here, Adam? With Cristina? It is Cristina, isn't it?'

'No, we've taken a place owned by a friend of Max's. It's in Cley-next-the-sea.' Adam looked at his father as if he was seeing him for the first time. 'We'll need to get back after a quick drink.' He ordered them each a pint of Adnams and a glass of white wine for the two women which they carried back to the table. 'White wine. What Mum always had,' he said to his father.

'Yes, it was her favourite.' He turned to his father and touched him gently on the arm. 'We're staying a couple of days. I need to get back into the office and write that article. Pulitzer Prize stuff you know...' He paused and scratched his nose. 'Cristina is helping me with all the back story, the life and crimes of her grandfather, that kind of thing. Shocking but she's pleased the truth has finally come out.' He looked towards the window. 'But the weather looks good. Maybe tomorrow I could swing by, and we could ... walk the pipe?'

'I would like that, Adam, I really would.'

***

They met at the small carpark just down from the church. Adam was carrying a small backpack. He approached his father and gave him a clumsy hug.

'Let's not walk the pipe this time, let's take the path across the marshes to the seal colony. The bridges walk,' said Hugh.

At first neither spoke, then Adam said, 'A couple more days and the article should be done. I've sent Max a rough plan and he seems impressed. Cristina has been a great help.'

They paused to walk single file across the first of the wooden bridges that crossed the creeks.

'I owe you an apology, Adam for chasing after you like I did. If I'd had any sense, I'd have realised that losing a phone hardly warrants such action but what with Mum dying, I think I wasn't myself....and couldn't face losing you too.'

'I don't think any of us was ourselves, Dad, but if you hadn't come you wouldn't have met Julia...'

'And what do you think about that? Too soon after Mum has gone?'

'I think Mum would be happy, that you won't be lonely in your old age...' He laughed.

'We're not rushing into a quick marriage or anything, Adam, but I think I will find a sense of peace – happiness even – with her, and I think she likes you and Cristina.'

'I had to get away for other reasons too, not just to research the article, but to create some sort of distance between us...'

'...Distance...?'

'Yes, with Mum I always felt close, able to be myself, but with you it always seemed more difficult. I don't mean to be unkind but when I lost the phone, I suddenly felt a huge sense of freedom, that I was on my own at last.' He stopped and crouched down. Carefully he gathered a small bunch of blue flowers.

'Mum's favourite flowers. Let's turn back, the creeks are filling fast, and we don't want to be caught out.' Hugh moved closer to his son as they walked back in the direction of the church. They entered the churchyard and made their way to the grave. Adam added the flowers to the vase. For a moment neither spoke. 'Thanks, for coming to find me, Dad.'

Hugh said nothing, gently touching the arm of his son. Across the marshes, a harrier flew out towards the wind turbines. Rain clouds had scurried in from the west. As it flew through the clouds and on towards the horizon, it gradually disappeared, and then reappeared, and then finally disappeared.

***

ACKNOWLEDGEMENTS

There are a number of people whose assistance made this book possible. Pedro Llosa Vélez, a gifted Peruvian writer provided the foreword, assisted by Sharon Duncan. Thank you both for your kind words. José Manuel Abastos, a Lima-based lawyer provided expert knowledge of the Peruvian legal system, in particular the working of a Superior Court judge. Seb Powderham, a helicopter pilot, advised me on the nature and types of helicopters likely to be employed in South America, and friends from the Lima Writers' Group provided lots of invaluable local knowledge of what life was like during the time of the war between the Shining Path and the State. I must also thank the Museo de la Memoria in Ayacucho, a museum dedicated to the disappeared of Peru.

As an introduction to the Shining Path, I consulted the *Shining Path of Peru*, a collection of essays edited by David Scott Palmer (1994); *The Shining Path: A History of the Millenarian War in Peru* by Gustavo Gorriti (1999); *Mourning Remains – State Atrocity, Exhumations, and Governing the Disappeared in Peru's Post-war Andes* (2017) by Isaias Rojas-Perez. Perhaps the most remarkable and insightful account of the conflict is given in the extraordinary memoir of a child soldier who fought on both sides of the conflict, *When Rains Became Floods: A Child Soldier's Story* (2015) by Lurgio Gavilán Sánchez.

In England, I would like to thank the writer, Nicholas Binge, for his kind review and another writer, Max Porter, who gave me invaluable feedback during the early phases of writing. A huge thank you to my editor, J. David Simons, who offered both detailed and generous advice, and to Jeff Weston of Thinkwell Books who had faith in me and my book.

Thanks to friends and family, too, who regularly appeared and then fortunately, disappeared during the writing of this novel.

Finally, a big thank you to Claire, who supported me during the research and writing of this book in Barranco, Lima. *Gracias, senora*.

***